MURDER AT MANASSAS

MURDER AT MANASSAS

A HARRISON RAINES CIVIL WAR MYSTERY

Michael Kilian

BERKLEY PRIME CRIME, NEW YORK

MURDER AT MANASSAS

This is a work of fiction. Names, characters, places, and incidents are either the product of the author's imagination or are used fictitiously, and any resemblance to actual persons, living or dead, business establishments, events or locales is entirely coincidental.

A Berkley Prime Crime Book
Published by the Berkley Publishing Group,
a division of Penguin Putnam Inc.,
375 Hudson Street
New York, New York 10014

The Penguin Putnam Inc. World Wide Web site address is
http://www.penguinputnam.com

First edition: January 2000

Library of Congress Cataloging-in-Publication Data
Kilian, Michael, 1939–
Murder at Manassas : a Harrison Raines Civil War mystery / by
Michael Kilian.
p.   cm.
ISBN 0-425-17233-3
1. Manassas (Va.)—History—Civil War, 1861–1865 Fiction.
I. Title.
PS3561.I368M8   2000
813'.54—dc21   99-33286
                                                        CIP

PRINTED IN THE UNITED STATES OF AMERICA

10   9   8   7   6   5   4   3   2   1

Author's Note

This is a work of fiction. Harrison Raines was not an actual person. Neither were Caitlin Howard, Boston Leahy, Caesar Augustus, Major George Pleasants, Louise Devereux, or Colonel Phineas Gregg.

But this is also a historical tale, intended to transport the reader back to another time—indeed, a period of considerable consequence to this nation. Many of the characters were living persons—Abraham Lincoln, Allan Pinkerton, John Wilkes Booth, Belle Boyd, and Clara Barton, obviously, but also Ella Turner, William Howard Russell, General Barnard Bee, and Congressman Ely.

Every effort has been made to portray them as accurately and true to life as possible and to place them exactly where they were at the time of actual events—including their positions in battles. Though I am weaving a mystery story into the fabric of real history, it's been my goal not to allow the fiction to interfere with or alter that history in the telling. I have also sought to make the context and setting of this story as authentic as possible, and so have consulted Civil War–era menus and Washington street plans, as well as walked all the areas of the landscape described, and visited Booth's house in Bel Air to boot.

I hope I have succeeded.

Michael Kilian
McLean, Virginia

Acknowledgments

I am greatly obliged to historians William Seale and John S. D. Eisenhower, the late author Cleveland Amory, writer David Elliott, and photographer Ernie Cox for their help, guidance, and encouragement in the preparation of this Civil War mystery series and the pleasure of counting them as friends. I want very much to thank Gail Fortune for her peerless performance as editor and agent Dominick Abel for twenty-one years of happy collaboration. I must thank Barry Neville for a brilliant idea. I am grateful to my wife, Pamela, and sons, Eric and Colin, as only they can know.

For my son Eric,
and battlefield days

MURDER AT MANASSAS

Chapter 1

July 1861

"THEY say the war shall be won tomorrow," Caitlin Howard said, setting down her whiskey glass to take up the two cards Harrison Raines had dealt her.

"Dear lady, they've been saying the war's about to be won every day since Sumter," Raines replied, after pondering his own poker hand. "I don't think they know for certain there's even to be a battle tomorrow."

"Someone must be certain, Harry. Half of Washington City's going to be out there to see it."

"Finding sport in watching men die."

"Call it what you will, Sir. I should like to be with them."

He let that pass. They were alone in Caitlin's small, stuffy sitting room in the quarters she rented at Mrs. Fitzgerald's boarding house just off Pennsylvania Avenue, idling away the hours of another hot Washington July night. Harry preferred euchre or whist for pastime, considering poker serious business—in fact, his principal line of work. But it was Caitlin's game of choice. As always, he indulged her.

Caitlin had made a wise choice in her landlady. Mrs. Fitzgerald was wonderfully careless about her enforcement of the rules of proper conduct, and didn't object to these late night tête à têtes, which provided Harry some of his happiest moments. He didn't feel he was compromising Caitlin's reputation. As an actress, Caitlin had small reputation to worry about, man in her chambers or no.

Harry had drawn only one card and stared at it unhappily through his gold-rimmed spectacles. The Queen of Hearts he normally considered lucky, but it was a poor mate to the four spades he had kept in his hand.

He pulled a handkerchief from his sleeve and once again wiped the sweat from his brow. They had tried having the window open, but there was no breeze, and the smell of Washington in the summer was a worse thing to endure than the heat.

"If there is a battle tomorrow," he said, "I expect it's only going to aggravate the quarrel, not end it."

"No matter who should win?"

"These armies are so green, I'm not sure either one can win a fight."

There was a gleam in Caitlin's gray-green eyes from the gaslight, adding mischief to her famously lovely smile. "And which side would be yours, Harry? Have you at last decided upon a 'we'?"

It was a question with which she had regularly taunted him since Virginia had joined the Secession parade. Despite his protestations of neutrality, there were those in Washington City who thought Harry Raines a Confederate agent, with Lafayette Baker, chief inquisitor of the Provost Guard himself among the most highly suspicious.

Washington was acrawl with Southern sympathizers, and Harrison Grenville Raines had been born and raised on a Tidewater Virginia plantation that was home to more than one hundred owned Negroes. Upon coming of age, he'd moved away to Richmond, where he'd acquired the reputation of a wastrel and dandy. Here in the Federal City, he lived well with no apparent means of support other than gambling, occasional horse trading, and vague "investments."

Most suspicious of all, his father and brother were officers in General Longstreet's brigade of the Confederate Army. Despite his excellent horsemanship and potential as a cavalry officer, Harry had declined all offers and pointed suggestions to become part of the Union forces, refusing to bear arms against his home "country" of Virginia, much as his father's friend Robert Lee had done.

In their last encounter, Baker had threatened to have him arrested as a possible—which to Baker's mind meant "probable"—spy. He'd not yet made good on that threat, but Harry presumed he was serious.

The truth was, Harry detested the notion of a Confederacy as much as he bore affection for Virginia. Like Caitlin, who was English born and the child of fiercely liberal London actors, Harry openly hated slavery and had voted for Abraham Lincoln as the one politician he thought might have the moral fortitude and cleverness to uproot the "peculiar institution" for good. He had left home because he'd fallen out with his family over the issue. His exile to the Federal City was the eventual result.

Harry was sick at heart that it had now come to war, much as his kin in gray proclaimed it "the Second American Revolution." He saw little good or noble to come of such a conflict. Only death and devastation and no resolution of the problem.

"You know very well why I take no side," he said to Caitlin, still squinting at his poker hand. "Not while the one side is the United States and the other Virginia."

"But this is war, Harry. Over slavery."

"If you find me less than handsome without brass buttons, Madame, I would remind you that your magnificent Mr. Booth wore a borrowed uniform of the Richmond Grays just so he could attend the hanging of John Brown two years ago, but has not been seen in one since, and we've been three months at war."

At the mention of Booth's name, Caitlin's smile vanished and her look turned hard.

"I would never think you a coward for not becoming a soldier," she said. "It cannot be an easy thing to kill another man, and I respect you for not wishing to do it. But I find no courage in your refusal to take a side."

"Booth is on what you hold to be the wrong side, yet . . ."

"The bet, Sir, is ten cents," she said, coldly.

It was the price of a matinee theater ticket, or half a pound of butter. Harry looked once more at his failed hand. There were few things in life as unsatisfactory as two-handed poker, except perhaps for loving a woman who would have him only as a friend. A woman who loved another.

Raines was considered a man of most agreeable countenance—even handsome—among his circle of saloon, theater, and artist friends, with or without his spectacles. Nearly six feet tall, he had sandy hair worn long in the Southern fashion, and a long cavalier's moustache, though no whiskers. His eyes were an amiable brown. His manners were remarkably genteel, even for a member of Southern "chivalry."

But he was small match for John Wilkes Booth, whom the newspapers had proclaimed "the handsomest man in America." A look from that actor's coal-dark, burning eyes caused women to wilt by the regiment, even those like Caitlin, who knew at first hand Booth's callous disregard for their sex once his pleasures were taken.

Harry had hope, but it resided less in his own attractions than in the more loathsome aspects of Wilkes Booth's behavior. Some day Caitlin would tire of the actor, his maddening narcissism, and frequent absences. Or if not that, at least of her endless, pointless wait for some return of her affection. In the meantime, Harry would stay near. He could have escaped Lafayette Baker's threats and harassment simply by moving to Philadelphia or New York, which remained under civilian rule and were outside Baker's jurisdiction. He could support himself, even thrive in these cities—whose civilization appealed to him far more than that of the bumptious national capital, with its crude wooden sidewalks, muddy streets, and wandering pigs and livestock.

But no place was truly civilized without a Caitlin Howard in it.

She was not prospering in this season. She earned forty-five dollars a week or more as an actress in good times, but only one of the city's theaters was open for the summer months. That house was staging a new drama, *Eily O'Connor,* but Caitlin had not been cast in it. Until Grover's Theatre reopened, she'd be living on savings.

"I raise your bet ten cents more," he said.

"Done," she said, with a malicious grin, and laid down a hand with three jacks in it.

He tossed his own cards on the table facedown, but she took them up.

"A pair of sevens? You'd bluff me, Harry?"

"Not well, Ma'am."

"I thought you a better player, for you are a good actor. Yet I gain nearly four dollars from you tonight."

He shrugged. "Small loss. I've had your company for the evening. That's gain enough for me."

"The hour is late," she said.

Caitlin had unbuttoned the jacket of her green dress because of the heat. Rising, astounding Harry, she now removed it, revealing bare arms and shoulders, corset and camisole. This was without precedent in their relationship, but of course no invitation to amour, much as he might have wished it. Their friendship was as much a barrier to intimacy as was her still smouldering passion for Booth.

"You're a bold lady tonight, Kate," he said.

"No. Merely a hot one. You men love the corseted dresses we wear. These pesky hoop skirts and piles of petticoats. The more cloth on us, the grander possession we make. But you've no idea how much we women hate these clothes. In our own rooms, we commonly go about in undergarments—as I suppose you've amply discovered. I yearn for the Empire gowns of my mother's time. In summer, when she was abroad in sunny climes, she often wore nothing underneath."

"Then that's a yearning I'd share," he said.

"The yearning you may have, Harry, but nothing else."

Raines knew many actresses, but few surpassing Caitlin in beauty, despite her age, which was now thirty—two years beyond his own. Not the flirtatious and fetching Agnes Robertson or the regal Lucille Western. In Washington, only the young, raven-haired New Orleans born Louise Devereux was considered a greater beauty on the stage.

None surpassed Caitlin in talent. Maggie Mitchell was perhaps more a master of comedy and the aging Charlotte Cushman more varied in her range. But Caitlin could hold her own on stage with anyone, and thrill the audience with mere tilt of head and cast of eye. She was decidedly a better actress than the famous Laura Keene. Some compared her to the young Fanny Kemble.

A remarkably tall woman, some nine inches above five feet in height, Caitlin had large, beautiful eyes and perfectly groomed light brown hair worn with side curls in the still-lingering fashion. Her figure was not full, but her carriage was splendid, even now, when she seemed much fatigued.

Caitlin went to a low chest of drawers, atop which was a decanter of whiskey and a pitcher.

"Would you like more apple tea?" she asked, pouring herself a glass of liquor. "Or would you have stronger spirits now you've lost in our game?"

Harry had gone to the window, pulling the drape gently to the side. Caitlin's rooms overlooked 6th Street, but he could see to the corner and the Avenue.

No one was there. That had not been so earlier.

"Neither, Ma'am. I should be leaving."

Harry pulled forth his pocket watch, a gift from his now dead mother on his twenty-first birthday. The present his father had given him on that occasion he no longer possessed—a male slave named Caesar Augustus.

"Indeed, it's past midnight," he said. "Not an hour for a gentleman to be seen leaving a lady's rooms."

"Nor an hour for a gentleman to be in 'em—but you would occasion no surprise in this house," Caitlin said. She turned toward him and sipped from the glass, leaning back against the chest of drawers. "What will you do tomorrow?"

He thought upon it. Rise at eight or nine o'clock. Breakfast at the hotel where he resided, the National. Perhaps take the train to Baltimore, an hour and three quarters away, where he owned some real estate and from time to time dealt in horse trading. Perhaps not.

"Nothing in particular," he said, returning his spectacles to their hard-backed case and slipping it into the breast pocket of his linen frock coat.

"You won't go to Centreville for the battle?"

"Kate, why do that?"

"Several of the folk in our little troupe plan to attend the show. Members of Congress are going—and taking their ladies! I think all the newspaper correspondents have left for there, or are about to. Have you not noticed how empty are the saloons?"

Indeed, McDowell's army, thirty-five thousand strong, seemed to have dragged along a large part of the city's one hundred thousand population with it, like a dog whose tail had become ensnared by a brambly vine.

"Hell, Kate, the fight may not be until next week. It may already have commenced. Instead of Centreville, it may be at Warrenton, or at the gates of Richmond. We've no idea."

She drained her glass and set it down hesitantly on the top of the chest, as though she might take it up again for yet another refilling. Wilkes Booth had been away from the city for days, and this depressed her.

"I'll offer you a reason," she said. "You're a gentleman. Would you allow a lady you've sworn always to defend make the journey to such a dangerous place unescorted?"

"You've no business there, Kate. You've always told me you hate to watch men fight—that you detest the sight of blood. Why drive thirty miles into Virginia in a hot July to watch them stick bayonets into each other?"

A smaller, more perfunctory smile now, as though she were blithely trying to make light of something she held serious.

"It's history. The thing could be decided right there, before our very eyes. But, I—Harry, there will be people in attendance about whom I have concern."

"What, you now have an army officer among your beaux?"

"No!" She turned in a whirl of skirts to pour herself another whiskey.

"A sergeant then?"

She ignored this. "I am going out there, Harry. Will you come with me?"

He still hoped to find a way to talk her from this—or somehow prevent their departure. But not at this moment. He bowed, with a theatrical flourish. "Of course, dear lady. Always. Anywhere."

"Can you hire a gig? I shouldn't want to sit a horse all that way."

There would be no gig nor carriage left in the city for hire. He doubted there was a night soil wagon still available. "You don't require a coach and pair? A barouche for the fairest lady in the Federal City?"

"As I must ask you to pay for it, Harry, I would wish something less dear. And nimbler. I'm told the country's rough."

"No great hills, but rough. Yes, very rough. And dangerous. Brigands, worse."

She sipped, thoughtfully. "You'll be armed, I trust. I had a pocket pistol among my things, but it seems to have gone astray."

"That pepperbox of yours would be about as useful as an apple out there," he said. "If I can't talk you out of this folly, I'll bring my Navy Colts." Reaching into his coat again, he stepped toward her. "Until you find the other, please take this."

He handed her, gently, his own gambler's pocket pistol—a single-shot percussion derringer. It was loaded, but better in her hands than his. As she had demonstrated on more than one country outing, she was a much better shot than he, particularly when he wasn't wearing his spectacles.

She examined it. "One shot. Mine fires two bullets."

"As memory serves, yours is .36 caliber. This is a .44, which should do the work of two. But let us hope you'll have no need for even one."

"You are a kind man, Harry. I'm happy to have your friendship."

He looked at his watch again. "It's so late, we'd do just as well to head for Virginia this very hour." She was exhausted, barely keeping her eyes open.

"No, Harry. I would sleep awhile. Let us depart at, say, half past four. Those damned army reveille drum rolls by the Capitol always wake me at four o'clock, no matter what. I'll be ready in time for us to be well across the Potomac by first light, and I'll bring refreshment for the journey." She extended her hand to be kissed, a habit of theirs. "A good night to you then. I would be out of these suffocating clothes this instant."

Harry left flushed and frustrated. He'd make an effort to

acquire a conveyance. She'd be furious with him if he did not. He'd go to the best livery stable in Washington. But there wouldn't be anything available. He was sure of it. In the morning, he'd console her on the disappointment, she could return to her bed, he could go off to Baltimore, and that would be that. The soldiers could have their brawl without them.

THERE was a steamy mist to the air this hot night, and Harry ambled more than strode toward the stable, which lay many blocks away along Pennsylvania. On the other, disreputable side of this broad, tree-lined thoroughfare, which everyone in Washington called simply "the Avenue," were red clay brick rowhouses, saloons, bawdy houses, and gambling parlors. They ran past C Street down to the foul City Canal. As he walked, he could hear the assorted sounds of carouse and exuberant sin.

But the northern, respectable side of the Avenue was home not only to his expensive National Hotel but the elegant Metropolitan, the Kirkwood House, and the palatial Willard. Here were the best saloons, restaurants, ice cream parlors, and oyster bars in the city. The street on this side was nearly deserted. Harry could hear his own footfalls.

And another's. He paused, and took a quick look over his shoulder. In the shadows of a tree at the corner was a vaguely glimpsed figure of a tall, sizable man. The fellow was back.

The stranger had stopped, though there was no ostensible business on that deserted corner to occupy him. Harry had seen the man earlier in the evening, following along behind when he had set out for Caitlin's, but had tried to dismiss him from his mind. Now he was made exceedingly nervous by the fellow.

With the loan of his derringer to Caitlin, he had no weapon with him save a small folding saloon knife. The city did employ some fifty policemen to see to the safety and order of the streets, but they were all political hires who went off duty at sundown and hung about in the safest places no matter what. Another force of fifty who worked for the federal government took over in the hours of darkness, but their charge was the protection of federal buildings, not the local citizenry. The nearest to him now were over at the Treasury Building several blocks away.

There were a few soldiers about, but they were to be regarded as more potential menace than security. Two of them loitering across the street seemed quite drunk and quarrelsome. As always and everywhere in Washington, there were some Negroes lounging, small help to a white man. It was foolish to walk these streets so poorly armed at such an hour.

Harry quickened his step, glancing back again to see the tall figure moving forward and matching his pace, boldly and brazenly. The livery stable Harry was bound for was at the farther end of the Avenue near the baseball field and the President's Park. He decided to stop in first at the bar of his hotel before proceeding, in hopes his pursuer might think him retiring for the night and so be thrown off.

Only four men were in the National's bar, one a gambler Harry knew named Big Jim Coates, two strangers, and the photographer Matthew Brady.

The bartender, a Welshman named Maddox, had poured a glass of Harry's favorite for him, not apple tea but Old Overholtz '55. Harry debated whether to take it. The unease at being followed and the excitement of Caitlin's company required calming. He accepted the drink and put a coin down to pay for it.

"Few about tonight," said Maddox.

"All off to see tomorrow's grand martial pageant."

"Surely there'll not be fighting on the Sabbath?" The Welshman laughed, then moved to some labor at the end of the bar.

Harry turned to face the room. The photographer was seated at a table by himself. He had given Harry no notice, though they knew each other.

"May I join you, Mr. Brady?"

The photographer looked up. His spectacles were foggy, and he had to peer over them. "Harry Raines, is it? Yes, please. Sit. Sit."

Brady was a celebrated man, more so in New York than in Washington City, but fame and success had brought him small content. Harry thought him fidgety, and Brady drank over-much.

"Surprised you're still in the town," Brady said, as Harry seated himself.

"No more surprised than I am to find you here. The battle should be a worthy subject. Though I wonder how you would photograph a war. Soldiers don't stand very still in a fight."

"I am going to the battle. Yes, indeed. My assistant Mr. Gardner and I will be there. You may be certain. But I've no clear idea how I'm going to get a single useful exposure. You're quite right. Unless I can get the armies to stand per-fectly still, there'll be little to photograph."

"They'll be perfectly still when they're dead."

The thought seemed to depress Brady even more. He pulled at his beard, as if to straighten it. He was in a great fidget.

"I am uncertain even where to go. I have maps. I have a wagonload of equipment. But armies move hither and thither. Are you going, Raines? You know Virginia. I should be glad for your company, for your guidance."

"I am sorry, Mr. Brady. I am going, but I'm to escort a lady—if I can find a rig to hire."

"Have you a pass? A military pass?"

He did not. Harry hadn't thought of that. It would be a marvelous excuse. No pass. He shook his head.

"If you come with me, Raines, you won't need one."

If he remained there much longer, Brady would have him in his wagon. Harry stood. "Let me buy you a drink, Sir. But I must be going. I've an errand still to attend to. A good night to you."

"But tomorrow, where should I go?"

"To Centreville, Mr. Brady. Once you're there, head for the sound of the cannons. But don't let it get too loud."

"What do you mean?"

"I mean don't get so close you find a cannonball in your lens."

Harry finished his drink, signalled to Maddox for refresh-ment of Brady's glass, set another coin on the table, and walked to the door. Sticking his head out cautiously, he found himself staring into the face of the tall, muscular man who had been following him.

IT was a rough and very Irish face, with nose and cheekbone slightly misplaced as though from some old, odd injury. The man wore a black coat and a bowler hat. His clothes were cheap, but a city dweller's. Though tall and broad-shouldered, he was in no way stout. What bulk there was looked all muscle. In rougher clothes, he might have been a teamster or dockyard laborer.

Harry stepped outside. "Who are you?" he asked. "And why do you follow me?"

"Why do you think, you goddamned Rebel," the man said. His voice was as Irish as his face—and as mean. He gruffly turned and moved on toward the next corner. "Good night and to hell with you, Harrison Raines."

"What? You leave me now?"

"There are others to watch you."

Not a comforting thought, somehow. The fellow's knowledge of his name gave Harry a clammy feeling, but he shook it off. As the man disappeared up 6th Street, another came around the corner on a large gray horse. Harry recognized him immediately, as much by his fine horsemanship and flamboyant style as anything

Booth. The National was his residence as well. Wherever he'd been, he was back.

In addition to handsome, the actor was a splendid athlete. It was for that reason that men came in such crowds to join the swooning ladies at his plays. He swung his right leg over the saddle and landed on the street in a graceful leap. Without further pause, he touched his hat, muttered a quick "Raines," and started into the bar.

"A moment, Sir," Harry said.

Booth stopped. He was wearing a pair of fine kid gloves despite the heat, and polished riding boots, only lightly touched with dust. "What do you want, Raines? A drink? I am buying for the house."

"It's a small house to buy for, but no thank you. Miss Howard has asked me escort her to Centreville tomorrow. General McDowell is expected to do battle and she wishes to see it."

He hoped Booth would protest. Another excuse.

"If there's a battle," said Booth, his mellifluous voice booming out into the street as though to an audience, "then you and Caitlin shall see the triumph of my country. You are welcome to that pleasure, Sir. Have a care to the lady's safety."

With that he swept into the bar.

His "country," indeed. Having begun his acting career to small success in Philadelphia, Booth had moved to Richmond and prospered, remaining there for two years. But that was all he could claim of Virginia as "country." He was a Marylander. His father, the great mad drunken actor Junius Brutus Booth, had brought his large and illegitimate family up on a farm in Bel Air near Baltimore and in a grand house in that city as well. Both of Booth's parents had come from England.

Harry had met and much admired Wilkes Booth's brother Edwin, a fine and poetic tragedian. Edwin was as hostile to slavery and supportive of Lincoln as Harry was, and if Edwin claimed a country, it was New York.

Harry stepped off the walk and passed beneath the trees into the street. The corner at 6th remained deserted, but that didn't mean he was safe.

Directly across the way, next to the Murray Hotel, was the Palace of Fortune, this night sounding as lively and busy as the National's barroom was not. Harry knew the tawdry establishment well, and the location of its back door.

With studied casualness, he walked across, pausing at the entrance of the gambling hall to look up 6th Street again with some care. It was all in darkness, lacking gaslights. Harry could sense nothing moving, or lurking, except perhaps a dog or two, and the usual scurrying rats. He put on his spectacles. Still nothing at all, though he heard a bit of laughter coming from a house south of the Avenue. Situated in Marble Alley, it was the establishment of a Miss Julia Deen, declared by the Provost Marshal's office to be one of the most reputable disreputable houses in Washington City. It boasted eight female inhabitants and was seldom without visitors.

Harry turned away. Pushing open the doors, he strolled into

the gambling emporium, nodding to a few acquaintances. He ordered and paid for a drink at the bar, but left it untouched as he excused himself to use the necessary in the rear.

Someone had gotten to the privy first, but Harry actually had no need of it. Moving as swiftly as he could manage in the gloom, he slipped into the yard of the Murray next door. No one came after him.

Stepping over what proved to be a sleeping pig, squealing in its sudden wakefulness, he crossed the yard and made his way behind the St. James, crossing C Street and following the back lane that led past the fish wharves on the canal. On this hot night, the canal itself smelled worse than the stocks of fish. He wondered how many dead bodies had been dumped into it that week. There were always cats and dogs to be found floating in its muck, and horses were not uncommon. Neither, especially with so many soldiers now calling the city home, were humans.

Harry was passing by the rear of a row of shabby small hostelries of the most dubious reputation when a gunshot boomed out, echoing off the shadowy brick walls.

Thinking the source of it the belligerent Irish tough who'd accosted him, he flattened himself against a wall, upsetting a box of bottles and other rubbish, but he quickly realized the shot had come from the side, from one of the backyards. The round had gone high. He'd heard the ball whizzing well above his head.

Carefully checking behind him, he crept forward until he could see the building from which the round had been fired. There was an open doorway—a faint glow of candlelight visible deep within. He expected another shot to follow the first, but instead came a loud, clear, angry voice, highly-pitched and likely a woman's:

"Don't you dare!"

Those three words. Nothing more.

He wondered what he could possibly have done to give offense in this strange quarter, then saw that he was not the supposed malefactor at all. There was a man down on his hands and knees in the dirt ahead of him, sent there either by the bullet or fear of it.

Harry knelt quickly at his side. "Are you shot, Sir?" he whispered.

The man was angry, scared, and not a little drunk, but appeared unhurt. That condition might not endure for long if another bullet were dispatched his way—and Harry's. Grabbing the fellow's arm, Harry hauled him erect, hurrying him away from the alley and across the Central Market, not stopping until they were at the foot of C Street. He was a soldier—an officer with much braid.

"Who was shooting at you?"

"None of your concern."

"Two feet lower and it would have been."

The man's uniform was in much disarray, coat unbuttoned, and shirt out of his breeches, but Harry could see his rank. In the light from the open market square, he could also see his face, and recognized him as Major George Pleasants. He was well known in Harry's fancier haunts as an incompetent gambler and successful ladies' man. His wife was the daughter of a powerful U.S. senator who was a friend of Lincoln's.

Neither the President nor the Senator would be much approving of the Major in his present condition and circumstance. The house he'd apparently stumbled from rented rooms by the night and hour, and provided companions. Run by a voluptuous blonde woman named Mollie Turner, it was on the Provost Marshal's list of bawdy houses—rated a "1" on an official rating scale that ran "1," "2," "3," "low," and "very low."

They had stopped to catch breath.

"You are known to me, Major," Harry said.

The officer stared at him, blinking, then scowled. "But I do not know you, Sir."

"We've met over cards. At the National, and in the Palace of Fortune. You were perhaps distracted, as you were losing both times. I know your regiment. It left for Virginia three days ago."

Pleasants pulled himself up straight, standing without assistance. "I left with it," he said. "I've come back on business. Private business. Urgent business."

Here was also a handsome man, and a remarkably blond

one. Pleasants' hair and moustache were as bright yellow as his uniform sash, now dragging along behind him. He was more blonde than Mollie Turner. Almost as blonde as Mollie's beautiful young sister Ella.

"Were I you, I'd rejoin your regiment without delay," Harry said. "All the world is expecting a battle tomorrow. An absent hero will miss out some on the glory."

"A soldier doesn't need a civilian's instruction on where he should be and when. I will be found leading the first rank when the order comes to attack."

"McDowell's at Centreville. A long ride."

He wobbled. "I know! I was on my way."

"Where is your horse?"

"At Naylor's Livery, up by the President's Park."

"Then we go to the same place. And it's well there are two of us."

Hastening along C Street, with Harry gladdened by the paucity of towering, glowering Irishmen in bowler hats behind them, they passed the rear of even cheaper hotels and more unsavory saloons and gambling halls. Reaching the diagonal of Ohio Avenue and the sprawl of Negro shanties between that dirt street and the canal, they were at the district called Murder Bay, and well named. There was small comfort in Pleasants' sidearm. In his condition, he'd be a worse shot than Harry.

This slum was a settlement mostly of freed slaves, who were taking to Washington City as a refuge from the surrounding "slavocracy" in increasing numbers. One of them Harry knew particularly well, as he had freed the man himself.

They were spared any perambulation of Murder Bay in search of Caesar Augustus' dwelling place, however, as the former slave would now be found where he worked as night boss of Naylor's Livery.

The door quickly opened to their rapping. Caesar Augustus, a shorter man than Harry, though immensely more powerful, was up working late. They had interrupted his repair of a harness.

Caesar Augustus glared at them, eyes flicking from one to the other, then admitted them. "You come late, Marse Harry. What you be after wantin' dis night?"

"Please stop talking that way," Harry said. "You know it makes you sound a cretin."

At great effort and risk, not to speak of paternal displeasure, Harry had violated the laws of Virginia by teaching Caesar Augustus to read and read well. The man could recite lines from Shakespeare.

The black man grinned with inner triumph and returned to his harness work. "What for you, then?" he asked. "I'm pretty well busy, as you can see. Everything with wheels and hooves that hasn't gone to Virginia is bound there tomorrow, which it almost is."

Pleasants looked confused by the variance in the Negro's speech and attitude, and by the nature of Harry's remark and his relationship with the black man. But he made no comment. The major seemed a man who kept his mind on his own problems, which were many.

"This gentleman would like you to fetch his horse, a chestnut with military saddle and regimental blanket," Harry said. "I need to hire a rig for the morning. The very early morning. By four o'clock."

The major was now paying scant attention, concentrating on staying erect and awake.

"His horse I can get pretty quick," said Caesar Augustus. "As for you, Marse Harry, ain't got no rig for the hire."

"You're sure?"

"Yes sir. Not a stable in the city got equipage ain't spoken for."

Harry sighed. "Just as well. I'd need a military pass, and I have none. No chance of getting one at this hour, is there? I suppose I'll have to forget the whole thing."

The major's chestnut gelding was brought forth, well fed and groomed. The officer needed a boost into the saddle, but once there, sat well enough, though Harry wondered if he'd reach even Fairfax City.

"You've a long ride, Major," Harry said. "Best have a care to stay awake. There may be roving bands of Confederate irregulars behind the Federal advance. Some little better than bandits. Your uniform marks you a target."

The man's uniform was still a mess. Harry hoped he'd attend to it before reaching his regiment.

"I would have your discretion," Pleasants said, steadying his mount. "About our encounter."

"Are you asking it or demanding it?" Harry said.

"I would be grateful for it."

"Then you have no worry."

"Obliged, Sir," the officer muttered, then paused and reached into a saddlebag, retrieving an order book. Taking pencil from pocket, he quickly wrote a few lines on a blank page, then ripped it out.

"A return of favor," he said. "There's your pass. Get you all the way to Centreville. Though I suspect you may not need it. This battle, Sir—a big frolic."

With a touch of rein, he clattered off.

Harry looked to Caesar Augustus. They had known each other all their lives.

"You say you can't provide me a rig?" he asked.

"They're all spoken for and most gone. And near every horse. This is a powerful big do tomorrow, Marse Harry. I 'spect all the town's goin' be there to see it. You already got a beautiful animal of your own. What you need with a hired rig?"

"It's not just for me. Miss Howard wants to attend this affair and I am supposed to accompany her."

"Miss Howard! Well, that do make a difference. For her, I'll find something. You ought to have a rig like that English reporter, Russell, has hired himself. He's goin' out there in a carriage and four, all kinds of eatin's and drinkin's, two revolvers, a rifle, and a saddle horse tied on behind. He's got both driver and servant."

"What a comfortable war. Well, good night, friend."

"Wait, Marse Harry. There's a buggy out back. It's pretty much a wreck. Hitch's broke, and the seat's loose."

"As I say, good night."

"But if you'll help, I think we can fix it."

"Surely not by four?"

"Anythin' for Miss Howard."

"That doesn't leave much time for sleep."

"Well, Marse Harry, just think about all those poor soldier boys in Virginia havin' their last sleep on Earth tonight."

Chapter 2

THE nearest Potomac crossing to Caitlin's boardinghouse was the Long Bridge that spanned the river from the end of Maryland Avenue to the Virginia shore, hard by the Greek-columned hilltop mansion that was Robert E. Lee's Arlington. But Harry decided on a different and he hoped faster route out of Washington. Heading west through Georgetown, he drove the gig along the north bank of the river, crossing by means of the Chain Bridge up by the rapids at Little Falls. The span was guarded by what looked to be a full platoon of Union infantry, but the soldiers, mostly green recruits, questioned them only briefly and let them proceed without even glancing at Harry's pass. The soldiers' concern was more for people trying to enter the capital, such as they showed concern at all. Victory was in the air. The war was all but over.

Yet, once on Virginia soil, Harry felt no such complacency. These gentle hills had been his home ground the year before. Now this seemed an alien, menacing country. Armed men were on these roads, anxious to use their weapons.

A cleverer fellow would have found a way out of this trip. He blamed the late night for having thoroughly dulled his senses. But no matter what his state of mental keenness, he was never a match for Caitlin when she was bent on something.

It was cool in the early morning darkness. Though the buggy seat slid back and forth on its ramshackle mountings when the wheels bumped over ruts, the ride was tolerable.

Once they'd ascended the bluffs on the Virginia side of the river and were rolling along through the piedmont, Caitlin came against his shoulder and went to sleep. He put his arm around her to add to her comfort, though the act only discomfited him. It was maddening to enter an embrace with her solely as pillow.

She was dressed in a fawn-colored riding skirt and white cotton blouse, worn beneath a brown linen jacket. Her face had been very pale and drawn when he'd collected her, though he'd thought that simply a sign of fatigue.

He guessed that the main roads leading to Centreville from Alexandria and Falls Church would be crowded with army traffic and spectators from Washington. So he'd picked a more northerly route, following roads that led to Lewinsville and Vienna and the Little River Turnpike. The long spell of hot, clear weather had dried the mud and left the traveling surface hard and fast, but the dust was prodigious. As the sun rose, Harry found his coat turned yellow with it. Caitlin had chosen her colors well.

Once on the turnpike, a major thoroughfare, they encountered substantial military traffic, with express riders thudding along in both directions and sutlers' and teamsters' wagons bunching along to westward. Harry got his rig around one particularly long line of vehicles by swerving out behind a fast-trotting troop of cavalry, and past another by turning through an opening in a snake rail fence and bumping over a farmer's newly mown hayfield to avoid a crowded crossroads.

With the sun rising high and hot and so much noise about them, Caitlin was now fully awake. She offered to take the reins and let Harry sleep, but there seemed so many hazards about he was reluctant to put her to that burden.

Stopping by a ford at a creek called Rocky Run, they went at the lunch Caitlin had prepared—roast beef, cheese, bread, and whiskey—resting themselves for a brief time on the grassy bank. Then they remounted the buggy and clattered on—he reluctantly, she with grim anticipation—joining a stream of military and civilian equipage that seemed endless in all that hanging dust.

Their conversation had been intermittent, and mostly to do

with the stage. Her fellow English-born actress, Laura Keene, was managing a theater in Boston and had asked Caitlin to join her company for the new season. Kate had never worked with the actress universally known as "the Duchess," let alone for her, but knew many who had and not liked it. Keene had deserted Edwin Booth in the middle of a play's run in Hawaii six years before, and the great comedian Joseph Jefferson had complained that Keene had thrown a goldfish at him in some towering rage, which with "the Duchess" were frequent occurences.

Still, a female theater manager was a rarity and to Caitlin's mind a bold idea that should be fostered and supported. Part of Keene's reputation for shrewishness stemmed merely from her exacting approach to stagecraft—a stern insistence on perfection that in a man would seem an admirable quality.

Keene had promised Caitlin the roles of Lady Anne in *Richard III* and Beatrice in *As You Like It*—and a salary of fifty dollars a week. But Keene also had on her bill the tiresome Tom Taylor farce *Our American Cousin*, which Keene herself had already played in some five hundred times.

"That ghastly old thump of comedy," Caitlin said. "I'm not sure I could bear five minutes in it. The thought of it weighs me quite the other way."

"You've been in worse," said Harry.

"That remark is not gallant, Sir."

"Then I withdraw it."

He knew very well that Caitlin would not accept Keene's offer for a hundred a week, plus all the thrown goldfish she could catch. It would mean prolonged absence from the spellbinding Wilkes Booth, no matter how little attention he paid her.

There was a distant rumble to the southwest. The sky was hazy, but Harry doubted it was thunder. The hour was still too early for a summer storm. The sound's impart was grimmer than inclemency.

"I fear that's the battle," he said.

"You think so?"

"It's not bad weather, and there's been nothing to occasion a ceremonial cannon salute."

"Dear God."

"It's why you wanted to come."

"I'm not complaining, Harry."

The wagon ahead of them lurched, and began to move faster. Harry flicked the reins to urge their mare to close the interval.

"This is a good time for you to tell me just why you're so keen to be out here," he said.

"I told you, Harry. I hate this brawling between the states. I want it over. That could happen here—today."

"It could happen just the same with you safe in your rooms."

"I want to see it happen."

"There's more. You mentioned a concern for someone here. Yet you denied having a soldier beau. Who then? Is your Booth here? No one's heard of him so close to musket ball before."

"It's no soldier and it's not Wilkes. My concern is for Louise Devereux." She bit her lip, looking away, then turning back. "I fear I betray a confidence."

The Devereux woman was not so good an actress as Caitlin but more beautiful, and younger. Harry had flirted with her once or twice, but without much result, or real interest on his part. His ardor was for Kate.

"I will keep it close," he said. "You know that."

"She has a soldier beau. She vowed to be out here with him. She was mad to do it. I could not dissuade her, though I tried. God, but I tried."

Harry laughed. "There may be fifty or sixty thousand fighting men on the field, plus all us gawkers. How do you expect to find such a needle, no matter how beautiful, in so big a haystack? And that's presuming we can get close enough even to see the army."

"She said only that he is with Howard's Brigade. So we must find it."

"In this confusion, I think a whole division will seem a needle."

•   •   •

THEY reached Centreville to find it looking like both a military camp and a county fair all tossed together. Cannon and caissons crowded the way, and down one little street they could see the wagons of a baggage train followed by a herd of beef cattle, stopped in their forward progress. Several houses on the east side of the town had been shelled and burned, their stone walls standing gaunt and gutted, but the damage did not look to have been done that day.

The present battle was still something to be heard rather than seen, but its ruckus was now much louder than before. The artillery sounded in successions of kettle drum bursts, and Harry thought he could hear the rip and rattle of musketry, though he didn't think them that close to the fighting.

The mingling of military and civilian here was remarkable. By a small church, they heard a sergeant bellowing profane oaths at a clumsy file of soldiers not ten feet from two fine Washington ladies with parasols, who paid the loutish fellow no more mind than they might a passing cloud.

Caitlin seemed quite anxious now, constantly turning this way and that to look among the crowd. Louise Devereux was a small woman, but a beauty to stand out in any gathering, especially with her penchant for going about in public with her long black hair undone in a cascade over her shoulders. She also owned a very large bay horse—the gift of a now departed admirer—with distinctive markings.

But no such comely vision came into their view. Making their way on through the town, they discovered there was a limit to the army's tolerance of spectators. A knot of men in civilian clothes stood about before a young officer who barred their way.

One of the men was known to Harry—the somewhat portly British reporter named William Howard Russell, a veteran of numerous British campaigns about the world. They had played at cards in the Palace of Fortune just four days before. At the side of the road was Russell's open carriage, a handsome black saddle horse tied behind.

Harry alighted from his buggy, careful not to expose the two long pistols he wore beneath his coat, lest he be deemed someone dangerous.

"What's amiss?" Harry said, going up to Russell.

"This young fool won't let us go beyond the town," said Russell, stepping aside from the group. The man's face was a cheery English red above his graying whiskers.

"He's just trying to keep you from the bullets," Harry said.

"It's our damned job to be among the bullets," Russell said. "If this were the Crimea, I'd have this boy taught a harsh lesson. I'd . . ."

His imagination failed to bring forth a suitable punishment for the officer, who at all events now seemed to be changing his mind. The other men there, presumably newsmen also, suddenly broke away, many of them now smiling—though one or two looked even less happy than before.

"They're allowing us to go up to a stone bridge near the battle!" shouted one, to Russell. "It's at our 'official risk.' "

Russell started to hurry after them, but Harry held him back.

"Do you know where Colonel Howard's brigade is?" Harry asked.

"Howard? Colonel O. O. Howard? I think he's with Heintzelman's Division. But I've no idea where in blazes they are. It's all so deuced chaotic, I don't think General McDowell himself could answer you."

Caitlin had overheard some of what had been said and had guessed the rest.

"Let us go forward with those men," she said. Her words came out boldly, but she looked decidedly worried. He took her distraction for fear, but erred, for it was urgency.

"This is no frolic, Kate. People are going to die today."

"I know! I just don't want Louise to be one of them."

"I guess there's no arguing with you." He climbed back into the seat and clicked the reins. The nervous horse jolted forth and at once broke into a quick trot.

THEY pressed on, in train with a handsome rig containing a dashing figure Harry recognized as a New York congressman named Alfred Ely, and a wagon full of reporters trailing behind. Passing a nearly empty Union Army camp to the side of the long, straight turnpike, they paused a moment to ask a soldier left on guard what unit he represented. Harry was told the Second Wisconsin, of Colonel William T. Sherman's Brigade and General Tyler's Division. Howard's Brigade had been camped the other side of Centreville but was on the march, though the man knew not where. Sherman's men would be on the march, too. They were going into an attack just as soon as General McDowell came up.

The soldier made a poor sentry. If Harry were a Confederate spy, he could make good use of such information when within reach of the Rebel lines.

Wherever those were.

They crossed a small stream called Cub Run over a rattlesome bridge and then commenced the slow ascent of a long rise sloping up to a wooded ridge. Passing through the trees, they at length broke out into the clear at the top. Artillery batteries were arrayed in open fields to either side, but none were firing. The road ahead led downward again into a wide valley with a meandering stream curving through it—Bull Run.

Harry had brought a spyglass. He turned the gig off into the meadow, taking care to park to the rear of the cannon muzzles, in a clear space where a number of other civilian carriages had drawn up. With care, he studied the terrain below. There were puffs of smoke in the distance, looking like odd whisps of cotton—and moving blue dots and lines. Plainly visible through the glass was the stone bridge dead ahead at the bottom of the slope.

"That's it," said Harry. "But, with or without the army's permission, I've no mind to visit it. This is the road to perdition, m'lady."

"Do you see Louise?"

"Only soldiers."

Not for long. The congressman, reporter Russell, and a few other newsmen trotted by on their way down to the bridge, or some vantage point closer to it. Harry noted Russell had switched to his saddle horse.

"Perhaps they can tell us something when they come back," Harry said. "If you want to wait that long."

"I do."

Another young officer, with a bristly black moustache and eager eyes, approached them, recognizing Caitlin from the stage and apparently drawn by her celebrity. With a bow and gallant sweep of cap, he introduced himself as a captain of signals and an admirer of her stagecraft. For all her desperate worry over Louise, Caitlin seemed a little pleased and flattered.

The officer had no idea of the whereabouts of Howard's brigade, but claimed knowledge of much else, and offered to explain that battle unfolding down in the valley. Gesturing off to the right, he noted that Sherman's brigade was going out that way to turn the Confederates' flank from the north and that the Rebels would soon be on the run—possibly all the way to Richmond. The sputtering fracas down by the bridge was merely a rearguard demonstration, the captain insisted, designed to discourage a Union pursuit.

"There'll be a victory parade in Washington tonight," he prophesied.

He then drew attention to an odd contraption rising from the hillside behind them—a wooden tower topped by dangling, hinged arms. This he described as a signals telegraph that communicated with the crews of other hilltop devices just like it by means of changing the position of the dangling arms according to a code. Such devices had been introduced to modern warfare by Napoleon, he said.

Harry, a voracious reader, especially of military histories, knew that these signals had indeed originated with the French Revolution but they predated Napoleon's rise to power by several years. He politely remained silent.

No other thing did. At that moment, the area down by the bridge erupted in noise and smoke. Turning quickly to present the glass, Harry saw clusters of glints—orange for musket fire, silver for bayonets. Of a sudden, a thick line of gray-clad figures rose from the brush and grass just across Bull Run. Figures in blue appeared in the nearer grass and began walking or running back. The smoke and gunfire increased as though stirred by bellows. Then, quite near them, the air was rent by the percussive roar of a cannon. A quick, startled glance informed them that it was a long-range rifled Parrot gun, whose crew was now hurrying to reload.

"Kate," Harry said. "We cannot stay here."

"What about Louise?"

Harry flicked the reins sharply across the horse's rump, turning their conveyance back toward Centreville.

"She's not here," he said, prodding the horse to a swift trot. "And Howard's Brigade is not here. But the Confederate Army is here and so it's time for us to be elsewhere. Fast. I'd choose home."

Caitlin glared at him with a hardness he had not seen since she last played Lady Macbeth.

"I will not leave until we've seen to Louise," she said. "The girl's been in a terrible state. Very upset. I fear for her."

"But we don't know where she is!"

"Someone in this stupid army must know where they've put Howard's Brigade."

Clattering into Centreville town again, Harry caught sight of two other newsmen from his wide acquaintance—a reporter and an artist from *Harper's Weekly*. They were of limited help, knowing nothing of Howard's location. But they'd heard that a large part of the Federal Army was on the march off to the north, crossing Bull Run behind the Rebel left flank at a place called Sudley Springs Ford. The two newsmen were preparing to head there themselves.

Harry knew this country. He had land and kinfolk up the Potomac Valley near Shepherdstown and had often ridden this way on his visits to them. Back by the stone bridge, he'd seen some Union cavalry turning off the pike onto a side road just shy of Cub Run. It led north and would likely take them toward Sudley's. It would be the shortest way.

Dispatch was of the essence. All he wanted was to find the headstrong Louise and secure the safe return of all three of them to Washington City as fast as humanly possible. Something about this battle struck him with foreboding. He knew in his bones there would be no victory parade.

Before they could depart the town, another citizen came galloping up, a bald fellow minus his hat, who proved to be yet another of the journalistic persuasion. His news was good.

The Union troops had beat back the Confederate attack and were still in possession of the stone bridge. There were casualties, and one of them was Congressman Ely. It appeared he'd been captured.

"Some prize," said the *Harper's Weekly* reporter. "I think the Rebels would much prefer to have that bridge."

Harry leaned close to Caitlin.

"Do you still want to go around to the north?" he asked.

"Yes!" Her eyes were desperate, about to break forth with tears.

"The way takes us near the battle again."

"If that brings us nearer to Louise, then let us go!"

Chapter 3

As they cantered north along the Cub Run road, the sounds of war diminished, and in time an odd, false serenity came over them. Caitlin, among many others, believed the war would come and go just that way—a brief spell of noise and violence, the affair quickly settled, then fading swiftly away, an aberration in the general progress of civilization, soon to be forgotten.

But Harry could see already that the wish was folly. Caesar Augustus had spoken a harsher but more reasonable truth: this fight between the states would not end until the last African was freed of shackles. And that day could be hastened only by the bravery and resolution of the soldiers of Abraham Lincoln.

Caitlin's words of the night before continued to sting him. With his carefully crafted neutrality, Harry certainly wasn't adding anything to the Union's supply of courage and resolve. Many of the men in blue arrayed upon these hills and fields were three-month soldiers whose enlistments were about to expire. Could Harry find it in himself to step up in replacement? Or would he continue to content himself with merely objecting to the "peculiar institution," smug in his principles? He supposed he had risked his life once or twice on behalf of escaping Negroes before the war, but had done little on their account since its commencement.

It gnawed at him, his not doing more. But he was vexed

and troubled, too, by the prospect of taking up hostile arms against his own father and brother, against so many old friends, adding to the blood that would likely now drench his native state, which he truly did think of as "country." Were his mother to rise from her grave and see him trod upon Virginia soil in the blue of the invader, what spectral clamor would that arouse?

"Why have you slowed?" asked Caitlin.

"Why, indeed," said Harry. A snap of the whip, and the horse went from slow trot to pounding canter.

Cresting a rise, they descended to the very incomplete beginnings of a railroad line, and, bumping over that, they were shortly at the Sudley Road. All the movement on it was one way—south. Harry joined the flow.

In a very short time, they were approaching Sudley Springs Ford, with clumps of Union soldiers spread out to either side of the road and vehicles and horses everywhere. But there was no sound of war, save a few oaths and imprecations and a distant sound that could just as easily have been thunder.

The shallow river crossing here had become a bottleneck, compelling soldiery and citizenry alike to wait their turn, resting where they stood or lay. A few groups of soldiers looked as though they had let their turn at crossing come and go several times. Men in uniform were sprawled beneath the trees, their packs and equipment scattered around them, looking like simple idlers on a summer's day, not warriors deciding the affairs of a great nation. The army term for such fellows was "skulker."

Harry pulled the gig to a stop at the side of the road, on a small slope that canted it slightly toward a ditch. That distant thunder was now discernible as cannon fire, over the ridge that rose from this gentle valley to the south. Harry took them to be Union artillery pieces firing away towards the enemy, but he had no way of knowing for certain.

He commanded Caitlin to stay in the buggy—as much as anyone could command Caitlin to do anything—then dismounted, heading for the nearest soldiers. A half dozen or so enlisted men were lounging around one large oak.

One plump private seemed to be truly suffering from the

heat, lying faceup and still, his face in pallor, his breaths coming in shallow gasps. The others around him appeared simply slothful. Only one of them answered his greeting. The accent was New England.

"I'm looking for Howard's Brigade?" Harry asked.

"And who be you?"

"I seek a friend." He didn't want to bring up the fact that she was a woman—and a beauty at that.

"You don't sound like a man who'd have any friends among Maine boys."

"If they're up the road fighting," said Harry, "and you're still hangin' back here, you're not going to have many friends among 'em, either."

"We'll move up," said the lone sergeant among them, a very large man with bushy eyebrows and scraggly beard whom Harry vaguely recalled from recent poker games. "Soon as we get our rest. We come a long, hard way. No other regiment's carryin' the load our fool officers got on our backs." He gestured at his kit, which he had strewn on the ground beside him. "Lookee here—rucksack, blanket, cooking pot, rations. Full pack. Wool uniforms. And the sons of bitches had us at the double quick comin' down this road! We had to fall out or die of the heat and dust. Look at poor Goldsborough. He's more dead 'n alive!"

As memory had it, Harry had won money from the man. He wondered if the fellow remembered.

Harry glanced at the sergeant's thick uniform coat and shook his head. He pulled a small glass flask from his pocket and tossed it to the sergeant.

"My gift to you, Sir," Harry said. "For what you've been through. Now where can I find Howard's Brigade?"

The sergeant took a swig, then shared the little bottle. "You've found Howard's Brigade. That's us. You can tell by how much we're all sweatin'."

Harry looked at his pocket watch. It would be dark when they got back to Washington—even if they left for it that very instant. He sighed, with deliberate emphasis.

"I'm only a civilian with no knowledge of military matters," he said. "But I had thought a brigade somewhat larger than six men. If there are others of your regiment besides you, where might I find them?"

"Your name?"

"Harrison Raines, of Washington City. And yours?"

" 'Sergeant' will suffice, for you. And your trade?"

"Horses."

"You come out here to trade horses?"

"I merely seek a friend, Sir."

The man wrestled with some thought. He might soon be shot for desertion or malingering, yet here he was worried about Harry's bona fides.

"Well," he said, finally, reaching to pick some insect from his beard. "Rest of the boys were headin' for a place on the Warrenton Pike called Groveton. They was followin' behind Porter's New Yorkers. Past the ford there, that road's supposed to branch twice. Second fork takes you to Groveton. Or so the captain say, and he got the map. That's where we're headin' when we're cooled off and rested up. Which I promise will be soon, should any ask."

"Thank you."

"Obliged for the whiskey."

Something jarred Harry's memory.

"Do you know a Major George Pleasants?"

The sergeant looked to the others. But none spoke.

"He has yellow hair," said Harry. "Bright yellow. Same for his whiskers and moustache."

"There's an officer like that up front. He was absent at muster this morning but came gallopin' up when we were marchin' outta Centreville. The colonel gave him a noticeable talkin' to—and put him up front as punishment. But I think ours goin' to be the last brigade onto the field, so it ain't goin' to hazard him none."

"May be more hazard than one finds here." Harry grinned, to show it a pleasantry.

"They ain't movin' fast. We'll be catchin' up to 'em soon enough."

Harry gave the group the slightest of bows and turned for his hired rig. When he reached the ditch beside it, he paused. A small, flat box was lying amongst the leaves there. He picked it up, recognizing the label. There were six or seven cheroots inside, still fresh.

Caitlin had dismounted, and was talking to a lady and gentleman in another carriage. A freight wagon that had been blocking the ford had finally attained the opposite bank and traffic was moving again.

"They're just ahead, Harry!" she said, rejoining him. "Howard's Brigade!"

"So I've been informed."

"What are you looking at so seriously?"

"A box of cheroots I found."

"You don't smoke those, do you?"

"No. It's just that I recognize the tobacconist's label. It's a shop in Richmond."

"Why do you find that so fascinating? This is Virginia."

"Yes it is. But we're with the Union Army."

"Harry, I want to be with Howard's Brigade!"

He helped her back into the buggy, a little thrilled when her leg unintentionally came against him.

"It could be miles more," Harry said. "And Louise may not be there."

"Oh, she will be there. You don't know her if you doubt that."

Harry climbed onto the seat, taking up the reins. "Louise's beau—could he be an officer named Pleasants?"

Caitlin flushed, looking straight ahead. "I am sworn not to speak of this. But how would you know that?"

Harry had sworn no vow of silence, but was reluctant to relate his encounter of the previous night. The major was in sufficient trouble as it was.

"Tavern talk," he said.

DODGING caissons and cannons and galloping couriers, they advanced south now along the Sudley Road, following the sergeant's directions. Field guns were booming ahead.

Not far from the ford Harry saw one welcome sight: Matthew Brady's photography wagon, the proprietor thereof busy with something at the rear. Pulling off to the side and dismounting, Harry went over to him, having to shout over the din.

"Not only have you found the battlefield, Mr. Brady, but you beat me to it."

"Luck, Mr. Raines. Mr. Gardner has a camera back over by the creek, but I'm not sure what he will find there. I hope he does not stray too far, as the negatives must be developed when they are still wet, and our only darkroom is this wagon." He looked up, squinting up the hill. "They say our soldiers have gone on well past the turnpike. What am I to photograph? Empty fields? The distant cannon smoke?"

"Perhaps the tide of battle will turn in your direction—and favor."

"I'd rather a victory for Mr. Lincoln than a picture for me. All I have is a glass plate of General McDowell standing with several officers. And some members of Congress."

"That could yet be a prize."

Brady frowned, as though Harry's remark was an unsuccessful joke. "May you survive the day, Raines."

"I'll stand you and Gardner to a drink, Sir."

He set the horse on up the road, following a caisson. Dust or smoke or both hung over the summit like a curtain.

"Let us abandon this," he said. "Louise, wherever she is, has a whole brigade to protect her."

"No. We've come all this way. I will find her."

"Kate, please."

"We find her! Damn it! Show some courage, Harry!"

Her words stung. He slapped the reins. Their horse was full of fuss, but getting weary and unhappy. The more the sound of cannon increased ahead, the slower its progress. The beast was barely managing a walk by the time they got to the top of the next rise. There were artillery batteries there, all banging away, and troops—all belonging to Colonel Burnside's Brigade. Howard's, they said, was arrayed to the right of the crossroads that dominated the valley below. It was hard to tell. A curtain of dust was drawn over the scene as though across a theatrical stage.

Waving farewell, Harry fetched his spyglass, moving down

the road. Lifting her skirts, Caitlin followed. They stopped at a stand of trees.

Harry trained his glass down to the valley floor below. Despite the dust, he could see considerable humanity in it, most in blue, but surprisingly many in civilian black and fawn and white, and a few figures that might be womanly. Two carriages, one closed and one an open coupé, were parked in the lee of a small hillock.

The scene appeared too blurry. Putting vanity aside, Harry took his spectacles out of the case in his coat pocket and put them on.

Ahead now, spread out over the adjoining meadow, moved a file of soldiers, all by themselves, trudging through the thick dust on toward the fighting, wherever it was.

There was more cannon fire—booming rolls of it—and some rattles of musketry, but mostly off to the left, to the east. He raised the glass to a distant hill over that way and saw smoke, drawn out in a long line across the summit, on which stood a two-story white farmhouse. Whatever was going on there, the Confederates were holding fast.

Dust was rising all about them, but below, on the valley floor, he could still see Union troops surging forward, moving across the Warrenton Pike in a great sweep around the Confederate flank. Farther to the right, the regiments he'd been told were Howard's were moving ahead across a summer-yellow field, passing between two stands of woods and advancing upon a thicker one lying to the south. They moved slowly, doubtless still carrying those heavy packs.

"Here's your history!" he said, handing the glass to Caitlin. "Made before your very eyes. The Federals may actually win the day."

"Where are Howard's men?"

"Off to your right, to the west there, moving toward those woods."

"I don't see Louise."

"You wouldn't in all this dust. But I doubt they'd let her that near. More likely she'd be down the hill there, directly ahead of us. By those carriages, somewhere in that dust. I saw several ladies. A small mob of civilians."

"Let's go there."

"Kate, no. The horse needs resting. And I want to see how this plays. If it is a Union victory, we can gather Louise up later."

"It might be too late."

"Too late for what? Damn all, Kate, what's afoot here?"

The actress lowered the glass and bit down on her lip, but said nothing. Then at once she brought the instrument to eye again. A rider was cantering madly up the road toward them. He waved his hat as he passed by, shouting, "Victory! The Rebels run! We've whipped 'em! Whipped 'em good!"

Harry took the glass. The gray-clad troops on the distant hilltop to the left, ranged before that white, much damaged house, hadn't budged. Their regimental colors were where he'd just seen them.

"Harry!"

A new eruption of gunfire, all musketry, this time to the right, the noise joining with the artillery fire on the hilltop behind them and causing a great cacophony. The woods in front of Howard's slow advance now stood obscured by a curtain of abruptly rising smoke reaching from one side of the field to the other. From it, suddenly, came soldiers, many gray-backs, but some of them in blue. There were blue uniforms worn by both armies in this fight, which must have been causing profound consternation. The Union soldiers wavered, then turned, some of them not even firing. One or two, then more, then all of them suddenly broke in fright.

Firing burst forth at the center of the line now, just ahead of the crossroads below them, near a stone house. The fighting there looked savage. There was more wavering among the blue. Then more running, the tide of "victory" draining with it. Of a sudden, a large body of cavalry appeared to the right at the farthest extent of the line. Harry quickly realized it was Confederate. The day would be the South's, and very soon.

"What's happening, Harry?"

"A Rebel counterattack! You wanted to see history. I don't think you're going to like it."

"Oh God."

They stared, transfixed. The Federals at the center now

turned and ran, then stopped and held, then sagged, and gave
way once more. To the right, Howard's men, no doubt now
shed of packs, were in full tilt, hurrying back toward them.

Caitlin turned away, her back against the tree. "What's to
be done?"

"When they get across that little creek and reach the high
ground this side of the valley, they'll rally. They can stop the
Southern boys the way the Southerners stopped them."

But the Confederates had set upon Howard's brigade from
hiding in those woods, a surprise force thrown in at a critical
moment. As far as Harry could see, the Federals had no reserve force to fling into the action as a counter attack. Burnside
and Howard had marched here as a flanking move, and now
its momentum was spent.

Union cannon along the ridge to the left now began firing
with vigor, hurling shells at the Rebel advance, but shooting
too fast and high, missing. Howard's Federals were streaming
across the meadow back toward Harry and Caitlin. To his surprise, once safe across the pike, they formed, of all things, a
Napoleonic hollow square. In its midst, excited officers
mounted and on foot were scurrying back and forth, waving
swords, one of them appearing to be in overall charge.

"Some fool's been reading the wrong tactics book!" Harry
said. "Thinks this is Waterloo!"

Holding to the tree, as though taking some strength from it,
Caitlin stood on tiptoe to watch. She was seeing men fall now,
and appeared both stunned and fascinated.

"Louise," she said. He saw her speak the word more than
hearing it.

"Do you see her?"

"No. Only in my mind's eye!"

Harry took her by the shoulders.

"I'm going down there!" he said, yelling into her ear. "On
foot! You get in the rig and turn it toward the road! If I can
find her, I'll bring her back. If these retreating soldiers get
here first, you move out with them! Don't wait! I won't have
you harmed!"

"Harry . . ."

"Please!"

"Now I've put you in this peril."
"Kate. If you feel obliged to me, do as I say!"
She nodded vigorously, eyes fearful.

THE retreat was now in full, mad progress moving up the road as he came down it. Horses and running, weaponless soldiers kept him dodging, but he trotted on, looking ahead and to the right through the thick fog of smoke and dust. On the little hill by the crossroads, the Napoleonic square was melting. Like a sand castle before a curve of crested surf, its sides were trickling away.

He stumbled and fell, rolling into a ditch. These were Burnside's men running by. Holding himself to the side until the bulk of them were past, he then resumed his trek. Howard's men were coming toward him across the grassy slope, anxious for the road, yelling in fear. Then an officer galloped out from the left of the mob and curved around, moving out ahead of them.

Harry thought he must be the most flagrant coward of the lot, making full speed to be the first to safety. Once he reached the road, however, the officer hurled himself out of the saddle and landed hard on his feet, in a swift movement pulling his sword from its scabbard and sweeping his hat from head, waving it frantically at them as though they were to be stopped like cattle.

The man's hair was a brighter yellow than the flowers in the dry summer grass. Harry was amazed. It was Major Pleasants! How he had an ounce of spirit in him after his long night, Harry could not imagine, but he was making himself a one-man bulwark, bellowing at his frightened men to stop, to hold, to reform. One or two he struck at with the side of his sword as they stumbled by—including the officer who had been in charge at the Napoleonic square. That craven fool hit back at Pleasants, a look of absolute terror on his face.

That officer's poor example undid whatever success Pleasants had been having in stemming the rout. The flow of oncoming troops now simply parted around the major, then came together in a mob again behind him as they turned up the road.

But behind him, needing no slap of the blade, one or two halted. Then three or four more. Pleasants began shouting at them, gesturing at the milling crowd of frightened civilians still in harm's way. Others joined his little force. When he had about him a platoon-sized body, Pleasants turned and led them at a run down the hill toward the civilian carriages.

Harry stopped again, bringing up the glass. The Union retreat had spread from one end of the line to the other, but the Confederate pursuit had ceased. The graybacks had reached the turnpike and the crossroads at their farthest grope, but went no farther. There, and all across the field, they'd halted, content to rejoice at the pellmell withdrawal of their foe. If the Federals turned and set upon them once again, the day might still be theirs.

But there was small chance of that. The road behind Harry was now choked with Union blue, moving north like an undulating snake.

He pressed on forward. There was so much dust he could not make out quite where Pleasants and his brave little band had gone. More terrified soldiers kept emerging from the cloud, along with terrified civilian spectators. The two civilian carriages he'd earlier noted appeared one after the other and swept along with the retreating stream so swiftly they might have been carried on the soldiers' shoulders.

Lunging along behind one of them was a riderless black horse. Harry recognized it as Louise's bay from the oddly diagonal blaze across its nose. It was terribly frightened, rearing and snorting.

Harry snatched at its bridle, missing the reins at first grab but catching them up on the next. He pulled the animal to the side and tried to calm it. Perhaps this was serendipity. He'd mount the beast and retrieve its mistress, who must be just ahead. With transport now, they'd both get to safety.

The animal's sides glistened and there was froth about its mouth. The lady's sidesaddle would be ungainly, especially with two, but these were the direst of circumstances.

Putting foot to stirrup, he swung the other leg over. The moment his body thumped onto the saddle leather, the horse gave a screaming whinny and rose on its hind legs, pawing the air. When it came down again, Harry slid quickly to the ground. Something was wrong.

His left hand and knee were wet—and red. It was blood. The animal had been injured. Examining its shoulder, he saw a deep crease, welling crimson, cut along the muscle like a line drawn straight to the saddle. At that point, the leather and frame had been smashed—from the look of it, by a bullet.

Harry thought of dispatching the poor beast with one of his pistols, but hesitated. The animal was hurt, but not yet near perishing and not gone lame. Taking the reins, he led it forward. The size of the animal, at least, helped clear a path in the mad swarm of humanity still rushing up the road toward him.

All at once they were gone—every blue coat, every frock coat. Peering through the dust, Harry saw only two people still remaining on the road below. One was a woman, half bent over, sobbing madly, her long, dark hair a mad tangle. The other was a man, sprawled facedown. He wore no hat. The hair was bright yellow.

Pulling hard on the reins, Harry dragged the horse on. Reaching Louise Devereux, he grabbed her around her small shoulders and pulled her close, looking fiercely into her dark, shining, half-mad eyes.

"Louise! Do you know me?"

Her eyes now fixed on him.

"Louise!"

"Harry. Harry Raines."

"Yes. Louise, Caitlin is waiting for you. Up the hill. Take your horse and go to her! Do you hear me?"

"Horse," she stammered, finally. "Oh God. My horse."

"Hold the reins tight and walk it up. Go now before you perish."

She looked back to the fallen Pleasants. He had not moved. "George! . . ."

"I'll tend to him. Go! Now!"

He gave her a quick slap on her bottom, enough to concentrate her attention but not to hurt, as he might an anxious animal.

"Help him!" she said. "Help him, please!"

"I will. Please! Go!"

He wrapped the reins around her hand and pushed her on, then hurried to the officer, kneeling at his side.

Pleasants was very, very dead. The back of his uniform coat was covered with blood. Lifting the man, turning the body across his own knee, Harry saw runnels of blood about his nose and mouth, and another soggy crimson circle over the chest.

Harry heard yelling. He looked to the crossroads below and saw a dusty group of soldiers, wielding muskets and coming toward him at a run. All were in gray.

In a moment, they'd be in musket range.

Chapter 4

THE roads back to Washington City had become rivers of misery and fear. Ambulances loaded with wounded, white-topped supply wagons, artillery caissons, and all manner of civilian carriages were caught up in the struggling, blue-uniformed mob, whose strung-out units had lost all cohesion and were mixed together like toy soldiers strewn from a box. This was no longer an army but a mass of imperiled souls fleeing from their first glimpse of Hell—as though the Devil were hot after them.

There'd been little sign of pursuing Confederates, not even nips or forays by outriding cavalry. Yet the Union soldiers, their packs and muskets thrown down as impediments to speed, pressed on for the Potomac as though its farther shore offered their only hope for salvation.

Their initial mad panic had diminished to a steady desperation; the shouts and oaths and yelps had all given way to a grim quiet, broken only by the cries and groans of the wounded in the ambulances. The men trudged along, not wanting to waste their energies on chatter now, making sound only with their tramping, dragging feet.

It had been a fierce struggle getting Louise into the rig. She had been furious with Harry for leaving the major back on the road, and became violently disagreeable when he tried to convince her of the fact that her dashing officer was dead. Her wounded horse had broken away, dragging her into a ditch and nearly killing her before the reins came free of her hand and wrist. Once in the seat, she began screaming and wailing hysterically, until fatigue finally subdued her. Falling silent, she said not a word the rest of the long, horrible journey. As they rocked along, Caitlin held Louise tightly, to keep her from leaping or falling from the buggy.

Harry kept a hand close to one of his Navy Colts. His worst fear was that some soldier might decide to speed his deliverance from the Secessionist demons by pirating Harry's hired rig. A few of the men they passed looked frantic or murderous enough to try it.

Happily, none did. After sundown, Harry even slept in patches, the horse in harness needing little guidance from the reins as they moved along in the stream of defeated humanity. At one point he was awakened from his dozing by Louise's sobbing—and the soft moisture of a beginning drizzle.

"She loved him," Caitlin said.

There would be many such women this day.

IT was breaking a gray, ugly dawn when they crossed the Long Bridge and plodded into the Federal City. It had begun to rain in earnest, and their horse was barely lifting foot in the increasing mud. Harry kept on into the town, not halting till he pulled up at Caitlin's boardinghouse. Dismounting, he helped the two women to the street. Louise Devereux was quite wobbly and dazed, and the craziness had not fully left her eyes. Caitlin insisted the younger woman stay with her for the present. Louise said nothing, but clung to her friend.

"I am grateful to you, Harry," said Caitlin. "You are a brave man."

He bowed and kissed her hand, which was wet from the rain. "I'm just grateful we've returned safe. I hope you will not embark on such folly again."

She gave him a tired smile. "There's no longer any need. Goodnight, Sir."

"Goodnight, Lady." He looked up at the gray sky. "And good day."

•   •   •

IT was only with great difficulty that he got back to the stable, given the mass of soldiery crowding the Avenue. Some were setting up campsites right there in the dirt and mud, starting cooking fires, when the rain abated, with split logs taken from nearby wood yards and slats pried from fences.

There was much citizenry out and about as well. If the prospect of victory and celebration had brought them forth initially, fear and worry kept them there. Several called to Harry for news of the Confederate advance. Some seemed persuaded that Washington was about to be bombarded with shell and shot and then invaded.

Caesar Augustus seemed as downcast as any survivor of the battle.

"We got a dozen good horses still not come back," he said. "Two carriages missing. Mr. Naylor gonna be in a real fury."

"It was a disaster all 'round."

"So it's goin' to go on, then," the black man said, liberating the sorry, tired horse Harry had hired from its harness.

"The war? Oh yes. Oh dear yes."

Harry had slumped onto a hay bale. He could have gone to sleep right there.

"Them slavers make good soldiers, do they?" said his friend, resuming his work.

"Not all Southerners are slavers, Caesar Augustus. Most of them aren't. But yes, they surely proved themselves on this occasion."

"Well, Marse Harry, I for one welcome a long bloody goddamned war. All Lincoln's been askin' for is a return of the states to the family fold. Ain't said nothin' about ending slavery."

"You're a free man, Caesar Augustus. No one can touch you. You've got your paper, signed and sealed by the state of Virginia."

The remark prompted an exceedingly dark look.

"Yes, I am free. But I sure got kin who ain't. Lot of them the property of your kin. I don't want Virginia back in the Union like that."

Harry had no reply, and so merely rose and put his hand wearily on his friend's shoulder and bade him farewell. Trudging up Pennsylvania Avenue on foot, he was pleased to see no muscular Irishman lurking about in the throng. With luck, maybe that problem was over. The defeat was changing a lot of agendas.

The Welshman Maddox was up and tending the bar at the National, which like all the liquor stores, wine shops, and public houses had been opened for the gloomy occasion and had become crowded. Harry had a bit of a struggle getting through the mob of nerve-wracked drinkers—as many in uniform as not.

"A sorry day," said Maddox, setting down a glass of Old Overholtz.

The bartender could have been speaking from outraged patriotism or scorn of the U.S. Army. His lilting Welsh accent rendered his import unfathomable to Harry.

"You're open early," Harry said. The taste of the whiskey pleased him like few things on earth.

"Not early enough for most of 'em, and late it'll be when they're done."

"Good news for you."

"Only good news there is today."

Wilkes Booth was not in evidence, but there were Southern sympathizers in the room. One fool offered a toast to the victorious General Beauregard. Harry feared a Union officer might take out a side arm and shoot him, but all seemed far more fixated on their drinks.

At a table near the window, Harry saw better company—the English newspaper reporter Russell. He was drinking ale and looking over his notes.

"Ah, Raines! Glad to see you survived the debacle. And a first-class one it was. The Light Brigade at Balaclava was not this beaten."

Harry eased himself into the other chair at the table. "Green troops," he said.

"Aye, green—and cowardly. The entire Union right turned and ran. I'm told the President's already up and over at the War Department interviewing returning officers. Wants to know what started the rout. Many are saying it was civilians who got mixed up with the soldiery and panicked."

Harry sipped his whiskey, then tilted back his head, closing his eyes. "There was panic, all right. But it started with the troops, not the civilians. I was there. On the right."

"Were you, Sir?" Russell looked up from his writing. "I should be interested in hearing more. There's another report that blames the whole damn thing on a single officer. A Major Pleasants or some such."

"What?" Harry snapped forward.

"A quite reliable source, I daresay. One of the man's superiors—some lieutenant colonel from Howard's Brigade. Beals, by name. Encountered him at McDowell's headquarters in Centreville. The man said the entire regiment turned as one and fled, after Pleasants set the dreadful example. He said the poor devil was shot through the back by the pursuing Confederates, but it was too late to stop the rout. When the regiment went, the entire division went. And finally the entire right wing of the Army."

"That's nonsense, Mr. Russell. I said I was there. When I last looked on Major Pleasants alive, he had sword in hand and was leading a few brave men back toward the rebels."

"And he perished?"

Harry nodded. "I had to leave his body on the field. I barely got away myself."

"He was shot in the back as they say?"

"That I could not say. There was blood both back and front. I hadn't time to look at him further to determine which part the ball went in." Harry emptied his glass, and set it down hard. "But he conducted himself bravely, Mr. Russell. There were few on that field who did."

The Britisher had begun writing in his notebook, with some vigor.

"This is very interesting," he said. "And where on the right flank did this take place?"

"Along the Manassas-Sudley Road, north of the crossroads. Up a long hill from an old stone house there."

"That was a key point in the battle, I'm told. What happened 'round that house, and also some place called Henry Hill nearby. I stayed at the stone bridge, until that became untenable. Congressman Ely was captured, did you know?"

"The North will survive," Harry said.

"I'm not sure it will survive all the congressmen Lincoln is making generals." Russell laughed, a little sourly, then stood up, pocketing his notebook. "I must find out the why of this defeat. There were many more Confederates than expected. There's talk they were reinforced by railroad from the Shenandoah Valley. If that's the truth, then there'll be hell to pay for the general that let that happen. Think of it, though. Fighting wars by train."

Harry was looking out the window to where a group of soldiers were brawling in the street. "Will you write of Major Pleasants?"

Russell lighted a cigar. "I will—if I can find one more witness to corroborate your story. Do you know of any?"

Harry thought of Louise, doubtless now collapsed and sleeping on Caitlin's bed. "None whose name I could tell you."

"Hmm. Well, I'm off to the War Department. Good day, Raines. Glad to see you well."

HARRY climbed the stairs to his room, so weary he twice dropped his key. A week's uninterrupted sleep might not suffice. He collapsed on his bed without removing a single garment beyond his boots. It occurred to him he'd forgotten to tell Russell the most significant thing about Major Pleasants' mortal wound. Perhaps it was just as well.

HE awoke to darkness, and someone shaking him rudely.

"Raines! Damn you, wake up!"

"I am awake."

"Then rise. You're to come with me."

The voice was unfortunately familiar, the Irish accent quite pronounced.

Harry sat up, blinking. There was a faint light from the

drawn window curtains, enough to see the now familiar figure and recognize the shadowy face.

"Just who in blazes are you? Why do you haunt me?"

"My name is Leahy. I'm called Boston Leahy, but you will call me Mr. Leahy."

"And why is that?"

"Because I represent the United States government, and you are a man in trouble." He threw back the front of his coat, revealing the handle of a large revolver. "Do ye understand me, lad?"

"But why have you been following me?"

"No more questions, boyo. You just get yourself up and come with me."

DESPITE the lingering rain, the crowds were so thick in the Avenue that Harry supposed he might get away from the Irishman by making a break through them at an opportune moment. But the veteran gambler in him cautioned against such a play. Better to fold his rotten hand and wait for the next deal.

It came rather soon. Leahy led him directly to the Willard, steering him through the Pennsylvania Avenue entrance. Oddly, that southern-facing portal was the one used by hotel guests loyal to the Union. Confederate sympathizers preferred the F Street entrance, on the hotel's north side.

Leahy guided him up the stairs, ascending two flights and then prodding him down the long central hallway. At the end, Leahy knocked twice on a door, then opened it.

By the window, behind a large round table he'd pulled out into the room to serve as a desk, was a short, stocky man with a chinbeard but no moustache, dressed in black—as much by inclination, Harry guessed, as in conformity with the current fashion.

His eyes were dark—at least in this gloom. He gave Harry a quick but encompassing look.

"It's Raines," said Leahy.

"Sit down," said the man at the table, tersely, but with less hostility than Harry had expected. He introduced himself: "Major E. J. Allen."

Oddly, Harry thought he recognized him. He had an accent that was in part Scots but had also a touch of the prairies.

"You say you're with the Army?" Harry asked. The man was in civilian clothes.

Major E. J. Allen stared at him hard a moment. "I am with the U.S. Secret Service."

"What the devil is that?"

"It's an agency of the Federal Government called into being just this very day. It has the power to question people such as yourself and jail them if it serves a purpose. That's all you need to know."

Harry was beginning to feel bleary. He'd slept all day, which was to the good, but had had nothing to eat since the previous night. He was of a mood to tell this man whatever it was he wanted to hear, if he'd be let go when done.

"Very well."

"You're Harrison Raines. A gambler."

"Trader in horses."

"You're a Virginian."

"So is His Excellency, General Winfield Scott."

"What were you doing at Manassas?"

"Never got to Manassas. Neither, I might add, did the Union Army, vital railhead that it is. But I was in the vicinity. Honorably, Sir. I was escorting a lady who wished to see the battle."

The man peered at a piece of paper. "Actress. You went out with one and came back with two."

"The other lady was in much distress when the battle turned. She lost her mount."

"Her name is Louise Devereux," the man said. "She was born and raised in New Orleans. She resided for a time in the city of Richmond, as did yourself."

"She's an actress," Harry said. "They reside where fortune provides."

"The other woman you were with—Caitlin Howard . . ."

"No Southerner. She's English born. Why such close attention to my companions and movements when there was so much else occurring in that vicinity?"

"We want to know what happened."

"What happened? It was a disaster."

Major E. J. Allen leaned forward on his elbows. "Yes, disaster. We need to know why it happened. We know that General Beauregard was reinforced by General Johnston's entire army from the Shenandoah. By railroad. But that only evened the odds. By then the field was ours. We had the high ground. We gave it all away. Our soldiers ran." His last word came out like a cannon shot. "Why!"

"The troops had never been in battle before."

"That was true of both sides. Something spooked the Federals. And it all started on the right. With Howard's Brigade. Where you were."

"Among a number of civilians."

"We have reports the panic started with the civilians. We have other reports there were a large number of officers who ran first, setting an example for the men. You were among the last to leave the field, Raines. Why was that? You a brave fellow? If you were, you'd be in uniform. Maybe you were sending signals. Maybe you were meeting with the enemy. The big difference between you and most everyone else on our side there is that your father and brother are serving officers in the Confederate Army."

The directness of the man's gaze seemed so familiar.

"General Longstreet's Brigade," Harry said. "My father's with the 17th Virginia; my brother's with the 30th Virginia Cavalry, Langhorne's Troop."

"Both units were in the Confederate line at Bull Run."

"I was not aware of that."

"You weren't?"

"No. I've not spoken to my father since my twenty-first birthday."

"It's not what you might have said to your pa that concerns us, Raines. It's what you said there to the troops in our lines that's our worry. What you said to men in Howard's Brigade. You were seen speaking to several. A sergeant. A couple officers. Northern Virginia's acrawl with agents provocateur, Raines. So's this city. Lafayette Baker put you down on his list long before the battle."

It then dawned on Harry who this man was.

"You are not Major E. J. Allen," he said. "There may not even be a Major E. J. Allen."

The other pulled back, affronted, but curious. "I am that officer."

"No you're not." Harry sensed the Irishman Leahy moving up behind him. "Your real name is Pinkerton. Allan Pinkerton. You're a detective from Chicago."

For a moment, Harry thought the man might pull out a pistol and shoot him right then and there.

"How do you know that?" the other said. He spoke now softly, which was more intimidating than his hard edge.

"We met once. It was a dark night. There was only one lantern. But I remember you well."

"The hell. We've never met."

"No, it's true, Sir. I recall clearly, because I made a point of finding out about you, after you paid a visit to Virginia, to some friends of mine. You're from Scotland. You were the first detective on the Chicago police force. Then you established your own private agency. You protected the mails—and you were involved with a certain railroad."

"The Illinois Central."

"No sir. A railroad without tracks."

A long stare. Finally, "Go on."

"A very discreet railroad. Dangerous. What some call the 'Underground Railroad.' I'm very much acquainted with one of the 'depots.' A barn with an unusually large cellar—behind a farmhouse on the Potomac between Martinsburg and Shepherdstown."

"And how are you familiar with this farm?"

"I own it."

Pinkerton looked to Leahy. What the Irishman had been preparing to do behind his back, Harry could not know. But this was a signal to desist.

"I was told the owner of that farm was a sympathizer to the abolitionist cause who lived elsewhere. I assumed it was in the North."

"Washington City, Mr. Pinkerton, is certainly 'the North.' "

Pinkerton rose and went to the window overlooking the Avenue, peering out at it from the side curtains as though he had someone below under surveillance. He seemed not much higher standing than he had been sitting.

He turned back, folding his arms.

"I had Mr. Leahy check you out because we'd been told you might be a Southern spy, Raines. I'm satisfied you're not—at least until somebody gives me better proof you are. But I didn't summon you to talk about the Underground Railroad. We had another report about the defeat, and it's damned disturbing. It's said a single officer started it. Major George Pleasants. This isn't just from the saloons and taverns and alleys. It comes from his own comrades—officers and ordinary soldiers who were with him. You are the only person who's said to contradict this report."

"Did you hear this from Russell, the British correspondent?"

"We have many sources of information, Raines."

"Well, I'll say it again—to anyone you wish. Pleasants retreated with the rest of them when the Confederates counterattacked—and yes, he did run ahead of his men. But it was to turn them 'round, and he succeeded with a few. Then he led them back into the fight."

"And was killed in action. Though it's said he was shot in the back."

"No."

"You mean he isn't dead?"

"He's dead—as dead as any of them out there. But best I can determine, when he fell, he was out of range of the enemy fire. Well out. They took their time about their pursuit."

"Who shot him, then?"

"I've been puzzling over that." Here he lied. "And I've found no answer."

Pinkerton left the window and came back to the table, but remained standing. Harry sensed he was about to be dismissed. He was grateful.

"You swear this is the truth?" Pinkerton asked. "That he died a hero—not a coward?"

"Yes. That's what I'd tell the President himself."

"You could be asked to. Major Pleasants' wife is the daughter of Senator Quigley, one of the President's closest friends.

They served in Congress together. But the senator's a very worthy man in his own right. It's not seemly his son-in-law being called a coward—and blamed for this debacle. Doesn't sit well with the President. Not at all."

Pinkerton went to the gaslight and turned it up slightly, the better to study Harry's face.

"You could be of use to us, Raines—to the U.S. Secret Service."

"No thank you. I'm neutral."

"How can you be neutral if you were part of the Underground Railroad?"

"That was about slavery. This is war."

"Same thing, Raines."

Harry started for the door. "I bid you good night, Sir."

The detective raised a hand to stay him.

"Your cooperation will do you in good stead, Raines. These are perilous times. Southern sympathizers will find life hard here. Loyalty oaths are going to be required of citizens. I fully expect habeas corpus to be suspended in some cases. Already has been. The Provost Marshal's office is going to start rounding up people on suspicion alone. If Mr. Baker's of a mind to lock you up, there's little I can do about it—unless I can tell him you're with us."

"Understood. Goodnight, uh, Major."

HARRY managed a sort of meal in a restaurant—cabbage and boiled meat. Demand for food was high now and stores low. Then he returned to his bed, fully prepared to sleep through to the next morning.

But his slumber was interrupted once again—this time by someone polite enough to knock.

Harry, still in the same clothes he'd worn to the battle, staggered to the door. It was a porter, an elderly man with slightly crossed eyes.

"Lady downstairs wants to see you, Mr. Raines."

Raines rubbed his eyes. "What lady?"

"Very fancy lady. Handsome woman. Didn't give her name."

Harry looked at his pocket watch. Of course she didn't. A lady didn't call on a man at such an hour, even if she confined herself to the hotel lobby.

It would be Caitlin. It could be no other. He was thrilled to have her come to him but hoped it didn't mean more trouble over Louise Devereux.

He gave the man a nickel. "Tell her I'll be with her in just a moment."

Pulling off his shirt, he washed himself in swift and cursory fashion, brushed down his hair. Then he threw on another shirt and his coat, and thrust his stocking feet into his boots. He hurried down the stairs, almost stumbling.

There was only one woman in the lobby and it was not Caitlin Howard. The lady was primly but richly dressed—in black, with a veil. He wished he'd thought to put on his eyeglasses.

She rose—so stiffly it might have been part of a somber ceremony.

"Mr. Harrison Raines?"

"Yes."

"I am Mrs. George Pleasants," she said.

Chapter 5

THERE was something noble in Mrs. Pleasants' aspect—a dignity that spoke of suffering and pride, good breeding, and forbearance. Hers were the cool, careful, if charmless, good manners of New England—gracious, but constrained. Even in the dim light of this corner of the lobby, he could see she was a remarkably handsome woman, though severe, her face drained of animation, her mouth tightly set.

She kept her eyes firmly locked on his, tactfully avoiding any notice of his disheveled and altogether disreputable appearance.

"It is kind of you to meet with me at this hour, Mr. Raines," she said, with great formality. "I hope it is no inconvenience."

Her voice was as dignified and sad as her demeanor. Harry felt an immediate impulse to help her, whatever she wanted or needed. He put his resentment at her late intrusion aside.

"Certainly," he said. "Your husband . . ."

"Was among the fallen. I have so been informed." She glanced about behind her, to a plush settee, and settled upon it with a great rustle of skirt. She nodded to Harry to seat himself beside her. He did so stiffly.

"I was there, at the field of battle," she continued. "It was foolish to go there, I know. But there were many of us who did. I—I spoke to George. Just before. For all I know, I was the last person to look upon his face while he still lived. It was at the end of it, when the Rebels attacked, when there was so much confusion. I thought we were going to be captured or massacred. But suddenly, there was George. He was like an angel sent from Heaven, Mr. Raines—there at the door of my carriage, urging me to flee, helping turn the carriage, then sending me on to safety while he himself hurried on toward the enemy. A hero, who died for his bravery."

Mrs. Pleasants paused to lift her veil and dab at her eyes with a handkerchief, though her voice remained unchanged.

"If I had persuaded him to come with me, or if he had run like the other soldiers, he would have lived," she said, working over her eyes once more. "But he instead stayed behind. He chose a braver thing to do. And now I am informed he is dead."

One last wipe of the cloth and her eyes were full on Harry again.

"You know, of course, what is being said—that George was a coward, that he is responsible for the grave calamity that befell the Army."

Harry nodded.

"Yet I understand you have exposed the falsehood of that—in places where it matters."

He nodded again. "To a newspaper correspondent, and to the U.S. Secret Service."

"Yes. It was Mr. Pinkerton who informed my father of what you said. You do know my father?" The last sentence was uttered with some emphasis.

"He is Senator Quigley."

She looked down at the carpet, as if averting her gaze from something disturbing.

"Did you see my husband fall, Mr. Raines? Were you witness to his death?"

He gave her a solicitous smile, trying to be reassuring. "No. When I got to him, he was already . . ." Harry trailed off, his mind in search of words he could not fnd. "There were two or three carriages in all that confusion on the road. One was yours, Madam?"

She nodded. "Yes, a black coach with yellow wheels."

"I saw it. Your coachman. Perhaps he saw . . ."

"No. I asked him. His attention was elsewhere. There was so much noise. So many running."

"There was a girl . . ."

He'd blurted that out.

"What did you say?"

"A young woman. I mean, there were other women there besides yourself. It was not a suitable place for a woman to be."

"No. Most definitely." Her eyes held him very strongly now. "Mr. Raines, I would ask a very great favor of you."

She would be asking for a written statement, an eyewitness account of her husband's heroism. He would happily grant her that. He'd attend to it first thing in the morning—soon as that might be.

"I would like you to accompany me back to the battlefield, so that I may retrieve my husband's remains."

She might as easily have asked him to go steal Jefferson Davis' hat.

"Mrs. Pleasants, at this point, General McDowell wouldn't go back there with his entire army."

"Indeed not. President Lincoln has informed my father that McDowell is to be relieved. A General George McClellan is to take his place."

"Madam, you would not be safe in Virginia now had you an entire division for escort."

"Mr. Raines. I intend to go there and bring back my husband no matter what. I would hope that a woman traveling on such a solemn enterprise would not be harrassed or hindered by soldiery. I'm told you know the country and would make an excellent guide. You are a Virginian. And you know exactly where George fell. Your presence is not only recommended but absolutely necessary."

Harry shrugged. "Mrs. Pleasants . . ."

"I wish George to have a Christian burial, and I wish to have an end put to this monstrous lie about him."

"I'll swear it to whatever authority you ask. I'll write . . ."

"Sir. I wish to establish as incontrovertible fact that my husband was not shot in the back, fleeing from the enemy."

He sighed, thinking she might back away from this lunatic

quest if he were to reveal that Major Pleasants probably wasn't shot by the Rebels at all. Then again, that might spur her zeal for recovery all the more.

"It's been raining for a day, Mrs. Pleasants. The roads are . . ."

She sat so stiffly she seemed almost standing. "Mr. Raines, Mr. Pinkerton informs me your loyalty to the Union is a matter of some debate in the capital. I have the power to establish your legitimacy at the highest levels. But this sword I wield swings both ways, do you understand?"

Harry's mind wandered to a vision of the Old Capitol Prison sitting gloomily on Jenkins Hill.

"I do."

"Very well. My coachman will call for you promptly at six o'clock in the morning. I will pay you for your trouble. Generously."

IF he had no choice in the matter, Harry thought he would at least try to improve their chances with reinforcement. But Caesar Augustus wasn't at his place of employment—not because of the late hour but because he'd been discharged. The management had blamed him for the stable's losses at what was now being called the Battle of Bull Run.

"You don't think General Beauregard had something to do with it?" Harry asked.

"That Negro was in charge here," said the livery stable owner. "I left him in charge. Look what happened! I'm near ruined!"

"Caesar Augustus is a good man, about the best I know of with animals. You're going to need him to get what stock you still have back in hireable condition."

"Not going to need no Negroes ever again."

"Then I can only presume you're going out of business." Harry left the stable without closing the door behind him.

HE found Caesar Augustus in his little shack at the back of Miss Annie Wilson's bawdy house near Murder Bay. Harry had great difficulty finding the door in the dark and had to pound loudly upon it several times before it was answered.

The door opened to a room as dark as the night—Caesar Augustus's face visible mostly by the faint glimmer of his eyes.

"It's me," said Harry. "Were you sleeping?"

"If I was, I sure ain't now. Mostly, I was deciding whether to open the door. Washington City's gettin' a mite dangerous lately, all these damn soldiers and guns about."

He stepped back inside and leaned to light a candle. His cramped, shabby quarters weren't much better than what he'd had on Harry's father's plantation. A small furry thing darted along the wall and abruptly vanished in the shadows.

Somewhat tentatively, Harry stepped inside. Caesar Augustus shoved the one chair in Harry's direction and seated himself on the lumpy-looking mattress of his old rope bed. He had a billy in his hand—from the look of it, a leather sheath filled with round shot. He set it carefully on the floor.

"I went to look for you at the stable," Harry said.

"Then you did a dumb thing, Marse Harry, because I don't work there no more."

"So I gather. Did he give you any back pay?"

"He told me I cost him so much I got to work the rest of my days to pay for it all, and even then come up short."

"That's nonsense."

"I got angrier words than that."

"Do you have any money saved?"

"Got a little hid away, but that's for my future—unless I get real desperate about the here and now."

"Would you like to make some money?"

The Negro had a small whiskey jug. He reached for it and took a pull, then hospitably handed it to Harry.

"I told you, Marse Harry," said Caesar Augustus. "I don't ever want to work for you Raines folks again. Fact you might give me a little money don't much change the relationship."

"I need you to travel with me for a day or two."

"Travel where?"

"Virginia. Out to Manassas and back."

Caesar Augustus smiled. It was as though a second candle had been lit.

"Marse Harry. I spent my whole life gettin' away from that godforsaken place. Now you ask me to go back there straight into the middle of the whole damned Confederate Army. Headless chicken got more sense 'n that. What's this about?"

"Union officer's wife wants to fetch back his body. I was the last one to see him, so she wants me to go with her. As her father's a U.S. senator, I have little choice. She could get Lafayette Baker to lock me up for the duration of the war. She'll pay expenses. Her father's rich. They could be generous."

"What you want me along for? Carry a gun?"

Caesar Augustus was as good a shot as Harry wasn't. "Yes. And for something else."

The black man waited for Harry to explain, then offered the answer himself.

"You want me to act like I'm your slave, so you can pass yourself off as a Southern sympathizer—a true Confederate."

The fellow was indeed an excellent chess player. "Make things a lot easier, probably."

"That's just about the worst, most awfulest thing you could ask me to do, Marse Harry."

"I could hire another Negro, but he wouldn't be you. I still count you as friend, Caesar Augustus."

The other stared, his eyes brightly reflecting the candle flame.

"How generous?" he asked.

"How much would you want?"

"To go to Manassas? Five dollars."

"Ten." That was the sum Mrs. Pleasants had offered Harry. He'd no need of it, and Caesar Augustus surely did.

"Anything about this you left out telling me?" the black man asked.

"A small detail. The Union officer didn't die in battle."

"He succumbed to consumption right there on the battle-field?"

"He was shot, but not by the Confederates. They were out of range."

"Well now, that's mighty interesting. Does she know?"

"Not yet."

"Ten whole dollars?"

"Yes, Sir."

"All right. I'll go with you, Marse Harry. But as hired hand. I ain't gonna be your slave, or anyone else's. Not ever again. I don't care if it's pretend."

"Even if our lives depend on it?"

"Not even then."

Chapter 6

MRS. Pleasants' strict disciplines did not include promptness. Harry and Caesar Augustus stood at the curb beneath the trees of the Avenue for nearly an hour before her coach finally pulled up, splattering mud on them both.

It was an expensive and handsome vehicle, drawn by four matched horses and generating interested looks and stares from the soldiery still camped in the street. It would doubtless have the same effect on the Confederates. Harry wished she'd come in a farm wagon.

He was happy at least to see that she'd brought provender for the journey, as neither he nor Caesar Augustus had eaten the full makings of a meal in two days. To wash down these victuals, she'd provided lemonade and tea. Harry had whiskey, but decided to hold that in reserve.

He'd brought his Colt revolvers with him, and some extra ammunition. Caitlin had not returned his pocket pistol, and he'd deliberately left his rifle behind, fearing it might excite the curiosity and displeasure of the military, whether Blue or Gray.

It might have been wiser to have left all his weapons behind. Firing off a round for any reason where he was going would likely invite a reply in kind.

The lady raised no objection to Harry's former slave joining them, but insisted he ride up next to the coachman, a scruffy, nervous, red-nosed man whose clothes seemed much too large for him. Caesar Augustus said nothing—at least not aloud—but Harry found the arrangement disagreeable. So, apparently, did the coachman. He sat silently, obedient but sullen.

"And if it rains, Mrs. Pleasants?" Harry asked, as they moved off down the street.

"Many a brave soldier will endure worse than rain to defend that man's freedom," she said. 'I'm surprised at you, Mr. Raines. We will be traveling through Virginia, where a Negro riding inside a coach with his master is going to attract notice. My concern over where your man sits is nothing more than that. You are to be my guide. I should hope for better sense from you."

Harry accepted the admonishment without comment, letting the matter pass. As he thought upon it, she was probably right.

Heading for the Long Bridge with the horses still at a walk, they had progressed scarcely two blocks along the Avenue when they heard the shouts of someone pursuing them. Harry leaned out the coach window to see a man in spectacles, wide-brimmed straw hat, and black box coat, splashing along through the yellow-brown mud and calling for them to stop.

"It's Matthew Brady," Harry said. "The photographer."

Mrs. Pleasants called to the coachman to halt. Brady was breathless, and hung on to the window edge while he regained his wind.

"Raines," he said finally. "They said in your hotel that you're going back to Bull Run."

Harry had told no one about this journey, though he'd left a note for Caitlin. He doubted she'd even arisen yet—let alone tended to her mail—and wondered who could be spying on him.

"I am. In the service of this lady." He paused to make introductions, but Mrs. Pleasants volunteered that she had sat for a *carte de visite* likeness by Brady, and offered him greeting, though without much warmth.

"I lost everything out there," Brady said, turning back to Harry. "Everything. Camera, plates, chemicals, wagon, horse. I barely escaped with my life. Gads, poor Gardner's still not turned up."

Harry had witnessed Brady's rapid departure from the field in the confusion of the rout on Sudley Road, and recalled that the photographer had been among the very first civilians to turn and head for home—in his case, with such haste that he'd abandoned his wagon and fled the scene on foot. Brady's assistant, Alexander Gardner, had been nowhere in view. At this rate, Brady's patrons would see little of the war through his lens.

"I'll look where I can," Harry said. "What do you want back most? Your camera, the wagon, or Mr. Gardner?"

"Don't fret about Gardner. He'll make it back. He's a resourceful fellow. But my camera—and the plates! I've nothing to show for having been there, Raines. The greatest battle ever fought on this continent. The largest armies ever to muster on this continent! And I have nothing to show for it."

"I don't hold much hope, Brady. But it's to that spot that we're bound. I'll see what's there. Do my damnedest."

"Then I thank you."

"Just keep quiet about this journey."

"Whatever you want, Raines."

The photographer jumped back from the coach with a splat. Harry was surprised to see a slight smile appear on Mrs. Pleasants' stern lips. It proved fleeting.

THE morning's increasing sunlight and a freshening breeze began to dry the mud, but their pace on the Virginia side of the river remained slow because of the cordon of barricades, sentry posts, skirmish lines, and soldiers' camps that the Union Army had established there.

The defensive line now ran along the curve of the Potomac from Alexandria north to the Long Bridge and then around to the Chain Bridge on the west. It was thin in places, but troops were being shoveled into this position as soon as their units had been reformed and refitted. New outfits were coming in— three-year enlistees to replace the three-month men whose enlistments were expiring. It seemed ridiculous now that the government, and the general populace, had thought this rebellion might be put down in a mere three months. No one believed that now.

Mrs. Pleasants carried a pass signed by President Lincoln himself. They were accordingly treated with almost swooning respect by the Union troops they encountered, especially in the area around Arlington Heights, where Colonel Sherman— brother of a Republican senator—was in command. But instead of speeding them on their way, the presidential signature served to delay them by stirring unwanted attention. Though uninvited, a troop from one of the cavalry companies of Palmer's Battalion even followed them as escort out Columbia Pike all the way to Bailey's Crossroads, spurs and sabres jangling musically and making Harry nervous. This was just the sort of thing to attract an enemy cannon shell or sharpshooter's bullet.

But the troopers spooked upon reaching the intersection. The lieutenant in command gave the coach a hurried salute, then reined his mount around and put spurs to flank. His men noisily followed.

Harry and Mrs. Pleasants continued on unbothered for a time, but a few miles beyond, just shy of Fairfax Courthouse, they encountered their first Confederate picket, announced by a musket shot fired high that made Mrs. Pleasants blanch. Two young soldiers in ill-fitting uniforms and a richly-bearded sergeant emerged from the side of the road.

Harry handed Mrs. Pleasants the pass her late husband had written out for him.

"Put this and the President's safe conduct in a place where no gentleman would look," he whispered to her. "And let me speak for all of us."

"We're to be Southern?"

"Well, I certainly am."

"Just use good sense."

"Yes, Ma'am." He leaned out the window and identified himself to the sergeant by name, deciding it best to invoke also his father's and brother's names as well, and finally adding their Virginia military units. Before the sergeant could inquire further, he explained their purpose on the road by saying simply that the lady wished to recover her husband's body.

Lies were most successful when accompanied by as much truth as possible.

"He was at Manassas?"

"Yes. And we believe he lies there still."

The sergeant's beard had tobacco juice streaked through it. Harry disliked the habit and so had no chaw to offer in trade for the man's friendship and approval, but it occurred to him as a good idea for the future. He did have two cigars with him, and gladly contributed one to the cause. "Obliged," the sergeant said, putting the cigar in his half-unbuttoned tunic. "Where you people come from?"

"Near Arlington." That was true enough. They'd been in that place.

"Ain't that country in Federal hands?"

"Don't know for sure what's in whose hands from minute to minute. Didn't expect to come upon you fellows this close to the Potomac. I have a house near Martinsburg and travel through here frequently, but never been stopped by soldiers before." He smiled.

"Well, you get yourself used to it, Mr. Raines." The sergeant started to back off, then hesitated, looking into the coach. "Excuse me, Ma'am, but might I ask your name?"

Mrs. Pleasants' accent was decidedly New England. She was no actress, and there'd be no disguising it.

She found a way. Putting handkerchief to her face, she began to cry, replying between sobs. She might have been from Charleston itself for all the sergeant knew. Harry was impressed.

"I'm sorry," she said, with another sob. "My husband . . ."

The sergeant's touched his cap. "Sorry to trouble you." He looked up at Caesar Augustus.

"He your'n?" the sergeant said to Harry.

Harry and Caesar Augustus owed each other many favors from their long association, but Harry had forgotten which of them was in the greater debt. After this incident, Harry's obligation could be large, indeed.

"Yes," he said, after perhaps too long a pause.

"That right, boy?" the sergeant asked. "He's your master?"

For a long, unnerving interval, Caesar Augustus didn't speak.

"You hear me, boy? That your master?"

The former slave's shoulders hunched forward, but still he did not speak.

The sergeant's brow wrinkled into a very deep frown. "I ain't going to tolerate that kind of insolence," he said to Harry. "Now you answer me, you black son of a bitch. You belong to him?"

Harry closed his eyes, waiting. He supposed he probably could have hired any Negro off the street for this charade.

"Dat right. He my Marse Harry. I belongs to him."

Harry exhaled in relief—and amusement. Fortunately, the sergeant's ear was not so acute when it came to the sardonic. The man backed fully out of the way of the coach.

"You go on, now," he said. "But find yourself an officer and get you a safe conduct. Them Federals come out here again, this part of Virginia goin' to be a mighty dangerous place and ain't much going to be accepted on faith."

"Thank you, Sergeant," Harry said, touching his hat as the coach rolled on.

"How much more of that will we have to endure?" said Mrs. Pleasants, after they were out of earshot of the pickets.

"It depends. The most direct route'll run us head-on into the main Rebel army. There's a longabout way that'll let us get around them, but it'll take all day."

"What happens to us if we're taken prisoner?"

"Mrs. Pleasants, Ma'am, I'm afraid this is my first war."

She gazed out the window for a time, then turned to face him squarely.

"What will have happened to my husband's body?"

"Their army's moved on. Their first concern will have been their wounded, then ours. I don't know when they might have gotten around to the dead. I suspect he'll likely still be there."

"Then let us avoid the Rebel soldiers. By all means."

"We'll have to spend the night out here, and nearly all of tomorrow—even if we find him quickly."

"I don't mind any privation, Mr. Raines, so long as I get my husband back to Washington."

• • •

HARRY chose a new route that, in zigs and zags, led them generally northwest and around the Confederate Army. But there continued to be military traffic on the road—supply wagons and gray-uniformed dispatch riders, and along one stretch, a train of ambulances. No one gave them any bother. Harry wondered how long that would last.

As the sun rose higher and the heat increased, Mrs. Pleasants began to doze. Eventually, her chin came down to her chest and she slept soundly. Despite himself, Harry did the same.

When he awakened, the day had advanced into the afternoon, and Mrs. Pleasants was shaking him with a firm, authoritarian hand.

"We're at a crossroads, Mr. Raines. The coachman doesn't know which way to go."

A look out the window showed a road angling in upon theirs from the right, crossing a single line of railroad track in the process. A large oak tree with weird, elongated branches informed him precisely where they were. There was a stream nearby where he'd picnicked with Caitlin not too many months before.

"Turn left," Harry said. "We need to head south again."

Mrs. Pleasants instructed her driver accordingly, then adjusted her position, fidgeting somewhat in her seat. The heat made her dress stick to the leather.

To Harry's discomfort, she began to talk about her dead husband, recounting his fine and noble qualities, of which all but courage had eluded Harry's perception. Then, confounding him all the more, she began to ask questions. Had Harry known the man in Washington? What interests and pursuits had he out and about the town?

"He was popular, Madam."

"With whom?"

"With, uh, the prominent people in the city."

"You mean Southern people." Color had come into her face, and that odd little smile had returned. "Washington society has long been dominated by Southern families—haughty folk who style themselves as 'fine.' Are you saying he was popular with such as these? Southerners?"

Harry hesitated. "I don't think he had many Southern friends, Mrs. Pleasants."

"He has none this day, surely." She looked at him squarely. "Are you a gambler, Mr. Raines? Mr. Pinkerton said he thought that's how you made your living."

The coach lurched over a bump, jostling them together. Harry righted himself, making apology. She'd maintained her stiff posture, sitting as straight as a New England grave marker.

"I enjoy cards, and I make some money from them," Harry said, "but I have investments. I own land. And I trade in horses."

"Then I expect you'll become rich, as the army is going to need a great many horses."

"Expect it will."

"I refer to the Union Army, Sir," she said. "Or will you supply both sides, and make even greater profit?"

He sighed. "Perhaps it would be better if I rode up top."

The hardness of her expression softened, and she put a hand gently on his arm.

"Forgive me, Mr. Raines. I loved my husband very much. I am devastated to have lost him—and to have it happen right there, almost before my very eyes. I can't tell you the horror of that. I am easily made resentful now, especially toward Southerners. I'm sorry. I mean you no offense. You've done me no harm. You've been very kind. You . . ."

To his astonishment, she came suddenly against him, seeking the comfort of his arms, thrusting her face against his neck as sobs and tears came forth in a great, heaving gush, this time quite genuinely.

He held her until the torrent of sorrow had run its course, then gently moved her back.

"We've a while yet before we reach the battlefield," he said. "You must rest."

• • •

FOLLOWING Harry's circuitous route, they did not set hoof on the Sudley-Manassas Road until an hour so late in the afternoon that, in winter, it would have been dark. Once across the Bull Run ford, Harry did switch his seat, replacing Caesar Augustus up beside the coachman's. He wanted to see whatever they might encounter well before Mrs. Pleasants did, whether it was Secessionist military or Yankee corpses.

There were neither to be found in the place where he had left the unfortunate major. Harry had seen no other Union soldier fall there, but if any had, they like Pleasants had been carried away.

He had noted a wealth of army weaponry and equipment discarded and cast aside in the immediate aftermath of the battle, but the ground had been cleansed of that as well. What remained was wreckage and breakage. With Caesar Augustus' help, he poked through some of that scattered in the high grass at the side of the road. Though he came upon no flesh, they turned up at least part of what they sought. Brady's wagon and team had been confiscated, but his camera, equipment, and plates had been dumped on the ground where he'd been working.

There'd been some damage, but Harry had no way of judging its seriousness. He and Caesar Augustus gathered up as much as they could find and loaded it onto the roof of the coach.

Mrs. Pleasants, who had alighted to stretch her limbs after such long confinement, objected angrily.

"My husband is lying God knows where, and you stop to burden us with this rubbish?"

"Mr. Brady thinks of it as history, Madam. Let us indulge him, for it could prove to be the case."

"Where did my husband die?"

"Exactly here—at the side of the road."

"Where is he then?" She had made fists of her hand.

Harry looked down the hill to the stone house at the crossroads, then west along the Warrenton Pike. "A moment, Mrs. Pleasants."

He reached into the coach to where he had stowed his spy glass, then climbed to the coachman's seat and slowly examined the area, moving his focus to the halted wagon below.

Two men were by it, working as though loading cord wood. He guessed their load was flesh and blood.

Dried blood.

"We may be in luck," he said. "If you want to call it that."

MRS. Pleasants urged a gallop, but Harry didn't want to careen down so steep a hill—or alarm the burial detail, if that's what it was.

The two Confederate privates gave Harry no notice until he came close to speak to them. He figured they must now be far enough behind the Confederate army to be taken for Southern civilians at all times.

"There are still dead here?" Harry asked. "This long after the battle?"

A sickly odor was in the air.

The soldiers paused in their labor, looking glad of the opportunity.

"A few. Not enough."

"They're not Confederate?"

"There was Confederates on Henry Hill—a heap of them—but they're all buried. Them there're Yankee corpses."

Harry looked over the wagon's load, then back to the patch of woods, where he could see a sprawl of lifeless forms.

"Mind if I take a look at 'em?"

"Suit yourself," said the younger of the two privates. "If you can stomach the smell."

"Thank you," said Harry, starting for the trees. Caesar Augustus leapt off the coach to follow.

"What you want with ripe Yankee dead?" the other private asked.

"Just want to see what they look like," Harry answered.

"They look like what we want them to look like. Wish the whole damn Yankee nation looked like that."

The sickly smell was worse in the trees. Every fly in Virginia seemed to have found this place.

There were fewer bodies, though, than Harry expected. They'd been tossed close together, but were more strewn than stacked. All their useful possessions had been taken—boots, shoes, swords, bayonets, canteens, belts, shirts, braces—in some cases everything but their underwear and blue uniform coats.

Some were missing more than that. Major Pleasants was one of these unfortunate victims.

They'd taken his boots, sword, and side arm, but, perhaps in respect for his rank, had left everything else. Harry recognized him by his still-brilliant yellow hair and sash.

Some pigs were snuffling the ground over on the other side of the corpses. A large crow sat boldly on the shoulder of a man lying on his side, his head twisted around grotesquely. Harry picked up a piece of deadwood and threw it, missing the shiny dark bird but scaring it into noisy, squawking flight.

Caesar Augustus came up beside him.

"Must be a farm or two 'round here," he said.

"I think several," Harry said.

"Let their pigs run loose."

"Just like in Charles City County."

"Never liked pigs, Marse Harry."

"Let's go."

The black man started toward Pleasants' body.

"No," Harry said. "Let him be for now. We'll come back after sundown."

"You goin' to leave him like this until then?"

"I don't want that Rebel burial detail to note our carrying off a Union officer. And I don't want Mrs. Pleasants looking upon him in the light of day. She'll want to see his face."

The major no longer had one. As with several of the corpses here, the pigs had gotten to him.

When they returned, the Confederate soldiers had gone. Otherwise, all was as it had been, only far more ghastly in the flickering yellow-orange glow of the lamp.

"We'll have to remove his coat," Harry said.

"Why's that?"

"I want to use it to cover what was once his face."

With some struggle, and no help from the scruffy coachman, they got Pleasants' remains back to the coach and up on its roof. Mrs. Pleasants demanded to see her husband but Harry warned that they were in danger traveling this country at night and urged her to save her farewells for a proper funeral.

Grimly, she obeyed. Retracing their route, they were descending the other wise of the hill when a gunshot rang out. The ball whizzed by without striking anything. It was followed by a shout.

"Halt! You stop that team, you son of a bitch!"

A moment later, a man on horseback appeared beside the coach, his cuffs and sleeves decorated with gold braid. He was soon joined by what looked to be an entire squadron of Confederate cavalry.

Chapter 7

HARRY had planned to return to Washington by way of Maryland, avoiding both armies by going directly north to Leesburg and crossing the Potomac the next morning at a ferry, where he knew the boatman.

The Confederate cavalry patrol altered his plans considerably. After a brief and churlish interrogatory by the lieutenant commanding the troop, a lanky, shiny-faced fellow who seemed little more than a boy, they were taken by another road to Upperville, Virginia. The Rebel cavalry rode close escort on both sides of the coach as well as front and rear. They'd given no official explanation for this arrest; only oaths, jeers, whoops, laughter, and melodramatic mutterings about spies.

After Bull Run, the Confederates were certainly enjoying themselves.

Mrs. Pleasants was fiercely indignant about everything, forcefully impressing upon the young officer the morbid nature of her visit to Southern territory and the outrage she felt at his interfering with it. Worse, as Harry had feared, she let the boy know in no uncertain terms that her father was a United States senator.

Harry attributed her irrational behavior to her emotional state. If he were bringing back the body of Caitlin Howard, he supposed, he'd be just as recklessly intemperate.

After many miles of bumping through the darkness, they

were brought to the yard of what appeared to be a small farm. Mrs. Pleasants was escorted into the main house. Harry, Caesar Augustus, and the coachman were put into the barn. A soldier was posted at the door, which was shut though not locked. They were not allowed a lantern, and so sat in the dark, though a bit of pale light from the house was visible through cracks between the wooden slats of the barn wall.

"What now, Marse Harry?" said Caesar Augustus, quietly. The churlish coachman had moved away from them toward the back of the barn.

"I'm afraid that's up to the Confederate Army."

"They might want to hang us or shoot us."

"They won't bother you. You're just property to them."

"Marse Harry, if they shoot you as a spy 'cause you're out on the roads at night with a dead Yankee officer on the roof, I become a slave again."

"Very well, Caesar Augustus. For your sake, I won't let them hang me. But if we don't get Mrs. Pleasants back to Washington City as safe and sound as she left, we both could come in for some hanging and shooting on that side of the river."

"Don't you fret about that woman," her coachman said. "She'll have these boys wishin' they were elsewhere before this night's done. You ain't come in for it much yet, but she's got a tongue like a bullwhip."

The coachman's voice was coming from the rear wall. Harry could hear him moving around as he spoke. There was scarcely light at all, but vaguely, dimly, Harry could see the man's form—a shifting shadow.

"How long've you worked for her?" Harry asked.

"I don't. I work for Senator Quigley. But she moved back in with him after her husband went off to war, so now I haul 'em both wherever they want to go. Sure wasn't my idea to come out here for the battle."

"She must have loved her husband very much to have come out here alone."

"She warn't alone." There was a scraping sound.

"What are you doing?" Harry asked.

"It's stone," the coachman said.

"What is?" asked Harry.

"The barn wall. It's foundation stone. It was hard to see pullin' into the yard here but I think this barn's part dug into a hillside."

"Then we'll be able to keep cool if we have to stay here through the heat of another day."

"That ain't what I'm thinkin', Mr. Raines. I'm thinkin' the upstairs part—the loft up there—those walls are all wood. And if you broke through one of them you'd be on solid ground on that hill, out of sight of them Rebels below."

"As a coachman, I guess you know your barns."

"You're not gettin' his meaning, Marse Harry," said Caesar Augustus. "He don't plan to pass another day in here."

"We could kick out a board or two up there and be on our way 'fore they'd know a thing," the man said.

"And Mrs. Pleasants?"

A pause. "We could go for help. Get the Union Army."

"Friend, the nearest Federal troops'll be on the other side of the Potomac, which from here is close to fifteen miles away. And if we show ourselves near that house they'll shoot us down before we can call out her name."

"You still got a Colt revolver," Caesar Augustus said. "They only took the one."

Harry now wished they'd taken both. He'd stuck the second one in his belt at his back, and its metal bulk was hurting him. If they found it now they probably would shoot him.

"A short-sighted gambler, with a six-shot saddle pistol, taking on a whole troop of cavalry? Those are pretty poor odds."

"Those horse soldiers went back out on patrol," the coachman said. "Maybe there aren't so many left around here."

"This is some kind of headquarters," Harry said. "There'll be soldiers enough.

The latch on the barn door rattled and of a sudden the door was pulled open wide. Three enlisted men stepped in—two carrying muskets and the third, a corporal wearing a holstered pistol that drooped below his formidable stomach, holding a lantern high. Most visible in the pale circle of orange-yellow light was the coachman, caught climbing partway up the vertical ladder leading to the hayloft. One of the soldiers quickly raised his musket and took aim at the man.

"Get down now, or we'll shoot you off that ladder," said the corporal with the lantern. "First shot directed arseward."

The coachman came down quickly and hard, landing on his backside. He got to his feet and stood cursing loudly a moment, then looked anxiously to the three soldiers. The fellow seemed some petty villain out of Charles Dickens.

"Sit down!"

The coachman did so with a thump—his eyes dark little points in the lantern light.

"You come with us," the corporal said to Harry.

"Where?"

"Not far."

It was raining when they stepped back into the yard, softly but steadily. He glanced about, hesitating. If they actually were going to shoot him or hang him soon, they'd have his arms bound tightly by now. Certainly, if he were in charge of such a party, he'd have his prisoner secured that well, but these fellows now seemed to treat him with a little respect. When they shoved him, it was gently enough for him to keep his feet.

He was led through the back door of the farmhouse, down a short hall, and into the front parlor. A captain, a rather tall man with huge dragoon boots that came up over his knees, sat sprawled in a wooden chair beside a small marble-top table with some papers on it. He had long black hair that fell over the collar of his unbuttoned uniform tunic. In his hand was a metal drinking cup, which he raised to his lips as Harry entered.

"You may sit, Sir," he said. "That horsehair sofa by the wall is tolerably comfortable."

"Thank you." Harry went over and seated himself carefully. The sofa was worn and lumpy with some bare patches in the upholstery, but he was happy to be on it.

"Refreshment?"

Harry wanted to keep his wits about him, what wits there were.

"No thank you. Sir."

The Confederate captain had been reading a newspaper. Without a further word to Harry, he picked it up and resumed his perusal. Harry might as well have been waiting for his turn at a barber's. He took advantage of the moment to close his eyes and doze awhile—but it proved a short while.

"An amazement," said the captain. "Truly an amazement."

"Sir?"

"We're Swann's Batallion of the 1st Virginia Cavalry. Detached now, but we were at the Battle of Manassas. Part of Early's Brigade. Rode flank when Early's men were brought across Henry Hill to stop the Yankee's afternoon attack. I got sent by General Bee to find Colonel Elzey when General Smith was shot, but I remember clearly Bee being mad as hell at General Jackson. You ever hear of him, General Thomas J. Jackson?"

"No, I'm afraid I haven't."

"Mean son of a bitch. Crazy, too. Always suckin' on lemons. Good soldier, though. That's what they say. And his Virginians sure fought well later in the day. But before, when I was there with General Bee—well, Jackson had all on his own pulled his men out of the line on the right and brought 'em over to where the Yankees were attacking. Did it just on his own say-so. General Johnston didn't tell him nothin'. But he gets his brigade up on the hill and then stops. He has his men settle in there and won't budge an inch farther, even though General Bee wants to attack. Bee sends two dispatch riders to urge Jackson forward, but there he stands—unmovable. Bee, he was furious. He throws down his cap and says, 'There stands Jackson like a stone wall!' Then Bee charges down the hill toward the Yankees without Jackson's Virginians so much as throwin' a rock. And Bee gets himself killed."

Harry stared without comprehension. "My condolences."

"You don't understand," said the captain, waving the newspaper about. "This Richmond paper here, they got it all wrong. They have Bee calling Jackson a stone wall, but in the meaning of a general who don't skedaddle. They make him out a hero, when I think Bee would've had Jackson relieved of command if he could. An amazement, Sir! The fact turned right around like a two-wheeled cart! It's our history these newspapermen are writin', and look what they do to the truth."

Harry still stared, but his incomprehension was aimed at something else.

"If I may ask, Sir. You're holding me here as a possible spy, yet you talk about all these things as though I were a fellow Confederate officer. Why speak so freely?"

The Captain drank some more liquor from his cup. "Hell, Raines, I know you're not a spy. You've been vouched for."

Harry blinked. "Vouched for? By whom?"

"By your kin."

"My kin? Do you mean my father and brother? They're in your army—with Longstreet."

"So you told my lieutenant. But Longstreet's over in Fairfax County, scarin' the hell out of the Union Army. No, I'm talkin' about your cousin."

"Cousin?" He had piles of cousins, but none living near Upperville.

"Your *famous* cousin!" He held up the newspaper, rattling it. " 'The Heroine of Front Royal.' Killed herself a Yankee soldier just two weeks ago—on the Fourth of July in fact." The captain studied him a moment, as he might an idiot. "Marie Isabelle Boyd. *Belle* Boyd!"

Harry snapped fully awake. The use of "cousin" here was a stretch of the word. He had a third cousin in Falling Waters, Virginia, who had married into the Glenns, who were cousin kin to Belle's mother, Mary Glenn Boyd. Belle had always tried to improve upon the relationship, even when she was a little girl. When he journeyed to Martinsburg, she'd tag along behind him wherever he went, sometimes on her pony. When she was old enough to ride an actual horse, she'd fly to Shepherdstown on the merest word that he might be at his farm near there—or was expected soon. She talked constantly of their marrying someday.

She had just turned eighteen in May. As far as Harry was concerned, he was now in two predicaments.

He took the newspaper to hand. Union troops under General Patterson had come into Martinsburg on July Fourth and she'd shot and killed one in her house with a large saddle pistol.

"Where is she?" he asked, hoping it was by now some distant place.

"Right upstairs—talking to that disagreeable Yankee woman you had with you."

A clatter of feet was heard on the stairs. Harry wondered if Belle has been lurking up there, listening.

"Cousin Harrison!" she exclaimed, with more theatrics than Caitlin would have dared use on a stage. "It fills a lady's heart with such joy to lay eyes on you again."

There were those who regarded Belle as a powerfully attractive young woman. She was tall and slender, though otherwise notable for her exceedingly buxom form. Her mouth and eyes were large and wide, but the latter were of an arresting blue-gray color that attracted as much attention as her figure. Her nose was prominent—indeed, commanding, worthy of the bow of a ship—and her jaw was as strong. But she had an abundance of golden brown hair, wit and charm, a grand style, and a bold esprit.

Harry had always liked and admired her, though the older she got, the more nervous she made him. He'd failed to persuade her that his heart belonged to quite another woman, even though the woman didn't seem to want it.

Belle was an extraordinary horsewoman—better at a gallop than Harry. He'd once seen her canter a level field actually standing on the saddle of her horse, Fleeter. Whoever she eventually married, the man wouldn't stand a chance.

"Hello, Belle," he said. "I see you've become famous—for killing a man."

"I was defending our family home, Harrison Raines," she loudly proclaimed. She turned toward the officer. "Captain, I should like to walk outside a moment with my cousin. Would you oblige me?"

The officer responded with a bow. "No one's goin' to deny you anything in this headquarters, Miss Boyd."

She gave him her grandest smile, then pulled Harry after her out the front door of the house. There was a sentry outside very near sleep who paid them no mind, but she continued on until they were on the muddy dirt of the road.

"I had no choice, Harry. That Yankee brute was threatening

my mother, and there was no man in the house to defend her."

"Didn't need one with you around."

She smiled, then returned to seriousness. "I did not mean to kill him, but he died anyway. Some colonel ordered an inquiry but I was found guiltless—by the Union Army, Harry. I'm no murderer. Merely a patriot."

Belle slipped on a wet patch and caught his arm. She kept her hand there as they proceeded.

"How is it you've 'vouched' for me?" he asked.

She squeezed his arm. "You're kin, if only by marriage," she said. "They shot a railroad engineer at Manassas as a saboteur, just because he couldn't get his locomotive runnin'. I surely would not want that happening to a lovely man like you. So I told them you were a spy for us in Washington City—that that's why you were with this woman, findin' out important things that only the daughter of a friend to the monster Lincoln could know."

Wearily, he shook his head. "Belle, I'm not a spy for anybody. I've taken no side. I came out here to help this woman find her husband. I'd escort a Southern lady to a battlefield in the North in the same circumstance."

"Of course you would. But Confederate spy you're goin' to be. Leastwise here in Leesburg. And if they ask you about shoes, tell 'em the arrangements are being made."

"Shoes?"

"War's not three months old, and our glorious army's runnin' out of shoes. It needs thousands of shoes, for the new men comin' in. You keep this a dark secret between us, but there's supposed to be someone from the North goin' to find some for us—someone in Washington."

"In the Union Army?" If the Confederacy was going to employ such chatterboxes as his "cousin" as spies, its cause was doomed.

"Don't know—but if anyone here asks if it could be you, say yes. That'll do you more good gettin' back than a fistful of passes signed by Jeff Davis. And if you do find out about any shoes, you let me know quick."

"Belle . . ."

She turned them back toward the farm house. "You are

obliged to me, Sir. Possibly for your life. Now, I'm goin' to see that you, that woman, and your servants are given safe conduct and set on the road to home. But Harry, I want something in return. Aside from shoes."

Of course she did.

"Best thing I could do for you right now, Belle, is get you back to your mother and daddy. There's a real good chance of getting yourself killed around here—member of the fair sex or not."

"My daddy is an officer in the Confederate Army—just like yours. Just like you should be, Harrison Grenville Raines. He's with Jackson's Brigade not two hours' ride away. But what I want from you—darlin' cousin—is help gettin' through Yankee lines. I mean to get back to Washington City, where I'm to stay with Miz Rose Greenhow. I believe you know the lady."

"I know her too well. She's going to find herself in Federal trouble, if she's not careful. And the same could happen to you—if we get stopped by the wrong Union officer, somebody who doesn't take kindly to young ladies gunning down soldiers in her parlor."

An owl called out from the dark woods across the road from the farm. It was an eerie but incongruously peaceful sound to be hearing in the midst of an army camp.

"By what road are you returning?" she asked.

"My intent was to cross the river by one of the fords north of Leesburg. It's the long way around, but has the fewest soldiers."

"Then let's strike a bargain, cousin. I'll help you get through all this hostile country to a ford, and, once across the river, you get me by the Yankee patrols."

"Belle, Mrs. Pleasants will have you clapped in jail the instant she finds out about that soldier you killed. She's mourning that dead husband of hers pretty hard. She's in a mood for revenge. You don't want to be too handy."

Belle stopped and thought a moment. They were nearly to the farmhouse door.

"All right, Harry. I'll take leave of you somewhere on the

road in Maryland—afore she can get ahold of a newspaper. You just get me across that river."

"You just promise me you won't shoot any more soldiers— or use my help to do some harm to the Union army. I'll have no part of it."

"Your 'neutrality' is a disgrace to Virginia, Cousin. But I'll give you my word. For now."

THE captain, perhaps realizing it would do him no good whatsoever attempting to obstruct Belle Boyd in any of her inclinations, readily agreed to her wishes. Mrs. Pleasants, her carriage, and Caesar Augustus were swiftly produced and all of them sent on their way along the road north.

All of them except for Mrs. Pleasants' coachman. True to his promise, he had made his way to the barn loft and escaped over the hill.

Chapter 8

THEY returned to Washington at daybreak, the weather much the same as that which had greeted them there after Bull Run—sticky, hot, and moist with hanging, gloomy mist. It made a fitting background for the first place they stopped—the Union military hospital in Georgetown.

Mrs. Pleasants leaned to peer out the window of the carriage. "Why do we stop here?"

These amounted to her first words to him on the entire return journey. She had not spoken at all while Belle Boyd was with them; her sullenness continuing even after Belle had parted company at Poolesville, riding off to destinations unspoken on her horse, Fleeter. Harry got the sense Mrs. Pleasants was disappointed that they had not slain at least one of the Confederates they'd encountered in revenge for her husband's death. Belle, she gave strong indication, would have served the purpose nicely.

"This is a hospital," he said.

"I know that. My husband is beyond its help, is he not? We can smell that much, can we not? I want to take him to an embalmer. There is much to be done. There are arrangements to be made. I don't want to tarry! As is more than evident, we have tarried too long as it is."

"Mrs. Pleasants, our purpose in going to Virginia was to redeem his honor. To show the lie of the calumny against him. There is a doctor here I know. Your concern is for the military record. The major should be examined by a military physician. This one's a friend."

"A friend?"

"We play chess weekly. Or did, before the war intruded."

"No. I want to go. I hate this place. I've seen enough dead and dying."

"The killing's hardly begun. As a good Abolitionist, you should understand that."

"You speak of Abolition like the Southerner you are."

"Mrs. Pleasants—please! You don't want to ride through the streets of Washington with a corpse on your roof! People will think you mad. We won't be long. Your husband must be examined."

Her eyes were as much full of sadness as anger now.

"You insist."

"I must."

"Very well, Mr. Raines. But he's to be taken to an embalmer's directly."

"I'll arrange it. Consider it part of what you're paying for."

There were ambulances and wagons drawn up in the yard of the hospital—breathing soldiers coming in, the expired moving out. Nearly all the wounded from Bull Run had been retrieved, but for many, the journey had been merely to change their place of dying. Camp disease was beginning to take a toll as well.

Inside, despite the early hour, it was busy—mostly to do with the morning cleanup of the wards. Orderlies, male nurses, and the ambulatory patients crowded the main corridor. A few less well were lying on cots against the wall. Smells of sickness and ammonia mingled strongly. Some sort of breakfast seemed to be in the making as well. The aroma did not make Harry hungry.

Something else about this place weighed upon his nerves. A sound, discernible above the thumps and bangs and clatter, something like a low and constant wind.

He realized what it was—the moans and groans of a hundred or more maimed and dying, blended together into a single, piteous, heart-rending drone.

Quickening his step, Harry made his way to the end of the

corridor, where he was surprised to find a woman on duty. There'd been talk in the saloons about how this might become necessary, and ribald notions of what might result from having the fair sex employed among so many men.

He smiled at this lady, a stern-faced crone ladling some fluid from a large bucket into a smaller one.

"I'm looking for Doctor Gregg."

She gave him barely a glance.

"In the surgery. It's three doors back up the hall, on your right. We got more ether in. Otherwise, you could tell it by the screaming."

HE found Brigade Surgeon Phineas Gregg hard at work, wearily sawing off the lower leg of an anesthetized young soldier. When the doctor was done, much more quickly than Harry had expected, he looked about, as though for another customer. Relieved and pleased to find none there except Harry, he stretched and yawned, then picked up his uniform coat—brightly new colonel's eagles on the shoulder straps.

"Hello, Harry. I hope you've not come for a game. Or are you ill?"

"No game. No illness. Just a morbid errand that requires a favor."

"Coffee first. I've not yet been to bed." Doctor Gregg led him away from the surgery, and down a side hall. "Do you know who came by? President Lincoln himself! Don't know whether to say it was earlier this morning or very late last night, but here he was. Came all alone except for that German Nicolay fellow who works for him. Said he wants to visit all the hospitals. I'm afraid I told him they'd likely be building them faster than he could visit them, but he seemed to take no offense. I like that man."

"Are there more wounded?"

"The same wounded. Succumbing to their wounds. Even with the best amputations. It's a frustration, Harry. It breaks my heart. You fix them up, they take them away, and then they bring them back to you. And then they die. We're getting a lot of sickness now, too. Men who came in looking fairly fit but move swiftly to an infectious and malarial state."

"What's the cause?"

"No one knows. I have a theory. Clean bedding seems to have a salubrious effect. Perhaps there'll be enough time before the next battle to experiment with that." They paused before the door to a dining hall. "There's coffee in here. Will you have some?"

"Yes. Much obliged, though I can't stay long. I'm afraid I bring you another patient."

"Is he badly injured?"

"Doctor, it's Major Pleasants."

Gregg's eyebrows lifted, but he said nothing immediately. Taking two steaming cups from an orderly, he handed one to Harry, then stared into his own before finally reaching into a coat pocket and taking out a small flask. When Harry declined a share, Gregg poured a large portion of its strong contents into his cup, then slowly, savoringly sipped, leaning back finally in his chair.

The doctor was a short but most distinguished-looking man, with a gray, well-trimmed beard and silver-framed spectacles. He was so tired the circles under his eyes extended below the frames.

"Pleasants," he said, at length. "The 'villain' of Bull Run. I thought he'd been killed—shot running from the enemy."

"His death is a fact, but his villainy is debatable. I bring his remains here for help in settling the debate."

"Harry, I barely find time to sleep. I've not been out of these clothes in two days."

"Mrs. Pleasants is the daughter of Senator Quigley, good friend to Mr. Lincoln. She feels strongly it will save his reputation if it can be shown he wasn't shot in the back."

Gregg looked up. "That's easy enough. I'll go out and take a look at him as soon as I finish this." He raised his cup.

"His face is gone, Doctor. Food for Virginia pigs. I'd prefer if he could be examined in here, and then taken to the embalmers. His wife waits in the coach. She's not aware of his condition—except that he's dead and quite fragrant."

Gregg wrinkled his nose, causing his moustache to go up.

"Very well."

"Another favor, Doctor. Do you know anything about ballistics?"

"A little. It's not a complicated science, I don't believe."

"If you can recover the fatal round, or at least make some judgment from the wound about its size, I'd be interested, very interested."

"Why is that, Harry?"

"I want to know if he was killed by a Confederate musket ball."

Gregg studied him, curiosity dispelling his tiredness. "Why bother with such a fact as that?"

"Because I don't think he was."

LEAVING Caesar Augustus to drive Mrs. Pleasants home in her coach, Harry entered the lobby of the National Hotel barely able to totter. His mind was on his waiting bed.

That, alas, was not all that awaited him. As he passed the round banquette at the center of the lobby, a large dark form rose from the other side, bowler hat in hand and revolver visible in belt. Leahy had also done without sleep, and his face was meanly creased.

"Where in hell you been, Raines?"

Harry glanced over at the desk, where the clerk quickly busied himself with another matter.

"Doing odious duty," Harry said. "I've fetched back the body of the infamous major."

"Why'd you do that?"

"Mrs. Pleasants, who employed me for the purpose, wished it so. She needed escort to the battlefield."

Leahy gripped Harry's shoulders as though with blacksmith's iron tongs. "You took Senator Quigley's daughter out to Virginia! Damnation, man."

"You haven't met the lady. If you had, you'd know I had little choice."

The Irishman stepped back, folding his arms on his chest. "Well, what have you discovered?"

"The poor devil most definitely was not shot in the back

fleeing the enemy. I do believe he was murdered before the Confederates reached his position."

"How do you know that?"

"I don't *know*. But I do believe it. I'll know more presently. I'm having the body examined by a surgeon."

Leahy stared at him hard. "Mrs. Pleasants is unharmed?"

Harry thought it wise to avoid mentioning their capture by Rebel cavalry.

"Yes."

"Major Allen will want a full report. Directly!"

Harry was beginning to sway from side to side from his fatigue. "Yes. As soon as I can. Where?"

"Old Capitol Prison. It's where he's established himself for the day."

"Oh."

"Goin' to be a crowded place, Raines. Good day to you."

AFTER a few hours' sleep; a sort of bath; a change of clothes; a sizable meal of oysters, roast beef, and corn bread; and two glasses of Old Overholtz, Harry felt much restored.

He took the horsecar up Pennsylvania Avenue, noting the progress on the addition to the Treasury and the activity around the gray-painted brick building that was the War Department. At the hospital, he was told that Gregg had gone to his quarters, but had left a small package for Harry and an accompanying note.

It said just what Harry thought it would. He pocketed both note and little parcel and then set out on foot back crosstown to the large house on the hill near the Capitol that was home to Senator Quigley, keeping a promise he'd made to Mrs. Pleasants on parting. The walk was long and hot, but he wanted to think.

A maid answered the door. Harry handed her his card and was ushered in almost immediately to the parlor. He stood a moment, taking note of an oval oil portrait of Mrs. Pleasants as a very young and extremely attractive woman hanging above the mantel. He had the impression she might be an only child.

The senator entered from the hall behind Harry, announcing himself with a polite cough. Harry turned to see a man as handsome as his daughter and bearing much resemblance to her. Quigley, one of the founders of the Republican Party, had been said to have harbored presidential ambitions. He certainly looked the office, unlike its ungainly current occupant.

But Quigley had readily deferred at the 1860 convention to his old friend Lincoln, swinging votes that gave the nomination to the Illinoisan on the third ballot. The two had served in Congress together during the Mexican War and had vigorously opposed that conflict, in the belief its intent was to wed Manifest Destiny to the spread of slavery.

The senator extended his hand, shaking Harry's stiffly.

"I want to thank you, Sir, for your kind offices on my daughter's behalf. I have friends and blood relations who wouldn't have performed such a service so gladly."

"I knew the major—a little. I'm glad to see him get some justice. If we can manage it."

"And do you think we can? I understand you delivered the remains to the Union hospital. Your doctor friend, did he . . . ?"

"He performed an examination. It's his judgment that the Major was shot twice—once in the back, and once in the chest."

The senator's brow crumpled into a frown. "In the back? You're certain? The doctor is certain?"

"After the last few days, Doctor Gregg probably knows as much about bullet wounds as any surgeon in the army. One round hit the major's heart and exited through the chest, striking only flesh. The other struck the spine. It's his opinion that was the first. He thinks the major then spun around and was hit by the second, which killed him."

"This is distressing news. I was hoping these calumnies could be put to rest."

Harry shrugged. "There are a dozen brave reasons to be shot in the back, Senator. Turning to rally your men is one of them.

But in this case, there's a more compelling reason. He was shot long before the enemy got to him."

The senator had taken a small cigar from a case in his pocket. He halted midway through lighting it. "What do you mean?"

"Murdered, Sir. Shot by someone on the Union side of the lines."

"That's astounding. But can you prove it?"

"I hope to—and soon. But the best proof is to find the person who did it."

The senator's hand went to his collar, loosening it slightly. His face had flushed. He seemed a trifle dizzy with this news.

"How do you propose to accomplish that, Mr. Raines?"

"Start with witnesses. There must have been a hundred people around him when it happened—civilians as well as soldiers. Someone must have seen it. I'll start with his men. His fellow officers."

"One of them, his immediate superior—Lieutenant Colonel Beals—he's been spreading the lies. Do you think there's a possibility that . . . ? I wish I'd been able to get to the battlefield. I'd have seen it all. Maybe have prevented it."

Harry shrugged. "That's something no one can know. Doctor Gregg retrieved the bullet. It's of a small caliber—.31. Not an officer's side arm. Perhaps a pocket pistol. Such as a gambler might carry."

"You're a gambler."

"I am. But my pocket revolver has a larger bore—.44 caliber. The same as my saddle pistols. It's unusual. I carry that formidable a weapon because I'm not a good shot. Most content themselves with something lighter. Whoever killed the major was a very good shot—or stood very close to him."

"No one was close to George—except me!" Mrs. Pleasants entered with a great rustle of skirt.

Harry bowed, making a sweep with his arm in Southern cavalier fashion. "Good evening, Ma'am. I hope you are well rested."

"Good evening, Sir. I am most unrested. If what I heard you say is true, I will not rest until George's murderer is brought to his deserved fate."

"I would expect nothing less of you, Ma'am, having witnessed the tenacity with which you stuck to your purpose in Virginia. But you cannot say you were the only one close to your husband. People were running every which way. There was dust. And you were inside your coach. Your view was limited by the frame of the door and window. Everyone on that road must have been carrying some kind of weapon."

She looked to her father. "Joseph was armed."

The senator nodded. "Our coachman. He and Major Pleasants were on bad terms."

"Has he returned?" Harry asked.

"No!" said Mrs. Pleasants. "And I doubt he shall." She seated herself, gingerly, as though she'd become frail. Harry's own backside was a little delicate, after so much time bumping over Virginia roads

"Mr. Raines," she said, "we would like to engage you to resolve this matter."

Harry wanted to be elsewhere. He hadn't spoken to Caitlin now in days. "I am not a policeman. I'm not a detective."

"But indeed you are. Look what you have discovered thus far. In but a single day."

"I'd like to think upon it."

"Of course. But do not delay overlong. We are firm on this."

Pinkerton would want him to take the job. The arrangement might serve to keep the vexing Lafayette Baker off his back. The money would permit him to provide a few days' employment for Caesar Augustus.

And, if he was judging matters correctly, Caitlin would be greatly pleased to have him be the one to settle this business— given her strong friendship with Louise Devereux.

"Very well. I'll do it."

The senator gave Harry a careful, dignified smile. "This will take you from your ordinary business." The smile widened. "Your several businesses. And you will incur expenses. I will see to it you have generous compensation."

"Thank you."

Harry nodded in courtesy to both and prepared to leave, but Mrs. Pleasants raised her hand to stay him.

"The embalmer urged that my husband be buried as soon

as possible," she said. "I am sensible to your reasons now for preventing me from looking upon him. There will be a memorial service at St. John's Church Saturday. I would be obliged if you would attend."

Chapter 9

RETURNING to his hotel from a late breakfast the next morning, Harry found a letter awaiting him at the front desk of his hotel. It was poorly handwritten, but on official paper. He read it over quickly.

"Who brought this?" he asked the desk clerk.

"Some soldiers. A sergeant and two others."

Harry glanced around the lobby. "They still here?"

"No, Sir. They left directly."

"Then I suppose I'm not arrested."

"Wouldn't know, Mr. Raines. Hope not—least until you pay your bill." He smiled, then turned to speak to another guest.

Harry folded the paper carefully. It was a summons to report to the Provost Marshall's office at the Old Capitol Prison. There was no time given, but the wording was so terse he could only assume the meaning was immediately. "Major Allen" was becoming impatient.

He would have to wait. Harry had more compelling business calling upon his attention.

CAESAR Augustus was seated on the doorstep of his shanty, whittling some small wooden figure from a piece of board. Harry's family had acquired the man's mother from Haiti, and she had been a practitioner of the spooky Voudon. Harry's father had found this so disagreeable—especially when she began sticking nails and needles into little figurines of this sort—he'd banished her to the fields and eventually sold her. Though Harry had no notion that he'd ever been a target of his friend's indulgence in Caribbean witchcraft, it always made him nervous when these carvings came to hand.

"Who's that for?" Harry asked.

Caesar Augustus widened his eyes menacingly as he glanced up. "How 'bout the whole damn Rebel army?"

"My father and brother are in the Rebel army."

The black man dug the knife point into the incipient belly of the piece he was carving, then held it aloft. "Then maybe they oughta start thinkin' 'bout deserting." He yanked out the knife and set the wooden figure down. "What you want now, Marse Harry."

Harry sat down on the step beside him. "Senator Quigley has hired me to investigate the major's murder."

"You all sure it's a murder now?"

"Doctor Gregg said he was shot twice—probably with a pistol." Harry reached into his pocket for his grisly souvenir. "He dug this out of the man's back. Too small to be military."

"How's this my worry?"

"It isn't, except the Senator's offering to pay considerable money. Enough to provide you with some employment for the present if you're of a mind to help me."

Caesar Augustus nodded over toward the river. "I ain't goin' back to the Southland, Marse Harry—not if he's offerin' a hundred dollars a day. The Mason-Dixon line run between Pennsylvania and Maryland—a good forty miles north of here. I'm too damn far south as it is."

Caesar Augustus' shack sat on a slight rise that, down the alley and between two slat wooden fences, gave a view of "The Island" past the Canal and the red brick "Castle" of the Smithsonian Institution beyond the trees in the distance, not far from the unfinished obelisk intended to honor the great Washington. This mall-like expanse was a public common— the stretch in front of the Castle euphemistically termed "the Smithsonian Pleasure Garden." Now, white canvas soldiers' tents were appearing there, with many more to come.

"I'm not asking you to go back into Virginia," Harry said. "I want you to hire on with one of these Army units here— one of the Maine regiments. Pleasants', if you can. They're paying Negroes to fetch water and firewood, clean equipment, generally make themselves useful."

"They pays their Negroes Negro wages," Caesar Augustus said, picking up his half-carved wooden figure again.

"You'd be paid twice for the same labor, and on my account quite generously."

"And what would I be doin' for you whilst I'm fetchin' wood and blackin' boots?"

"You'd be listening. And asking some careful questions."

"I been listening. I can tell you they've given the Army to McClellan, that they're goin' to close the saloons and bar-rooms to soldiers, that there's a Confederate battery down-stream on the Potomac bluffs that's got the whole river closed to Union boats and ships."

"How do you know that?"

"Newswalkers."

Unlike the similar, commonplace references for prostitute, the term was unfamiliar to Harry. "You mean 'newsboys.' "

"No, nothin' to do with newspapers," said Caesar Augustus. "They're just soldiers. They walk through the camps from unit to unit, askin' for news and sharin' what they have. They're how come so many of soldiers find out about their orders 'fore the generals do."

"It sounds like they're what's responsible for all the outra-geous rumor mongering that's been going on. They're prob-ably the reason Major Pleasants is being held such a villain."

"Maybe so, but they're no worse than the newspapers in that regard, Marse Harry. If you want to know what the sol-diers are thinkin' and sayin', I'd be listenin' to these boys."

There was a filthy goat puttering about the weeds of the lane. Caesar Augustus tossed a pebble toward it, striking the ground by its forefoot. The animal ignored this.

"All right, then. That's what I want you to do. You be my newswalker. I'd like you to tell me anything and everything the soldiers have to say about Major Pleasants. All the camp talk. I want to know it all: Who speaks ill of him. Whether he had any enemies in his regiment. What is the general run of thought upon the matter of the retreat. There was a colonel or lieutenant colonel at the head of that rout. I think his name may be Beals. I want to know what they say about him."

Caesar Augustus picked up another pebble, this time to throw aimlessly, at nothing. "I was thinkin' about army work before you wandered up here. I need work, sure enough." Another pebble. Then he resumed whittling. "What about you, Marse Harry? Not like you to want to work for anyone else. You're the worst man for takin' orders I ever knew. It's a blessin' for both armies, you're not joinin' up for the war."

"This job is a brief inconvenience. And I prefer it to moving to quarters where Provost Marshal Ward Lamon or this Lafayette Baker are host. And it gnaws at me that one of the few men to show any gumption and gallantry on that battlefield gets tarred as a coward and poltroon."

"How much?"

"Dollar a day."

Caesar Augustus let a little grin sneak onto his face. "I can sure enough live on that. But I ain't goin' back into Virginia."

"The Army will be going back. That's for certain."

"Well, dey goes widout dis Negro." A particularly violent slash of the whittling blade took off the head of the figurine.

"Just who *is* that you've beheaded?"

Caesar Augustus grinned. "Jeff Davis maybe. Maybe Mr. Linkum—he don't start some emancipatin' pretty soon."

Harry rose, yawning. It would take the year to restore the sleep he'd lost in all this foolishness. "Did you bring Mr. Brady back his camera and boxes?"

" 'Course I did, Marse Harry. I'se yo obedient servant."

"He have anything to say?"

"He wasn't much happy."

"He never is."

BRADY'S gallery was just off the Avenue on Seventh Street, on the third floor above Gilman's Drug Store. Harry found the man hard at work with two assistants—neither of them Mr.

Gardner. As the photographer explained, with so many soldiers and their relatives in Washington, the demand for daguerreotypes and *cartes de visites* to memorialize the occasion had been unceasing.

"I thought I'd buy you a drink," Harry said, stepping aside as one of the assistants bustled forth with a box of glass plates.

Brady, standing in rolled-up shirtsleeves at his work table, paused, giving the invitation about five seconds' consideration. Then he resumed his labors.

"Tonight would be more likely," Brady said. "Though I'm not sure I'll be able to take supper, so much work to be done."

"I was interested in what you brought back from Bull Run."

Brady gestured at a mud-flecked sword leaning against the wall to Harry's side. "There's that. I found it on the battlefield. Well, near the battlefield. It belongs to a Zoave unit, same bunch that found me when I got lost in the woods. Those New York firemen recruited by Colonel Ellsworth."

"What woods? When last I saw you, you were on the Sudley Road."

Brady dabbed at an exposed plate that he'd removed from a tray filled with liquid. "Yes, yes I was. But the road went north. My desire was for the east, so I set off through the woods. I couldn't get across the creek, and then I got lost. I could hear Rebels coming. Thought I was to perish. Then the Zoaves found me. Rough fellows, but they saved my life."

Harry picked up the sword and pulled it out of its scabbard. It was very plain, a noncommissioned officer's weapon.

"I had your camera and some plates brought to you," he said. "As you asked and as I promised."

"Yes you did. My apologies, Raines. It is I who should buy you refreshment. If I weren't so busy, I'd do so now." As if for emphasis, his elbow knocked over a bottle of some chemical. Brady leapt back, exclaiming with a rare, profane oath, then snatched up a rag and worked away at soaking up the fluid.

"You said you didn't get much out there?" Harry asked.

Brady stopped, sighing. "An image of McDowell and a few generals in Centreville. A glimpse or two of trodden field. And this."

He shifted to the side and removed a glass plate from beneath a cloth. It was of a soldier—a cavalry trooper from the look of him—lying on his side on a grassy slope. His head was twisted up at an odd angle, as was his left leg. Harry realized the young man was dead.

"Useless," said Brady. "Totally useless. Nobody will want to look upon that."

Harry stared at the image, tilting it slightly to better catch the light. "Where did you take it?"

"On a road outside Centreville, on the way up to the battle. Poor fellow must have been thrown by his horse or shot. They just left him there. I told the first officer I came upon. I guess someone came and got him."

"Then he was among the fortunate dead." Harry looked more closely. The picture made him profoundly sad, but fixated him as no work of art he had ever gazed upon—and he was much taken with paintings. "Nothing more? Nothing of the battle?"

"No. Perhaps Gardner has something, wherever he may be. You don't know what this art of mine entails, Raines. It's most complicated. I need a man with me to mix chemicals and pour them over the plates as I use them. The chemicals have to evaporate, then I sensitize them by placing them in another chemical, and I must do this in darkness—in my wagon and under a cloth. Then the sensitized plate is put in a closed holder and inserted into the camera. After exposure, the plate must be rushed back into the darkness for developing. If I wait more than a few minutes, the image is gone."

Stroking his moustache, Harry walked over to the window. A troop of cavalry was trotting down the street, raising dust.

"Is this commonly understood?" he asked. "About the taking of photographs."

"No. Not by most. Why?"

"People will be curious. I surely am. Will you tell me when Mr. Gardner returns, as I hope he does?"

"He'll be happy to tell you himself, if your offer of refreshment includes him."

"It does."

"I fear he may be leaving me. The war has brought so many

to the city. And they all seem to want their photograph taken. How about you, Raines? I'd charge you nothing. I'm obliged to you for the return of my camera and equipment."

"Perhaps later, when I have more time."

"Mr. Booth has had his portrait done. I'm printing *cartes de visites* from the plate. I expect to sell quite a few of his likeness."

"No doubt."

DOWNSTAIRS, the door to the drug store was open in hopes of a breeze, and Harry could hear voices from within as he passed. One stopped him in his tracks—Caitlin's.

He stepped inside. She was standing at the counter, talking with the druggist, who was moving about his shelves of jars. Without making sound enough for her to notice his presence, Harry came closer. He was unhappy to see the nature of her purchase. When the proprietor turned away again, Harry stepped beside her.

She gave a start.

"Harry!" Her hand went to his arm. "The man at your hotel said you'd gone back to Virginia. I feared you'd made your choice of allegiance at last."

"You know me better than that."

"There are times when I wonder if I know you at all. But I am glad to see you. I was fearful."

"Your words make me happy."

She ignored the intimacy of the remark, glancing impatiently at the man behind the counter. "Where did you go in Virginia? To visit your family?"

"That event will likely have to wait until the end of the war."

The druggist wrapped her purchases in paper, tying the parcel with string. She paid him, her hand nervous and clumsy with the coins. She quickly turned to go. He reached to carry her package for her, but she would not let him.

Outside, on the brick sidewalk, he took her arm and leaned close. In his mind was the well remembered image of her lying on a sweat-soaked bed in only a chemise, her skin as sickly white as the sheeting.

"Why did you buy laudanum?" he asked. "You promised me you were through with that."

"I am, Harry." Her tone was a little scolding—for his doubting her. "This is for another."

There was only one person that could be.

"Louise is still with you?"

Caitlin shook her head, sadly. "I wish she were. She's returned to her quarters. But she shouldn't be alone. She is sorely vexed by this. I fear she is a little mad."

He tapped the package. "So you bring her this?"

"A temporary curative. It will bring her sleep—blissful sleep. She tried to kill herself, you know."

An overloaded coach was careening down upon them along the Avenue. Harry pulled Caitlin back, raising his arm to ward off a muddy clot kicked up by one of the horses.

"When did she do this?"

"Last night. She was drinking. I told you my pistol was missing? She'd taken it—days before the battle. I caught her holding the barrel to her breast, staring at it with this demonic look upon her face."

"Did she try to fire it?"

"No. She hadn't cocked it. I wrested it away. She left me— God, what vile language that young lady knows. Went to her boardinghouse. I stopped by this morning. She was unharmed, but fretful. Too mild a word, that, for her state. I'm very worried, Harry."

"Where's your pistol?"

"At home. I should return yours."

"I'll come with you."

CAITLIN apologized for not offering Harry refreshment, but she didn't want to tarry long in getting on to Louise's. He stood in the doorway of her bedroom as she went to her dresser. Something new had been added to the souvenirs and sundries she kept on top—a framed daguerreotype of Wilkes Booth.

Damn Brady. Damn Booth.

Harry retreated into her parlor.

"Here you are," she said, placing the derringer in Harry's hand with care. "Have a caution, for it's still loaded. I'm so relieved there was no need for it in Virginia."

"I'm relieved, too. For a while there, the need was breathing down our necks." He glanced over the little weapon, then slipped it into his coat pocket. "And yours? Was it fired?"

She had started toward the door. "I told you, Harry. I got it away from her in time."

"Your pistol has two barrels."

Caitlin paused. "Yes it does." She returned to her bedroom, this time with Harry following her into it.

He came close behind her as she opened the drawer. Taking up the gun, she clicked the little catch that broke it open.

"Well?"

"It—it's been fired."

"Both cartridges?"

She handed it to him. "No. Just one." Her eyes lifted, challenging.

"May I borrow the piece?"

"Whatever for?"

Before she could in any way prevent him, he slid the cartridge out of the chamber and into his hand. "Curiosity."

"Harry, I know what you're thinking."

He gave her back the pistol. "If you knew what I'm thinking, you'd stop looking at me like that. You'd know I mean Louise Devereux no harm."

IN the summer months in Washington, Harry had adopted the practice of carrying a pocket handkerchief scented with cologne, a habit that increased his reputation as a fop and dandy.

But this was less affectation than fastidiousness. His livestock and gambling dealings often took him to the other side of the canal, and he could not bear to cross that fetid, stagnant, putrescent waterway without some sweet scent against his nose to distract his sense of smell.

Even with it, he crossed the 12th Street bridge with alacrity. There were two dead pigs afloat in the slimy water—the blank eyes of one of them turned toward him.

Live pigs roamed on the open ground beyond, as they did throughout the city. Growing up in the country, he had early on developed a superstition about crows as harbingers of doom or evil. After the encounter with Pleasants' remains, he'd now add pigs to that. It was no wonder that the Muslims and Jews avoided their flesh. It was a wonder that puritanical Christians didn't.

It occurred to him that these strolling, rutting beasts might be in for a little doom themselves. The number of tents on the mall was increasing. After a few more days of Army food, the soldiery would be happy for some fresh meat.

No matter what the creature had been dining upon.

CAESAR Augustus was seated on an upended empty cracker box halfway up a street formed by two rows of tents. Ignored by the milling troops, he was polishing an officer's boots.

"I see you've found a job all right," Harry said.

Caesar Augustus lifted his head, then lowered it to his task again. "For today. Maybe more work tomorrow."

"Have you learned anything yet?"

"Learned it's too damned hot for this Negro to be blackin' another man's boots."

"Nothing more?" Harry glanced about cautiously, feeling unwelcome in this camp.

"Learned what I said to you before is all true. McClellan's cuttin' off the soldiers' liquor sure enough. The Potomac's closed to Union river traffic because of that Confederate battery on the bluff, and they're afeared the Secesh in Baltimore's goin' cut the railroad. Washington City's what'd you call marooned."

"I suppose it's a good thing the Army decided to hole up here then. Otherwise the Rebels'd move right in."

"President Lincoln wants McClellan to take the troops back out into the field—push the Rebs back a little. But the general wants to wait until he's got 'em all ready."

"How do you know that?"

"How's dis Negro be knowin' sech things, Marse Harry? He heered it from dat same captain what sticks his feets into dese here boots."

"Sorry."

"You asked me to find out what I could. Bet you Jeff Davis like to know what I just told you. And I've only been here a few hours."

"I'm not faulting your abilities in the slightest, Caesar Augustus. But my interest is in Major Pleasants."

"He was in the next battalion over, so I ain't learned a lot. But he was a gambler, and he had a lady friend. Maybe more. And he was a drinker."

Harry sighed. "Those things I already knew. What about enemies?"

"From what I heard so far, he had some, but not too many. He had a bad temper when he was drunk, but he was good to his men. Not harsh about their bad behavior. That colonel, Beals. He didn't like Pleasants much. Something to do with the colonel's young and comely wife. The major had a wanderin' eye, just like your friend Booth. I hear sometimes their eyes done wander to the same woman."

"When you finish those boots," Harry said, "I'd like you to come with me. It won't take long."

"What'll I tell this captain here?"

"Ask him if he'd like you to fetch him some whiskey. Tell him that, though McClellan's declaring the saloons off limits, you know a man who can get him a bottle."

"This captain's not partial to whiskey. His name's Kelleter, and he's real partial to following orders."

"Tell him you were following orders."

THOUGH the summer sun was still above the horizon, Harry found many soldiers in the forbidding back streets south of the Avenue—patrons of the cheapest bawdy houses and "hotels." The Provost Marshal had rated many of the establishments in this district, especially those on C Street and in Fighting Alley, "very low"—the most unsavory rating he could bestow. Harry was glad of Caesar Augustus' company.

Whores in various stages of undress were seated unprettily on back porches and in doorways, a few of them calling out to Harry because they thought him a more generous prospect than their uniformed customers. Several rough-looking men lounging along the way eyed Harry just as speculatively, and for the same reason.

"Not a district for a daily perambulation," Harry said.

"These're my neighbors, Marse Henry. Only my quarters ain't nearly so grand."

THEY had reached the rear of Mollie Turner's establishment, from which Major Pleasants had emerged in such disheveled haste. Though there was raucous noise and singing coming from the building next door, this place was as quiet as a church.

Harry went to the rear door and stood on the stoop with his back to it, squinting across the dingy little street. There was a slat-wood shed directly opposite—about a story and a half high. He pulled the pocket pistol from his coat and extended his arm, taking dry aim.

"What in Hell are you doing, Marse Harry?"

"At the moment, trying to divine the intent of a hysterical young woman."

The first question was whether the shot that night before the battle had been fired from one of the Turner house's windows or the back door, which had been ajar. He decided a person pursuing the major in anger would be following him to it.

The next matter was whether the round had been fired with a desire to kill or one simply to frighten. Shooting directly into the air would have sufficed for intimidation, yet Harry had heard the round whizzing over his head. His best guess was that anger had brought the shooter close to an aim to kill, but other emotions had intruded, lifting the aim at the last instant.

Then, too, she might just have been a bad shot.

As best he could recall, he'd come upon the crouching officer at a spot in the street directly opposite the door—affording a look straight down the dimly lit hall. Harry turned, tried the latch, found it free, and slowly pushed open the door, relieved that no one was to be found within. He took visual and mental measure as he looked down the little corridor, then back to the street, and up to the shed wall and roof.

Behind him came the clang of some heavy object dropped, followed by curses, bellowed by one woman, and returned by another. He stepped back toward the yard and closed the door again.

"Marse Harry . . ."

Harry put a finger to his lips and, in measured pace, crossed from the doorway to the street. Having established two points of an imaginary line, he followed it across to the shed, then with his eyes pursued it up the wall. About three feet above his head, just by the eaves, was a splintery pockmark produced by neither knot nor notch.

"If you wouldn't mind," Harry said to Caesar Augustus, "I'd appreciate a boost up this wall."

"We could get shot for thievin'."

"Won't take long."

Caesar Augustus locked his hands together, but that lifted Harry insufficiently. Finally, Harry was compelled to stand on the other man's shoulders, amazed at his friend's strength. He bore Harry's weight as he might a bird's.

Harry took out his spectacles, put them on carefully, then produced his New Orleans saloon knife—unfolding it and locking the blade in place. It bore the smith's name on one side and the word "Widowmaker" on the other.

Probing with the blade point, he hadn't dug far when it came up against something very solid.

"A moment more," Harry said.

"It ain't the effort, Marse Harry. It's the indignity."

Digging with a circular motion, Harry felt the object yield. There was a "sprang," and it flew out over his shoulder, landing on the hard dirt behind him. Putting a hand gently to his friend's head, Harry leapt down to the ground.

He retrieved the spent bullet, glad to find that it had not been greatly flattened. Taking out the small parcel left him by

Doctor Gregg, he removed from it the expended round that had been taken from the major's body and held them side by side in his hand.

"Just so," he said.

"What'd you find?"

"I found that they're not the same."

Harry pocketed both bullets, paused in thought a moment, then looked up and down the street. There were some people moving about farther to the east, but to the west, it was deserted.

He walked back to the Turner doorway, studied the shed, then took out Caitlin's little double-barreled pistol, pointing it at the top of the building.

"What're you doing?" said Caesar Augustus.

"I need to fire this round into that shed."

The black man came toward him. "Marse Harry, that there shed is the barn whose broad side you can't hit. Gimme that thing."

He took the pistol from Harry, aimed it, took a deep breath, partially exhaled, then held, then fired. A puff of dust appeared near the roof.

As Harry discovered climbing on the man's shoulders again, this new round had struck within a foot from the earlier one—an amazing bit of accuracy with such a short-barreled weapon.

Working quickly now, he got this fresh bullet out, finding it still hot to the touch and dropping it. Sliding to the ground, he picked it up with his handkerchief, into which he also set the two from his pocket.

"Very good," he said, without looking to the other man. "These two *are* the same."

Caesar Augustus made no reply but to shake his head. Harry turned slowly and saw two stout women and one of the young toughs standing in the street looking at them. Several soldiers were hurrying along in their direction from farther down the street. In the other direction, some barking dogs were bounding toward them, with some boys in pursuit. As he observed their progress, an older, dirty-looking man stepped outside from the house next to the shed, carrying what looked to be a shotgun.

Directly behind him, peering out the doorway of the Turner house, was a young woman wearing only a shift.

"Caesar Augustus," Harry said quietly. "It's not my custom, but I think we should visit a whorehouse. Quickly."

Chapter 1 O

HARRY asked the young woman to close and latch the door behind them, which she did with some reluctance—as she might comply with a customer's peculiar request.

"What were you shootin' out there?" she asked. "Somebody after you?"

She was a small and scrawny thing, not much washed or dressed.

"I discharged a pistol accidentally," Harry said.

The girl flicked her eyes back and forth, taking in Harry's fine clothes and Caesar Augustus' well displayed muscles—and color. It made her nervous. "What you men want here?"

"I'd like to speak to the proprietor," Harry said.

"Miz Turner? She just went out. Good thing for you. She don't much like shootin'. Been too much of that, lately."

"How do you mean?"

She slipped past him, moving on toward the front of the building. He followed, thinking there might be a small lobby or desk, but there was only a front parlor with the drapes drawn against the daylight.

"Has there been shooting here, in the last few days?"

"Always somethin' goin' on. Now, you want to spend some time with me? Hope so, 'cause I'm all there is right now."

"I'd just like to ask a few questions."

"About what I can do?" Upon close examination, she seemed no more than sixteen or seventeen.

"I need some information—not about that. You do rent rooms by the hour?"

"Surely do. You want to rent one? For me and you?"

"I mean to people who aren't your customers. To, uh, couples."

"Surely do. But you don't have a woman with you?" She shrank back. "You don't mean with him?"

Harry scowled, shaking his head. "Have you been renting one to an army officer?"

She looked at Harry as though she feared she'd allowed a raving lunatic into the place.

"Whole army of army officers been comin' here."

"I mean with a lady. Renting a room."

"Guess so." She stared down at her bare feet.

"A Major Pleasants?"

She shrugged, still pondering her feet.

"Do you have a guest register?"

"Miz Turner got a account book, but she keeps it locked up."

"Do you recall an officer with yellow hair—blond hair, long like mine, but yellow?"

Another shrug. "Had a Swedish soldier last night. From Minnesota. He had real blond hair. Almost white. But he was kinda bald. And he was a private."

Harry heard a thump from upstairs and a woman's voice, though he could not understand the words.

"Was there an officer with yellow hair who came here with another woman, his own woman—and rented a room? In the last few days—just before the big battle out in Virginia?"

"Who are you, Sir?"

Harry spun around, looking to the hall and the stairs. A vision stood where none had been—a blonde young woman in the budding bloom of sixteen or seventeen. Certainly not yet twenty. He'd heard that Mollie Turner had a beautiful young sister named Ella. He'd no idea she was such a dazzlement.

"I am Harrison Raines, Miss. I am inquiring after a, er, friend, Major George Pleasants, who fell at Bull Run. I am trying to find a woman he was with the night before."

The blonde stepped farther into the room. She was wearing a most elegant green gown that perfectly matched her eyes, but one far more seemly for the evening than this bright of day.

"Well," she said. "No need to bother our Nancy here." She turned to the girl. "You may go." It was instruction.

The wench fled, looking grateful, but still curious.

"Would you know the answer to my question?" Harry asked the blonde.

She shook her head. "I merely reside here, Sir. This is my sister's establishment." She extended her hand, and he kissed it. "I am Ella Starr, though I must confess, that is the name I use on the stage. My born name is Turner."

Harry was a habitual theatergoer, but could not recall this lady as actress in a play. He would have remembered.

"I think," he said, releasing her hand, "that the woman's name might have been Devereux, Louise Devereux. If you are an actress, you must recognize it, for she has become one of the great ladies of the Washington stage, though her years must be as few as yours."

"Devereux? I never heard it." A sweet smile.

There was a creak of wood. Harry thought it might be from the floor above.

"Are you sure? She's dark-haired—from New Orleans. An extraordinary beauty. Like yourself."

There was another creak, and this time Harry realized it came from the stairs. He guessed there might be someone up there, listening, waiting for him to go. He resisted the impulse to bound over to the staircase to look.

"I have no recollection."

"Did you hear a pistol shot that night? Out the back?"

"In this rough neighborhood, Sir, there is often that. Especially now. All these soldiers in town."

"This would have been very late at night."

"That's when it's worst."

Another creak on the stairs. Her eyes flicked toward them.

"I think, Sir, as you are not engaged in business here, you had better go. My sister is not on the premises."

"Miss, I'm only interested in some information." He produced a large coin and proferred it.

"How dare you, Sir! Please leave at once."

Caesar Augustus gave him a look expressing agreement with her sentiment.

"You have brought your Negro in here, Mr. Raines. This is contrary to the new ordinances. There's a young lady employed at Mina Bearing's house who was just arrested by the Provost Marshal's guard for cooperating in such an offense—'cohabitating with a Negro.' "

"Marse Harry," said Caesar Augustus, "I think we better bid our farewell."

Harry pocketed the coin but put one of his calling cards into Ella Turner's hand.

"If you remember anything more," he said, "I'd appreciate your getting word to me."

She just stood there.

Caesar Augustus beat him to the door, hurrying to the street. With more dignity, Harry closed the door behind him and joined the other man on the street.

"Someone up those stairs," Caesar Augustus said, glancing back at the building when they had moved on from it.

"Could have been anyone," said Harry. "Another bawd. Maybe her sister."

"Someone who didn't want us to see 'em."

Harry looked back at the house's front door a moment. No one appeared.

"You want me to look around back?" said Caesar Augustus. "Case someone leavin' by that way?"

"Just keep clear of trouble. I'll meet you on the Avenue—on the corner by the *Washington Star* office."

Caesar Augustus nodded, then disappeared down a dirt lane between two wooden fences.

THE *Star* had posted its front page for the afternoon on a board set up outside for the purpose. Harry took a place behind a short man and, after putting on his spectacles, leaned forward over him to read the headlines.

There were conflicting stories side by side—one about the Union Army on the march adjoining another warning of a possible Confederate invasion. Neither thing seemed to be in the offing.

On a lower part of the page was what he was looking for. The major was still in the news, this time the subject of a possible congressional inquiry into the causes of the defeat and rout.

He felt a tap on his shoulder and moved aside to make room for the person, but the tap came again, this time more insistent. It was Caesar Augustus.

Harry drew him back toward the curb.

"I don't know if it was her hidin' up those stairs, but I saw someone comin' from the back of that place, just like I thought. And in great distress."

"One of the whores?"

"I guess there's some who'd call her that. But I wouldn't. No. She's an actress."

"Actress? Who?"

"It was that Louise Devereux."

"That can't be."

"Well, it was so, Marse Harry. There she went, right down the street."

"Where did she go?"

"Can't say. When she saw me, she turned 'round and went the other way—lickety-split."

HARRY sent Caesar Augustus off to return to his captain, then went straight to the stable where he kept his saddle horse, Rocket, a big bay, even darker than the mount Louise had lost at the battle.

The gelding was misnamed. Though Harry traded in racing horses, for his own transport he'd happily dispensed with speed in favor of strength and stamina for the long ride. His decision had served him well in the past. Rocket had once carried him out of the Blue Ridge Mountains in a blizzard that would have foundered a lesser mount.

He seated himself on a bale of hay while the stable boy

fetched and saddled the animal. Taking out the spent bullets from his pocket, he contemplated them sadly.

"You be gone long, Mr. Raines?"

Rocket had had little exercise in recent days and seemed not much interested in any this hot day. Harry swung himself into the saddle wearily.

"I hope not."

It was a short trot to Louise Devereux's boardinghouse, but a long wait for someone to answer the door. Finally, the square, lined face of an old German woman appeared, the mother of the owner, wispy white hair straggling forth from beneath an unkempt bonnet.

"She is not here," said the old woman, preparing to close the door.

"I'm not calling on your daughter," Harry said. "I'm looking for Miss Devereux. Louise Devereux."

The old woman squinted at him disapprovingly. "I know. I know. Everyone looking for Louise Devereux. She is nicht zu Haus. Not here. She not here for days."

"Thank you," said Harry, bowing slightly, with a sweep of hat.

He gathered up Rocket's reins, but refrained from mounting, pondering his next destination, wondering if he might best take his horse into the alley a few houses up the street and wait in that vantage point for Louise to come home. If that had been her on the stairs of the bawdy house, he wished she'd come down to talk with him. He had some good news for her, if she was in fear of the Provost Marshal's law.

He lighted a cigar, puffing contentedly until an alarming thought intruded upon his pleasure. If Louise was not home, as Caitlin had said, for whom had Caitlin bought that laudanum?

Harry had a good guess as to the answer to that and didn't like it one bit. Clenching the cigar between his teeth, he thrust himself into the saddle and turned Rocket hard, goading him into a lunging canter up the slope of the street.

• • •

No one answered the front door at Caitlin's boardinghouse, but he found Mrs. Fitzgerald in her backyard, hanging laundry with the help of a young black girl.

As usual, Harry bowed, with his customary sweep of hat. "I'm looking for Miss Howard, with some urgency."

"Well, you won't find her here, Mr. Raines."

"Are you certain? I was talking to her on the Avenue a short while ago."

"If I warn't certain, Mr. Raines, why would I say it?"

"Perhaps she went to her rooms while you've been out here. If I could but knock on her door."

"Won't do you no good. She ain't here. She did come back for a little while, but then she went out again. In a big hurry."

"But where?"

Mrs. Fitzgerald went back to her labors. "She didn't say. She left with Mr. Booth."

"Booth?"

"And a young woman. He had a pretty young woman with him. An actress, like Miss Howard."

"Louise Devereux."

"Right. That's the one."

Harry sat his horse a long moment, then headed slowly down toward the Avenue, his thoughts despondent.

They worsened. There at the corner, astride what looked to be a huge dray horse, was Boston Leahy, looking a little ridiculous in tight-fitting black suit and bowler hat. There was a revolver in his hand, resting on the saddle pommel.

Chapter 1 1

THERE were six or seven black men waiting outside the room in the Old Capitol Prison that Pinkerton had requisitioned for interrogations. They proved to be John Henrys, as the soldiers referred to them—slaves liberated by the Union advance into Virginia, inept and unsubstantial as it had been. Pinkerton was seeking information from them on the Confederate strength and movements. Harry thought this daft. The Rebel high command was not inclined to take its Negroes into confidence. But Pinkerton listened raptly to their every word. There was a steady stream of such people coming into Washington, and the chief of detectives seemed bent on talking to all of them.

If the North wanted good intelligence, it should use the kind of operatives the South did—women.

Pinkerton was at least aware of that fact.

"Are you acquainted with a Mrs. Rose O'Neal Greenhow?" he asked, after Harry had been presented to him.

"Of course I am. She is one of the leading hostesses of Washington City."

"A Southerner."

"It's a southern town."

"I think she's a spy."

Belle Boyd had made that perfectly clear to Harry. "I've had no personal experience with that, Sir."

This drew a hard look. It softened. "We may have to arrest her. Would that offend you, Mr. Raines?"

"That would depend on the extent of her crimes—if crimes there are."

"Would you be willing to undertake an investigation to determine that? My detectives can't get near her."

"Aren't you at all interested in the matter of Major Pleasants?"

"Of course I am! That's why you're here. What have you found?"

Harry related his discoveries concerning the officer's fatal wounds.

"Murdered," said Pinkerton, leaning back in his chair. "D'you believe that, Leahy? Murdered on a battlefield?"

The Irishman met his boss's steady gaze, then nodded. "He showed me the rounds. They weren't from a musket or rifle."

"Have you any other proofs?" Pinkerton asked.

"I'm looking for the principal one."

"What d'you mean?"

"The murderer."

"You're not a policeman."

"I've been privately engaged by Senator Quigley and Mrs. Pleasants for that purpose. They want some justice done."

Pinkerton searched among the papers on his desk and then snatched one up. "That explains this." He held it up, but not for any close examination. "It's from the President's secretary, John Nicolay. He asks that when we have acquired any information at all on the matter of Major Pleasants we should bring everything pertinent to the President's House as soon as is convenient. I surmise the President has been talking to Senator Quigley—as well as reading all these damned newspapers."

"I haven't reported anything to the senator yet."

"Presidents come first, Raines." He took out his pocket watch. " 'As soon as convenient.' That's now, Mr. Raines. Unless your loyalties lie with a different president."

"I'm not working for either president, only Senator Quigley."

He paused, reaching into a pocket and removed a folded sheaf of printed papers. Withdrawing one, he laid it upon the desk and wrote out Harry's name in a blank space at the center, then handed it to him. The form had already been signed by Secretary of War Cameron.

"That pass will allow you transit through any United States military command or district," Pinkerton said. "I'm only giving it to you because you are working for the senator. Guard it carefully, as they are hard to come by."

Harry was already well acquainted with Secretary Cameron and the ingenious wartime uses to which he had put the capitalist system.

"I'm surprised the secretary's not out selling these in the streets," Harry said.

"Talk like that," grumbled Pinkerton, "is seditious."

For the first few months of Lincoln's presidency, there'd been a constant traffic in and out of the mansion—a mixed and largely unsavory swarm of politicians, job and favor seekers, purveyors wanting contracts, officers asking assignment, friends and cronies wishing to bask in Lincoln's glory.

Since Bull Run, this flow had abruptly diminished, with the posting of extra military guards at gates and portals and the requirement of official passes for entry. Harry suspected the flow of guests would increase to normal levels as more of those passes gained currency.

Pinkerton and his little party were admitted without much bother.

Instead of proceeding from the north door to the Cross Hall, and thence to the Grand Staircase at the west end of the house, the detective led them through a side door off the foyer and thence up some service stairs to the second floor.

On that level, they passed into a small vestibule with doors leading off to the left and right. Harry started to turn in the latter direction but Leahy motioned him back.

"Private quarters that way," he said. "We're going to his office."

With that, they turned left and entered a large reception room with comfortable chairs and a two sofas. Two white-haired, important-looking men were already waiting there, not happily.

A young man with neatly trimmed European-style moustache and beard poked his head out a doorway. Pinkerton went up to him and they spoke quietly for a moment. The young man disappeared, then returned very quickly, nodding to them to follow. Leahy remained behind in the reception room.

The President's office was a large chamber, facing south with a view of the river. There was a sofa and some chairs against one wall and a large, rectangular table in the center, with a map of Virginia on an easel beside it. In one corner was a smaller, round table with a single armchair next to it. In the opposite corner was a rolltop desk, with numerous documents sticking out of the various pigeonholes.

There sat the President, wearing spectacles and bending over a piece of paper. He wrote something on it, then slowly turned.

He'd been barely noticeable at first, but when he rose to greet them, he seemed suddenly to fill the room. Harry had seen Lincoln only at some distance, and was surprised at the strength apparent in his shoulders and long arms—and in the grip of his hand.

The man's voice was another surprise. The pitch was high and there was a western twang that spoke of the wilds of Kentucky and Illinois. Woodsy or no, this President was well spoken. Harry guessed he was a reader. There were many books about the room. He recognized a volume of Shakespeare.

The President, folding his long frame, seated himself in the largest of the chairs, nodding to the others to follow his example. Harry took a seat near the map and easel. The positions of the Union and Confederate armies were marked upon it with bits of ribbon. Where he had taken Mrs. Pleasants was deep behind the enemy position. It seemed a little frightening now to look at it that way.

The President coughed politely, then spoke. His luminous gray eyes were wise and gentle—and curious. His remarkable face was lined and creased from worry and fatigue. Harry wondered how he might look when this war was done, whenever that might be.

"Senator Quigley informs me you are assisting him in learning the circumstances of poor Major Pleasants' death in battle."

"Yes I am, Mr. President."

"And you escorted Mrs. Pleasants into Virginia to bring back his remains?"

"Yes, Sir."

"That was very intrepid."

"More on Mrs. Pleasants' part than mine, Mr. Lincoln."

The President leaned back a little farther in his chair, rubbing his bristly new beard. "It strikes me as nonsensical, this notion that a single man who turns rabbit should set an example for an entire army to follow. But the public sometimes likes to seize upon the simplest excuse and explanation for a calamity, no matter how ridiculous. The newspapers do it all the time. If you can fit the blame into a single wheelbarrow, all the more easy to cart it away."

Nicolay gazed raptly at Lincoln. Pinkerton seemed fidgety.

"But, as they like to say back home, if the Lord gives a man a pair of cowardly legs," the President continued, "how can he help their running away with him?"

Nicolay laughed. Harry smiled.

"They say the first man back from the battlefield was a member of Congress. I suppose he wished to be here in time to chastise our panicky soldiers as they returned."

More careful, polite laughter.

"Reminds me of a story," Lincoln said. "I never knew but one man who could run like this congressman. He was a young man out in Illinois who had been sparking a girl much against the wishes of her father. In fact, the old man took such a dislike to him that he threatened to shoot him if he ever caught him on the premises again.

"One evening, the young man learned that the girl's father had gone to the city, and so he ventured out to the house. He was sitting in the parlor with his arm around Betsey's waist—the girl's name was Betsey—when he suddenly spied the old man coming around the corner of the house with a shotgun.

Leaping through the window into the garden, he started down the path at the top of his speed like greased lightning. Just then a jackrabbit jumped up in the path in front of him. In about two leaps he overtook the rabbit. Giving it a kick that sent it high in the air, he yelled, 'Git out of the road, gosh dern you, and let somebody run that knows how.' "

Nicolay's laughter was drowned out now by Lincoln's own. He slapped his knee, rocking back and forth, letting his hilarity roll out like something being poured. Falling silent finally, he removed his spectacles and wiped his eyes with the heels of his long, bony hands. When his eyeglasses were returned to their proper place, he was all somber again.

"Mr. Pinkerton assures me I can count on your discretion and confidence," Lincoln said. "As proof he offers an incident before the present hostilities, when you put yourself at some risk to assist in the deliverance of Negroes to free territory—such as there was any for them after the lamentable Dred Scott decision."

Pinkerton nodded. Harry did the same.

"The Army didn't run because of one man," Lincoln said. "It ran because the soldiers discovered they had cowardly legs. They were not ready for that fight. They never heard bullets and cannon shot coming for their heads like that before. General McDowell was hopeful, but not confident, about taking them out there. General Scott was reluctant, most reluctant."

"Too damn reluctant," said Pinkerton, sharply.

"But the issue must be pressed," Lincoln continued. "This rebellion must be stopped before it grows into a thing so monstrous we cannot defeat it. We could have put an end to it at that creek. We would have done that had our soldiers been more ready for a fight. As it was, we came within a whip tickle. If our troops were green, so were theirs. They were all green together. We could have done it."

He leaned forward.

"I have a general now who I think will make this army ready. If he can bring it into engagement with the enemy soon, we may yet prevail. But the soldiers and their officers must understand that the mistake was of their own making—that nothing will find improvement if all the blame is bestowed on one man. And an innocent man upon all."

"He was innocent at Bull Run, I'll swear to that," Harry said. "And he was not shot down by Rebels in the back."

"How can you say how he was shot? Were you witness to it?"

"No, Sir."

"We have two witnesses," said the President, a little tersely. "*Official* witnesses. Major Pleasants' immediate superior, a Lieutenant Colonel Beals, has submitted in his official report the notation that he observed the major struck by enemy fire while fleeing the line. And this observation was sworn to by a company sergeant. What was his name?"

"Fetridge, Mr. President," said Pinkerton.

"But Pleasants was out of range of the Confederate line," Harry said. "That much I did see, Sir. A surgeon friend of mine removed one of the fatal rounds. He was shot in the back, all right, but up close, and likely with a pistol. He took another round from the front—through the heart. And I saw him dead long before the Confederate advance got near him."

"He thinks it's murder," said Pinkerton. "And my man Leahy agrees."

Lincoln fixed his eyes on Harry, waiting. A. Lincoln, attorney at law, intellectually interested in the puzzle.

Harry removed the bullets from his pocket and placed the one that Doctor Gregg had extracted from Pleasants' back upon the table before the President.

"This was taken from the back of the major," Harry said. "Lodged against the spine. It's a pistol round, Sir, .31 caliber."

Lincoln picked it up, somewhat daintily, and brought it close. "How do you know this?"

"On the word of the surgeon and a gunsmith he consulted for the purpose," Harry said. "It's a science called ballistics."

The President's eyes became sad. "It grieves me to think how many of these will find our soldiers' flesh. Theirs, too." He set the round back upon the table with a tiny click, then sat back, still staring at it. "Is there any chance this was done by some Confederate scout, or spy, who worked his way to the major's side?"

"I don't think so, Sir. There was a higher ranking officer nearby, and I believe some members of Congress. More likely as candidates for assassination. But that's a dishonorable form of war. And the South's a region that prides itself on its honor. Perhaps to a fault."

"Treason is dishonorable," said Pinkerton. "This rebellion is high treason."

"Not as they see it," Harry said. " 'The Second War of Independence,' as they call it."

"You're a Southerner, Mr. Raines? A Virginian?" Lincoln asked.

"Yes, Sir. But that describes my birth, not my politics."

Lincoln grinned, an expression that became him. "I'm a Kentuckian by the same measure, and your words fit me as well." The grin diminished, and the lawyer in him returned to the fore. "What are those other objects you had in your hand, Mr. Raines."

Now Harry felt truly stupid. Why hadn't he put the other bullets in another place? He'd only fumble his thoughts and words if he tried to lie now. And he'd no wish to be dishonest with this man on any account. But he didn't want to involve the fair Louise in this when he believed her to be innocent.

"I haven't told Mrs. Pleasants this and do not intend to tell her," Harry said, "but her husband had a, er, friend. A lady friend. An actress named Louise Devereux."

"I know of her," said Lincoln. "Has a fine comedic sense."

"And a dramatic one as well," Harry said. "The night before the battle, they had a quarrel, and she discharged a small pistol in his direction in her wrath. But it was fired high, with no intent to harm. I retrieved the bullet and the weapon and fired the only other one in its chambers into the same wood—for comparison. They are alike, Sir. Exactly so." He held them up in the palm of his hand. "And they are of a significantly larger caliber than the bullet taken from Pleasants."

"How do you come by knowledge of her and this weapon?" Lincoln asked.

"She's a friend of his," Pinkerton said. "He rescued her from the battlefield when things went bad. She was there on the Sudley Road."

The President's large eyebrows went up a notch. "She was present at his death?"

"She is innocent, Sir. The pistol she carried, borrowed from a friend of mine, was a two-barreled, two-chambered derringer. One bullet was fired in her angry outburst the night before. The other was not fired. And neither match the fatal round we recovered."

Lincoln looked at him hard. "You'll keep on with this? Working with Senator Quigley?"

"Yes, Sir."

"I wish you success. Swift success. These newspaper stories must end. We must get on with this war." He rose, a great tower, then reached with his long arm to shake hands. "Thank you, gentleman. I fear I have other claims now on my time."

With that he returned to his desk.

Outside the front gate, Pinkerton, Leahy, and Harry stood a moment. Harry found himself feeling not a small thrill at having at last met this man.

"Where does she live, this Devereux?" Pinkerton asked.

"On Third Street, in a boardinghouse. Why?"

"I want you and Leahy to examine the premises."

"But she's innocent! I've proved that!"

"Well, go prove it some more. And if you won't go, Leahy'll take care of it himself."

Leahy was already walking in that direction.

BOTH the old German woman and her daughter, the landlady, were on the premises, and not much of a mind to admit either Harry or Leahy. But the Irishman made short work of that. Brandishing some sort of badge and a very official looking warrant—apparently made out appropriate to all circumstances and occasions—he pushed past them into the vestibule. When the landlady continued her objections, he leaned over to put his face down by hers and demanded: "Do you want me to come back with soldiers?"

She shrank back.

"Show us Miss Devereux's room! Now!"

• • •

WHEN the woman had unlocked Louise's door, Leahy sent her back downstairs. Motioning to Harry to follow, he stepped inside, glancing about before closing the door behind them.

Louise had just the single room, and it looked like someone had already searched it. Several pieces of clothing lay about the floor, and one of the drawers of a chest against the wall was pulled open. A theatrical trunk against a wall stood agape as well. There was a faint smell of cigar smoke.

Leahy went to the chest. "You ever done this before, Raines?" he asked.

"Only in my own chambers, when I forgot where I'd put something after a night of too much drink."

The Irishman pulled the top drawer open fully. "The trick of it is to be thorough and methodical. Look at everything; miss nothing."

"I wonder if someone's been here ahead of us."

Leahy held up a woman's undergarment. "I don't think so. Things taken. But most things undisturbed. It's my guess t'was simply her. Leaving this place in a considerable hurry."

"Then why are we bothering?"

The detective pulled open another drawer. "There's always something." He lifted up a stocking. "And if there ain't, then we'll all feel that much better about Miss Devereux, won't we?"

Turning from the other, Harry went to the night table beside the bed. In the only drawer, he found a book in French—poetry, from the look of it—and beside it, a small stack of letters, bound with ribbon. Sitting on the bed, which he found poorly mattressed, he slipped off the ribbon and pulled forth the first folded sheet of paper.

It was signed, with great ardor, "George." Glancing quickly over its contents, he refolded it and put it back with the others. Biting on his lip a moment, looking up to see Leahy now shifting to the theatrical trunk, he put the entire stack into a pocket for later perusal.

This was theft, trespass, and worse, but it couldn't be helped. Harry realized that at the moment he had indeed become a detective, or spy, or agent, or whatever term might best apply for this skulduggery. The difference between him and Leahy was that he was yet detective and spy without a master. Senator Quigley was not going to get a peek at these for his money.

At least not yet.

Harry watched Leahy pull out all of the drawers of the trunk and reach behind, then tap along the sides.

"False bottoms. Hidden compartments."

"Oh."

"None here." Leahy stood. "You checked that table?"

"Yes."

Leahy paused, looking carefully around the room, then strode to the bed. "Get up, if you please."

Harry did so. "What?"

The Irishman knelt and lifted the mattress, reaching beneath it and feeling back and forth. He worked his way down to the foot, then moved to the other side. Finally, he stood.

"Shall we go?"

"Wait," Leahy said. Another look about the chamber, his eyes fixing on the small rug beneath the dresser. "That's oddly placed."

He went to it, lifting the chest by its leg and pulling the rug free. Then he began running his hand over the floorboards, pushing them down in place.

"Ha!" he said. In a moment, he had lifted one of the boards and set it aside. A moment later, he retrieved a small metal box.

Harry stared, fascinated, as Leahy undid the clasp and opened the lid. The Irishman swore. "Empty! Worst surprise of all."

It was time to go. Moving toward the door as Leahy returned the box to its hiding place, Harry noticed for the first time a dressing gown hanging on a hook on the back of the door. He touched it, moving it to the side. There was an odd weight to it. He pulled it back and let it swing forward. It struck the wood of the door with a thunk.

Leahy, having heard the sound, was watching him. With a sigh, Harry found a pocket in the garment and reached within.

He pulled out a small caliber, six-shot pocket revolver.

Chapter 1 2

LEAHY broke open the revolver to examine the chambers.

"Three shots fired," he said.

"Three?"

"Yes. If you'd hand me that spent round y'been carryin', I'd be obliged."

Harry hesitated. Leahy was not pleased.

"Damn you, Raines. I'm a detective in the employ of the U.S. Secret Service. You, Sir, are a damned civilian, goddamn it! I thought you were helping us with this."

"I am, Mr. Leahy, but . . ."

"You can't ignore the obvious, lad, and you can't put off the inevitable."

Harry handed him the desired object. Leahy removed an unfired cartridge from the revolver and held the two of them in the palm of his hand, toward the light.

"Ballistics, you call it."

"Yes."

"They look the same to me."

"The same caliber. That's all we can say for sure."

"It's enough, Raines."

"What of Colonel Beals' report? Eyewitnesses saying they saw Pleasants fall to Rebel fire. Shot in the back running from the enemy."

"You know that's a lie. We've proved that's a lie. And now here's proof again."

"But it's an official military report, his superior officer's word—corroborated by that sergeant."

Leahy looked like an angry but indulgent parent, confronting a misbehaving child. "Raines. Do you know where to find this woman?"

"No."

The Irishman carefully put the revolver into the breast pocket of his coat, then turned his eyes on Harry hard. "The President wants to put an end to this matter. That appears to me what we have in hand. And it's to Mr. Pinkerton I'm taking it."

"I don't know where she is. I came by earlier, and she was gone. I've no idea where. That's the truth."

Leahy started for the stairs. "If you ask me, Raines, her leaving is just another proof of what you and I are both this minute thinking."

HARRY stopped at the bar of Young Gadsby's Hotel at 3rd and Pennsylvania, ordering oysters and a beer at the bar. Like everyplace else now in Washington, the establishment was crowded, though there was no one in the throng of sweaty, thirsty, noisy men he knew.

Finishing his quick lunch, he ordered up coffee, taking it to the door and leaning against the frame as he watched a cavalry regiment jangle by. Judging by the horses' lathered flanks, and troopers' slumped backs, they'd come far. Harry wondered if they were bound to or from Virginia. He wondered the same of himself.

He'd been beating his brain for a way to save Louise Devereux, but Leahy seemed to have blocked every path.

Glancing up and down the Avenue, he saw others observing the military procession as well. Up toward 2nd Street, lounging against a tree, was a familiar figure—the familiarity deriving most from the insouciance of his pose. Harry pulled out his spectacles and put them on.

Booth!

Harry set down his cup on the wooden floor and stepped

outside. Because of the noise made by the cavalry, he reached Booth's side without the other noticing.

"Good day, Sir."

The actor turned his head only slightly, as though annoyed to be distracted from this equestrian pageantry.

"Ah, Raines. A sorry looking lot, aren't they? Not like the horsemen of Virginia."

Harry let that pass. "Where is Miss Devereux?"

"Louise? Why, her rooms are just up the street. Surely you know that? You fetched her home from the battle."

"I know where she lives. I've just come from there. I want to know where she is."

Booth had been smoking a small cigar. It had gone out. "Now, how would I know that?" He struck a match, then flicked it into the street when done.

"Because you and she called upon Caitlin, and then you all went somewhere."

"Miss Howard and I went for a ride. Just the two of us."

"A hot day for that."

"What's your interest in Louise Devereux, Raines? I had thought it was another woman who struck your fancy."

"Damn it, Booth. I need to find her. She's at great hazard. There are Federal detectives looking for her. Or will be soon."

"Whatever for?"

"For murdering a Union Army officer!"

Booth smiled broadly. On stage, he would have caused half a hundred female hearts to flutter.

"No crime that, surely, Sir. Good day to you, Raines."

He strode off. Harry could have hit him, though there was nothing to be gained from that. Certainly not from Caitlin.

A screeching train whistle sounded behind him. The Baltimore & Ohio Railroad depot was four blocks away on the other side of Tiber Creek. A locomotive was visible, though mostly by a sooty black cloud chuffed high above the rooftops.

Booth had come from that direction.

Harry began to run toward the tracks.

•   •   •

"BOOTH?" said the ticket agent. He shrugged.

"The actor. Famous actor. Man with shortish hair and a moustache. Dark hair. Black. Eyes to match. Clothes as handsome as he is."

"Oh yes. That fella. Rich man. Goes to Baltimore all the time. Actor, you say?"

The ticket agent led a small, narrow life.

"Did he travel to Baltimore today. To there? From there?"

"Mr. Booth?"

"Yes!"

"Nope. Bought a ticket, though."

"Did he use it?" Harry asked, as patiently as possible.

"Manner of speakin'."

"How is that?"

"He bought it for someone else."

"A small, dark-haired woman? Long dark hair? Very pretty?"

"Yup. That'd be the one."

"She took a train to Baltimore?"

"Yup." The agent glanced up at the wall clock. "Oughta be there by now. Was more'n two hours ago."

Harry stepped back, with a sigh, then abruptly came up to the window again. "Is there another train to Baltimore?"

"There's two. Got one departing five o'clock."

"And the other."

"That'd be the one behind you there. It's leavin' right now but it's a local. Won't get you there 'til after four."

Chapter 1 3

THERE were military guards posted throughout the train, and, as they neared Baltimore, many others were visible along the railroad right of way. They were among the milder manifestations of the U.S. response to the attacks made upon Union troops by pro-Secessionist citizenry when Pennsylvania and Massachusetts regiments had crossed through the town that spring in transferring from one railroad to another.

Ten soldiers and eleven civilians had been killed in that clash and the rioting that had followed. Lincoln had ordered the suspension of civil rights in the city, a precaution that was still observed. Worse, the President had sent in General Benjamin Butler to restore and maintain order. "Beast Butler," as some Marylanders now called him, had seen fit to jail the mayor, the police marshal, four police commissioners, and a newspaper publisher, among dozens of others—and the prison rolls were increasing.

Harry was glad to have the new military pass signed by Cameron in his pocket, though he doubted Pinkerton would approve of the use to which he was going to put it. He had no intention of bringing Louise Devereux into Federal custody. Caitlin would never speak to him again if he did that. But, before seeing to her liberty, he ardently wished to talk to her—and to free her from any ties to that damnable Booth.

The actor wouldn't have sent her to an address within Baltimore. Not if his intent was to spare her the infelicities of

Federal justice. The city was acrawl with troops and Marshal's detectives.

Harry had a much better idea where Booth would have Louise go. Caitlin had gone to this place herself with the actor. It was the country house his father, Junius Booth, had built outside Bel Air, a country town just to the north of Baltimore. "Tudor Hall," it was called. Caitlin had said it was Tudor in architecture, and Shakespearean in aspect. Booth's room in fact had a balcony from which he could leap either to the ground or to the limb of a great tree.

Arriving at Baltimore's Camden Station, Harry took the horsecar along the waterfront to the President Street Depot, where he'd switch to the Philadelphia, Wilmington, and Baltimore Railroad. Baltimore stank in the summer even worse than Washington, no matter that it was on the water at the head of the wide expanse of Chesapeake Bay. Looking out the open window of the street car, Harry looked at the docked sail and steamships rather wistfully, dreaming on their destinations.

Looking across the harbor, Harry saw that the high hill on the southern shore had been turned into a Federal fortress. Cannons poking out of embrasures seemed to be aimed at every point in the city. Reassuring for the likes of Mr. Pinkerton; no doubt terrifying for Louise, if she had passed this way.

There were still bullet holes in the wall of the President Street station, inflicted upon it in the spring brawl. Two broken windows had been left boarded up against the possibility of another riot. Harry had used the station often in peacetime. It had been an actual stop on the old Underground Railroad. He'd once shipped an escaping black man to Philadelphia from the depot in a large crate.

The station master here knew Booth well, but could not recall seeing him in recent days. He did remember seeing an attractive dark-haired woman that afternoon, alighting from the horse cars and buying a ticket for Bel Air up the line.

THE "station" at Bel Air was little more than a bit of platform with a peaked roof over it. Once the locomotive and train had chuffed on up the line, Harry crossed the tracks and started up the road to the village. It led generally uphill, and in the heat he found himself having to pause at the crest of the first ridge to rest himself and cool off. He hoped this mad hunch would bear fruit.

Tudor Hall was famous in the vicinity, and Harry had to ask directions only once. A farmer was happy to stop in his late afternoon labors to provide Harry with them—along with some disapproving comments on Booth's politics, which the farmer apparently found too Yankee! He had in mind, apparently, elder brother Edwin Booth, Mr. Lincoln's stalwart admirer.

Harry turned right at the crossroads indicated, then ascended another hill, turning left at its summit onto a narrow dirt and gravel lane that curved into some woods. Emerging from them on the other side, he saw across a rolling stretch of meadow a gabled house looking almost precisely as Caitlin had described it.

Moving on along the curving drive, he halted of a sudden. To the side of the house, bending over some flowering bushes, was a dark-haired woman in a light-colored dress. She wore her hair pinned up and bagged in the current fashion, not shoulder length as was Louise's habit, and had on a hat besides. But that could be disguise.

As he came closer, Harry stepped off the gravel and onto the soft grass. Slowing, he came up behind her without her noticing, reaching to take her by the shoulders. Before he could get a grip on them, she whirled about, looked into his face, and screamed.

Chapter 1 4

HARRY managed little sleep on the return rail journey, what with the soot and incessant lurches and rattling. Upon reaching Washington, he proceeded on foot from the B & O depot down D Street, not minding the strange sounds and skittering movements he encountered in the shadowy darkness. Growling panthers would not have distracted him.

A chorus of startled, irritable barking erupted when Harry knocked, then pounded, on the door to Mrs. Fitzgerald's. The hour was late, but that had seldom been a concern of this house in the past.

"Such a ruckus, Mr. Raines!" said the landlady, from the partially opened door. "What in hell's the matter with you? Have ye lost yer mind, or are ye drunk?"

"Neither, Madam. I need to speak with Miss Howard on a matter of some urgency. Has she returned?"

"She has."

He started toward the door, but she did not yield it.

"She don't want to talk to you, Mr. Raines."

Harry paused, but impatiently. "Now, how would you know that, Mrs. Fitzgerald."

"I know 'cause she told me. She said I wasn't to admit you."

"But . . ."

"My son, Samuel, is asleep in the back, and he's as drunk as he gets. But I can awaken him, Sir, and then you will be sore sorry you stopped by this house tonight."

Harry stepped back as the door was slammed in his face.

•   •   •

THERE was a message in his box for him to meet with "Major E. J. Allen" at "the initial place of encounter" as soon as was convenient. That place, of course, was the Willard.

After a hurried but cooling sponge bath from the basin in his own room, he dressed in fresh linen, shirt, and suit; dashed on a few drops of cologne; and put his derringer in an inner pocket.

His chamber was in some disorder. He supposed the house maid had not been by. For what he paid for these quarters, he expected better.

On the way out, he stopped again at the desk.

"My rooms have not been attended to."

The clerk's eyebrows lifted. "Sorry, Mr. Raines. Thought they had been."

"Is Mr. Booth here tonight?" he asked, nodding toward the door to the hotel's bar.

"No, Sir. I believe he has left the city."

"Left? He was here just a few hours ago."

"That's what he told us."

Harry nodded his thanks.

HE knocked on the door at the Willard where he'd had his first audience with Pinkerton, and got no response. After another attempt, he inquired at the desk and was told Major Allen had not returned for dinner. Harry asked for Leahy's room and was informed that Leahy did not reside at the Willard but at the less savory Globe Hotel next to Naylor's Livery and across the Avenue from Grover's Theatre.

The Irishman answered his door wearing only the bottom half of a suit of red underwear. He was otherwise barefooted and barechested, and covered with sweat.

"Where've you been, Raines? Major Allen wants to speak with you!"

He allowed Harry inside. The reason for his odd appearance was readily explained. There was a set of weights in the center of the room. Leahy went to them and resumed his calisthenics.

From the look of the weights, they were more than Harry could heft in that manner for more than a few minutes, yet the Irishman went at them with a seemingly effortless relish.

"I went looking for Pinkerton," Harry said. "He's not in his room."

"He's down at Old Capitol Prison, interrogating a new arrival." Leahy continued the rhythm of his exercise.

"More freed slaves?"

"No, not slaves. Where've you been, Raines?"

"In Baltimore."

Up and down. Up and down. "Baltimore? There and back since this afternoon?" Up and down.

"The train schedule was accommodating. I was looking for Louise Devereux."

Leahy's arms stopped motionless, extended with the weights high above him. "Did you find her?"

"No. It was a foolish impulse to go there. Very foolish."

"Indeed it was, laddybuck. For she is taken."

"Taken?"

"She's been arrested, Raines. By Mr. Pinkerton himself. He's taken her to the Old Capitol Prison. She's lucky she didn't get put up in the Old Blue Jug."

His reference was to the city jail at 4th and G, which derived its name from the blue paint which covered its stucco walls. It was a hellhole aswarm with rats, roaches, and every other kind of vermin, and many human prisoners of a not much higher order. The Bastille had been Versailles compared to it. The merest thought of a woman like Louise Devereux resident in such an institution made Harry shudder.

"Where did you find her?"

"At the National Hotel."

"In Booth's rooms?"

Leahy slowly lowered the weights to the floor, then sat up. "No, Sir. She was in yours."

Harry decided he didn't want to hear another word about this until he could do so with his hand around a glass full of strong drink.

•   •   •

"SHE was drunk, half-mad with laudanum, generally hysterical, and tearing your rooms apart looking for something," Leahy said. He lifted his glass, swallowing half its contents, which were lemonade. Leahy, Harry was surprised to learn, was something of a temperance man—at least as concerned his own refreshment.

They were in the bar of the National, which was still quite full of patrons despite the late hour. McClellan's whiskey ban had been about as effective as his war plans.

"What was she doing there?"

"You're the man to answer that, now aren't you, Raines?"

Down went the rest of the lemonade. Harry stood him to another.

"I would have supposed she'd take up residence in Mr. Booth's quarters," Harry said. "They appear to be on intimate acquaintance."

"The desk clerk told us they'd come in together, but Booth was alone when we came upon him. He suggested we might try your rooms."

"He directed you people to her?"

"A patriot."

"A gallant." Harry's sarcasm here was inescapable, but Leahy ignored it.

"Right desperate she was," Leahy said. "Put up a nasty fight."

Harry pondered his whiskey glass, thinking upon Louise's return visit to the hotel down by Murder Bay. What had she sought there? What could she be looking for in his rooms? The same thing?

"Has she said anything?" Harry asked. "Explained herself?"

"Nothing a man can much comprehend. Raged on incoherently about Major Pleasants and her love for him."

Harry took a swallow. "Do you suppose Pinkerton would let me talk to her?"

Leahy took his bowler hat from the bar and set it carefully low upon his head. He barely moved his back in doing this. It was so straight it seemed a heavy oaken board.

"Yes, I do suppose that," he said, "if it's in the service of the Union, and not some stupid, ill-thought scheme to secure her freedom—for I know your thoughts on the matter, Raines. You think her an innocent. But you are wrong, Sir. And were I you, I'd keep a distance from that woman. She's a spy—Confederate spy. It all comes clear now. She went to Manassas to spy. Same reason she went to bed with Pleasants. He found out about her and died for his trouble."

"I think otherwise."

"Then you're a fool. All the evidence points to it."

"And Mr. Booth pointed to it."

"I suppose he did."

Harry finished his drink and set the glass down sharply. The woman he had accosted at Tudor Hall in Bel Air was Booth's sister Asia. When he'd calmed her down and explained himself, she had said she had been worried about Booth's "friendship" with Miss Devereux, for she feared the actress was a spy who would get her brother into trouble.

"I'm going to go see her," Harry said.

"Like I say, laddybuck. Mr. Pinkerton will be pleased to see you. But I warn you. We've enough evidence now to hang that woman twice over."

Harry started away, but enroute to the door someone caught at his sleeve. It was Matthew Brady, at a table with another bespectacled man.

"Raines!" he said. "Look who's here!"

Harry squinted. "Mr. Gardner!"

Alexander Gardner grinned, a little loosely. He and Brady had apparently been celebrating his return.

"I came back through Alexandria," he said. "Perilous journey, Sir. Perilous."

"Raines," said Brady, trying to pull him into a chair. "He brought back plates! He has two plates from the battlefront! You must come see them."

Harry got himself free. "Tomorrow, Mr. Brady. I must now go see a lady."

Chapter 1 5

PINKERTON was in the yard of the Old Capitol, standing by his horse and talking with two soldiers. Harry rode up very close to them, forgetting how intimidating Rocket's height could be.

"That's a sizable horse you have there, Raines," said Pinkerton, backing away a step. "I believe that animal could carry Winfield Scott."

Harry dismounted. "He has his uses, but transporting three-hundred-pound generals hasn't been one of them."

"You heard the news about Louise Devereux?"

"That's why I'm here."

"She won't talk to us. Not to me. Not to anyone. Keeps muttering lunatic things. One line in particular—over and over. 'But dead they are, and devilish slave, by thee.' Ravings, but those of a murderess."

"The ravings, Sir, of a great writer. William Shakespeare. *Richard III.* I know it for it's from one of my favorite scenes, where Richard as Duke of Gloucester seduces the Lady Anne over the corpse of her husband, whom he himself has murdered. The words are Lady Anne's. Not the murderer's."

The last time he had seen that play was at Grover's. Booth had been Richard and Caitlin, Lady Anne.

"Well, it makes no sense to me."

"I'd like to speak to her," Harry said.

"Are you throwing in with us?" Pinkerton pulled himself

up into the saddle, then squirmed a little to get the seat right. "You ready now to join the Secret Service? Tell me now because I must return to Cincinnati."

"For now, I'm in the employ of Senator Quigley."

"You are a foe of slavery, Raines."

"So you've noted in the past, Sir. But I must honor the prior commitment."

"You'll tell Leahy, whatever this woman says?"

"Yes. Of course."

That could prove a lie, but it was a necessary one.

"All right. Speak to her. But be careful, Raines. She is a spy."

"What is to happen to her?"

"That'll be up to a military tribunal. Murdering an Army officer is a hanging crime."

"What about Booth?"

"Booth? He's left the city."

"You don't think he's mixed up in this business?"

"How could he be? He told us where to find her. Did his duty, Raines. A good example for you."

If the Old Capitol was a prison, it was a capacious and comfortable one. There was a large central lobby that was used as a common room. Instead of cells, the inmates had been given sleeping chambers—some with sitting rooms. Prisoners were not confined to them, but free to move about within the institution as they pleased. Despite the late hour, several gentlemen were seated about the common area.

Harry recognized some of them. He wondered what was their crime—if there was any. He supposed he wasn't very far from one of those chairs himself.

Louise Devereux the warders took more seriously. A Union soldier was posted at her door, which had a bar across it.

"She been troublesome," said the sergeant whom Pinkerton had designated to escort Harry.

"I've no doubt."

•   •   •

THE soldiers left the door open but Harry defiantly closed it behind him. Then he walked carefully up to the bed in the corner, where Louise, fully dressed despite the heat and closeness of the room, lay facedown, gently sobbing.

"It's me, Louise. Harry Raines."

The sobbing stopped, but she said nothing. Aware of how violent she could sometimes be, Harry cautiously took a seat beside her on the edge of the bed. With even greater care, he put a hand on her small shoulder.

"Have they treated you well?" he asked.

"Go away. It's thanks to you I'm in this awful dungeon."

"That wasn't my intent."

"But here I am nonetheless, you villain. 'Thou mayst be damned for that wicked deed!' "

She sat up. As Shakespeare had writ, she bore 'a load of moan,' and looked it. Her dark eyes were reddened, her olive skin splotchy, her hair a tangled thicket, her lip rouge smeared to one side.

And yet, she looked to him to still be one of the loveliest ladies of the town. For all the apparent havoc wreaked by doses of laudanum, brandy, fatigue, terror, desperation, frustration, and anger, her beauty suffused her as though its source was something burning within.

Harry had given himself sage counsel, the first time he and Louise had met, that a man would have to be altogether insane to fall in love with her. Even if not, he'd soon be crazed enough from her company, for she was maddening in her every respect. Amour with Miss Devereux was amour with a whirlwind—as someone should have warned Pleasants.

But the temptation was powerful, perhaps overpowering. He felt it now as she reached and pulled his handkerchief from his sleeve, dabbing at her eyes.

"I went looking for you," he said. "All the way to Bel Air, north of Baltimore."

"Why go there?"

"Booth's house. Or I should say, his late father's."

"And why should I be there?"

"You were with Booth. That much I know for a fact. He'd been to the railroad station. I thought it was to see you off."

"He took his sister there—Asia—to see her off."

"I found her at the house. She spoke ill of you."

The handkerchief was lowered, revealing eyes now calm and cold.

"She's insanely jealous of all Wilkes' friends. I do believe she has an ungodly passion for him herself."

"She called you a spy, Louise."

Their eyes held each other, until at last she looked away.

"I am no spy, Harry. No secret agent. Just a poor woman unfortunate in love and circumstance."

He took the handkerchief from her fingers and gently wiped away a new tear from her cheek.

"They say they found you in my rooms," he said.

The dark eyes came on him flashing bright.

"Where is it, Harry? Where?"

"Where is what?"

"What? What? You came searching for it yourself—in that wretched hotel I now regret even passing in the street."

"I am still uncertain of what you speak."

"Damn you, Sir, it means my life! And you toy with me about it!" She pulled away, swinging her legs around and turning her back to him.

"I'm sorry, but I'm telling you the truth. I don't know what you are talking about. What is it? I want to help you, Louise."

He put a hand to her shoulder, but she shook if off.

"It's just a piece of paper. Not worth a damn to anyone, but I'm desperate to have it. If you find it, I'd be obliged if you do not read it, on your honor as a gentleman. If that's what you are."

"Granted. But what kind of paper? How will I know it's what you seek."

She thrust herself up of a sudden, dark eyes burning into his. "A paper issued by the State of Louisiana. Booth did not give you it?"

"No."

"You didn't find it with the major?"

"No. What are you talking about?"

"Never mind. Never mind. It's too late. Nothing matters.

I'm going to be shot by a firing squad. And all thanks to you. 'Never hung poison on a fouler toad!' "

He decided it would be best to take that as an exit cue.

"I'll get you out of here, Louise."

"Liar!"

He touched her shoulder and tried to draw her near, as he might a troubled child. At first she stiffly resisted, then suddenly came up close against him, pushing her moist cheek against his, reminding him oddly of Mrs. Pleasants and the scene in her coach.

"I will," he said. "I'll do it. I owe it to you. And Caitlin will not speak to me again if I don't."

"Caitlin? You'd help me only for the sake of her?"

"Louise . . ."

She screamed and threw herself back down upon the bed. The shrill sound summoned the soldier and Harry's sergeant escort. They opened the door with such violence it slammed loudly against the wall, causing Louise to scream again.

"This gets us nowhere," said Harry, as he walked quickly out of the room.

The scent of Louise's perfume lingered with him even as he mounted his horse.

Chapter 1 6

An incessant, insistent scuffing sound stirred Harry into wakefulness. He'd been dreaming—of Louise Devereux, not Caitlin—but his mind turned to images of marching soldiers. He could almost hear the tramp of their feet. Thwip, thwop; thwip, thwop.

He opened his eyes. The day was bright, and it took a moment for him to adjust to it. The sound continued into wakefulness. He thought at first it might actually be troops drilling in the Avenue outside his window, but it was nearer than that. Blinking, he took note finally of Caesar Augustus, who was sitting on the chair in the corner and brushing expertly a now highly polished boot.

"How'd you get in here?" Harry asked, lifting himself on an elbow.

"Waren't hard, Marse Harry. Someone's busted your lock open and the hotel ain't fixed it yet. When you didn't answer, I jes' walk right in."

"Why are you polishing my boots?"

"Like dat Mr. Linkum say, if'n I don't polish your boots, whose boots do I gots to polish?"

"You missed the joke. It turns on the word 'gentleman.' And stop talking like that."

"Yassuh, Marse Harry." He went at the boot with a burst of vigor, then set it down.

Harry swung his feet onto the floor, rubbed his eyes, then

went to his wash basin and poured in some water, splashing it liberally onto his face and neck. He peered at himself in the mirror, leaning close, for lack of spectacles.

"Do you think I should grow a beard?" he asked.

"Sure do. When you's an old man like John Brown. Right now, you're too young to look like a prophet."

Harry went behind a screen to use the chamber pot, then washed his hands again and began to pull on his clothes. There was much to do this day.

"Why aren't you with that army captain?" he asked Caesar Augustus, who had leaned back against the wall and was looking contented.

"I done resigned from the army. That line a work is pretty much like slavery, even for a nice officer like him."

"Your Mr. Douglass is agitating to have colored troops in the Union Army."

"Well, he's a fool, for all his good intentions. The Rebel army ain't gonna treat Negroes as soldiers, and I'm not so sure the Yankee Army would, either—way it's been treatin' me. 'Spect they'd all get put to liftin' and carryin', like I been doin'. That Captain Kelleter's a good man but he's got some mean sergeants. Could pass for plantation overseers if'n they had some whips."

"Before you tendered your resignation, did you find out anything more?"

"Ah sure enough did. 'Fact, Marse Harry, the main reason I've resigned is ah done got you what you acksed."

"You going to share this discovery with me?"

"Already have. On the dresser there, I got you a list of their names."

"Whose names?"

"The officers and men who them soldiers think might have a taste for killin' off the poor major."

Harry picked up the paper, which had been folded twice over.

"Damnation, Caesar Augustus. There are only three names here. I could probably think of twice as many who might want to kill me."

"These are what I come up with. Cost you some whiskey."

Two of the names were interesting, though obvious: Colonel Jeffrey Beals and Sergeant Leander Fetridge. The third was not known to him: Captain Marcus Colton.

"Beals was Pleasants' immediate superior," Harry said. "I don't know much about Fetridge—or this Captain Colton."

"He's the quartermaster. Camp talk has it he's on his way to becomin' a rich man in the service o' the Republic. Seems he's decided the Union Army has far too much in the way of supply than it needs. So he's found quiet ways to dispose of some of it. If'n there's somethin' you need and you gots de money, Cap'n Colton he fix you right up. Anyways, him and Major Pleasants had some kind of noisy disagreement. Some say Pleasants socked him one."

"Disagreement over what?"

"Ain't nobody knows—lessen it was over money. Major Pleasants owes damn near de whole regiment. He owe you, too, Marse Harry?"

"No, when he lost to me, it was with hard cash." Harry finished tying his cravat. "Why hasn't anyone reported this?"

"People have. This Captain Kelleter? He reported it to his commanding officer."

"Who's that?"

Caesar Augustus grinned. "Lieutenant Colonel Beals."

Harry turned around, smiling. "Caesar Augustus, I think you ought to go back to work for the Army."

"Marse Harry, whyn't you just pay me a nice ten cents for this beautiful shine I put on your boots and let me be on my way."

"Just for today. Just one more day. Maybe two. Please?"

"Why?"

"I want you to make one last really serious effort at finding someone who might have seen Major Pleasants get shot. All those soldiers there. Someone has to have seen something. They can't all have been looking at the Rebels."

"You was there, Marse Harry. You missed it."

"I wish I could get my hands on that coachman of the Quigleys. From where he sat up on that coach, he might have seen everything."

"If he did, he sure enough didn't want to talk about it much that night we were in that barn."

"Maybe we can find him—in Virginia."

The black man shook his head, then tilted it back, looking at Harry as he might the last card being dealt of a five-card hand.

"Why're you keeping on with this, Marse Harry? You hardly knew the major, and he wasn't no friend."

"Pinkerton arrested Louise Devereux last night."

Caesar Augustus' head snapped forward. "That pretty girl?"

"Pretty's a small word for someone that beautiful. They've got her in the Old Capitol. I want to get her out of there before things get more serious than they already are. They could hang her for either murder or spying."

Caesar Augustus' eye narrowed. "You sweet on that lady, Marse Harry?"

"I'm aware of her attractions, and sympathetic to her plight. But the answer's no. Let's just say that delivering her from this peril would make Miss Howard very happy. At the moment, she is very unhappy. Most especially as concerns me."

Caesar Augustus rose, wearily. "All right, Mr. Boss Man. I'll do this for you one more time—but I think you better double what you're paying me."

"Done." Harry started toward the door. "On your way back there, I'd like you to look around for Detective Leahy. Tell him to meet me in the bar of the Willard." He looked at his pocket watch. "At noon."

"Where you goin' now, Marse Harry?"

"To see if I can't get Louise out of jail an easier way."

HARRY was readily admitted to the senator's house, and ushered into the same parlor as before. Father and daughter were taking a late breakfast in a nearby room. Harry heard the clatter of crockery behind them just as they entered the parlor.

He rose, bowing to the lady and then shaking the senator's hand. These were people who seemed to put as much store by manners as Southern gentry did.

Mrs. Pleasants seated herself, but Quigley remained standing, a sign perhaps that he wished a quick interview.

"I've spoken with the President and with that man Pinkerton," the senator said. "I've read the morning newspapers. Excellent job, Raines. Splendid work. I certainly hadn't expected a result this soon. Yet here you've cleared up the entire sordid matter in a matter of days."

"I've what?"

"I was about to send a messenger to look for you. So we might conclude matters between us. As I say, Sir. Fine piece of work." Quigley went to a table and plucked up a folded newspaper, handing it to Harry. "Here. It's in the *Intelligencer*."

Harry took the paper and opened it. The story was on the front page. Pinkerton, or someone associated with him, must have let the reporter in on what was afoot early in the game.

ACTRESS SEIZED, the top headline read.

HELD IN MURDER AT MANASSAS

MAJ. PLEASANTS EXONERATED

REBEL FEMALE ASSASSINS

Harry read on, learning of an apparent plot to use beautiful Southern temptresses to woo important Union officers to their demise. The story's extraordinary lack of fact was compensated for with great measures of hyperbole and hysteria.

"This is astounding," he said.

"As I say," said Quigley, with a smile, "my daughter and I were surprised. But agreeably so. Very pleased with your work, Mr. Raines. Very pleased." He reached into his pocket and withdrew a large wallet, from which he took out six ten-dollar bills.

Harry held back from taking, hoping this did not seem bad manners.

"You are very generous," he said. "But the job isn't done. Far from done. I do indeed think Major Pleasants was murdered, but I believe the girl to be innocent."

"But she has been arrested and I presume charged," said Quigley, gesturing at the newspaper. "She appears to be a spy. I'm told by Secretary Cameron this morning that Colonel Beals and Sergeant Fetridge have amended their reports. They both now say that they must have been mistaken in the confusion of the retreat, and that it was this Devereux woman who killed him, not the enemy. The case is closed."

"I'm afraid it isn't with me, Sir," said Harry. "You asked me to find the major's killer and clear his name. Only half that task's been done."

"But it's been done to our immense satisfaction, Mr. Raines. Your work as far as we're concerned is done."

Mrs. Pleasants gave her father a sharp glance. Her poise and dignity had been fully restored. She comported herself coolly, but when she spoke, it was as a gracious hostess.

"Mr. Raines. May I offer you a cup of tea."

Harry didn't want any, but neither did he wish to be rushed from the premises just yet. "Thank you."

Mrs. Pleasants picked up a small bell and rang it twice. A black maid appeared almost instantly, then scurried off as commanded.

"Mr. Raines," she began, hesitantly. "Was my dear husband well acquainted with this Devereux woman?"

Harry couldn't decide whether the situation would be better served by being brutally frank or diplomatically devious. "I believe they were friends."

"And what occasioned this 'friendship'?"

"Major Pleasants was, uh, fond of the theater. Miss Devereux is an accomplished actress."

"Such an actress might make many men become 'fond of the theater,' don't you think?"

"She has her following. I count myself part of it."

"And you have a friendship with her as well?"

"I have a friendship with a young lady who has a friendship with Miss Devereux. That is the extent of my interest."

Mrs. Pleasants glanced at her father again, then lowered her eyes, staring at the carpet.

"Mr. Raines, I must be blunt," she said, finally. "Was my husband romantically involved with this woman?"

Her father coughed. "Elizabeth, please . . ."

"I have absolutely no evidence of any such thing, Mrs. Pleasants. All I can say for a fact is that they knew each other."

"Knew each other well enough for him to stop in the middle of a battle and talk to her?"

Harry shrugged. "He stopped to talk to you."

Her reply was like a cannon shot. "I am his wife, Sir!"

"Yes, Ma'am. I'm sorry. I don't know for a fact that he talked to her at Bull Run."

"Then how else would she get close enough to him to shoot him?"

The maid entered with a tea tray, which Mrs. Pleasants sharply instructed her to set down upon a side table. When she had gone, the major's wife sat as though nailed to her chair, showing no inclination now to offer Harry anything.

"As I said, Ma'am. I don't believe she did shoot him."

"The newspapers say the murder weapon is a revolver that was found in her room," said the senator.

"That's the sticky part of it," Harry replied. "That's why they have her locked up."

Now Mrs. Pleasants at last rose and went to her tea tray. But again she paused. "Mr. Raines, would you be willing to undertake an investigation to determine the exact extent of my husband's relationship with this woman? I understand there are agencies in New York City where one can hire agents to perform such an inquiry."

"I'm sure there are, Ma'am, New York being New York. But I have no interest in such an undertaking. It's not my sort of business."

She picked up a teacup. "The newspaper article says this Miss Devereux is from Louisiana—a Southerner. Is that why you're reluctant to do this?"

"Mrs. Pleasants, I wouldn't undertake such a thing if the lady in question were from Massachusetts or Maine."

The cup went back upon the tray with a bang and a rattle. The senator stepped forward, reaching into his wallet again. "I think the most agreeable thing, Sir, is to conclude our business now." He handed Harry the sum of sixty dollars. "As I said, Mr. Raines, we're much appreciative."

Mrs. Pleasants walked from the room without another word. As soon as she had slipped from view, the senator took Harry's arm and turned him toward the front hall and the door.

"I shall tell the President about your good work," he said.

•   •   •

HARRY climbed into Rocket's saddle, then sat a moment, contemplating the Quigley house, wondering if he would ever darken its door again. He felt a great sorrow for Mrs. Pleasants, but something about the senator repelled him, despite the man's reputation and efforts in the cause of Abolitionism. Something not obvious, but iniquitous.

He realized what it was. Quigley was much too quick with the dollar for an honest man.

From New England.

There was movement, a curtain in a window. Harry bowed to it, then gently turned Rocket down the street.

HE bought Leahy a lemonade, and himself a glass of Old Overholtz.

"What is it you want of me, Raines?" the Irishman asked.

"First of all, an honest answer. Do you believe Louise Devereux is guilty of murdering the major?"

Leahy gave him an honest look, at least, squarely eye to eye.

"I believe we found the murder weapon on her premises."

"That's not the answer I sought, Sir."

The detective turned away, sipping his cool drink. "I have doubts."

"Very good, Mr. Leahy. Then there are at least two of us of that mind in this city—three, if you count Miss Devereux."

Four, if he counted Caitlin, as indeed he must.

"Is that all you wanted of me? Hell man, I've other things to do. There's a bloody damn war on, you know."

Harry looked about the barroom. No one was paying them any attention—except the bartender, who was still trying to adjust to the reality of a man like Leahy ordering lemonade.

"No, I'd more in mind," Harry said. "I'd like you to help me conduct a search of a bawdy house. You seem a most excellent searcher."

Leahy smiled and shook his head. "Mr. Raines, Mr. Pinkerton is becoming a mite impatient with you. He'd like you to work with us officially on these matters, not larkin' about on your own like this. If you weren't retained by Senator Quigley, he'd put it to ye hard. Join us, or get out of the way. Or out of the country."

"I'm no longer retained by the senator and Mrs. Pleasants. We parted company just this morning."

"And why is that?"

"They are satisfied that the case is closed and the major's honor is restored. I've been paid in full."

"All this blather about Southern temptresses luring Union officers to their doom?"

"You don't believe that?" Harry grinned.

Leahy grinned back. "The major was killed on a bloody battlefield! Not in a brothel. These damn newspapers will print anything."

"And they're printing quite a lot of it. But the Southern temptress notion could be useful."

The Irishman finished his lemonade. He seemed uncomfortable in a saloon.

"How so?"

"To give you a reason to search that bawdy house. It's full of temptresses. I'll wager one or two of them is Southern."

Leahy stepped back from the bar. He was anxious for the street. "What is it you think may be found on those premises. Just what are you after Raines?"

"I want to find the major's true killer. I want this tale to end on a fact—especially if it's a fact that will free that poor little bird from her cage."

"You sparkin' her, Raines?"

"No, Sir. My heart belongs to another."

"Mr. Pinkerton is on the train to Ohio, if he's not there yet. I'll need his approval."

"Why? Didn't he leave you in charge? Doesn't he trust you absolutely? You can't go wrong raiding a whorehouse, Mr. Leahy. Bawds are a plague upon the Army, are they not?"

"All right. Give me the address of this establishment, and I will meet you there in one hour with a platoon of soldiers."

"Why soldiers?"

"Because the Secret Service now reports directly to General

McClellan, and we have authority over soldiery. I need not even ask Mr. Pinkerton, if I think it's justified. If we go there with only a copper or two, there'll be a big shrieking and running about and hulabaloo, with naught likely the result. With a couple squads of uniformed provost guard, we control the situation absolutely. No one and nothing will escape us."

"As you please then, Leahy. Just don't enlist any of your countrymen from those New York firemen Zouaves who are so much in our streets."

"And why not?"

"Because you'll never get them out of the place."

$\mathbf{A}$s it was, Leahy arrived at the appointed hour with only a squad of eight soldiers, led by a youthful corporal, but they proved equal to the task. Stationing half the group in the rear street behind the house, the Irishman led the other four through the front door in a sudden burst, with Harry tagging along discreetly in the rear.

There were some screams and curses, but not many and not for long. Within five minutes, one customer, four young women, and the proprietor, Mollie Turner, were assembled in the front parlor, all in some form of dress, though two of the bawds wore only dressing gowns. Ella Turner was not present. Her older sister Mollie was also blonde, but not so attractive.

"You all wait out in the back until we search the premises," Leahy said. "If you don't comply, I guarantee you'll be spending the night in the Blue Jug."

One of the girls began crying. Mollie began berating Leahy and offering questions as to his ancestry. He responded by having two soldiers take the woman by the arms and propel her down the hall to the back door.

"What are we after again?" Leahy asked Harry.

"Anything you think might belong to the major or Miss Devereux—which I suppose could be anything at all. It might also be useful to examine Madam's ledger books.

Leahy nodded. "Out! Everyone out!"

They found an officer's coat, but it bore a lieutenant's shoulder straps and appeared to belong to the lone customer then on the premises. While the other soldiers went through the upstairs rooms, Leahy, Harry, and the corporal perused the downstairs.

There was a strongbox in a small room off the parlor, hidden along with three ledgers behind a row of books, two of which had been set upside down. The box was locked, but one of the soldiers' bayonets sufficed to break it open.

"She's been making a tidy profit from this commerce in sin," said Leahy.

"It would be a poor businesswoman indeed who failed to do so with the town so choked with clientele," Harry said.

Leahy removed some business papers from the box, setting them aside as he began counting the money. Harry snatched up the papers.

One was a business license, signed by the Provost Marshal himself. Three letters of a highly amorous nature seemed to be addressed to the madam, but the signatories used only their first names. That was all.

"The woman has more than two thousand dollars here," Leahy said.

"You'd better call her back in so she doesn't accuse us of stealing any."

"Right." He turned to a soldier. "Haynes. Fetch that woman back. The mistress of the house." He smiled at his own joke. "I'd better look through the ledgers."

Mollie Turner came back in with a great bustle, the soldier hurrying to catch up with her.

"You thievin' bastards! You're robbin' me."

"No, Madame, we are not," Harry said. "Count the money yourself."

"Who are you? Were you in here yesterday?"

"We're the ones to be asking questions," Leahy said. He snapped shut one of the ledgers, then looked to Harry. "The fellow's name is in here. And not just once." He gave Mollie a sharp look. "We'll be taking these books for a while. You'll get 'em back after we've taken note of the entries."

"Those entries are my business. What right have you to come in here and . . ."

Leahy thrust the strongbox into her hands, then put the three ledger books under his arm.

"A good day to you, Madam. I would put that money of yours in a bank. There are criminals in this district."

Outside, he prepared to march his little army back to whatever quarters they had come from.

"What were in those papers you put back in the box, Raines?"

"Her license, and some love letters."

"You didn't take them? As evidence?"

"They weren't what I was looking for—at the least, I don't think so." Harry climbed into his saddle.

"Where you going now?" Leahy asked.

"To call upon Miss Caitlin Howard," he said. "If she'll receive me."

"Well, then, I hope she does."

But once again, she did not.

Chapter 1 7

PLEASANTS' regiment had been shifted from the camp-ground near the Smithsonian to a new site in Virginia, along the railroad that ran from Alexandria to Washington City. Riding across the Long Bridge, Harry worried whether a good mount like Rocket might run the risk of being requisitioned on sight by the Army, which was taking many liberties in the name of the national emergency—especially in Virginia.

But he found a soldier willing to watch the horse for him for a dollar. This detective business was producing far more expense than profit.

There were sentries posted in varying degrees of alertness about the camp, none of them bothering to stop Harry for a pass or bona fides. He sought out Caesar Augustus' Captain Kelleter, finding neither at the tent to which he was directed.

Inquiring further for the captain named Colton, he was sent to a government warehouse near the railroad that had been taken over by the brigade for quartermaster purposes.

Colton had been given an office that doubled as sleeping quarters, though most regimental officers were in tents. Both door and window were open in apparent hopes of a breeze, but there was none to be had, though the the warehouse was slightly cooler than the steam bath outside.

A smallish man, with glossy, pomaded dark hair and a wispy moustache, Colton was lounging behind his desk when Harry entered—his chair tilted back against the wall, a small cigar and a glass of whiskey in his hand. He gulped it down as Harry entered.

Movement to the side caught Harry's eye. A large, full-bearded sergeant emerged from behind a pillar—the very same sergeant Harry had encountered in the trees at Sudley Ford.

Harry nodded to Colton, but then turned quickly to the sergeant.

"Are you Fetridge?" Harry asked.

"I am Sergeant Fetridge. How be you knowin' my name?"

"I read it in the newspaper. You were on the Sudley Road when my friend Major Pleasants was killed."

Colton came forward in his chair. "You were a friend of Pleasants?"

Harry looked back to the captain. "I was coming to you in hopes you might be able to direct me to this man. And here he is."

"And who are you, Sir?" the captain asked.

"Harrison Raines."

"I think I've heard of you. You're a gambling man."

Harry returned his attention to the sergeant, who was looking very sour.

"I thought you were with a line company, Sergeant," he said. "Infantry. Not quartermaster."

"I was, but I got myself a better assignment." He made a sound like an animal rutting that Harry took for laughter.

"A reward for valor, no doubt," said Harry.

This produced frowns—from both of them. Colton was beginning to look irritated, and impatient.

"What's your business, Mr. Raines? We're busy here."

"I'm helping the major's family—his wife and her father, Senator Quigley—investigate the circumstances of his death."

It wasn't a lie. He'd simply used the wrong tense.

"That's already been investigated," Colton said. "They arrested some actress who was out there."

"Senator Quigley isn't satisfied with that." Now it was time to lie.

"Well too bad for him," the sergeant said. "And anyway it has nothin' to do with us."

"But you're an eyewitness to Pleasants' death," said Harry.

"According to the newspapers, anyway. Though I don't know how you got from Sudley Spring to the fighting in such a short time. Must have come up at the double quick."

"We done our duty. I put what I saw in a proper report."

"And then recanted, as did your colonel."

The sergeant came closer. He smelled of his lunch. "Look. I backed my colonel—lieutenant colonel—same ways he's always backed me. If he thought he saw Pleasants go down runnin' from the enemy, that's good enough for me. If he thought harder on the matter, and figures it happened some other way, then that's good enough, too."

"Did you actually see the major get shot?"

The sergeant grinned. "I sticks with the word of Lieutenant Colonel Beals. No matter what it is."

"Be satisfied with that," said Colton, rising to his feet. "There's a war on, Sir. We got a new general with Napoleonic ideas of how to run an army. There's much to do. So leave us now, please."

Harry moved out into the main part of the warehouse. There were high stacks of boxes, but he couldn't quite make out the writing on the sides.

"It certainly does take a lot of merchandise to put an army in the field," he said. "What do you have here? Canteens? Muskets?"

"Not muskets," said the captain. "We're quartermaster. Blankets, uniforms, canteens, too."

Harry moved close to one of the boxes. The word "shoe" was clear. As it was on the next box, and the one next to that.

"These are all shoes," he said.

"Shoes, too," Colton said, quietly.

"But all the soldiers I've seen already have shoes—brand-new army shoes. What're they going to do with these?"

"Oversupply. We're shipping them out of here."

"Where to?"

"What the hell do you care?" said the sergeant.

"I have some friends who need some new shoes. Seems to me that, if the Army's got so many shoes it doesn't need, maybe they could buy some."

Colton relighted his cigar, walking slowly up to Harry.

"Y'say you were a 'friend' of Pleasants?"

"Well, a card-playing friend."

"And you came here to talk to Sergeant Fetridge about the major's death out at Manassas?"

"That was one thing I wanted to talk to you about, just as card playing is one of my occupations—but not the only one. I have investments. I trade in horses. I trade in other things."

They were both standing near him now, and also blocking his path to the door.

"What else do I need to know about you, Mr. Raines?" Colton said.

Harry shrugged. "You might want to know that I'm a fair-minded man—open-minded, tolerant. Like you, I believe in the Union. But I have a brother who's in the 30th Virginia Cavalry, with Longstreet, and my father's an officer with the 17th Virginia."

"What're you trying to tell me, Raines?"

Harry grinned, then lighted a cigar of his own.

"I'm just trying to tell you I'm a fair-minded man," he said, between puffs. "And, if you'd like a friendly little game, you'll likely find me this evening at the Palace of Fortune, if you know it."

They both chewed this over, making no move to prevent his passing as he moved around them toward the door.

"Who knows you, Raines?"

Harry could feel the man's eyes on his back.

"I have a cousin in Virginia," he said, over his shoulder. "Name is Belle Boyd."

Harry could see soldiers being relentlessly drilled on the open space adjoining the tent city, but there were troops taking their ease along the company street as well, most of them in some degree of undress. Some were picking at bare feet or combing their clothing or persons in search of lice and other vermin. Some worked with great ardor at cleaning and polishing equipment, while others simply sat with faces upturned toward the hazy sun, imbibing their leisure as they might a spiritous drink.

One small group had a banjo and was singing an old Negro song: "Git out de way, git out de way, git out de way, ol' Dan Tucker, yore too late to get yore suppah . . ."

Harry harbored no yearnings to become a soldier. Sunny idylls such as this would soon enough be followed by bouts of cold rain and steel shot, depending on when General Mc-Clellan was inclined to get stirring. But he could see the attraction to it. Life's more burdensome cares could be put aside for the duration. One could live much like the animals in nature, dealing with exigencies as they arose while enjoying the intervals to the full. You didn't worry about the future. After Bull Run, the future wasn't the most wonderful thing to contemplate.

For many, once McClellan got going, there would be no future.

Caesar Augustus still had not returned to Captain Kelleter's tent, as Harry had hoped, but Kelleter was there—sitting in shirtsleeves and reading a book.

"Excuse me," said Harry, poking his head into the tent opening. "I was looking for my man."

The captain's eyes lifted unhappily from the page.

"My man is Caesar Augustus," Harry continued.

The captain stood up and reached for his uniform coat. "Your 'man.' Yes, indeed. I'd like you to come with me, Mr. Raines."

"Where is he? Is he in trouble?"

"Just come along, Mister. You'll see him soon enough."

Buttoning his jacket, he led the way out of the tent and down the company street. Soldiers' eyes followed their passage.

"Very talkative, this Mr. Augustus of yours. Full of questions," Kelleter said.

"That's not his surname. He has two Christian names, Caesar and Augustus."

Kelleter stopped. "He has no last name?"

"I don't suppose he does—not yet anyway."

"Not permitted one, is that it?" The captain shook his head in disgust and resumed his walk at a much faster pace, leaving Harry little opportunity to respond and not stopping until they

were at the tent of the brigade commander, Colonel Oliver
Otis Howard himself.

The colonel, Harry knew, maintained living quarters in one
of the finer hotels along the Avenue, but he apparently conducted his administrative business from this oversized tent. He
had a clerk and two aides de camp in there with him. In the
rear, tied to the chair he was sitting in, was Caesar Augustus,
as dejected as though he'd been consigned to the hold of a
slave ship.

"Begging your pardon, Colonel," said Kelleter. "I've
brought this man Raines. He came by looking for his Negro."

Howard looked up from a map he'd been pondering to study
Harry, with some contempt. This colonel was an exceedingly
handsome and tidy man, his dark hair, moustache, and whiskers very thick but neatly trimmed. His eyes signaled fairness
and honesty, as well as intelligence and perception.

Harry did not like the conclusion the colonel appeared to
have reached about him.

"I have lamentably had to keep your servant bound to that
chair, Sir, because, as a Federal officer, I am obliged to honor
all U.S. statutes, including the monstrous Fugitive Slave Act,"
he said. "But I will tell you, Sir, that I find this odious and
damn intolerable. We are fighting this war to defend the Con-
stitution. To my mind, its protections apply to this man as
much as any other. Involuntary servitude is . . ."

"Colonel Howard," Harry interrupted. "I agree with you
completely. Caesar Augustus is no slave. He is a free man,
earning wages with his free labor."

"But he claims to be your slave," said Howard, "in this
camp to do your bidding."

"Why would you do that?" Harry asked Caesar Augustus.

"Marse Harry, I . . ."

"He offered it as explanation," said Kelleter. "When we
wanted to know why he was asking so many of us so many
questions. Were he a white man, we might suppose this the
work of a spy—but he says he does it in your service. And
unless I'm very mistaken, you are Southern—from Virginia?
That's what he tells us and that's what I hear in your speech."

Harry did not like the direction this was going at all.

"I'm not a spy, Colonel, and neither is Caesar Augustus. His questions all had to do with the late Major George Pleasants, did they not?"

Howard looked to Kelleter, who nodded.

"Well, Sir," Harry continued. "That's all I'm interested in. How Major Pleasants died."

"What business is that of yours?"

"His family, Sir. I'm assisting them."

The colonel pushed his map aside and beckoned Harry to a seat. He seemed of a sudden very weary, as Harry supposed he was.

"How Major Pleasants died, Sir, is very simple. He died in battle, as many did. I'm told Union casualties have exceeded three thousand, Mr. Raines, including the wounded, and many of those men are now dying."

He gestured to his aide to release Caesar Augustus from his tether.

"I wish it were that simple, Colonel Howard," Harry said. "Honorable death in battle. The newspapers have been providing very different accounts, and . . ."

"The newspapers be damned."

"The newspapers this morning are blaming it on an actress, Louise Devereux."

"Exactly! They'll print any kind of nonsense. Which is why I ignore them."

"But Miss Devereux has been arrested, Colonel. She may be tried for murder."

Howard rubbed his eyes with the heels of his hands, then lowered them and shook his head sadly.

"If as much effort were put into wresting victory from those people across the river as we expend hurling calumnies and blame at each other, we'd have this thing won," the colonel said. "I am satisfied this officer fought well and died well. I said so in my report. I have it from an eyewitness."

"Lieutenant Colonel Beals?"

The colonel blinked and rubbed his eyes again. "No. Not him. Certainly not him. No, Sir, from a brave young officer who himself was wounded in that fight. Lieutenant Fox."

"Sir, an eyewitness is all Caesar Augustus and I were seeking. A truthful account to dispel all these foul rumors."

Now the Colonel looked exceedingly unhappy. "You'll find him at the Union Hospital in Georgetown, if he still lives. The boy lost a leg, and last I heard was not faring well."

"Thank you, Sir."

Howard had retrieved his map, but paused. "Mr. Raines. If your Caesar Augustus wishes some honest work in the service of the Army, he's more than welcome to it. But let's have no more spying and pesky questions. And I would warn you, Sir, that a civilian prying in Army affairs just now could find himself in great jeopardy."

But Harry needed to pry—just a little.

"Colonel Howard, did you have any problems with Major Pleasants? Problems having to do with his character?"

"Let us not speak ill of the dead."

"Well, have you had problems concerning missing supplies and equipment?"

This drew only a quick and exasperated look that came close to anger. "Yes! Thousands of them. We left supplies and equipment all over Northern Virginia. It may take months to replace it all."

"Yes, Sir. Thank you."

"I wish you luck, Raines. I wish us all luck."

ROCKET was big enough to carry them both with Caesar Augustus riding postilion. Harry kept the horse at a walk, worrying about the heat. Recrossing the Long Bridge, he could see a lot of Washington City in the distance—the unfinished Capitol dome on the right, the Treasury Building and President's House on the left, the spire of St. John's Church just to the left of that. What of this would be left standing when the war was done? Or would Richmond, of which he was quite fond, be the victim?

"What now, Marse Harry?" said Caesar Augustus, as they reached the District of Columbia side of the river.

The Long Bridge connected with Maryland Avenue, which ran on a diagonal to Pennsylvania.

"I'm going to stop by Mr. Brady's studio, and then Miss

Devereux' residence, and then ride over to the hospital in Georgetown."

"Well, I'm goin' to my little house, and rest these ol' bones."

"You're the same age I am, Caesar Augustus. So are your bones."

"These bones feelin' old all the same, Marse Harry, on account they been put to hard labor all the while you're amusin' yourself at games of chance and jauntin' around the countryside."

"Did that Captain Kelleter pay you for the work you did?"

The black man nodded. "He's an honest man, but not what you'd call generous."

"And now you're out of work again."

"Hot day like today, it's an agreeable situation."

They could smell the canal, though there was no wind, and they were far from it.

"How would you like to do some more work for me?"

"Marse Harry, if they ever let black men into the Army, like Mr. Douglass say, that's where I'm goin'. I mean to wear brass buttons and kill Confederates, long as there is any—and that means your friends and maybe your brother and Daddy. 'Long as you understand that, guess I don't mind takin' your money for helpin' you in this foolishness. A man's got to eat and you're a kind fool, if nothin' else."

"As no one seems much interested in having colored troops, I'll rest content on that question and be pleased with your decision on the other."

"So what you want me to do now?"

"Go rest your ol' bones. When the day cools, call upon me at the National. I'll be back by then. Now I'm going to look at some pictures."

H<small>E</small> found Brady, Gardner, and their assistants working feverishly in shirtsleeves and sweat, including two young ladies, who were busy retouching *cartes de visites*. Despite the incessant drilling ordered by General McClellan, the soldiers were finding time to be photographed. Brady might be frustrated by his inability to capture any meaningful image of battle, but he could well become rich of this war.

Harry's visit prompted a cessation in their labors. Brady sent an aide downstairs to the beer store for a bucket of refreshment, and they sat down to wait for it.

Gardner told his story. Unlike his chief, who'd made a perilous but successful escape, Gardner had been captured by the enemy in the great rout, and taken to Manassas Junction after the battle.

"They held me at General Beauregard's headquarters. When he saw my camera and heard I worked for Mr. Brady, he had me take a daguerreotype of him and his staff. They liked the plate and had me take more, then finally let me go. Pity I couldn't have kept them."

"Mr. Brady said you brought back plates."

"I came back by way of the battlefield. My equipment was mostly smashed up, but three glass plates survived, except one got cracked and a corner broke off another."

"May I see them?"

Brady shook his head, but to express his rue. "They're not much to look at, Raines. I don't think we'll be exhibiting them."

He led Harry into another chamber, with Gardner following. On a table near the lone window in the room were two of the plates, lying face up.

Harry studied them, both blurry images of fields and trees. In one, a mounted figure could be seen in the distance. In the other, a house.

"You said three."

Gardner went to a stack of plates leaning against the wall, taking up the outermost. He held it to the light.

"This is our only real image of the battle," Brady said, "but there's not much clear."

Harry leaned close. "They don't look like they're doing any fighting."

"They're not," said Gardner. "This was back by the Sudley Ford."

Putting on his spectacles, Harry leaned even closer.

"Do you have a magnifying glass?"

Gardner went to fetch one.

"If you're looking for yourself, Raines," Brady said, "I don't believe you're in it."

Harry said nothing, wiping some dust from the plate with a handkerchief.

"You're right," he said, straightening. "I'm not in it."

"Hard to make out who is," Gardner acknowledged, coming back with the magnifying glass.

"But one man here is identifiable," Harry said. "I think. Take a close look. Do you know who he is?"

"I do, but I did before I exposed the plate."

Harry stared at the plate as he might a fine painting. "Don't sell this."

"Don't know who'd buy it," Brady said.

MISS Devereux' German landlady wasn't very cooperative, but Harry managed to talk his way into her house and up to Louise's room, which Pinkerton's detectives had gone through again—thoroughly and messily. Harry gathered some of her clothes together and made them into a bundle, promising the landlady he would take them to Louise.

"One other thing," Harry asked. "Before the tall Irishman and I came here and found that gun, did Miss Devereux have any visitors?"

"She haff visitors, ja. Sometimes many visitors."

"Men? Women?"

"Ja. Both."

"What did they look like?"

"Respectable."

Harry thought a moment. "Did they come on foot or on horseback?"

"Ja. And one came by carriage."

"Carriage? Can you describe the carriage?"

"Ja."

DOCTOR Gregg was not on duty. The surgeon who was could not be disturbed as he was busy with an amputation, the horrifying screams of which seemed to carry everywhere in the building. They must have exhausted the supply of ether.

Wandering on his own through the corridors, Harry came to a small, plain woman occupied with the task of unloading fruit from a crate into several small baskets. She introduced herself as a Miss Barton.

"I'm not a nurse," she said. "Just a volunteer. But perhaps I can help you. Do you seek a relation?"

"I'm looking for a Lieutenant Fox. I don't know him. I come on behalf of one of his fellow officers."

She consulted a list drawn up on a long sheet of brown paper.

"Oh, yes. That poor boy. Come with me."

She led him to what he might have called "the hopeless ward," except he supposed all the wards could be called that to some degree. Most of the patients looked to be asleep or unconscious. Some were awake and watched him enter as though it was a major development in their lives. A few were sitting up and talking.

Fox was in a category all his own. He lay on his back, straight and stiff, arms at his side, vacant eyes staring straight up at the ceiling. He was missing his left leg. Miss Barton said he taken a minié ball through the knee.

He was a fresh-faced and comely young man, or had been once. Now he was terribly thin and sallow. Only the blink of his eyes indicated life.

"Can he hear me?" Harry asked Miss Barton.

"I think so."

Harry drew up a chair, then leaned close.

"Lieutenant Fox?"

The eyes turned toward him, slowly, with reluctance.

"My name is Harrison Raines, Lieutenant Fox. How are you feeling?"

It was a stupid question and he properly got no response.

"I need to ask you about Major Pleasants, Lieutenant. For the sake of his wife."

To Harry's amazement, the young man's lips moved. He heard the word "yes"—breathed more than spoken.

"Did you see him fall?"

"Y-yes." This time louder.

"Was anyone near him?"

"Y-yes."

Another stupid question. There'd been a swirling mob of people on that slope.

"W-woman."

"What?" said Harry, putting his ear by the youth's mouth. "He was shot by a woman?"

"Save her," said the Lieutenant. "Try to save the woman."

"What woman? Save her from what, Sir?"

"G-gun."

The eyes stopped blinking. Harry had used his last question.

He rose, and looked to Miss Barton. He saw tears on her broad cheeks.

"I still cry," she said.

Chapter 1 8

SERGEANT Fetridge drew two cards and grinned, looking across the table at Harry as cat to trapped mouse. Harry avoided replying in kind. He had already drawn two cards himself and was not unhappy with the result.

They were at the Palace of Fortune, at the large round table he favored in the rear of the large, boisterous establishment. Two of Harry's friends were in the game—the British journalist Russell and a magazine artist named Winslow Homer, a quiet fellow who nonetheless played for the sociability. Also at the table was another professional gambler, Big Jim Coates, and a Congressman Fowler, both of them playing with studied cautiousness. Fetridge had turned up about a half hour into the game.

"Bet's to you, Raines. Two dollars."

Harry took up his hand and peered at it closely. He had done something altogether stupid and foolish—broken a pair and drawn two cards. Gamblers like him viewed players that foolish as free meals sent by Divine Providence.

Yet he was winning! Except for folding a few times, he hadn't lost a hand all night. And now, the cards had come in again. The two he'd drawn had filled an inside straight to the jack. An amazement.

Something about Lieutenant Fox's dying, there before his very eyes, had moved him profoundly—moved him to recklessness. He was drinking freely, betting and playing like a wild man. He'd even written Caitlin a letter, saying all he'd meant to say in person and more—that he hadn't intended to do anything that might bring harm to Louise and that he would do everything in his power to free her from her prison. So bold was he that he'd declared his love for Caitlin, which he'd never been able to bring himself to do directly before.

"You done lookin' into the manner of that Major Pleasants' death?" asked Congressman Fowler.

Harry was staring at his hand. "Mostly."

"Oughta leave the poor devil in peace."

"Trying, Sir. Trying."

He knocked back his whiskey, savoring the swimming feeling a moment, then pushed out two dollars. Russell raised the bet by another two and when it came around to Fetridge the sergeant raised it two again.

A man of means, this common soldier. Harry had been playing with the money he'd received from Senator Quigley, not caring if it all slipped through his fingers. Whose money was this well-fed soldier employing?

Harry saw that raise and doubled it. He drained his glass of whiskey and poured more, waiting. The sergeant became more tentative. Finally, he called the bet. Everyone else but Harry and the congressman had dropped out. Coates was eyeing Harry strangely. They'd played together many times before, but never like this.

With a flourish, Harry spread out his straight. The sergeant held three queens. He'd likely drawn to a pair of them. There was always a certain insufficiency to three of a kind. It was a hand that always made one much too proud.

Harry waited for the sergeant to acknowledge the loss, then swept in the pot. "Looks like I'm Joe Johnston to your General McDowell, Sergeant."

Russell eyed him curiously. "Saw a man in India once win more then five thousand pounds in an evening's play—then lose it in four hands. Do you believe that? Four hands."

Harry made a quick mental calculation of his winnings. He had nearly quadrupled his "pay" from the Senator, all in the process of trying to lose it. That had been his resolve after his visit to the unfortunate Lieutenant Fox. To get terribly drunk and lose his Major Pleasants money as quickly as possible. But all his recklessness had achieved was enormous gain.

He'd keep trying.

"You may witness such a wonder again, Russell." Harry drank. "Though not such princely sums."

"You seem not yourself, Raines."

"Who is these days?"

There was a gunshot—outside somewhere—causing everyone at the table to jump, though random, unexplained gunfire had become a common occurrence.

Certainly, there was reason to be jumpy. McClellan had let it be known he feared an attack by the Confederates any day. He was desperately trying to bring in what he considered sufficient reinforcements to deal with the menace. He wanted a hundred thousand men just for the defense of Washington alone, fearing the Rebels had that and fifty thousand more just beyond the Potomac.

Harry thought that ridiculous, but he shared in the general unease. If the Union Army was to run from the Confederates here as it had at Bull Run, the United States would be a fiction. There was much to fear, if only from the conduct of Union troops.

Congressman Fowler asked to be dealt out of the game for a few minutes to permit a visit to the necessary. This prompted Russell to suggest a brief intermission for that same purpose and suggest that everyone replenish his refreshment. Harry, feeling a little dizzy, kept his seat.

So did Sergeant Fetridge.

"You have something to say to me?" the man asked.

"No, Sir. Except to congratulate you on the skill of your play. I see you still have money left."

The sergeant's cheeks reddened, and his brown eyes went into a dark glower.

"You said we could find you here. Do you have some business to discuss?"

"Gambling is my business."

"So I see. What about shoes?"

"Shoes? Never wear 'em. A gentleman belongs in boots, I always say."

"Damn you, Raines. Colton wants to talk to you."

Harry glanced around. The gambling palace was crowded, but he saw no uniform other than Fetridge's.

"Where is he?"

"Before I tell you, I need to know what you have in mind."

"Shoes, you said." Harry grinned, perhaps a little too tipsily. "Army's got to have shoes."

Fetridge looked around quickly. Russell had returned from the sinks, but had stopped to talk to someone at the faro table.

"We got an arrangement with someone else," the sergeant said.

Of course they did. "And who is that?"

Harry began idly but expertly shuffling the deck. A plump but pretty woman, her dark hair worn piled atop her head, was eyeing him amiably. She was a regular there and fond of winners. She'd been standing with a group of men near the bar, but now moved away from them—and nearer Harry.

"You better talk to Colton," the sergeant said.

"And where is he?"

"At the bar. He just came in. Didn't y'see him?"

The plump, pretty woman, who Harry recalled was named Nora, now sallied forth, approaching their table at an oblique sidle and then circling it, looking over the various-sized piles of money at each place as though she was shopping—which she probably was.

Fetridge did not find her presence agreeable. He gave her a sharp look. When that failed to ward her off, he growled to Harry: "Captain Colton's in a black suit. End of the bar. Don't worry, I'll watch your money."

Harry shuffled the cards one more time, then rose, plucked a five dollar greenback from the pile at his place, and bestowed it at a convenient place at the top of Nora's garment. After bowing to her, he made his wobbly way to the bar. He couldn't quite make out Colton, at first, but the captain quickly moved to his side.

He ordered whiskeys for them both.

"Thankee," said Harry.

"Just what in hell is your game, Raines?"

"Five card draw, most of the time."

"I mean about the shoes."

"Shoes?"

"You asked about the shoes. Isn't that why we're here?"

Caitlin had told him he might make a fine actor. Now was the time to give it a try.

"I trade in horses, both sides of the river," he said. "I'm thinking of branching out to merchandise."

Colton turned and gave Harry's face a quick study.

"I'm already talking with someone across the river," he said. "Now you show up."

"I'm an independent contractor."

"Do you want to talk price?"

"I don't know the quantity. I don't know how difficult the transport and delivery."

"You saw the quantity. Just about a whole damn warehouse."

"What about transport?"

"That would be up to you—and your friends."

"You'd expect me to get all that through Union lines?"

Colton sipped his drink. "I checked you out, Raines. You're on Lafayette Baker's suspect list. You are in truth Belle Boyd's cousin—and your pa's with Longstreet. But I'm still not sure about you."

Harry needed to fire his imagination at this point. Whiskey would have to do it. He emptied his glass. If nothing else, it gave him courage.

"I'm sure about you, Captain. Major Pleasants told me everything."

"And why would he do that?"

"I was looking for information to expand my business. He needed money. And he was drunk."

"That woman-crazy sot was always needing money. And almost always drunk."

"A poor partner. I'll make a better one." Harry smiled to himself. Perhaps Caitlin was right about his acting talent.

"Last thing I need is more partners."

"You've got to think in terms of progress, expansion. This war's going to make a lot of men rich, Captain Colton. You're not going to be one of them if you so blithely turn away from new opportunities."

Plump Nora had made another circuit of the poker table, but was now returning to her station at the bar, where Harry could see three or four well-dressed gentlemen awaiting her return. Fetridge was still in his seat, watching Harry and Colton. Nora apparently had no liking for his company, though she'd given Harry a friendly glance.

"I need to know your price," Colton said.

"I need to know where my friends could take delivery."

The captain made no response. Harry realized the conversation had reached a critical point. It needed a nudge.

"There's no way of getting that load through the Union lines in front of Washington," Harry continued. "And you wouldn't be sending a shipment that large north to Baltimore or east to Annapolis, as both places have almost as many blue-coated soldiers as the Alexandria front. You can't use ships because those Confederate guns south of Mount Vernon have closed the river below Washington. That leaves one direction. Up the Potomac. To the west."

His eyeglasses were somewhat fogged and smeared from the heat, but he thought he recognized one of the men standing with plump Nora.

"Too far upriver—say, past Cumberland—and you're into McClellan's old Department of the Ohio outfit and out of reach of the Confederate Army. But between there and Leesburg, all along the C. & O. Canal there, Federal troops are spread thin. There are grain sheds at Williamsport and a rail depot and some warehouses at Martinsburg—depending on which side is in possession of it."

Colton's eyes blinked hard, twice. Harry took it for a sign, though he wasn't sure of what.

"I know of another place even more convenient to your purpose," Harry went on. "A farm with a capacious barn—on the river between Martinsburg and Shepherdstown. It's off the beaten path, yet a short distance from Charlestown by back road. Convenient? I'd say perfect."

"And how would we have use of that?"

"I own it." Harry sipped whiskey, then took out his handkerchief and began wiping the lenses of his spectacles.

"How long you had all this figured out?" Colton asked.

"Not long. Not long at all."

"Let me think about it more," the captain said. He emptied his glass, without ordering another.

Not a good sign.

"Don't you want to know my price?"

"Not yet. I don't think you and I are talking about the same thing."

Wiping the lenses carefully, Harry secured his eyeglasses on the bridge of his nose with care, seeking the maximum focus. What he saw on Colton's face was distrust and impatience.

"As I am in the service of his widow and father-in-law, Captain Colton, there's one thing I need to know about Major Pleasants. Though I promise, not a word of it to anyone else."

"Good night," Colton said, turning to leave. Harry caught his shoulder.

"Just tell me," he said. "Was Pleasants your partner, or was he just privy to the nature of your business?"

"All you need to know about that man," Colton said, "is that he's dead. Now good night."

He pulled away. Harry let him go. He hadn't played this hand very well, but it hadn't been a complete loss.

The poker game had resumed. Russell and Fetridge were looking his way. Nora was moving back toward the table.

Her small group of admirers farther down the bar appeared scarcely to take note of her departure. They were listening to one of their number, who seemed to be telling a story. The face Harry saw through his now clean lenses was more than familiar. It was famous.

"Booth!" Harry cried.

The man stopped as though in mid-word.

"Booth!"

The actor's eyes connected with his—always an electric moment when this happened.

Then Booth vanished.

The Pennsylvania Avenue entrance to the gambling hall was to Harry's rear. Booth wouldn't strike for that. Harry guessed he'd make for the back door that led to the alley and C Street.

The actor got through it well before Harry could. By the time Harry reached the alley, Booth was lost to view again. Harry started forward, heading west, toward Murder Bay, pausing only once to check the load in his derringer.

For all the darkness, Harry sensed movement all about him—flicks and quivers of it in the shadows, some of it animal life, cats and rats, pigs and stray dogs prowling in the rubbish. But here and there were larger, human figures, lingering in doorways and silhouetted against lighted windows.

Booth suddenly appeared ahead, moving in and out of shadows. Harry's spectacles kept sliding from their perch as he hurried along, and sometimes the actor was lost to view. But then he'd reappear in the occasional gaslight, a dashing figure emerging on his stage.

He stopped, before a familiar building. Lacking or having forgotten his key, he was compelled to knock, his pause giving Harry time to reach his side.

One thing Harry knew for certain about Booth. Caitlin had told him. He wasn't really a coward. But he had an all-consuming fear of suffering injury to his face. It was his livelihood, his stamp upon the world—to his egomaniacal mind, his reason for being on earth. Small wonder he had no taste for soldiering.

Harry gripped his arm hard and pulled him close, clenching and raising his free fist and sticking it into the sacred visage.

"A word with you, Sir!"

He yanked Booth off the steps of the house and back into the shadow of the street. The actor tried to break free but became instantly immobile when Harry pulled forth his derringer and stuck the short barrel against Booth's celebrated nose.

"What did you tell them about Louise?"

"Tell who?"

"The detectives! She's been arrested."

"On your account, Raines, not mine. You found a gun in her room. Caitlin told me."

"But you told the detectives where she was, damn you! You

sent them to my rooms! Why?" He clicked back the hammer on the derringer.

"Because they asked! I'd no idea she was wanted for murder."

The front door to the building opened. Without relaxing his hold on Booth, Harry looked up to see the silhouetted figure of a woman in the doorway.

"Ella!" shouted Booth. "Get help!"

Instead, the woman came out onto the steps, her eyes widening in recognition of two men posed in violent tableau before her.

Harry grabbed Booth's jaw, his mere touch striking terror in the man.

"What was she looking for, Booth? Why was she in my rooms?"

"You don't know as much about Louise Devereux as you think, Raines."

"Damn it, Sir! What did she want?"

Ella Turner had disappeared. Harry would have to hurry. She might have gone back inside to fetch a gun. You could always count on one of those in a bawdy house.

"Booth! Answer me!"

The actor looked anything but handsome now. Harry wished there were some way that Brady might photograph this moment.

"I don't have it. I never had it."

If Booth said anything after that, Harry didn't hear it. The last sound to penetrate his ears was a reverberating bonk as something immensely heavy struck his head. There was a flash of white and a paralyzing spasm of pain and then all was gone.

HARRY awoke in darkness, to a duller, throbbing pain, and an awful stench. He opened his eyes, noting through the blur a few hazy pinpoints of light. Many minutes seemed to pass before he realized he was looking at stars.

The pain continued, but became no worse. He clenched and unclenched his fingers, and found they worked. His right leg functioned, and so, though it was twisted somewhat, did his left. It wasn't until he attempted to raise his head that the full agony of his injury overcame him again.

He let many minutes pass before attempting anything again. Then, gently, inch by inch, he turned his head instead of raising it.

Someone was lying beside him. Slowly, he reached out, his hand coming against the rough texture of a wool coat.

Booth, like himself, had been wearing linen.

With great effort, remaining on his back, Harry pushed himself up a bit until he judged himself even with the man's head. He reached again, with even more caution, and found himself touching cold flesh.

He called out, but got no response. Finally, wincing at the discomfort, he dug a small box of matches from his pocket and struck one.

There, just inches away, were the staring, glassy eyes of Sergeant Fetridge. They didn't move.

Chapter 1 9

HARRY had a vague sense of sounds. They came and went like idle thoughts—people shouting, clumping hoofbeats, the creak of a wagon, a sad woman's soothing, troubled voice.

His sense of the sight of things was similarly vague and drifting—a glimpse of dark sky, a soldier's musket stock, a pair of dusty boots, seen closely. In time, he saw faces, some strange, some comfortingly familiar.

One in particular. There, miraculously before him, were the fine English features of Caitlin Howard, as sadly cast and noble as a saint's. She looked down at him intently and remorsefully, her exquisite gray-green eyes somber and troubled, as though she was looking upon some cherished object she'd clumsily broken and could not possibly repair.

"Harry," she said. "Do you see me?"

He could feel her touch—a cool, soft brush of fingers across the bone of his right cheek. Something moist came upon his skin, a tear—possibly hers, perhaps his own.

"Yes, I see you. Am I dreaming?"

He moved his head, a calamitous mistake. A sword run through his skull could not have produced more pain. He gave a violent shudder, waiting for the agony to pass.

"Be still, Harry. Don't stir." Her voice had never sounded sweeter—not as Roxanne, not as Juliet.

"What happened to me?"

"You've been badly hurt," she said. "Someone attacked you. They found you in Murder Bay."

"They? Who found me?"

"Wilkes—my friend Mr. Booth."

"Booth? Booth *found* me? He . . ."

Her fingers pressed gently over his lips, stilling them. "Wilkes sent for help, and he also sent for me. I was going to seek you at all events, but . . ."

"Is he here? Booth?"

"Please, Harry. Do not agitate yourself."

Flicking his eyes from side to side, he saw dingy brick walls and many shadows. "Where am I?"

"No good place, but you are safe. And you are with me. You need not worry about anything else. A doctor is coming. Your friend Doctor Gregg."

"I wrote you a letter, Kate."

"Yes. I am thankful for it."

"Do you believe me? About Louise? That I didn't . . ."

"I do. How could I disbelieve a man who has suffered so much on her account? And on my account. I am sorry for my anger with you, Harry."

"I love you, Kate."

She looked away, then back, frustrated. "I feel a most loving friendship for you."

"I suppose I must content myself with that."

"Be still, Harry. We don't know how badly you're injured."

"Where is Louise?"

"She's still in prison. Where did you think? We are waiting to hear about a trial."

"And Booth? Where did he go?"

"Harry, the doctor's here."

"You said Booth found me. Where was I found?"

"I told you. In Murder Bay. Next to the canal."

He remembered now the stench. "Did Booth say . . ."

"Hush now, Harry. Here's Doctor Gregg."

She held his hand a lingering moment.

"Kate . . ."

"I'll return to you in the morning."

Ignoring the pain, he tried to lift his head. A shadow of

anguish crossed her face, and she restrained his further movement and eased him back, then leaned forward, and, so gently
it seemed a touch of breeze, she kissed him on the lips. Caitlin
had never done that before.

"I promise," he said. "Louise will be free."

There was little more than resignation and irony in her farewell smile, which vanished as she turned away.

He could hear Gregg's voice. There were other sounds—
booted feet on wooden floors, the clank and clink of metal
against metal, gruff commands, odd echoes, the skittering of
tiny clawed feet, uncomfortably near. He had thought he might
be in a hospital. Now he knew better.

Finally, two familiar faces appeared above him—from his
position, seeming upside down.

"I hope you're not as sorely damaged as you look," said
Gregg.

"Sore, certainly."

The face next to Gregg's belonged to the woman from the
hospital—Clara Barton. Harry wondered if she was going to
give him an orange. Instead, she began ever so gently to dab
at the side of his head with a wet cloth. It might as well have
been a pick axe.

"Can you move your arms and legs?" Gregg asked.

"Yes." He demonstrated, biting hard on his lip.

"Good. Hold still now."

The physician began probing the side and back of Harry's
head with some sort of small, unpleasant instrument, while
Miss Barton held him still.

"Every cent I have, Doctor—my horse, Rocket, and my
farm in Virginia—if you never do that again."

Harry was rewarded with a grin of sorts, but it quickly went
away. Gregg straightened, then rubbed his well-groomed
beard. Miss Barton began cleansing the wound again. Harry
tried to be brave and not cry out, but it was hard work.

"Hmmm," Gregg said.

"What in hell does that mean?"

"I don't think anything's broken—skull, neck, spine, all reasonably intact. There may be injury to the brain, but you seem fairly sensible. The pupils of the eye are normal. It's a sign of damage if they aren't." Gregg leaned back. "You were struck only once, and the blow scraped along the side of your head. I'd say that was lucky. Had it hit directly I suppose you'd be dead now."

"If I were lucky, Phineas, I'd be at the Palace of Fortune, raking in my chips, or back in my rooms, sleeping peacefully."

Gregg sighed. "Do you know who did this to you?"

Harry tried to recollect what he could of the incident. He'd been holding Booth, keeping the derringer in the actor's face. He remembered that his attention had been drawn to Ella Turner, her face contorted and wild-eyed with anger and fright. But she was in front of him, on the steps to her building. The blow that struck him had come from behind.

"No," he said, at length. "In that neighborhood, you might find a thousand people to suspect."

"You were alone?"

He'd promised Caitlin he would secure Louise's liberty. If he were to secure instead her beloved Booth's incarceration, that kiss she'd given him would very definitely be his last.

"I think so," Harry said.

"Miss Barton and I are going to help you sit up," Gregg said. "I want to see if you can manage it."

He managed it about as well and happily as McDowell had managed his army at Manassas, but at length he was seated upright, held in place by the ever helpful Miss Barton, whose solicitous gaze reminded him of his mother's when he'd been ill or injured as a child.

She was such a small person, she'd make a suitably sized wife for the stubby Pinkerton.

There came a sudden wave of dizziness, but it was not overwhelming. The pain at the back of his head was dull now, throbbing, but more bearable.

"You have two choices, I'm afraid," Gregg said. "My hospital, or remaining here."

Harry thought upon the house of horrors in Georgetown. "Not the hospital, thank you." He glanced about the small, dank chamber. There was a lantern hanging from a hook on the ceiling and another sitting on a crude wooden table next to his cot. The only window was in the thick wooden door, and it had bars across it. "Where am I?"

"You're in the basement of the Treasury Building," Gregg said. "Mr. Lafayette Baker's using it as his own private jail."

"Jail? Baker?"

"I regret to say you're under arrest, Harry," Gregg said. "On Mr. Baker's orders."

"They say you murdered an Army sergeant," said Miss Barton. "And that you are a Southern agent."

"Sergeant Fetridge," Harry said. "He's dead?"

"Shot through the chest," said Gregg. "I'm going to examine the body now." He leaned a little closer to examine Harry's injury one more time and stood back. "If you were alone, and you didn't kill him, how did you end up lying next to him?"

"I left him playing cards in a game at the Palace of Fortune. I don't know how he came to join me. I don't know how I got to the canal."

"They found a small pistol on your person. One chamber was fired."

"Not by me."

"That's sure enough true. Even Mr. Baker hasn't been able to explain how you could shoot anyone with your head half stove in like that."

"Unless I shot him first."

"And then what, hit yourself in the head from behind? He's a damn fool, Baker."

"Not my friend."

"He is not. I'll leave you some brandy, Harry. It's all the painkiller I can give you." Gregg set a small flask down next to Harry and then turned to leave, waiting for Miss Barton to precede him.

"Doctor, wait."

"Yes?"

"If you would—a message to a man named Leahy. Goes by Boston Leahy. The Willard will know his whereabouts. I must speak to him. Soon."

"Is he a lawyer, Harry?" Gregg asked.
"He is more useful than that."

LEAHY'S arrival some hours later was announced by a loud
disagreement between the Irishman and someone in authority.
Leahy prevailed. A moment after, he swung the door to
Harry's room wide open, banging it against the brick wall.

"You alive, Raines? I must say, you do not look it."

Harry sat up, slowly. Amazed to find that his watch had not
been stolen, he consulted it. The hour was nearly five o'clock
in the morning.

"I am alive, but I hurt so much I almost wish I wasn't."

Leahy took the lantern from the table, held it above Harry's
head, and then set on the floor. He eased his big frame onto
the table top, for there was no other seat.

"These sons of a bitches have declared you a criminal," he
said. "You must have made an enemy of Lafayette Baker."

"This is his jail."

Feeling weak, Harry leaned his shoulders back against the
wall, careful not to let his head touch the bricks.

"Not an official jail," Leahy said. "But I guess that don't
make it any more comfortable."

"Can you get me out of here? You're a policeman."

"A Federal detective," Leahy corrected, "Lately under the
authority of the Army and General George B. McClellan. Not
a policeman. Hell, Raines, Baker reports directly to General
Scott. He pulled some slick stunt before Bull Run that has
impressed them all. Got himself to Manassas and Richmond
posing as a photographer. The Rebels took him prisoner
twice—he was interrogated by Beauregard and Jefferson Davis personally—but he managed to persuade them to let him
go. Came back with a bushel of observations on Confederate
troop strength and cavalry activities."

"Fat lot of good it did come the battle."

"It was slick spy work, no matter what you think of the
man. Scott thinks Baker's the best we got. If we're not careful,
he could end up running the U.S. Secret Service. Or anyway,
this city. Right now, he's sure the boss of this place, though

officially he's only an employee of the State Department. He says you're going to be charged with enough offenses to hang you ten times over—murder, espionage, treason, creating a disturbance, committing mayhem. He rants on, the gloating bastard. Must take you real seriously, though, if he's talking about formal charges. He's been holding some people here without any charge at all."

"If my head weren't bashed in, I think I would create some mayhem. I did nothing wrong. I don't know who killed the sergeant."

"What were you doing at the canal?"

"I don't know. Last I remember, I was outside Mollie Turner's whorehouse—having an earnest conversation with John Wilkes Booth and Ella Turner. I gather they are intimately acquainted."

Leahy's expression grew hard. "I can have those two arrested on my own authority."

"No, no," said Harry. He reached to touch his wound, which Miss Barton had covered with a sort of bandage, wound around the top of his head. The pain was easing a little.

"Booth has no doubt fled the city," Harry continued. "And the lovely Miss Ella had nothing to do with any of this, as far as I can figure. I would like to speak with him, but don't drag them into this. I have a friend who admires Booth greatly. She'd hate me for it."

"She need not know you had anything to do with it."

"Please. Leave them be."

He paused, remembering the flask Doctor Gregg had given him. Finding it in a coat pocket, he raised himself up and took a long pull. It was reviving.

"I do believe I can put an end to this matter, Mr. Leahy," he said. "But I can't manage it from here."

"I am sorry, Raines. There's not a damn thing I can do."

"Where is 'Major Allen?' "

"Still in Cincinnati—performing some task for McClellan."

Taking another sip of brandy, Harry decided his brain might actually be functioning again. "Can you reach him by telegraph?"

"Imagine so. He's never far from a telegraph key. But he

can't help you, Raines. I told you, Baker's got big friends."

"Pinkerton can get to someone Baker can't ignore."

"And who would that be?"

"General McClellan. No one in Washington City's going to interfere with his orders."

"Raines, McClellan won't even permit the President an audience. And under no account is he going to let the accused murderer of a Union soldier walk free on his own say-so."

"I'm not asking that."

"What then?"

"You said this isn't an official jail. I'd like to be transferred to one. The Old Capitol Prison."

Leahy rose. "You sure? That'd make your incarceration real official."

"I'd prefer that to this."

"Very well. I'll telegraph him this hour."

CAITLIN did not come as promised in the morning. No one at all came to visit him—friend or foe. His only words were with the Army private serving as guard, when the man brought his miserable breakfast.

No one brought him lunch or dinner. He was not disturbed at all until late in the evening. This time his caller was an Army sergeant.

"Can you stand?" the man asked.

"I can. If you'll be patient."

The sergeant looked him over, frowning. "Can you make yourself more presentable?"

"There you ask too much."

"All right. Guess it can't be helped. Come with me."

"It can't be time for my hanging already."

He meant it as a joke. He wished the sergeant had laughed.

THE sergeant led him from the basement dungeons to a spacious office overlooking the corner of Pennsylvania Avenue and 15th Street. Baker, wearing a dark civilian suit, was seated behind an enormous desk, frowning over papers that seemed of great import. Though Harry was about to collapse from the effort of walking from his cell, Baker left him standing for several minutes.

Suddenly, he set down his papers, looked up, and smiled. Rising, he gestured to the other end of the room, where Harry took note of a table set elaborately for late supper.

"Please join me, Raines. It's time we had a conversation."

It was indeed a decent meal that Baker had spread upon the table—perhaps the finest Harry had seen during his residence in Washington. There were oysters, deviled eggs, a crab soup, capon, Virginia ham, candied yams, and—pleasing Baker most of all—terrapin, prepared without a fleck of flour.

"That is how General Scott likes it and that's good enough for me," said Baker, tucking a napkin into his collar after seating himself. "You will find, Sir, that I keep a table as good as his in every respect, and there's no better in the town than his."

Harry eased himself into his chair with great care. He had slept for much of the day and it had proved something of a curative, but he was still wobbly.

"Will you have some of this fine wine, Raines?" said Baker, proffering a ruby colored bottle.

"Yes. Some of the fine wine. Please."

Baker poured. The taste was unexpectedly rich and mellow.

"It's excellent, Mr. Baker. No jail could boast better."

Baker frowned, hesitant, then grinned to show his appreciation of the joke. "Five dollars says you cannot guess where it came from."

Harry took another sip. "France? No, Italy." He really had no idea, as he was not much of a wine drinker.

"Wrong, wrong, wrong," Baker said, enjoying this. "It's from the same place I am."

"New York?" said Harry, remembering something he'd heard about the man.

"Certainly not. New York was where I was born. Michigan is where I lived for a time. But California is where I'm from. And so is this wine. Can you reckon that? The Italian settlers. They brought cuttings. It will be the glory of our nation, California wine."

They both took another sip.

"To what do I owe this splendid hospitality?" Harry asked. "A short while ago, I was an enemy of the state and a murder suspect."

"You still are, Raines. You still are. To be very sure. But I want your family in Virginia and all their kind to know how good we've got it here. I expect they'll be eating paté of swamp rat soon enough."

"I doubt I'll be talking to any member of my family until this war's over."

"Sure you will, Raines—unless you're hanged. You must talk to them all the time. I count you've made two trips to Virginia since Bull Run. You got caught by Rebel cavalry and they let you go. You're a spy for the South, Sir. I know it. You know it. And now you're where you belong."

Harry began eating, figuring his opportunity to do so might prove fleeting.

"If you will consult with President Lincoln, or Mr. Pinkerton," he said, after downing three oysters, "you will discover that I have a better reason for my travels than that."

"The President, I'm sure, has no idea who you are, Raines— not being a patron of whorehouses and gambling halls. As for Pinkerton, he is a railroad detective running errands for General McClellan. I am in the service of General Scott, and he has entrusted me with gathering intelligence for the defense of this capital."

"And he's given you the basement of the Treasury as your own private jail?"

"As the President says, we must do whatever's necessary."

"Including locking me up without even investigating the case? I couldn't possibly have shot that sergeant."

Baker shifted the plates around, shoving one stacked with roast meat in front of Harry. "I've had my eye on you, Raines. Many of us have. The capital swarms with Rebel agents, and you have impressed me as one of the most dangerous."

"Then you should move me to the Old Capitol Prison, with all the other dangerous agents."

The other man leaned back in his chair, eyeing Harry over the rim of his wineglass. "What's your game, Raines? Why would you want to go there?" His lips curled up at the corners. "I know you've tried to reach Pinkerton. Someone telegraphed him for you."

Harry shrugged, causing a pain to run up his neck to the base of his skull. He waited for it to pass. It took a long time doing so.

"It's that woman we've got in the Old Capitol, isn't it?" Baker leaned forward, full of certainty. "Louise Devereux, the one we've got locked up there for murder, just like you. She's one of your fancy women, ain't she?"

Harry hesitated, then set his sail on a course. "Yes."

"But you've got a barrow full of 'em, don't you? There was another one by this morning. An actress like Devereux."

"Caitlin Howard? She came by today?"

"Howard, yes. A well-mannered woman. You would have thought her a lady. I told her you could have no visitors. Your injury." He grinned, trying to look malicious.

He succeeded.

"Did she have a message for me?"

"She's the one you're partial to, isn't she, Raines? This other one's just a little bit of sweetmeat on the side."

"They are both my friends."

Now the grin was salacious.

"You do not look well, Sir," said Baker. "I fear this rich food does not agree with you in your present condition. I'm going to have you moved to the Old Capitol without further delay."

He finished his wine and rose. He studied Harry for a long moment, then came around to Harry's side of the table, pulling up a chair and moving close.

"Do not think it will be better for you there, Raines. W. W. Wood is the superintendent, and he is a friend of mine. It could go harshly for you in that establishment. It is no hotel."

"No California wines."

Baker ignored the sarcasm. "One word from me, you know, and General Scott could have you before an Army firing squad. He'd do it on my say-so. The city's frightened. He's in a bad temper. A different word from me and you'll be sent to Fort Delaware. It's an island fortress in the Delaware River from which there is no escape."

"I had thought you only some sort of clerk in the State Department."

"Don't be impertinent, Raines." He leaned back. "I am willing to make you an offer. I can't set you free. A military judge would have to see to that. But I can hold back any action against you for the time being. Maybe suggest to General Scott that this case is less than it seems. Who knows, you might eventually go free. But you must provide me with what I ask."

"An introduction to Miss Devereux?"

He'd now succeeded in making Baker angry. The man's face was turning the color of the wine.

"I want her confession, Raines! And I want names! When I send you to Old Capitol, I will expect you to spend your time there in the extraction of information from Miss Devereux. Names, names, names, Raines. I want the name of everyone involved in the conspiracy."

"What conspiracy is that, Mr. Baker?"

"It's been in all the papers. The Rebel conspiracy to murder our best officers using prostitutes and female assassins."

Harry gazed at him blankly, then realized the man was actually serious.

"Very well, Baker. I'll do it."

"I'll keep my part of the bargain. Bring me names, and your situation could improve."

"You didn't answer my question. Did Miss Howard leave a message?"

"She came back with a letter for you."

Harry brightened.

"And you may have it, Raines—as soon as you've done what I've asked."

Chapter 20

THE transfer was performed that night, by means of a closed carriage with black curtained windows, which Harry discovered could easily be pulled aside to admit the view.

It wasn't much. Looking out to the right, at the less reputable side of the Avenue, there were only the usual drunks, lowlifes, and skulks. Looking to the left, there was no one to be seen on the street at all, though the bar of his hotel seemed well patronized. He wished himself there, but he had work to do.

Curiously, there was only one guard assigned to him in addition to the driver of the coach and both men rode on top. It appeared remarkably easy for Harry to escape from the vehicle. But Baker did not seem a stupid man. Was he hoping Harry would bolt so that they would have justification to shoot him? Or was this a test to see if he'd head directly for the Confederacy—proving suspicions beyond all doubt.

Those were questions he'd leave unanswered. His path, if he was to reach its end, led through the gates of the Old Capitol Prison.

HE was given a decent room, and in the morning, an edible breakfast. Though the inmates were confined to their individual quarters at night, at daybreak they were free to wander the common areas of the building—and a walled section of the grounds. As a supposed murderer, he was lucky to be here.

Gathering in the common room seemed the general practice. Harry recognized a few of the people walking and standing about within it, some of them people of consequence in Washington society.

Most were men and diehard Secessionists. Two were card players. Harry soon found himself in a game.

Louise Devereux did not show herself, though one of the guards assured him she was still a resident. Dealing himself out of one hand, he asked to be brought to her, but was told she wished no visitors and that, in her mental state, none would be allowed. He asked if he might send her a note, but that too was denied.

Leahy turned up at midday, informing Harry he had attended the funeral service for Major Pleasants. He said there'd been many on hand for the ceremony, which was held at Congressional Cemetery. Most of the guests were curiosity seekers, though, attracted by the celebrity Pleasants had obtained through the newspapers. Only a few military men had come, among them Colonel Howard and Captain Kelleter. Colton had been conspicuously absent.

"The major was already underground," Leahy said. "The widow took care of that as soon as she got him back to Washington. Seems a peculiar thing to have done."

"If you had seen the body, you would not say so," Harry said.

They had walked out into the walled yard. There were two women with parasols idly strolling on the other side, but neither was the dark-haired Louise.

Harry remarked on his inability to gain an audience with the young actress.

"You'll see her soon enough," Leahy said. "They're going to haul her before a military judge on Monday and formally charge her with the major's murder. A trial's to follow soon after."

Harry stopped in mid-step and turned to face his new colleague. "That can't be true! We talked to the President."

"Orders came from Secretary of War Simon Cameron himself. Said he wants to set an example for all who would be assassins—male or female."

Harry took out a long, narrow cigar, causing Leahy to step back when he lighted it.

"And what about me?" Harry asked, through a cloud of smoke that hung almost motionless in the still, moist air.

"There is no word of your being charged."

"No matter I was found with a dead sergeant shot with my gun?"

"For the moment, it's Pleasants that's the grand issue."

"You know what they say about Cameron?" Harry said.

"Aye. That he's a man for the main chance and is not expected to go poor in the nation's service."

"What has he to gain from this? There's no money in hanging Louise Devereux."

"Maybe he's doing it out of patriotism."

Harry took another puff. "I must talk to her, and soon. There's a lot I must do soon, Leahy."

"Pinkerton'll be back tomorrow. You'd help your situation if you'd officially throw in with us. Swear an oath. Accept a badge."

"No thank you. But I appreciate the invitation. In another circumstance, I would be pleased to be your colleague, Sir."

Leahy paused, then reached into the breast pocket of his coat. "I forgot. You got some mail, Raines."

Harry looked through it quickly. There was no letter from Caitlin. Only bills and an advertising circular—and a letter from the man who managed his farm near Shepherdstown.

"These were at my hotel?"

"The clerk was obliging."

Stuffing the rest of the mail into his coat, Harry opened the letter carefully. To his surprise, the brief note from the farm steward was wrapped around another page of writing, in a different and more educated hand.

He smiled, and turned away to read.

"Mr. Leahy," he said, finally. "Are Shepherdstown or Martinsburg within Union lines now? Can I get a letter posted there without trouble?"

"Maybe. But not without delay. The mails are irregular."

"If sent by dispatch rider?"

"In whose name?"

Harry thought on this. "Mr. Pinkerton's. Or if you will, Major E. J. Allen's."

"He might not like that."

"But then again, he might, if the result is what I hope. And if I might trouble you further, Mr. Leahy, I'd be obliged if you could use the Army telegraph to query the Springfield Arms Company in Massachusetts."

"About what?"

"The handgun we took from Miss Devereux's room. It was of their manufacture and, as I recall, quite new. If there was a recent shipment of these revolvers to Washington City, it would be useful to know which gun dealers received them."

"To what end?"

"To ask if they remember selling one to Miss Devereux. Brady has copies of her *carte de visite*. You could show it around."

"You make a busy day for me, Raines."

"If you'll indulge me, Mr. Leahy, I'd make it busier still. There are several thousand pairs of surplus army shoes in a regimental warehouse in Alexandria—in the custody of a Captain Colton. I should like to know if they are still there."

"How in Hell am I to determine that?"

"Find my man, Caesar Augustus. He's working for the Army as a laborer in Pleasants' outfit. He will know."

"And if the shoes are still there?"

"Then I'll rest easier—for now."

HARRY obtained his audience with Louise that evening. Waiting near her room as her supper was brought around, he noted that the attendant left the door unlocked and unlatched upon departing after his delivery was complete. Harry slipped inside, took coffee and a bit of food from the wooden plate, then set the plate outside the door and shut it fast.

She lay on her cot, face to the wall. The cotton sheet that had served as coverlet had been wrestled from her body in her sleep. She wore only corset and chemise. Her legs and feet were bare.

Harry set himself gently on the edge of the cot. She stirred slightly, but her eyes remained closed.

"Louise." He touched her bare shoulder. "It's Harry, Harry Raines. I've come to help you."

Her eyes opened but looked only upon the wall. They closed again, and then she spoke: " 'He is betray'd and I am undone.' "

"Louise? Who's betrayed?"

" 'O, banish me, my lord, but kill me not!' "

"Louise! I'm not here to kill you! It's me, Harry."

" 'Kill me tomorrow; let me live tonight.' "

Her words struck him with some familiarity. What was she trying to tell him?

"I want you to live a hundred thousand nights, but Louise, you must talk to me." He looked about the chamber. On a table was a small cup and an opaque brown bottle. "Have you been taking laudanum all this while?" he asked. "Have they been letting you?"

" 'But half an hour. But while I say one prayer!' "

Harry realized the source of her words. Shakespeare. The lines were Desdemona's, from the scene in which Othello decides to kill her, and does so. In fact, her last words were the cue. The Moor replies "It is too late," and performs the mortal deed.

Reaching to grasp her right shoulder, Harry lifted her carefully and held her sitting in his arms, supporting her with some difficulty, for she remained very limp.

"Louise, this is not Othello. It's me, Harry Raines. You needn't die. I've come to get you out of here. I think I've found a way."

She did not speak, but her eyes began to show awareness of him. Then at once she began to cry.

He hugged her close. To his annoyance, the door opened, and the uniformed guard stepped within, his mouth agape. "What goes here, Mister?"

"She is distraught."

"She's near naked."

"I am a friend. I have Lafayette Baker's permission to be with her."

"I don't know no Lafayette Baker."

Harry sighed and released Louise from his arms. He went to the guard and handed him a silver dollar. "Mr. Baker thinks you are insufficiently paid."

The guard puzzled over this, then smirked and withdrew. Harry guessed he might have half an hour with Louise.

Closing the door again, he returned to her, sitting on the edge of her cot but not touching her. She had fallen back upon the sheet and was staring up at the ceiling.

"Louise," he said, seeking her attention. "Matters have taken a serious turn. They're going to proceed with prosecuting you. You're to be charged in less than two days' time. Then quickly tried. We've no way of knowing their disposition toward capital punishment for women, but there's hazard of your hanging. Do you understand? Your life's in danger."

She continued to stare. He leaned closer.

"Do you understand me, Louise? The hangman's noose!"

Her eyes closed, then reopened to lock on his. He thought that at last he'd penetrated her veil of madness and drugs, but then she spoke.

" 'Hang there like fruit, my soul, till the tree die.' "

"Louise!"

" 'It seems she hangs upon the cheek of night, like a rich jewel in an Ethiop's ear; Beauty too rich for use, for earth too dear!' "

He turned and sank his head into his hands, careful of the tender area behind his left ear.

"Are you ill?" She sat up, and came close. He felt her warm hand upon the back of his neck.

"At times. I wait for it to stop."

"Poor Harry."

He looked at her between his fingers. "You know me, Louise?"

" 'A little touch of Harry in the night.' "

"Damnation."

She reached and gently turned his face toward hers, a searching curiosity in her eyes now.

"Harry, why am I to die?"

This was no mad recitation.

"Louise, you do know me?"

"Yes. You are Harry Raines, my friend. But why are you here? This is a prison."

"To help you. Your friends are trying to help you."

"Wilkes? Wilkes Booth? Where is he?"

"Never mind him. He's of no use to any of us. Louise, I know this is upsetting, but have you any recollection of what happened when Major Pleasants was shot?"

"George was shot?"

"Yes! Twice. At Bull Run. You were there."

"Yes I was. A thousand times I've wished I had not been. He was coming to my rescue. There was so much noise. Cannons and smoke. Soldiers running. I was in frightful terror. I thought I was to die."

"Why did you go out there?"

"George was coming for me. He was running. My horse was as frightened as I. He was almost to me when my horse rose up and began this mad dance. I flung myself off and fell to the ground. When I'd gathered my wits, George had fallen in the road."

Harry gripped her shoulders. "Louise. Did you go to the battle to kill George Pleasants? The night before, you were in a violent rage. I was in the alley with him when you fired that shot."

Her full lips began to quiver. She shook her head. "No, I did not. 'Which the fair heart would fain deny, and dare not.' "

"Louise!" He shook her. She pushed him away, her eyes afire.

"No! I had no weapon. I did not kill him! I loved him!"

She commenced sobbing again. He waited for it to end, and this took considerable time.

"Louise, then tell me why you went to Centreville?"

He offered her the handkerchief from his sleeve. She took and held it, then began dabbing at her eyes.

"I went because I didn't want him to die in battle thinking I hated him. He left me, Harry. He caused me harm. That's why I fired that shot from Miz Turner's. But I took no aim.

Dear God, how could I do that? I loved him, Harry. The night before, he told me he was going back to his wife. That he had no choice. Her father had found out about us, about many things. He'd threatened George."

"Threatened him how?"

"The senator had been paying his debts, but said he would no more. Unpaid debts, Harry. South of the Avenue, a man can be killed for that. But now George is slain all the same. And the fault is mine. He was struck down as he came to my rescue." She turned away. " 'Pray for me, and what noise so-ever ye hear, come not unto me, for nothing can rescue me.' "

The words struck Harry's ear as odd, and thinking upon them, he realized why. They were not of Shakespeare's au-thorship. Indeed not. They came from *Doctor Faustus*. With his head so dented, he could not recall who had written it, but he remembered the work. And an apt one it was. George Pleas-ants' life had been a kind of Faustian pact. He, too, had not been ready to pay the price for it.

Harry put his arm around her shoulders, providing both comfort and steadiness. "Louise, did the major ever mention the subject of shoes?"

"Shoes. 'A surgeon to old shoes.' No." She swung forth her leg, looking to the foot. "He said that I had pretty feet, and he wished them always naked. But he never spoke of shoes. Or gave me any."

"A Captain Colton?"

She shook her head.

"A Colonel Beals?"

"He spoke of this man derisively. He did so once or twice. Nothing more."

"Did the major come recently into a sum of money?"

She laughed, bitterly. " 'Cast away care, he that loves sor-row, lengthens not a day, nor can buy tomorrow; Money is trash, and he that will spend it, Let him drink merrily, fortune will send it.' " She took note of her near nakedness as though for the first time. Reaching for her dressing gown, she pulled it on clumsily.

"Did fortune send him some?" Harry asked.

"A thousand dollars would last him no longer then ten. You

know that, Harry. I'm sure there's some of his money in your pockets."

"Why have you feigned madness, Louise? You're as sensible as I am."

She gave him a mad look, ruffling her long dark hair till it seemed to grow from her head like a bush. "Shall I scream for the jailer? Would that persuade you?"

"I'm trying to help you, lady."

"For Caitlin's sake."

"For all our sakes. I need to know, Louise. Have you committed some crime in this?"

"None that I need answer for."

"Are you working for the Confederacy? In any capacity?"

"Who says this? I'm accused of murder, nothing more."

"Asia Booth. Wilkes' sister."

"She told you this?"

"She said Booth told her."

Louise looked as though he had struck her a sharp blow. "Who else says it?"

"No one. Unless perhaps Booth himself."

She took his hands in hers and brought them close to her breast, imploringly. Her dark eyes showed fear and welled with tears again. Her emotions changed like the clouds of a spring sky.

"You've been searching, Harry. You and your Negro and that big detective. You came into Mollie Turner's in search of something. Did you find it? What did you find?"

"Nothing."

"You went through his uniform—the major's. Did you find it?"

"Find what? I didn't go through his uniform. There wasn't time. The enemy was advancing. What are you talking about?"

She bit down on her lip, releasing his hands, sinking back against the wall.

"I seek a piece of paper, Harry. An official document. One bearing a woman's name. Find me it and I will tell you all."

"Tell me now. If I'm to gain your liberty, I have to know as much as there is to know."

"You can't know this."

"Louise . . ."

She came against him, the flesh of her bare arm very moist and hot now. "Harry, please stay with me this night. I am afraid."

"It's not allowed."

"All things in this place are allowed—except the singing of 'Dixie.' All it requires is money. And you have that, Harry. You're not like George. You always have money."

"I can't, Louise. I . . ."

She looked down at her loosened garments, then up at him. "I ask you not to take my virtue, but to guard it. This place . . ."

"Caitlin . . ."

"Of all the people in all this world, Harry, Caitlin would understand."

She took his hand again, clutching it tightly, then lay herself down again, assuming much the same position as when he'd entered.

He'd taken clean clothes from her room, but they were now in his own quarters.

HARRY slipped from her side at some hour in the dead of night. The door was open but they'd not been disturbed. The dollar he'd given the guard had bought much.

Stepping into the corridor, he looked both ways. No guard was in view, and now he wanted one.

He started down the hall, moving quietly. There was a tiny office at the end—a blue-uniformed soldier sleeping in a chair tilted against the wall. Harry put his foot on it and brought it down sharply. The man's head snapped forward, and he wakened. He had a musket against the wall and a revolver on the little desk, but was too startled to reach for either.

"What do you want?"

"I want to speak to Mr. Baker, as soon as possible."

"It's the middle of the night."

"He'll want to speak to me. I have the information he sought."

"You're a prisoner."

"Not for long. Send for him. You won't regret it if you do. You will if you don't."

Chapter 2 1

HARRY was brought back to the Treasury Building in the same black coach, and placed in the same chamber as before, where he was greeted by what looked to be the same rat. Ignoring the creature, he collapsed into sleep so swift and deep it erased his pain for all the hours of the night.

Baker did not send for him until well into the morning. The man was at the table again, occupied with an elaborate breakfast. He offered Harry coffee, nothing more.

"You spent the night with the woman," he said, between mouthfuls of fried egg.

"Most of it."

"Did you find time to converse?"

"In a manner of speaking."

"And you have her confession?"

"Of course not. If she were guilty, she'd not give it. Being innocent, she could not."

Baker struck the table with the butt of his fork. "Damn you, Raines. If you haven't her confession, why did you ask to see me?"

"To tell you that I am surer than ever that she killed no one."

"That's all you have to say?"

"Except to repeat that I didn't shoot that sergeant."

Baker threw down his fork this time, scattering bits of egg across the table top.

"You do not help me!"

"Help you to do what? Hang innocent actresses? What sort of war is this that we make women participants?"

"It was her choice!"

"You're the damned murderer, Sir! You're bent on putting a rope around that beautiful neck."

Baker stood up, his chair falling behind him. He ignored it. His voice quieted, but his temper had increased.

"I can have you put in irons, Raines. We have a room here with no windows and no light. Talk."

Harry looked to the windows of this room. There were bars.

"Louise Devereux is not an assassin, Mr. Baker," he said. "She had no wish to kill Major Pleasants. I do not believe she has ever killed anyone. Neither do I think she is a spy. I don't believe she could tell a field mortar from a knapsack. But there is something I can tell you. Something I've pieced together from many places. A conspiracy, involving treasonable Union officers. And Confederate agents."

Baker shoved a plate with fresh bread upon it in Harry's direction. Next came a basket of apples. "Which army officers? What agents?"

"I think one of the officers may have been Major Pleasants."

"I thought you were hired by Senator Quigley to clear that officer's name."

"Only as concerns his conduct on the battlefield. And that I intend to do."

"What Confederates?"

"I don't know."

"Is she one of them?"

"No!"

"How do you know she isn't if you don't know who they are?"

"You saw the answer yourself when she was imprisoned. The lady is not entirely of right mind. She has become distraught and distracted, and now she doses herself with laudanum. She rambles, and speaks in lines from plays, as you may have observed. Of what use is such a spy to anyone? But I have heard elsewhere—on my forays into Virginia—that there's trafficking in U.S. Army goods. Some agreement has been made with Southern operatives."

"What sort of goods? Muskets? Powder?"

"Nothing so obvious, or lethal—but something important. Best I can determine, it's clothing. Shoes I think."

"Shoes?"

"They are a valuable commodity, Mr. Baker. An army cannot march without shoes. The South has small capacity to make them. And both sides are calling for more men. They must have shoes."

"But one can't just hand thousands of pairs of shoes over to the enemy. How would they get through the lines?"

"There aren't troops everywhere. One could ship them someplace where the enemy could get at them. Set me free and I'll get you every particular."

"Set you free, and you'll skedaddle to Virginia."

"Very well. Set her free and jail me."

"Shoes?" Baker began to rub his chin, as though that would aid comprehension.

"Shoes, Mr. Baker. Thousands of genuine U.S. Army government-issue shoes."

"Sorry, Raines. I just don't believe you. I'm going to send you back to the Old Capitol. You will both stay in jail until you obtain her confession. You have until her trial to do so."

"And when is that?"

"I haven't decided."

HARRY had made no real plan, but he'd certainly established his priorities. Number One was escaping the reach of Baker's authority—and if at all possible, removing himself with great haste from this city and to a place far up the Potomac Valley.

The coach that was to take him back to the Old Capitol was the same as before, but the driver and guard had been changed. This time, the guard was a cautious sort who rode inside with him on the facing seat, a long-barreled revolver in hand. Harry smiled at the man, who gave no response in kind. As they trotted down the avenue, swerving from time to time to avoid the inevitable pedestrians and wandering animals, Harry found himself at a loss as to what to do. The Old Capitol Prison was not where he needed to be just now.

Someone had once told him that the most successful generals were not those with the most brilliant plans but those who were always prepared to take advantage of opportunities. Looking out the window, Harry saw one in the making. Two drunken soldiers, both in the gaudy uniforms of the New York firemen Zouaves, were reeling along toward them in an effort to cross the dusty Avenue, almost oblivious to traffic. They seemed at just the right point between sobriety and stupor to suit Harry's purpose.

Harry put his head out the window, careful to keep his wound from the wooden frame.

"Hey, you dumb Irish bastards!" Harry shouted. "You're breaking General McClellan's rule! No liquor is to be served to soldiers. You sots!"

The two Zouaves stopped, staring at him in some disbelief. The coach driver kept the team going, though at a walk.

"What are you idiots celebrating?" Harry continued. "T'was your fault we lost at Bull Run. You should be doing penance."

One of the men made an obscene gesture at Harry. The other began moving faster toward them, calling out words Harry could not quite make out, though he guessed they were likely profane.

"You Irish louts, you're no more brave than mice!"

His guard leaned abruptly forward, pressing his pistol barrel down hard on Harry's arm. "Lay off that now," he commanded. "Enough!"

Harry tossed off one more at the Zouaves. "Bogtrotters! You all got faces like potatoes!"

This parting shot sufficed. The soldiers broke into a lumbering, slightly inaccurate but purposeful lope, heading straight for the coach. Harry heard the driver snap his whip, but no sooner had the vehicle been jolted by a break into a faster pace than it lurched into a slow one again.

He could see why. One of the men had reached the coach and was standing on the step, reaching inside for the latch to the door. The other, Harry guessed, was running near the horses, trying to stop them.

The one hanging nearest was having trouble holding his balance as he tried to open the door. Harry's guard had leaned across to stick the barrel of his revolver into the soldier's stomach.

"Get off the coach! We got a prisoner here!"

The soldier was reaching for the door latch. Harry got his hand to it first and yanked the handle. The door swung back, with the soldier clutching it. He began to sway.

Harry snatched the revolver from the guard and kicked the door, sending the drunken soldier backwards into the street. Trusting no one was on the coach's roof, he fired off a shot through it, just for effect.

It was what he desired. The guard, startled, shrank back against his seat. Outside, the gunshot had commenced drawing all manner of firemen Zouaves into the street. A cry had gone up about the fallen soldier. Someone shouted, "He's been shot!"

"What mischief is this?" the guard asked. "Are you a lunatic?"

"I'm getting off here," Harry said. "If you don't want to get your head split open, I'd do the same. And now!"

The soldier looked to the window. The view was all of Zouaves, rushing forward as though in battle charge.

Harry slid to the other side of the coach, snapped open that door, and without further comment, leapt to the dirt. A knee gave out beneath him but he was quickly back on his feet.

He was a block from the National. The Zouaves were occupying the attention of Baker's men—the coach aswarm with fezzes and rocking back and forth. He would have several minutes—he hoped—before they sorted this out.

Fighting off a momentary dizziness, Harry plunged into the flow of pedestrians on the brick sidewalk and made his way quickly up the Avenue to his hotel, rushing past the desk clerk before the man had a chance to speak.

His door was unlocked, but with happy reason. Caesar Augustus was in a corner chair, reading by the gaslight. He looked up.

"I am pleased to see you," Harry said, heading for the bedroom and his dresser. He began pulling out clean shirts and linen. "But I am surprised."

"Mr. Leahy said I should wait for you here—asked me if I would," said Caesar Augustus from the other room. "Or for him. Whichever came first."

"It was looking like he'd beat me here by a year," Harry said.

Harry searched for his small portmanteau, remembering finally that he had put it under his bed.

"And where is he?" Harry asked.

"Gone to Baltimore."

"Baltimore?"

"After them shoes. Turns out Colton loaded four or five railroad cars with shoes, and sent them to Baltimore."

The small suitcase had a sort of false bottom—an extra fold of cloth under which he had hidden a cache of traveling funds in the event of an emergency. This surely was that. He pulled out a sheaf of large bills and a small leather bag of coins, putting both in his pockets. Then he began stuffing the bag with clothes.

"Wait," he said, after a moment. "Baltimore's the wrong direction."

"Baltimore's full of Secesh, Marse Harry."

"They wouldn't dare rob a military train. After the riots there last spring, they'd be shot down before they could take a step toward it. Even if they'd succeeded in getting their hands on all those shoes, they'd never get them from there into Virginia. They'd have to go through the entire U.S. Army."

Finishing his hasty packing, Harry went to his dresser, pouring water from the pitcher there into a large china basin. He splashed water over his face and neck. His time here was running out.

"The B & O don't only go to Baltimore," Caesar Augustus said. "The main line from the yards there runs west to Frederick."

"And from there to Harpers Ferry and Martinsburg. I am bound for that place myself," Harry said. He dropped his two Colt revolvers plus the gun he'd taken from the coach guard into his suitcase, then quickly looked around. "As fast as I can."

He remembered his extra pair of spectacles, but had forgotten where he had put them. Going into his other room, he began pulling open the drawers of his desk. Caesar Augustus held up what Harry sought.

"On the book by your chair," he said.

"Thank you." He slid them carefully into a pocket.

"Marse Harry, are you escapin' from jail?"

"Precisely what I'm doing." Harry went to the window, peering out from the side. Several Zouaves were rushing toward the National's main entrance. He watched them disappear beneath the awning below. "And I am tardy."

Harry started toward the door.

"Why you going to Martinsburg?"

"To call on my 'cousin' Belle."

"You walkin'?"

"I may have to. If I try for the stable, they'll see me."

"Won't matter if they see me, Marse Harry. They don't knows me."

Harry opened the door, then paused. " 'A horse, a horse. My kingdom for a horse.' "

"Where'll I meet you?"

"Behind the market at Northern Liberties—those shacks and sheds near New York Avenue."

"I expects to be paid."

"Of course." Harry fled.

HE heard the soldiers coming up the main stairs as he turned the corner of the corridor and flew down the back. A moment later, he was in the alley, and not long after, at the rendezvous point.

Caesar Augustus arrived as promised, leading Rocket, but riding a mount of his own.

"Why have you hired that horse?" Harry asked, climbing wearily into the saddle.

"It's on your account, Marse Harry. Thought I'd escape the summer vapors of the city and take to the country air."

"Well, let's take to them fast!"

Chapter 2 2

W HEN Harry and Caesar Augustus rode into the little town of Martinsburg, it was still firmly in the hands of the Union Army, as was Harpers Ferry downriver. The B. & O. Railroad was a vital lifeline between Washington and the west, and for all its fecklessness and foolishness, the Army's high command had recognized that fact to the extent of fortifying these Potomac river towns considerably. Entering Martinsburg on the road from Falling Waters, they'd encountered a Federal artillery battery with its guns facing north. Harry was sure there'd be others around the town, aimed at every point of the compass.

"Ain't no Confederate raiding party goin' to come shoppin' for shoes in this place," said Caesar Augustus. " 'Less they bring their whole army."

"You're right. Maybe 'Cousin' Belle can suggest a likelier destination."

There'd been rain, but it had diminished to a drizzle. They walked their horses down Queen Street, the hooves slopping in the mud.

Lights glowed in most of the downstairs windows of the wooden house despite the later hour. Belle herself answered the door, brandishing a shotgun. Not recognizing Harry at first, she brought the barrel to the fore.

"Shoot, and you'll have one less friend," he said.

"Harry! I was writing you a letter. I was of the mind we

should meet in some discreet rendezvous. Now, you show up on my doorstep."

"I should like to leave it, for a place a little drier."

Flustered, as she so seldom was, Belle moved aside with a sweep of skirt and pulled the door open wide to admit them. She seemed not surprised to see Caesar Augustus, but, to Harry's displeasure, started to direct him to the kitchen.

"He is with me," Harry said. "He came on this journey of his own free will."

"But I cannot have him in the parlor, and that is where I would receive you."

"Dat's all right, Marse Harry," said Caesar Augustus, heading for the kitchen and its inviting smells. "Dis darkie wants to be close to dem eats."

"I've ham and cheese and bread—whiskey and coffee," Belle said. "I'll make you both a quick supper. Harry, wait in the parlor. Mother's upstairs asleep, so we must be quiet. She knows nothing of any of this. She's been fearful, ever since the Yankees came."

WIPING his lips in a mannerly habit, Harry pushed his plate aside and reached for the mug of whiskey-laced coffee, easing himself back on the horsehair sofa. Belle was seated beside him.

"I am comfortable for the first time this day," he said. "I thank you."

"Explain yourself, Harry. Why are you here so soon? Why didn't you wait to hear from me."

"Louise Devereux will soon be on trial. I couldn't wait." He decided to say nothing about his flight from Lafayette Baker's custody. He didn't want this chatterbox boasting of his having allegedly killed a Union sergeant and escaping a Federal jail all over the Virginia Piedmont.

She touched his arm in Southern coquette fashion. "Ever the gallant. Louise Devereux is lucky to have you for a friend."

Harry let this pass. He'd been anything but luck to Louise thus far. "In your message, Belle, you said you could be of help in the case."

"Oh indeed I can." Her hand went to his arm again. "I have evidence that she was not the shooter of this Major Pleasants—that she was almost a victim herself."

"So you said in your message. What evidence is there for that?"

"Her saddle. It holds a bullet that just missed her leg. I asked General Jackson for his help, and he recovered the saddle for me. Also, all of the major's personal effects, including a handsome watch taken by some wretched private from the 7th Louisiana."

"Are there papers?"

"Yes. Some letters. And *carte de visite* photographs of Devereux and a woman I take to be his wife."

"May I see them?"

"I'll fetch them."

LOUISE was favored far more by the camera than was Mrs. Pleasants, who looked so cold and severe on the paper print she might have been a statue. Louise's dark eyes gleamed with lurking passion and urgency. Both pictures had traces of blood on the cardboard backing. The major must have carried them facing his heart.

Harry looked through the papers, finding a list of the major's debts and creditors, Big Jim Coates and Congressman Fowler among them, as well as two letters. Both were from Louise. He read through them hurriedly, finding much anguish in the words, but little revelation.

"This was all?" he asked Belle.

"All that could be located. My request for these things was approved by General Jackson himself—and I'm told he would do anything for me—so I'm sure if the major had more, I would have it. The general's aware of those dreadful newspaper stories in Washington—about female assassins and murder conspiracies. We must put an end to them before some action is taken against the Southern women in the capital. We have many friends among them, do we not? They could be compromised. There's peril for them in this."

Peril seemed to be what Belle enjoyed most in life.

"Louise is desperate to have some paper, some document perhaps, that was in the major's possession," Harry said. "I must see that paper, whatever it is, before I can be finished with this. I must know its import."

Belle shrugged. "I cannot help you about it, Cousin." She rose. "I'll show you the saddle."

Taking a cloak from a wall peg in the hall, she lighted a lantern and led Harry through the small back yard to the stable, where Fleeter and another animal stood contentedly in their stalls.

"Here," she said, hefting a woman's side saddle onto the door of the lone vacant stall. "You see. The bullet dug this track through the leather and struck the wooden frame of the pommel. It's in there still. She could not have fired it at herself. Take it, and show those Federal scum what fools they are."

Harry ran his finger along the groove. "The bay horse?"

"It was crazed from the wound, they say. Someone shot it. Fool thing to do. It might have healed. They say he was a fine animal."

"What of Senator Quigley's coachman?"

"Who is that?"

"The man taken prisoner with us—until you came to my rescue. He escaped from the barn where we were held. His name is Joseph. I don't know whether surname or Christian."

"Oh that poor man. He was shot dead that very night, by a fretful sentry."

"I wish I could have talked further to him. I think he would have been of use to me."

"I'm sorry, Harry. But it was not your fault."

She moved close to him. Her hand came to his arm again, and remained. At seventeen, she was fully woman, and it made him nervous. There were times when he would have wished for close kinship to her—as a defense.

For the moment, he had something better to deploy.

He stepped back, turning her to face him, holding her by the shoulders but keeping her at arm's length.

"Isabelle," he said. "I have serious news for you, but I must ask something from you in return for it."

"What do you ask? I'd grant you anything, Harry."

"The news first. Your friend Rose Greenhow. They suspect she is a spy. She may be arrested. It could happen any day. She must flee to the South. If she stays in the capital, she cannot be safe."

"She won't leave—not while she thinks she can be useful to the Cause. And she has been wonderfully useful."

"She won't be useful to anyone if she's in the Old Capitol Prison. You, too, Belle. You must flee. Get beyond the Yankee lines."

She stepped back. "But, Harry. I *am* in the South. This is Virginia—our sacred soil."

"You are called a murderess in the Northern press. The rumors of female assassins feed as much on your Fourth of July deed as on the calumny against Louise."

"I killed a Yankee invader! He threatened my own mother in this very house!"

"Belle. I do not know for certain what they will do to Southern women they consider spies. But murder is a hanging crime, and tempers are high. Get away from here. If nothing else, go to your aunt's in Front Royal."

Turning away, contemplating some far-off point as might an actress on a stage, she addressed him coolly.

"Thank you, Sir, for the intelligence you bring. What is it you wish in return?"

"I wish to know where the Confederate army is going to take delivery of that trainload of Yankee shoes."

Belle whirled to face him, her composure briefly lost, and recovered too late.

"Why, Harry, whatever are you talking about?"

"You know very well what I'm talking about—as must every Confederate agent in Virginia. There's a load of shoes about to be made available. They've been sold to the Confederate government by a crooked Union officer named Colton. Major Pleasants was part of it."

"And with this information, what would you do, betray your Country, Sir?" Her pose was again theatrical, but her anger and passion were real. This child/woman was as much a patriot as the South possessed.

"You know that I am neutral in this fight, Belle. I would not raise my arm against Virginia, nor would I to defend slavery. I want to be there so that I may learn who on the Southern side Colton was dealing with. I believe this person can tell me why Pleasants was killed—and why Louise was made scapegoat for it."

"Scapegoat? She's part of it!"

"How would you know that?"

"He told me himself!"

Her unintended revelation struck her like a stick. They stood a long moment, staring at each other in understanding silence.

"It is *he* who I seek," he said. "Who is *he*?"

"I misspoke."

Harry stepped forward, putting his arm around her as a gesture of reassurance.

"No you didn't, Belle. I'm not here to give over anyone to the Federals. In fact, if I get to them in time, I mean to tell them it's a trap—that Union troops in large numbers are coming for them."

"It's true? A trap? I must warn them at once."

He pulled her close. "Belle, your name is on lists! You are suspect. I'll get word to them. Just tell me where to go, who to see."

"I promised him I'd not tell anyone. He asked my help and I gave him that along with the promise to say nothing. He's not a man I'd dare betray."

"Belle . . ."

"But I can tell you this: '*Petit Orleans.*' "

She gave both words a French pronunciation.

"That's where? They told you this?"

"Do not betray me on this, Harry."

"When?"

"Sir?"

"The shoes. Just tell me when, and I'll bother you not a moment further. And I promise you, Belle, no harm will come to the Confederate cause from this—if they heed my warning."

"Then I shall ask you for something."

"Anything."

She smiled, fully the coquette again. "A kiss."

He bestowed what she asked. It was not an embrace to have engendered much jealousy in Caitlin.

"It's tomorrow night," Belle said.

THE night air was moist, but the rain had stopped. They wiped their saddles free of wet before mounting.

"You haven't said where we're going," Caesar Augustus said.

"Upriver. Pretty far."

"How far? These bones are tired."

"Past Hancock, Maryland. There's a town on the Chesapeake and Ohio Canal called Little Orleans."

"What's there?"

"The Potomac has so many bends up there the railroad crosses the river five times in the space of a few miles. It's a perfect place to stop a train."

"Marse Harry. No place that far from here is perfect."

They followed the B & O tracks all the way to the town of Bath, on the Virginia side of the river, where Harry stopped at the telegraph.

He sent two messages—one to Leahy to be shared with Pinkerton, and one to Captain Kelleter to be shared with Colonel Oliver O. O. Howard. The messages were the same. A train bearing surplus shoes bound for Ohio via Frederick and Martinsburg was going to be waylaid by Confederates at the bends of the Potomac at Little Orleans, Maryland. Troops should be sent at once by the fastest means.

"You signed that wire Harrison Raines," Caesar Augustus said, as they rode out of town, heading north for the Potomac.

"It's my name."

"But now they'll know where you are."

"If that brings Federal troopers quicker, all the better."

Chapter 23

THERE was a ford across the Potomac just upriver from the hamlet of Cacapon. They found it unguarded and crossed without hindrance. Harry had expected to encounter mounted patrols and sentries, with both railroad and canal running so close to Confederate territory here. But not a military man was to be seen from the Cacapon crossing on. Keeping their horses to the level, easygoing C & O Canal towpath, they finally relaxed a bit, talking idly, as though they'd left the war far behind them.

Yet he knew that if his suspicions were correct, there was a substantial little dose of war waiting for them just ahead—after a few miles more of winding and turning river as it cut through the hills and mountains.

Throughout the hot, cloudy day, they saw only the occasional lock tender and farmer. It was dark again when they finally reached Little Orleans, a cluster of dwellings overlooking the banks of Fifteen Mile Creek where it flowed into the Potomac just west of a high, steep ridge called Sideling Hill. This mountain country had been the wild west in George Washington's youth. He'd blazed trails and fought French and Indians here. It seemed to Harry he could almost hear their ghosts in wooded darkness, and he was glad to be in a place of habitation.

There were only a few buildings in the village proper—a lock tender's house, a grocery and tavern, a stable, and a dozen or so cottages—strung along either side of Little Orleans' lone street. Here, too, it was tranquil and soldierless; yet the village sat on the line that divided Union from Confederacy. The newspapers had said there were several thousand Rebel troops in the mountains southwest of this place. Harry had heard there were some Southern cavalry in a small command down there. There might be Rebel patrols only a few miles distant, a short ride.

They dismounted in the middle of the street. There were lights in a few of the buildings, but little sound save a couple of listlessly barking dogs, and no one moving about. And mosquitoes. He'd slapped his neck and ears red trying to defeat their thrusts and parries—all without success.

Otherwise, all was so still as to be eerie. Harry wondered if Belle had misunderstood—or if she'd deliberately misinformed him. There could be no great occurrence in such a place this night.

"What now, Marse Harry?"

"I'm thinking."

"You got some plan?"

"None at all, except maybe to get something to eat. I'd thought we might find elements of the Confederate Army here, trying on shoes."

"Ain't no army, but there's two horses tied up at that tavern."

"A tavern seems as good a place to think up a plan as any."

"Will I be sent to the kitchen?"

"This part of the country's not much a place for slavery, Caesar Augustus. Even across the river there. That part of Virginia really ought to be part of the North."

He started toward the tavern. The yellow light from the window seemed inviting.

"Marse Harry?"

"Yes?"

"You're not wearing your spectacles."

"I'm not here to play cards."

"You can't be worried about comin' upon some pretty girl in a place like this."

"Pretty girls grow where they will."

Leaving the black man to tie up the horses, Harry pushed through the low doorway of the tavern, finding himself in a long, narrow, dimly-lit room. A broad plank set on two barrels did for a bar, with an oil lamp at one end providing the room's principal illumination, though there was also a candle set on the table at the other end of the chamber. Two men were seated there, visible mostly in silhouette. A third man, with an enormous beard, stood behind the bar. Stepping up to him, Harry guessed he was his own best customer.

He plunked down a silver dollar. "A bottle of your best whiskey, Sir, and two glasses. Have you food?"

Though he'd not quite heard their voices upon entering, Harry sensed that the two men at the table had ceased talking.

"Got cold corned beef and yesterday's bread pudding." The barman gestured over his shoulder at a cloth-covered bowl behind him.

"It will have to do."

The tavernkeeper set down two wooden cups and a whiskey jug. While Harry attended to the pouring, the man brought forth the bowl, pulling off the cloth and causing a cloud of flies to take flight in buzzing circles. He then stuck a wooden spoon into the pudding.

"I'll charge ye fer what ye eat."

"Two spoons, then. You mentioned beef."

"Aye."

He produced a cloth covered plate, adding to the swarm of flies when he removed it.

Caesar Augustus entered singing a song Harry had never heard from his lips before: " 'Dance, boatman, dance. Dance, boatman, dance. Dance all night in the broad moonlight and go home with the girls in the morning . . .' "

One could have taken Caesar Augustus for a canal boat hand, Harry supposed, but the pose was of little use. Harry looked precisely what he was.

As one of the men at the table quickly noted.

"By God, it's Raines!"

Harry turned slowly, and he hoped confidently, to face the two. Both rose from their chairs, one of them walking toward him, keeping his hand near the opening of his coat. The other moved to the door.

"Good evening," Harry said. He still could not quite make out who they were.

Then at once he could—at least the one who stepped close. The man had a pistol in his hand.

"Captain Colton," Harry said.

"You have a rare talent, Raines, for locating yourself inconveniently."

Harry smiled, wishing now he was wearing his spectacles. Caesar Augustus had moved slightly to the rear of Colton, but Harry wasn't sure what he intended. His actions would have to be circumspect, for the man at the door had a full view of everything, and was likely armed as well.

"I thought you'd been jailed," Colton said. "Arrested for murdering my sergeant."

"They got the wrong man," said Harry, still smiling. "As you and your friend might have reason to know."

Whoever the other man was, he seemed to find Harry's words disagreeable—wishing to hear no more of them. The door swung fully open, and an instant later he was gone.

Caesar Augustus of a sudden bolted for the door and disappeared through it as well. Colton turned, but too late. He fired off a shot, but the bullet flew off into the darkness, giving no sign of striking a thing.

Harry reached for his own revolver, but the barrel caught on his wide leather belt. By the time he yanked it free, Colton had turned back and was on him, striking Harry hard on the back of the head with his pistol—an area of his skull that had already suffered more than sufficient injury.

Harry crumpled at once, not so much from the force of the blow as to escape another. Collapsing onto the floor, he put his arms over his head, trying to ward off further nastiness.

He failed. He felt a kick, not one intended to injure, but to roll him over. He complied with the intent, struggling to focus on the man who stood above him. Like the fellow who had so hastily just departed, Colton was dressed in civilian clothes, including a black coat and broad-brimmed hat.

"Damn you to Hell, Raines. Did you follow me here?"

"No, Sir. I'm just looking to buy some shoes."

Colton kicked him again, this time trying to inflict pain and succeeding in his effort. Harry rolled over and retreated beneath the plank.

"I want no shooting in here," said the tavernkeeper, who apparently was aware of something Harry wasn't. Had Colton cocked his weapon?

"There's a war on," Colton said. "You better get used to shooting. The Rebels shot a railroad engineer down near Manassas for letting his locomotive break down when they needed it during Bull Run."

"No Rebels here," the tavernkeeper said. "This is Union country."

Harry wished it was Union country enough to have some Yankee soldiers on hand. This Colton seemed of definite mind on the question of killing him. Harry supposed his only doubt was whether to leave the drunken barkeep a witness or victim, too.

"I'm a Federal officer, on a special mission," said Colton, having decided, apparently, that Harry's extermination would suffice for the moment. "This man's a Southern agent. I'm taking him with me."

Colton reached beneath the plank to grab for Harry's arm, catching only his sleeve. Harry pulled it away. If this rogue captain meant to get Harry outside, he certainly wasn't going to cooperate an inch in that direction.

Harry hadn't the strength to do much, but next time Colton reached for him, he kicked out at the man's shin, striking a glancing but still painful blow.

Colton replied by pointing his long barreled revolver directly at Harry's face. It was a single-action piece, and it was cocked. There'd be no evading any projectile it might send his way.

Staring at Colton's trigger finger as best as he could focus on it without his spectacles, he thought he saw it begin to tighten. There was a moment of hesitation, and then, as best Harry could make out, the finger relaxed again.

Hoofbeats! Distantly heard, but many of them. Harry as-

sumed his telegraph from the town of Bath had produced re-
sults. He felt a joyous sense of salvation.

Colton lowered the pistol and turned away. The hoofbeats
increased, the riders sounding as though they were charging
right at the tavern. Voices could be heard in the confusion,
and then the stomp of boots on the wooden doorstep.

The door slowly opened. A cavalry officer, wearing high
dragoon boots and a plumed hat, stepped inside, looked at the
three of them in quick turn, and then all about the room. Whatever or whoever he sought, he didn't find it.

"Was there another man here?" he asked.

"Yes, but he went off," said the tavernkeeper.

The officer came forward into the lamplight. He wore the
gray of the Confederacy, though Harry couldn't tell much
more about him.

"Who are you?" the Rebel officer said to Colton.

"You've come for the shoes? Did you bring wagons?"

"I asked who you were."

"You don't know? I'm Colton."

"I don't know any Colton." The officer gestured at Harry,
who began to edge forth from beneath the bar. "Who's this
man?"

"He's a Union spy. I just caught him."

The barkeep, having partaken in a large gulp of whiskey,
commenced to sputter out the words: "You just said he was a
Southern agent!"

The cavalry officer came closer. Feeling somehow safer,
Harry began to rise, just as several other Confederate soldiers
entered the room.

"I tell you he's a Yankee." Colton said.

The officer peered down at Harry, then of a sudden reached
to help him to his feet.

"I know you," he said.

Harry recognized the officer as well—the same who had
briefly been his captor at the farm near Middleburg.

"I'm Belle Boyd's cousin," Harry said. "You remember
her."

"So you are. So you are. And who still in possession of his

senses could not remember that lady. What happened to your head? What are you doing here?"

Harry gestured at Colton. "He happened to me. He's a Union officer. You'll find a U.S. Army military saddle on his horse out there."

Colton stepped up to them both, still holding his revolver in his hand. He gave the Confederate a hard look.

"I'm the one who's making this 'delivery' possible. The one you owe the money to," he said.

"I'm supposed to meet a 'Mr. Gloucester.' "

"Gloucester be damned. I made this possible. I'm risking my neck for this. I'm the one to be paid."

There was a clatter and then shouts outside. A sergeant thumped up to the door.

"Wagons're here, Captain."

The officer turned to attend to this duty, directing that the conveyances be sent up the towpath to the trestle where the railroad first crossed the canal and river.

"And have them put some hurry into it!" he shouted after, as the sergeant ran back to the little street.

Colton's eyes flicked about the room, but he did not appear to be in search of escape. He wanted his money. Harry and Caesar Augustus had upset the commercial arrangements he'd so carefully set in motion. No wonder he was so bent on dispatching Harry.

"Captain," Harry said, stepping away from Colton with a slight hobble. "It's true what he says. He's a Union officer engaged in the sale of U.S. government property to the Confederate States of America. He had three partners. Two of 'em are dead, and the third has fled from this place just ahead of you, I know not to where. I gather he might be your 'Mister Gloucester.' "

"He left no message?"

"No, but I bring you one—from my cousin Belle. I promised her I'd tell you. You don't want these shoes, Sir. They're no good to you."

"No good? They're good as gold!"

"No, Captain, the soles are no better than glue and dust. They're shoddy."

"That's not true!" exclaimed Colton, who still had his pistol in his hand. "They're regular Army issue! As promised."

The Confederate captain seemed a little bewildered—and irritated.

"You've been warned, Sir," Harry said. "You don't want those shoes. And you don't want to linger in this vicinity. There's a Federal force on the way to catch you."

"How do you know this?"

"I've come here from Washington."

"The man lies!"

Harry looked to see the barrel of Colton's revolver once again pointed at his head. Before Harry could duck, it discharged, but the Confederate captain managed to knock it to the side. The round struck the wall of the tavern, prompting the flies to start buzzing about in the smoke from the firearm.

A strange sound intruded. Listening carefully, Harry realized it was a train whistle. So did the captain. Snatching Colton's firearm from his hand, he summoned a soldier forward.

"Put these two in a wagon. We'll take them with us. Keep a weapon on them and shoot them if they bolt."

THE railroad tracks ran on a level substantially above the canal along this stretch of the Potomac. When the train finally came, it seemed to be flying above them, a noisy, heavy-breathing dragon, spitting sparks and clouding the night sky with its billowing, black smoky breath.

As the train passed, Harry looked for guards, but none were visible in the darkness. There were just more sparks and an infernal din of chuffing and rattle, augmented by a blast of whistle that seemed to blow leaves from the trees. Then it was gone, the sound diminished to echoes and rattles.

Colton stared at it as he might some cherished possession.

They were sitting side by side in the back of a wagon. The private—a revolver held on his knees—sat facing them at the forward end, watching them attentively. The overcast sky above had parted to reveal a slice of rising moon, which as the train smoke dissipated now softly limned the tree branches and curving towpath before them, a tiny glitter of it dancing on the otherwise murky surface of the canal.

The Potomac was very close here, its waters rushing over a wide, shallow rapids. The path was narrow, and the creaking wheels came near the edge on both sides.

Harry lighted a cigar, puffed on it a savoring moment, then offered one just like it to Colton. The man glared at him, making no move to accept the gift. Harry tossed it instead to the soldier, then went back to his contented puffing.

"My apologies for interfering with your commerce, Colton," he said. "That wasn't my intent. All I'm after is the name of Major Pleasants' murderer."

"I've nothing more to say to you. These soldiers will find what they seek. My expenses will be attended to. And you'll be hanged."

"Who's this Mr. Gloucester then? I've never heard of any Gloucester in Washington."

Colton turned away, as might a petulant child.

"If I'm to be hanged, why not tell me?"

"Damn you, Raines! He was right in front of you."

"The light was dim."

"You two stop that chatterin'," said the soldier, as the wagon lurched over a large stone or hump in the path. "This is enemy territory. Damn wagons makin' enough noise as it is."

They rumbled along then in relative quiet, the last wagon in the file. There were two cavalrymen bringing up the rear behind them, moving at a slow trot and passing a bottle or flask back and forth. One of them laughed. He didn't think western Maryland enemy country.

"Did he kill Sergeant Fetridge, this Gloucester?" Harry asked, trying to keep his voice to a whisper.

"This is an honest answer," Colton said. "I do not know. For all that I do know, it could have been you, General Scott, or the sainted Abraham Lincoln. I do not consider it my affair, except that Fetridge worked for me, and I do not like the fellow I've been given in his place."

"An honest man, is he?"

"A stupid one. Same thing."

"Major Pleasants was not stupid."

"Nor honest. A man of many weaknesses."

Because they had lowered their voices, the private let them talk. He held his revolver loosely in his lap, now, with the barrel averted. Harry suspected that Colton was still armed. When they'd been jostled together by that hump in the path, he'd felt something hard and sharp-edged beneath the captain's coat. Harry still had a derringer in an inside pocket of his coat the Confederates had not found, plus a knife in his boot. In close quarters, that could account for itself better than a firearm.

"All I need to know is this," Harry said, trying to keep his manner friendly. "Was Pleasants an active participant in your conspiracy? Or was he only aware of it?"

"There is no conspiracy. I have merely shipped some surplus Army shoes back to a depot in Ohio."

"Shipping them over a river crossing where a Confederate raiding party is waiting to grab them. Conspiracy enough for you to be out here chasing the money you're claiming for it."

Harry could not quite make out Colton's expression, but it seemed to him the man might be smiling—in careful, subtle fashion.

"Do you have another of those cigars?" Colton asked.

Harry gave him one—his last. The captain lighted it with care; the rosy glow illuminated his face. It was an intelligent countenance and bore no outward signs of venality, though some grim bitterness was discernible, as it had been on the occasion of Harry's first meeting with the man.

Colton was a career army officer. Others holding his permanent rank in the regular army had recently been promoted to colonel and given brigades. Some with nothing more to commend them than friends in Congress were being made generals.

"Obliged," Colton said, as he took a long puff of smoke that came luxuriantly to Harry's nostrils. As the wagon bumped along, the three of them in its bed sat in silence and smoked. They might have been travelers on a holiday.

"Whatever happens tonight," Harry said, "I won't hold you to account for it. I'll promise you that much. But I need to know how much Pleasants was involved. Louise Devereux's going to be formally charged tomorrow, and they won't wait long on a trial."

"Why you so heated up about her? She was Pleasants' woman. She yours now? You have yourself some amusement in the Old Capital Prison?"

Harry fought to keep his temper. His head was aching.

"I am sworn to save her, Sir, and I must know all I can. Was Pleasants killed for his part in your business?"

Colton puffed some more. "Had the man lived, it would not be necessary for me to be here this night. He needed money. As you probably know, he owed a lot of money—to gamblers like you and larcenous men. But it would not have profited them to have shot the sonofabitch. Just the opposite, for he stood to improve his fortunes from these transactions."

"Transactions. You mean there are others? Were others? Will be others?"

Colton didn't respond. His eyes were on the military procession ahead. They passed through an open space that gave a view of the dark, rushing river to the left, then were back in the woods again.

"That girl knows everything," he said, finally.

"Louise? How can that be? She's just an actress. What would she know of army shoes?"

"She was Pleasants' mistress, that's how. He talked a lot."

There was a crack of thunder, but it wasn't that. The night sky ahead and off to the left turned bright orange in a fleeting burst of light. The sound that followed came to them as a great thump, followed by the staccato pops of what had to be musket fire.

"Your transaction," Harry said, "is under way."

Chapter 24

THE sound of the fighting quickened both man and beast. There was a jostling in the column of wagons ahead and then the clipping sound of horses moving into a trot, including their own. At this point, their wheels were but inches from the riverbank on one side and the canal on the other, but there was no caring. The sooner this act in the drama came to a close, the sooner home to safety—for the Confederate raiders, at least. Harry still could only guess at his and Colton's fate, knowing it very well might not be the same for both.

Ahead—and from the sound of it, above them—the musket fire continued, increasing in volume and frequency, though there were no more explosions. Some angry shouting was mixed in with the gunfire. As they drew nearer still, a scream rose above all, and—for whatever reason—the battle abruptly ceased. In the following silence, there were three splashes in quick succession. Something—or someone—had dropped from the trestle that carried the railroad over the Potomac.

A moment later, their wagon bumped to a halt, throwing Harry and Colton together again. Looking up, Harry saw that they were at the base of the trestle, the track and train high above them. Upon it, illuminated by a hellish, orange glow, he could see two boxcars of the train and a portion of a third. Confederate soldiers were moving alongside the cars, opening the doors. Whatever Union guards had been aboard were not in view.

Their wagon creaked forward again, then stopped.

"Gotta get out," said the private. "They're gonna fill the wagon with somethin' more useful than the likes of you."

"What of us, then?" Harry said, clumsily clambering over the side. He twisted his ankle slightly on landing and cursed the moment he had agreed to any of this.

"That's up to the captain," said the private.

"And where is that gentleman?"

"Dunno. You two stay here until he says otherwise."

The soldier, more boy than man, waited till both of them were on the ground, then vaulted with revolver in hand over the side. Colton looked like he might seize the instant's opportunity to effect his departure, but hastily reconsidered, his eyes darting back and forth. His chance had come and gone. The soldier's pistol was on them once more.

A small flurry of gunfire was heard from across the river, but quickly died away, as the orange glow was doing. The Confederates had obviously staged their ambush by setting off explosives on the trestle just as the locomotive slowed for the crossing, an action calculated to stop the train without damaging it. Then they'd rushed it from the rear and sides, in the manner of train robbers. Men had died there, and Harry guessed they were mostly Union.

A Confederate officer ran by, shouting to the teamsters and soldiery to hurry. A commotion commenced farther up the towpath, where the river and canal diverged sufficiently to allow space for turning the wagons around. The lumpy ground was soft and marshy in places. Much of the commotion involved loud swearing.

Harry looked above. Men were hauling boxes off the cars, opening them, and dumping the contents over the side into one of the wagons.

"They planned this well," he said. "An excellent site for an ambush and also for the unloading."

"I had nothing to do with it," said Colton. He glanced about. The private was watching the wagon maneuvers.

"We could both spare ourselves a lot of trouble now," Colton said, lowering his voice.

The private remained distracted.

"You mean run?" Harry asked.

"Ease into the canal, make our way quiet like along the bank, then move to the other side and skedaddle into the woods. Once we were gone, they'd pay us no mind. This is Union territory. They'll want out of here fast."

"You mean to go back to Washington?"

Colton paused, stepping back slightly to remove himself further from the private's hearing.

"That'd depend on you. If you want the scales balanced some, I'll tell you who Gloucester is."

"That for my silence?"

"This Rebel captain'll likely believe what you say because you're Southern and a Virginian. But your word don't count much in the Federal City. I checked that much out. You could accuse me of pretty much anything, and nobody would do much about it."

"But maybe not."

"Gambler's chance, but I'm willing to help you in return for your making no trouble for me."

"What about the money owed you?"

"I'm an optimist."

"I'd ask more. The promise that you will never, ever—in uniform or not—engage in such commerce again."

"Done," said Colton, his eyes fixed hard now on the Confederate private.

"All right, who's Gloucester."

"Captain Robert Kelleter."

This was a falsehood insulting in its blatancy.

"I believe you misspoke," said Harry. "I believe that is not the correct name."

A large load of shoes came tumbling down into a wagon bed. Colton, ignoring it, reached within his coat and then slowly produced a small revolver. He kept it to his side, but it wouldn't take him but a second to aim and fire.

"Into the canal now, Raines," he said, softly. "We'll sort this out later."

He took a small step to the side, then, as did Harry. Silence fell upon all the men at this place. They turned, wherever they were, listening.

From the east, downriver, came the unmistakable sound of another locomotive, moving fast.

The Confederate captain appeared up on the tracks, bellowing to the men unloading the cars to work faster. Then he waved to other soldiers to follow him and hurried at the double quick toward the oncoming train.

He might better have had them follow him in a jump from the trestle. The approaching engine, its headlamp an eerie golden eye, came careening along full throttle, then at once commenced a screeching, scraping slide along the rails as the engineer tried to slow and stop it. Harry could see flashes of musket fire coming from its roof. When it had slowed sufficiently, dark figures began dropping from the passenger cars hitched behind. It was hard to tell in the dark, but Harry figured there was at least a company of Union soldiers aboard this train—twice as many fighting men as the Rebel commander had with him besides the wagon crews.

Colton made his move. He was there, and then he wasn't. The splash he made going into the canal was barely audible in all the shooting. By the time the Rebel private noticed, the wretch was out of sight—likely moving downriver.

"Where'd he go?" the private asked Harry.

"He was your prisoner, Sir, not mine."

An ill-chosen remark. The private had his revolver now on Harry and seemed prepared to use it, exacting compensation for the trouble he'd be in for letting Colton bolt. Harry supposed he had no choice.

"Is that him?" Harry said, looking to the canal bank just behind the soldier.

The youth looked over his shoulder, turning the handgun in the same movement. Managing more celerity than he'd thought possible what with all the abuse his mortal coil had lately suffered, Harry leapt at the boy, smashing him against the back of the wagon. Gripping the private's arm with both hands, he knocked the bony part against the sharp edge of the wood. The youth cried out as the revolver fell to the ground.

Pushing the boy to the side, Harry snatched up the weapon.

"Run, boy," he said. "Get yourself across the river. You're

outnumbered by these Yankees, and you're going to end up dead or a prisoner if you don't move now."

The private looked about wildly, seeking some last military action available to him in his embarrassing situation. Finding none, he took Harry's advice, breaking into a lunging run for the riverbank.

Harry, making sure the boy wasn't watching, flung himself into the canal and started downstream after Colton. He kept his head low, as bullets were beginning to zing overhead. Even when he was down in the water, a minié ball sang by his ear, hitting the grassy bank with a *thwat* that scattered dirt in his eyes.

He wiped them clear with his hand, hunkering low as the battle swept past him. Soldiers sloshed and swam across the canal ahead of him, clambered onto the towpath and came running toward him—one of them halting to take aim with his musket and fire at the Confederates by the trestle.

The flash from the gun brought bright spots to Harry's vision, making it even harder to see. He rubbed his eyes, then at last pulled his spectacles from his coat pocket. The lenses were wet, and he had nothing dry to wipe them with, but they provided some improvement. After the party of soldiers had run by, Harry started slogging forward again, grabbing at tufts of grass and small bushes along the bank to pull himself along.

This began to seem useless. Colton would be far ahead now. Harry really had only one choice if he was going to catch up to the man.

He looked back to the melee by the trestle, then all around him, then pulled himself up the bank onto the towpath, keeping his purchase there despite the weight of water in his boots and sodden clothes. He rose to his knees, looked about once more, then broke into a slow, painful, loping run, keeping his eyes to the canal bank. Colton might well be lurking in weeds somewhere along it just as Harry had been.

"You there! Stop!" The voice came from behind him.

Harry ignored it. There was no time for that now. A shot cracked the air, the bullet striking the dirt ahead of him. He would have to ignore the man's musket, too.

A trained soldier could get off three shots in a minute. This fellow had not attained that level yet. It was probably half a minute or more before the next round came, and it was even farther off the mark.

He ran hard, huffing and puffing like a railroad engine, realizing suddenly how much noise this was making. Slowing to a shuffling trot, he kept on. There was no more gunfire, at least not directed his way.

In short time, he passed far enough from the shouts and shooting to hear more familiar night sounds again—crickets and frogs and night birds and flitting and skittering creatures to which Harry could give no name. He stopped, taking a few deep breaths, then proceeded at a more merciful walk.

The sliver of moon slid out from behind a cloud. Harry clearly saw the path ahead of him, and that it rose and took a slight turning. There was what looked like a wall across the canal just ahead, which he realized was a canal lock. There'd be a lock tender's house nearby, though he saw no light. The canal company liked to hire family men for these jobs, so they could count on someone always being on hand to perform the duties. Someone would be there, possibly someone who had heard Colton passing and could tell him how long ago the man had gone by.

Harry walked on, trudging up the rise to the next level. There was a small swing bridge across the canal there just behind the lock gates. On the other side of the dark water was a two-story, whitewashed house, a small barn to the side, doubtless housing a spare tow mule or two.

Harry climbed onto the bridge, hesitating in the middle, listening for what his eyes might fail to perceive. Instead of rousting the lock tender, he might do better to steal a mule and proceed with the chase mounted. Little Orleans, with Rocket waiting for him, wasn't quite two miles distant.

The sound was almost imperceptible, almost lost in all the insect hum: a small, metallic click. Harry recognized it instantly as that made by a hammer being cocked.

He dropped to the wooden boards just as the weapon discharged. Yanking his head around, he saw a pale white face below in the shadows by the wooden watergate. Colton stared at him, as though angry at his missed shot, then grabbed hold of the stone wall of the lock behind him. Still holding his weapon, he began to climb. Harry scuttled on to the other side of the canal on all fours, rolling off the end of the bridge into the little yard in front of the whitewashed house. He pulled his derringer out from his sodden coat, bringing it to bear as Colton's head and shoulders rose from the lock.

If he fired at that distance, considering the shortness of the pistol barrel, the darkness, and his poor night vision, he might miss, and Colton would have time to fire before he could reload.

If he stood up and ran away, as he was strongly inclined to do, Colton would have a clear shot at him. If he tried for the lock tender's door, he might find it locked.

Colton was standing now at the other side of the bridge, his arm extended and a small pistol in hand—aimed, it seemed, at Harry's head.

"That your work, Raines? Sending for a troop train?"

"If I were you, Colton, I'd not worry about who's to blame for your situation. Not going to change it any."

Colton took a step closer. His pistol was probably as inaccurate at this range as Harry's. A few more steps and he might manage a killing shot, however.

"If you mean to kill me," Harry said, "would you at least carry a message back to Washington for me."

Colton now took that next step, but did not fire. "A message for whom?"

"A woman."

"Louise Devereux?"

"No. A friend. Another actress. Caitlin Howard."

"Beautiful woman. She the one you're in love with, Raines?"

"Yes."

"Well, I won't do it. You have made a ruin of this night for me, you son of a bitch, and now I'm going to do the same to you."

All this talk indicated a hesitancy, if not reluctance, to commit the murder, though Harry wasn't sure why. There were no witnesses to it. Harry might be considered just another casualty of the skirmish.

"Just this then. Before I perish, tell me who murdered Major Pleasants. You must know. I do believe you know."

"All I'll tell you, Sir, is that you got this comin'."

Harry heard someone running, coming toward them from up the canal. Colton heard it, too. He looked toward the sound, keeping his pistol raised and aimed in Harry's general direction.

Harry could probably fire his derringer now with some effect, but he couldn't bring himself to do it. He wondered how many soldiers at Bull Run had felt this way.

Perhaps there was yet opportunity to resume their clumsy negotiations—to talk themselves at last into an arrangement whereby they could both walk away.

"Colton . . ."

Harry spoke too late. An instant later, there was a shuddering blast of gunfire that came from behind Harry. Smoke rolled before his eyes. When it cleared, Colton had vanished.

In his place, standing just the other side of the canal, was Boston Leahy, dressed as always in black suit and bowler hat.

Yet he carried no weapon.

Harry whirled about. Standing just behind him, a freshly-fired double-barreled shotgun held out straight before him, was a man in a nightshirt and big boots.

"Who are you?" Harry demanded.

"I'm keeper of this lock," said the man. "We have orders to protect the canal from Southern agents."

Harry got to his feet, deciding to put his pistol away. "Well, you just killed yourself a Union officer."

Leahy, removing only his hat, jumped into the canal with a loud splash. He turned this way and that, then plunged beneath the surface. An instant later, both he and Colton emerged, the latter limp. Harry had feared the man might now be headless, but he seemed largely intact. Leahy propped Colton against the wall of the lock and tried shoving him up onto the bank, but the Irishman had no purchase for his feet, and accomplished little.

"Come on," said Harry to the lock keeper, starting back across the swing bridge. "You shot him. You help."

"Jest who the hell are you?"

"Never mind him!" Leahy said. "I'm a Federal detective with the U.S. Secret Service. Get over here!"

With Leahy pushing, Harry and the lock keeper managed to haul what remained of Colton onto the bank, turning him on his belly so whatever water he'd taken in might spill out.

The shotgun had taken off the larger part of the man's shoulder. He was bleeding prodigiously and there wasn't much there to hold his arm.

"He must be dead," Harry said.

"I think he lives," said Leahy, after pulling himself from the water with amazing ease.

Colton was breathing, barely, and with difficulty. Some canal water trickled forth from his mouth, and he sputtered and coughed, then lay still. One eye opened. Harry got back down on his hands and knees, and leaned close, eye to eye.

"We'll get you to a medical officer," Harry said. "I'm sorry. I didn't mean for anything to happen."

The eye, still holding a spark of life, gazed at him. Another dribble of water came forth with a shallow breath.

"Tell me," Harry said. "Please, tell me now. Who killed Major Pleasants?"

More water. Another bit of coughing. Then effort. Then a single word.

"Fool."

"What?" said Harry.

"Died for love."

Harry leaned as close as he could. "What?"

"Love."

His last word.

THEY persuaded the lock keeper to provide them with a spare tow mule from the barn, then carefully put Colton's mangled body over its back and followed the canal back up to the trestle.

Captain Kelleter was in charge of the Federal soldiers who had rushed to the attack on the second train. They were now in full possession of both trains and the river shore on the Maryland end of the crossing. The Confederates had mostly fled, leaving behind about a dozen wounded and three dead. The Union detachment had suffered five wounded and one dead, not counting Colton.

The casualties had been surprisingly light—because of the darkness. Were any of the newspapers to get wind of the little clash, they'd doubtless elevate it to the status of battle, especially as the Union side had prevailed. But that would only stir up more public inquiry into the activities of Major Pleasants and his friends. Kelleter, at least, didn't seem much disposed to permitting that.

"From what Detective Leahy tells me, we're obliged to you, Raines," said Kelleter.

"And I to you, Sir. I am particularly glad you were on that train."

"Why is that?"

"Because then you could not possibly be 'Mr. Gloucester.' My judgment of character is not flawed."

The Union officer pondered this uncertainly, gave Harry a quick, odd look, then turned to go about his business—which was considerable. Both trains had to be backed up and the trestle repaired. The dead and wounded had to be cared for, and the discarded muskets and other weaponry recovered. The shoes that were the central concern of this business were scattered all over the ground and had to be gathered up and re-sorted.

All this by the light of a few torches.

Kelleter picked up one shoe he found caught in a low tree branch. He turned it over, back and forth.

"I suspected there was something amiss," Kelleter said. "We had men in need of new shoes, but Colton refused to issue any. Not a pair. Not a boot or brogan."

"Maybe he was just trying to do your outfit a favor," Harry said.

"What do you mean?"

"Maybe it would have been better for the Union cause to let them pass into the hands of the Confederates."

"What in Hell are you talking about, Raines?" said Leahy.

Harry stepped closer and took the shoe from the captain. He gripped the sole with one hand and the toe with the other.

"Shoddy," said Harry.

With a quick twist, he was able to separate the one from the other.

"Wouldn't last two weeks," he said.

HARRY and Leahy took one of the Confederates' abandoned teams and wagons and set off back down the canal towpath, trailing the mule they'd borrowed and intended now to return. The lock keeper, fearing some penalty for his deed, had gone off into the woods and night. His wife, an agreeable lady, accepted the animal, expressing no little amazement at having it come back.

Reaching Little Orleans again, Harry was himself amazed to find Rocket still tied to the tavern hitching post, though Caesar Augustus' mount was gone, as were Colton's and "Mr. Gloucester's."

According to the tavernkeeper, whom they were required to rouse from deep slumber, there were only three routes the two could have taken—the railroad, the road that led north and east, and the continuing canal towpath, which led to Indigo Neck and a ford crossing into Virginia.

"Your mystery man wouldn't use the rails," Leahy said. "Too many soldiers. They'll be bringing both those trains back down the lines anyway."

"So what are you betting on? The road or the canal path?" Harry asked.

"Let us bet on both," Leahy said. "I'll take the team and wagon up the road, and you follow the towpath. I'll meet you in Hancock."

Harry climbed into Rocket's saddle. This night was turning out to be exceedingly long.

"Hancock it is," he said. "There's a telegraph."

"Don't you be using that again. Lafayette Baker's got the Provost Guard out looking for you, and there's no point giving them directions."

"Perhaps I should just abandon this enterprise now and disappear into the Confederacy as they expect me to."

"Suit yourself, Mr. Raines. It's a free country—or used to be."

Harry looked down the shadowy towpath. As the fracas at the trestle had brought home, anything could be waiting in those woods.

"Hancock," Harry said.

Chapter 2 5

CLOUDS began crowding into the night sky again, obscuring the moon. Upriver, pale lightning limned the horizon in flashes, the thunder making Harry think of war, not weather.

Harry slowed Rocket to a walk, keeping a careful eye to the canal's slippery bank. He'd gone no more than two or three miles when he heard his name called.

"Marse Harry?"

He stopped Rocket with a quick pull on the reins. All about him were bushes, weeds, and darkness. He could discern no human form.

"That you, Caesar Augustus?"

"Why no, Marse Harry. I'se General Pierre Gustave Toutant Beauregard."

Harry dismounted, leading Rocket forward.

"What are you doing here?" he asked, still unsure of his friend's exact location.

"As you can plainly see, if you got them specs on for once, I'm sitting here at the base o' this big oak tree, keepin' this great big Navy Colt revolver you loaned me aimed up at the top."

Harry looked more closely, blinking. So he was.

"Why?"

" 'Cause dat's where he done climb."

"Who is he?"

"Dat man I bin chasin' from de tavern. He's sure nuff a

wily cuss. Almost missed him when he let go his horse and take off up this here tree."

"But did you see who he is?"

"Plain as day, Marse Harry. It's Booth."

"John Wilkes Booth?"

"The actor—as I noticed right off. Thought you had as well."

"You impudent nigger!" came a godlike voice from the tree. "In this state, you could be put to death for what you've done!"

Booth's words carried through the trees as they might from a stage. Harry wondered if the man was always performing. Staring upward, he backed up a few paces. He still couldn't quite make out the man's form, but could see there were no other trees near enough for Booth to leap to and effect an escape.

"You've treed him good, Caesar Augustus. Just like that panther we came upon in Morgan County when we were boys."

"And I been just as careful about him."

Slowly, Harry reached within his coat. He'd failed to retrieve his other Colt revolver in the aftermath of the railroad fight, and was armed only with this mostly useless derringer. He tried to find encouragement in the fact that the night would mask its smallness and that, at the least, it would make an intimidating noise if he was compelled to fire it.

Withdrawing the little weapon from his pocket, he held it pointed aloft, hoping Booth would notice.

"Come down, now, Mr. Booth. We both have guns on you."

"You a Federal detective now, Raines? More treason to Virginia?"

"I've told you what I am. A friend of Caitlin Howard's trying to spare her friend Louise Devereux the scaffold."

"Well, Sir. I wish you well in that enterprise. I would assist you if I could. Now let me go. I can be of no help to you up here."

Harry could see him now. In shifting his weight, Booth had made a long branch sway. He was perhaps halfway up the tree.

"Careful, Booth. You'll fall and break your leg. Then where will you be?"

"You're a scoundrel, Raines. A man without honor."

This was a deep insult to a man from Tidewater, but the colloquy could go on through the rest of the night, and accomplish nothing.

"Is he armed?" Harry whispered.

"If he is, he ain't used anything on me."

"All right," said Harry, loudly enough to be heard by Booth. "We'll smoke him down."

"How, Marse Harry?"

"How do you think? Get some brush and leaves and stack it around the tree trunk. My mother used to smoke worms off her rosebushes this way. Wave a stick of burning pitch under 'em. Down would come the wiggly worms, just like Booth here will. Sometimes, they'd catch fire."

"Raines. You are an abomination," came the reply from above. Not quite the desperation Harry hoped to hear, but getting close to it.

"And if it should fail to work," Harry said, "the fire will provide enough light to shoot him by."

"Raines, you will regret this."

"Not so much as you, Sir."

Harry and Caesar Augustus made a great show of gathering combustibles, though their actual harvest was small—only enough to burn a brief while.

"Strike the match," Harry said.

Caesar Augustus did so. The tiny flame flickered and wavered, then caught and grew and began to dance.

"Raines!"

Harry stepped back again, looking up in the direction of Booth's voice.

"If I come down," the actor said, "do I have your promise not to kill me?"

"Better than that. I promise not to have you arrested by all these Federals roaming the woods hereabouts."

"And why are you so merciful?"

"The briefest answer is this: Caitlin Howard. She would not speak to me again were I to effect your death or incarceration.

You may not trust me, but you must trust my affection for her."

"You'll not have her, Raines. Not ever. She does not love you."

"Very well, Sir. I'll just go ahead with this fire then, until you drop and we find ourselves with a smoked actor—a little wiggly rosebush worm."

"Marse Harry, you gonna make me a happy darky." Caesar Augustus used his boot to stir the burning leaves into brighter flame. "This man been callin' me the most foul names all the time you been gone."

"Wait!" said the actor. "What do you want from me?"

"You come down now, Booth. Then we'll talk."

"Put out the fire."

"Come down lower first."

"Very well. I'm coming."

Caitlin had once told him something about Booth that came to mind now. She'd said his athletics on the stage had their origin in his childhood. Growing up in his father's mansion in Bel Air, Booth had had a balcony outside his bedroom window. Throughout his boyhood, he'd practiced leaping from it to the branch of a huge tree just outside, leaps that now thrilled theater audiences when he did them on a stage.

This recollection came a few seconds too late. Booth of a sudden hurtled down towards him. Harry flung himself backward, but one of the actor's boots caught him square in the shoulder, toppling him into the canal with a great splash.

He struggled to his feet in the water, happy to find it no more than four feet deep. Just as he lifted his head, Booth took a kick at him, but his footing was bad. Twisting his ankle, Booth himself came tumbling into the canal as well. Righting himself, he went at Harry in a fury. Harry would not have thought him so bold.

Moving to the side as Booth lunged at him, Harry felt a blow against his right forearm, one that stung. The wretch had a knife.

Harry grabbed the man by his coat lapels and hurled him back against the bank, then gripped Booth's wrist, keeping the knife back from his face. Booth started flailing at him with his free hand, causing pain. But he remained pinned against the bank long enough for Caesar Augustus to come from behind and whack him against the back of his head with the Navy Colt. He used the butt end. Harry feared he might have killed the actor.

Indeed, Booth almost slid beneath the surface before Harry and Caesar Augustus could catch hold of him. Harry propped him up as best he could when they did.

"I hope you have not killed this man," Harry said, "for then we would both of us be in very bad trouble. He's as famous as President Lincoln."

"I didn't try to."

"Help me get him up onto the towpath before he drowns."

Once sprawled on hard earth, Booth slowly regained his senses. Harry pushed his derringer against Booth's face—the barrel mouth flush against the side of the actor's much admired nose.

"You said you would not harm me," Booth said. "You promised."

"I said I would not kill you and that I would not have you jailed. But, damn all, Booth, I am more than willing to pull this trigger and send your famous appendage sailing off into the woods."

"You would do that—to me?"

Harry pushed the gun a little, causing the beautiful nose to bend to the side.

"I would, Sir. Caitlin would be displeased with me, sure enough, but in time her ardor for you would fade—unless you grew yourself an extremely bushy moustache."

"You are a barbarian."

"I am a man who needs answers and is running out of patience. Now, what exactly is your role in this wicked business? And what was Pleasants'?"

"I have friends in Richmond. That is my only role."

"So do I have friends there, but no one is shoving a pistol into my face—or expecting me to transact in U.S. Army military supplies."

"It was her doing—Louise's. She came to me and said she needed my help making contact with someone in the Confederate government, someone who could accept the receipt of a warehouse full of Yankee shoes."

"Louise did this? Of her own free will?"

"Of course."

Harry pushed the derringer hard enough against Booth's face to cause sharp pain.

"Maybe not freely," Booth said. "Pleasants had some power over her. He asked her to find him someone with friends in the Confederate government. All she could think of was me."

"And you have friends in the Confederate government?"

"I have many friends—in many places. But I shall name none to you."

"Why would she do such a thing? How could he make her do such a thing? Love?"

"Pleasants had some paper of hers—something important. She wouldn't tell me what it was but said it was powerful stuff."

"But if she loved him—and clearly she did—why would he need to do that? This poor woman went all the way out to a bloody battlefield, risking her life, for that man."

Booth managed to squirm his head sufficiently to remove his nose from the line of fire. Harry indulged him in this, at least for the moment.

"I don't know. It was some sort of legal document he either took from her or she gave him for safekeeping."

"If he loved her, he'd have given it back."

"He couldn't. His wife found it. And took it."

"Mrs. Pleasants? How do you know that?"

"Louise told me."

Harry rocked back on his heels, then rose, pulling Booth up to his feet. Caesar Augustus stepped close to the actor from behind, to prevent any more dramatic efforts.

"So in all this squalid business, there was only you, Pleasants, Colton, and Fetridge? With Louise caught up in it innocently?"

"What woman is ever innocent of anything?" Booth smiled, brilliantly, as though speaking some key line in a play.

Harry pushed the man away, causing him to stumble.

"Doesn't this shame you, Sir?" Harry said. "Sneaking

around in the shadows. Trading contraband shoes. Do you style yourself some sort of patriot? There's no honor in this sordid conspiracy."

"You know nothing about it."

"I know enough."

"I have taken no money and will not," Booth said. "My only interest is in serving Southern independence! Yet here you are in the pay of a powerful Union senator, engaging in the sabotage of the Confederate army, while your father and brother stand bravely in the sights of Yankee guns. How could you live with yourself, if word of that got back to your family?"

With a quick step, Harry was onto the actor again, this time grasping the man's shoulders hard.

"I am not your friend, Booth," he said. "But I'll give you this advice. If you want to serve your 'cause,' put on a uniform and do it honorably—like those poor men who were killed up by the railroad bridge, and at Manassas. These plots and conspiracies, these furtive little midnight meetings —there's no glory to any of that. And no good can come of it. Look at tonight's shambles."

"The shambles was your fault."

The fellow was incorrigible. "Tell me who killed that Sergeant Fetridge? Was it you?"

"No!"

"Who then?"

"I cannot say."

"I'm accused," Harry said. "I could hang for it."

"Then you'd best cross the river and get back to your country, Sir, where such deeds are lauded. I cannot help you. As for uniforms, Sir. I see none upon your back."

Harry wearily shook his head. With Caesar Augustus holding the big Colt to Booth's face, they made him remove his expensive English riding boots, then set him hobbling off down the towpath.

It was stony along this stretch. For all his wish to be away, Booth took a few hurried, dainty steps, then stopped.

"What will you do with those boots?" he asked Harry.

"Find an ill-shod soldier," Harry said, climbing into Rocket's saddle, "and make him a present of them."

Chapter 2 6

AT Leahy's urging, they took a military train back to the Federal City, leaving Caesar Augustus to bring in the animals. The Irishman was armed with an official letter, given him by Pinkerton and signed by General McClellan, requesting local officials to give them whatever assistance they might require in their mission. They used it to persuade their engineer to make a stop at Martinsburg for Harry to retrieve the saddle he'd left at Belle Boyd's.

Belle's mother had the tack waiting, but said her daughter had gone on to Washington ahead of him—on an urgent visit to Rose Greenhow.

"Urgent?" Leahy asked, as he and Harry walked back to the railroad a short distance from the Boyd House. "What's that about?"

"She did not say, and I do not consider it my business," Harry said. "Belle is frequently Mrs. Greenhow's guest in Washington."

"So are some powerful dangerous people, Raines."

"That's none of my concern."

But it was. He had set something in motion by passing that information on to his "cousin," by giving the zealous Mrs. Greenhow an opportunity to escape a justly earned fate. Harry seemed to be causing rocks to roll every time he turned around. Neutrality was going to be possible only if he moved to another country. And what nation now was uninterested in the fate of the United States?

"I'll not make a hard matter of it on this trip," Leahy said. "But that Boyd girl's bound for prison herself, if she don't watch it, and you'll not want to be tied to her when it happens."

"It's just a girl's playacting, Mr. Leahy. Nothing to worry overmuch about."

"This is no damned play, and she's no little girl. She's already shot herself a Union soldier."

"Another time, Leahy. Today, we let it pass."

The train rolled on down through the Potomac Valley without further delay or incident, giving both men a chance to sleep. They arrived at the Washington depot with the sun still up.

Pinkerton was there to meet them, along with several soldiers from McClellan's headquarters unit. Just down the platform, with a group of his own bluecoats, was Lafayette Baker.

It was Baker who got to them first. Harry had no more than descended to the platform when two of Baker's soldiers came onto him from either side, reaching for his arms, one of them dangling a set of manacles. Leahy was toting Louise's sidesaddle, and could not immediately intervene.

These soldiers were heavily armed. Harry dared not resist, but he thrust his hands into his coat pockets before the trooper could get the manacles around even one wrist. A few months before, there hadn't been a hundred soldiers in the town. Now they were arresting people as they stepped from trains.

"Unhand that man!" said the doughty little Pinkerton, arriving at last.

"He's a fugitive from Federal custody!" said Baker, turning to face the Scotsman. "He escaped during a prison transfer and started a street brawl that injured three of my men."

"Only three?" said Harry. "In a fight with the Firemen Zouaves?"

One of Baker's guards turned to hit him, but Leahy, reaching Harry's side, interposed, pushing the man off with a broad hand.

Pinkerton strained to gain height among so many quarreling tall men.

"Harrison Raines has performed a valuable service for the United States government, and his presence is required by the commanding general of the Army of the Potomac," the detective proclaimed, brandishing yet more folded paper.

"Raines is an accused murderer and a presumed spy," Baker growled back. "He is a fugitive, and he has been in contact with the enemy!"

"He is in my custody and will remain so!" replied Pinkerton. "My authority is General George B. McClellan, as you will discover to your sorrow, Sir!"

"And my authority, Sir," thundered Baker, leaning into Pinkerton, "is Secretary of War Simon Cameron! As you will discover to your ruination!"

Leahy had moved directly in front of Harry, shifting the saddle on his shoulder to the left, where it offered bulwark against Baker's cohorts. Of a sudden, Harry realized the Irishman was backing into him.

"The way we came, Raines," he hissed. "The way we came."

His meaning came to Harry slowly, and then all at once. The train.

He gave a quick glance to his adversaries, noting that Baker's men were for the moment transfixed by the debate with Pinkerton. With a backward step that almost ended in a stumble, he turned and clambered up the steps to the passenger car behind him.

Someone shouted. He didn't look. He whipped his thoughts as he might a horse. Leahy and the bulky saddle would block the way for seconds only. Baker's men were many. They'd be tearing through the railyards in both directions.

Harry turned left, leaping into the next car and making a great show of charging down the empty aisle. A conductor at the other end looked up, startled.

"There's a Southern agent on the train!" Harry cried. "After him!"

The man looked about. Conductors were armed now, but he reached for no weapon.

Harry ran by. "After him!"

Leaving the conductor to his confusion, Harry reached the next car platform and flew down the steps, reversing his direction and running back along the track. One car farther, and he reached the locomotive tender. A quick look back showed no pursuers—yet. He could hear shouts.

The engine was still quietly chuffing. Climbing onto the coupler and peering over the tender's open top, he saw the engineer lighting a cigar. Hoping it was sufficient distraction, he flung himself over the edge and onto the hard, piled wood. He was amazed that he had new places to hurt.

A s he had hoped, after Baker's crew had made a quick, futile search of the passenger cars on the run, the engineer moved the train out of the station and onto a shunting. The cars were uncoupled and the locomotive driven forward onto a side track and beneath a shed.

Harry waited until dusk, staring up at the holes in the slatted wood above him. He was near the Irish neighborhood of Swampoodle. The Tiber Creek marsh ran along it. He could follow that out to open countryside and make his way north to a friendlier city, there to wait until Pinkerton succeeded in sorting this out.

He raised his head slowly. A brakeman was ambling along the track nearby but proceeding away from him.

There was a locomotive next to his—the name "Baltimore and Ohio" painted brightly on its side. Something of Baker's exclamation stuck in his mind. A single word. He looked at it: "Ohio."

When the brakeman had gone, Harry clambered carefully down to the roadbed, then disappeared into the shadows.

H AD he Caesar Augustus to assist him, Harry might have employed more discretion in accomplishing his next task—using his friend to distract the Quigley cook and maid while Harry ascertained that the master and mistress of the house were absent, and, if that was the case, slipped into the house.

With Leahy at hand, he at least might have been more legal—
the Irishman brandishing his official papers about and intimidating the occupants of the residence to the point where they
offered no interference against Harry's search.

In the present circumstance, the only advantage Harry could
claim was speed. As soon as he saw the back door of the house
open and the cook waddle out across the yard to the privy, he
was up the rear steps and into the kitchen undetected.

Though not for long. The maid emerged from a pantry bearing a deep dish covered by a checkered cloth. The sight of
Harry at this late evening hour caused her such alarm she
dropped her burden with an enormous crash.

A complaining voice called out from within the house. The
maid, still frightened, said nothing, retreating back into the
pantry as though Harry were about to pounce on her.

Instead, he turned and went through the door into the central
hallway, where he found himself face to face with Mrs. Pleasants.

She backed up, then moved sideways into the lighted par-
lour. As Harry recalled, its windows looked directly out onto
the street. The floor-length drapes were pulled wide apart. Any
passerby could look in.

Mrs. Pleasants was in firm control of herself, but indignation
was visibly boiling within her. Her face had gone ashen at first
sight of him; now it was full of color.

"You were not announced, Mr. Raines."

"No, Ma'am. I'm afraid I am calling upon you in some
haste."

"I believe this intrusion could be considered a criminal act,
Sir."

"Lord knows I'm no stranger to such consideration at the
moment," Harry said. "I do apologize for your discomfort. I
need your help. It is in the matter of your late husband."

She stiffened, and retreated still further—closer to the street
windows.

"I have told you, Mr. Raines, that we no longer require your
services in that regard. We consider the matter laid to rest—
as is my husband."

"I understand, but I am still seeking justice for Miss Devereux—and I am very close to it. But there's something I need."

"I do not comprehend how I can be of any possible assistance in that."

She folded her arms, standing her ground now.

"Colton's dead," he said.

Her eyes widened, and stared. "Who?"

"Captain Colton. An officer in your husband's regiment. You don't know of him?"

She looked away. "There's much my husband did not share with me. I know little of his military life."

"Colton was a supply officer. He was killed last night in a skirmish up in the mountains."

The incongruity of a quartermaster falling in battle did not remark itself to her.

"I am sorry," she said. "So many die. Was he a friend?"

"Of your husband's. But I'm here regarding another matter. Mrs. Pleasants, did the major give you—or did you take from him—a legal paper of some kind?"

"Of course not. I am his wife. I've no involvement with his legal affairs."

"I was informed by a friend of your husband's that you had such a paper."

"This Captain Colton?"

"No, Ma'am. Someone very much alive. Someone well known to me. He spoke with great certitude."

She turned away, toward the windows. "There was something."

This surprised Harry. He expected her to deny going through her husband's pockets. She was such a proper woman.

"My husband's behavior had begun to worry me," she said, continuing. "Especially his gambling. Examining his possessions was my only means of assessing our true situation—short of hiring someone like you."

"You were aware of his debts?"

She wiped away a tear. "Of course." She turned. Both eyes were moist. "This paper had nothing to do with that. I don't know what it means."

"Do you still have it?"

"No."

"You destroyed it?"

"I gave it to my father, Mr. Raines. He is my counsel in legal matters."

"Where is he?"

She shrugged. "He is an important man, with important official business. You cannot expect a woman to be privy to these matters. I know only that he was to dine with Secretary Seward and Secretary Cameron this evening, and meet with others in the government afterward."

"You don't know where?"

"Someone's house. Possibly the Rathbones."

Harry looked at his pocket watch, holding it close. He suspected the senator might just now be lighting an after-dinner cigar.

The man's study was just across the hall.

Celerity was his only friend this night. He abruptly turned and strode from the room. The gas was turned off in the study, but there was light enough from the hall for what Harry intended.

Mrs. Pleasants followed him. "What are you doing?"

"Is it in this desk he keeps his strongbox?"

"Mr. Raines!"

He went to the hearth and took up a poker. Returning to the desk, he jammed it in the crevice above the center drawer, then pushed it hard. The rod slipped free, striking him in the thigh of a leg already bruised.

"Mr. Raines, if you persist, then I will have no choice but to summon police."

"That's certainly what I would do were I in your place, Ma'am."

She gave him a sharp but inquiring glance, then gathered up her skirts and whisked away. As he went at the drawer again, he heard the front door slam shut.

A second, more directed shove did the trick. The locked drawer came free with a splintering of wood, an action that freed all the other drawers in the desk. He commenced to look through the various papers he found in the upper space, then realized that, if the legal paper had any great import, it would be in his strongbox. The senator had to have a strongbox. As Harry had seen, he kept sizable amounts of money in the house.

It was in the double-deep bottom drawer. Harry lifted it to the top of the desk, then pulled out his derringer and held the barrel no more than two inches away from the box's lock, hoping this would not blow off a hand or fingers.

He pulled the trigger and a sharp, concussive report barked forth, echoing through the house. Through the gunsmoke, he saw that the lid of the box had lifted.

Harry of course left all the money the box contained, guessing there must be a thousand dollars or more in there. He found the legal paper he sought in a small, tied bundle of deeds, stock certificates, and lawyers' letters. Reading it over twice, he frowned, then shoved it into his pocket.

If haste was his only advantage, he was losing it. He fled the house into the night—fugitive murder suspect and now, thief.

MRS. Fitzgerald was used to late night departures from Caitlin's quarters, but not late night arrivals. She seemed to take hours to respond to Harry's urgent rapping. He was preparing to kick the door in, if he could manage that, when she finally opened it—all of an inch. He could barely make out her face.

"What in creation do you want with this house at this witching hour of the night, Mr. Raines?"

It seemed a safe guess that she had not heard of the various criminal acts of which he'd been accused.

"I am on important and discreet business, Mrs. Fitzgerald. If you do not admit me, I shall be forced to summon Detective Leahy of the U.S. Secret Service and let him have his way with your door."

She hesitated only a moment, then swung it open enough to admit him, but only just.

"I'm letting you in only because I don't want you lagging about out there, ruining my reputation."

He stepped aside as she pushed the door closed. She had a candle, but there were no other lights visible on that floor.

"I'm sorry, Ma'am."

"Miss Howard is ill. She has taken to her bed."

"That is unfortunate, but I will not disturb her for long."

The landlady shook her head, then turned to lead him up the stairs.

"Were it not for this war, I should not be allowing you in my house, Mr. Raines."

The logic of that failed him, but he made no comment. She refused to allow Harry to rap on Caitlin's door, claiming it would disturb her other boarders. She opened the door herself, pushing it ajar and stepping aside to let him pass, watching him as though he were some cutthroat with a Bowie knife.

There was a heavy scent of flowers in the sitting room. It grew stronger as he moved through the darkness toward the bedroom.

"Caitlin?"

Mrs. Fitzgerald was lingering in the hall behind him, listening.

He stepped into the bedchamber, gently closing that door behind him.

"Caitlin?" This he whispered.

He could hear her breathing. It was troubled, and there was movement. For a moment he wondered if she was with someone.

Harry moved closer. It was an unusually early hour for Caitlin to have retired. Even when not working in a play she would often stay up until dawn. Perhaps she was truly ill, and he should put aside his errand and send Mrs. Fitzgerald for a doctor. But if she were that sick, the landlady would have done that hours ago.

His eyes were adjusting to the dim light. Caitlin was alone and asleep. As he gazed down at her long body, she abruptly rolled over onto her other side, flinging an arm over her head and groaning.

It was not from pain, but from some dream, some disturbing nocturne. Barely had she settled in her new position when she changed it, rolling onto her back.

He could see quite well now, taking note of the abundance of hair spread out on the pillow, and of the unmistakable fact that beneath the thin coverlet she wore no clothing.

Reminding himself of his purpose, he pulled the covers up over her shoulders and then went to the gaslight and lit it, keeping the flame in the glass globe low, so that there'd be only enough light for her to see it was he, and not some dangerous intruder.

The powerful odor of flowers had a source. She had knocked over an open vessel of perfume, and it had run all over the top of her dresser. Two bottles on her night table were still standing upright, one of them looking to be containing gin. The other, of dark brown glass, he recognized as something even more lamentable.

"God have mercy," he said.

She had looked as though a shout would not have stirred her, but at these few words her eyes shot open. They seemed glassy, and when she spoke, her voice was frail. But she was alert, aware of her surroundings, and the nature of her company.

"Harry. You are dead. Or in prison."

Perhaps she was not lucid. He sat on the edge of the bed, keeping a discreet distance from her leg.

"No, Caitlin. I am neither."

"They've told me both. Something about a battle. Something about murders."

He took her hand. The flesh was moist. She was bathed in perspiration.

"I am well, Kate. All is well with me. But you . . ."

"I have been grieving." She closed her eyes. "Soldiers are looking for you."

"Not here."

"Yes here. Everywhere. Poor Harry. Poor me."

"Why poor you? What's wrong, Kate?"

"He loves her."

"Who?"

Caitlin fell silent, as though returned to her sleep. But then she moved her head back and forth, and spoke a single word: "Wilkes."

He rose from the bed and went to the window, turning from her to hide his rage. A troop of cavalry was trotting down the street—an odd sight at this hour, but perhaps now to become a familiar one.

"Kate, if Booth were arrested, or should be harmed . . ."

He heard her sit up. "No! It hasn't happened! Tell me so! Please!"

"It hasn't happened. His health and liberty are intact. But I . . ."

She had pulled the sheet up close around her. Her eyes were fixed on the opposite wall, as though at something far more distant.

"He spurns me, Harry. He loves her."

"Loves who?"

"Do nothing to harm him, Harry. Not for any reason. He's an artist, an actor. He does foolish things, but we must forgive him."

"Men died because of him, Kate. He didn't mean for them to, but . . ."

"I will hear no more of this! Not another word!"

"Very well."

"Did you come here to torment me?"

"No."

Harry turned up the gaslight full, then carefully took the folded paper from his pocket.

"Are you in danger?" she asked, as he returned to the edge of the bed.

"No, Madam. I am in danger only of being sorely inconvenienced before I finish my task."

"Your task." Her attention turned to the bottles on the night table. "Forgive me, Harry. I am in need of refreshment."

"You promised me, Caitlin. You said never again."

"Never again." Her voice became childlike. "But now, please, a small glass."

He sighed and rose. "Which bottle? The large, or the small."

"Both."

He performed the ministration, as might a doctor in distress. A very bad doctor. He felt sick with himself, as sick as she looked. But if he refused her, he could imagine the hysterical result.

"I am grateful to you, Mr. Raines."

The potion seemed to calm and relieve her. He waited until she was entirely done, then unfolded the paper he had pulled from his pocket and handed it to her.

"Have you seen this before?"

Her startled response to it answered his question "How did you come by this?"

"Major Pleasants in some way got it from her," he said. "His family had it, and now I do."

"This is dangerous, Harry."

"So I would suspect. But what is the meaning of it? Who is the woman named?"

"She did not tell you?"

"I've not had the chance yet to ask her. If I go near the Old Capitol Prison now I shall find myself an inmate again."

"I swore to her I would tell no one."

"I'm trying to help her."

"No you're not. You're after her. If I could with honor assist you, I would. She has destroyed me, destroyed my life. But what you ask I could never do."

"How has Louise destroyed you?"

"He loves her, Harry! He writes to her. Goes off with her. He has visited her in prison."

"Who? Wilkes?"

She began to cry. He waited for this to subside.

"Kate. That damned Pleasants knew what this paper means. Why can't I?"

She took a deep draught of the potion she had mixed from the two bottles, the glass having the color of molasses. Her eyes now had an odd cast to them. It was as though she could see through the yellowed legal paper, and the wall beyond, and was contemplating something far distant.

Something of great consequence.

"It is her mother," she said.

Chapter 2 7

HARRY left just at the first faint light of dawn, slipping out the back door of Mrs. Fitzgerald's and flitting across the yard into the alley. Dogs behind back fences hectored him as he passed, prodding him to move faster, so he'd pass by before anyone would awaken.

The day promised more heat. He desperately needed and wanted a bath. He hadn't eaten in nearly twenty-four hours. And he dared not go home. Baker would have someone waiting for him there.

But he had much to do yet to play out this hand.

If only he hadn't such a weight of sadness to carry in his heart. Caitlin Howard had been in his dreams almost since the day he'd first seen her. He feared now she'd be in his nightmares. The mixture of laudanum and gin was potent, and Caitlin had of a sudden fallen back asleep, as though struck by a blow. Dozing fitfully, Harry had spent the remainder of the night in an overstuffed chair across the room from her bed, listening to her thrashings and groans and mutters. She called out Booth's name from time to time and also Louise's. Never his.

When he could bear no more of her in this state, when he had the excuse of the coming day, he had left.

Despite the early hour, there was military traffic on the Avenue, including some trotting cavalry and a line of freight wagons, notable for its lack of decent draft animals. Were Harry to devote himself full-time to providing good horses for the army, instead of wandering off on these distracting adventures, he might become a wealthy man—and do so honestly.

Small opportunity he'd left himself for that.

He waited until the wagons and cavalrymen had passed, then hurried up the Avenue, staying close to the building fronts, turning finally up Seventh Street and stopping at the building occupied on the second floor by Matthew Brady's studio.

The street door was unlocked. The one upstairs to Brady's studio was locked very thoroughly, resisting all attempts to poke its mechanism open with his narrow-bladed sheath knife. He would have to wait.

Harry went to the next flight of stairs and lowered himself onto one painfully. Leaning against the wall, despite the small comfort, he went immediately to sleep.

SOMEONE was shaking him. He opened his eyes to a blur that became Brady's ever curious, bespectacled, anxious face.

"Raines? Are you all right?"

Harry straightened, a spasm of pain running from his neck and shoulder all the way down his back as he did so. He winced and rubbed his eyes.

"Good morning, Mr. Brady. Or is it afternoon?"

"It's not yet six. Good God, man, you look two frights. What has happened to you? Were you in another battle?"

"A small skirmish, way up the Potomac."

"What luck for you. No battles here. McClellan keeps drilling the army. I think he will wear out their shoes before they fire a bullet." Brady seemed apprehensive.

"Is something amiss?"

"Raines, they're looking for you. We had members of the Provost Guard come through the bar of the National twice last night. That reporter Russell says there's an order out to shoot you on sight."

"Surely an exaggeration. You know the press."

"Russell's a pessimist, but not an exaggerator."

Pessimist indeed. He'd written a piece for the *Times* observing that people who'd been present for the creation of the American Union would be alive at its dissolution.

"Don't worry, Mr. Brady. And have no fear I've involved you in some criminal activity. But I need something from you, urgently. May I see those glass plates Gardner returned with from Bull Run?"

"They're not good pictures. Why on earth do you want them?"

"Not *them,* Mr. Brady. Just one. And I'm not concerned with its aesthetics; only its subject."

Brady had forgotten where they'd been put and went on a bit of a rummage for them, finding them finally under a cloth, stacked against the wall.

The picture was as Harry had remembered—actually clearer, when one held it close to the eye.

"Brady, I must have this."

"They're Gardner's. He'll be along a bit later this morning. But there shouldn't be a problem. Didn't he offer them to you in the first place? Or was that for sale?"

"I don't remember. Whatever the case, I'll accept his offer. A good day to you, Sir."

"What shall I tell Gardner?"

"Tell him I shall return it, that I am obliged to him, and that he is about to make a significant contribution to the pursuit of justice. I think. Art and science in the pursuit of justice. Yes. Just so."

"Raines, it's you that justice is pursuing."

SOLDIERY was everywhere about the city now, but none Harry figured to be Provost Guard. Waiting as a drover moved a small herd of cattle toward 6th, Harry darted into the cloud of dust that it raised and made his way to the other side of the Avenue, taking a route through Marble Alley to the back door of the Palace of Fortune.

The bartender informed him that his winnings from the night of Sergeant Fetridge's murder had been substantial. They'd also been put in the proprietor's safe, and that gentleman would be absent until the afternoon. Harry accepted instead a bit of breakfast—hard biscuits, pickled herring, and a boiled egg—from the previous day's free lunch, washed down with a quick whiskey and a cup of coffee.

Finishing it all with great celerity, he excused himself to use the sinks in back, taking Gardner's daguerreotype with him. Returning, he stopped cold in the doorway. Two soldiers wearing the Provost Guard armband were at the bar, talking to the bartender. One of them noticed Harry before he could retreat.

But retreat he did, dashing for the kitchen and smashing through a window that led to the alley. Lunging along to the canal, he turned west and ran past the fish wharves, looking back to see both soldiers hot after him. They wouldn't dare shoot. There were fishmongers and others up and about the street. But they wouldn't relent. They had doubtless slept and eaten. This was a race he was bound to lose.

Turning back toward the Avenue again at 12th Street, he made a quick switch to the diagonal of Ohio Avenue, darting behind some carts and heading up 13th. At C Street, he recognized a doorway—Mollie Turner's whorehouse. At this hour, it would offer possibilities.

For whatever reason, the rear door was again unlocked. He flung it open, shouting oaths loudly. He had reloaded his little pistol and discharged it now for effect, which was immediate and chaotic. There were screams. Women, some naked, some in nightdress, appeared in the hall and on the stairs. One of them was the beautiful blonde Ella, wearing a green dressing gown. She stared at him—eyes hard.

He swept off his hat to her and proceeded out the front door, closing it quietly. Then he sprinted as fast as he could manage around the corner to the alley entrance, just in time to see the two soldiers enter Mollie Turner's through the back. There were more screams. Shouts and oaths followed.

Harry figured he'd bought himself at least five minutes. Moving on through a penny arcade and emerging once again on the Avenue, he slowed to catch his breath, heading west again, past the seedy Globe Hotel and Naylor's Livery.

Ahead, up 15th Street, its neoclassical columns looming over all, was the Treasury, its basement the lair of the dreadful

Baker. It would be a close run thing, but then, they'd certainly not be expecting him.

Head down, slowing now to a walk to appear less suspicious, clutching Gardner's image to his chest beneath his coat, he trudged on up the street and rounded the corner.

There, standing just outside the basement door, smoking a cigar and talking to a uniformed aide, was the all-mighty Baker. He stared at Harry as though at an apparition, then began sputtering.

With no choice now, Harry began to run again, all but flinging himself along Pennsylvania Avenue and the iron fence bordering the President's Park. There was shouting behind him and then gunshots—two quick ones and a third—all high, perhaps meant as warning.

He didn't heed them, but was startled so his balance went off. His ankle buckled and he lurched and then stumbled to the ground, dropping Gardner's daguerreotype. Hearing running footsteps behind him, he snatched up the plate and struggled to his feet.

There was the open gate and the circular fountain just beyond. Behind it, the majestic facade of the President's House. His pursuers were giving him no choice, but that didn't matter. This was his intended destination.

Chapter 2 8

"THE President is not here, Mr. Raines," said Lincoln's other secretary, John Hay. "And you haven't an appointment. And you shouldn't be up here. How did you get by the soldiers?"

"I was persistent. And told them I have something of importance for the President. Which I do."

"The President has gone to the hospital to visit wounded soldiers, and afterwards he is calling upon General McClellan. I believe he will not be back until noon, and then he has many, many appointments. Your visit comes at an awkward time."

"This is about the death of Major George Pleasants."

"The President has talked about the matter—and mentioned you. That's why I've allowed you to remain here as long as you have. But I can do nothing until he returns."

"As long as I can wait here for him, nothing will suit me fine."

He spoke too soon. They were in Hay's small office on the second floor of the President's House. Behind Harry, in the anteroom, there was some kind of commotion. Harry could guess its source.

"There you are!" Lafayette Baker stepped into the doorway like some conqueror breaching an enemy's fortress wall. "This man's a fugitive, Hay. He's coming with me."

Hay raised his hand palm outward to stay the intended action as though with magical powers—which as the President's chief assistant, he more or less had.

"I don't know what your official capacity is, Mr. Baker, or even if you have any. But this man is here because the President wishes it. Whatever business you have with him will have to wait."

Baker's face darkened. "Don't interfere in this, Hay."

"I am acting in accordance with the wishes of the President of the United States. If you want to act contrary to them, I can't stop you, but I can report the full particulars to Mr. Lincoln. I suggest you go back to the Treasury. And take those armed men with you. This is unseemly."

With sputterings and mutters and a vow to wait outside until Harry could be put in manacles, Baker left.

"If you will wait now in the anteroom, Mr. Raines. With the others."

"I need to have Pinkerton here for this, and his man Leahy."

Hay eyed him speculatively. "I know Mr. Lincoln wants this matter resolved. He has complained that it lingers on like some malady. But are you prepared to do that? Or is this just more bother without result—like the war?"

"I think I am."

"I hope so. The President is burdened enough."

LINCOLN'S arrival was announced by the shouting of small boys. One slightly larger and older than the other, perhaps ten or eleven, clung to the President's hand, looking at the men waiting in the upstairs lobby a little shyly. The other, riding on his father's shoulders, gave a whoop as the towering man bent nearly double to get through the doorway with his burden. The President wore black trousers, a rumpled white linen jacket and ill-arranged black tie. He'd left his tall hat downstairs, unless the child had knocked it off somewhere outside.

"Gentlemen," he said.

He lowered the smallest boy to the carpet, then glanced about at the occupants of the anteroom as the child commenced to run around him in circles.

His eyes settled finally on Harry.

"Hello, Raines. You look as though you have been long on the road."

"Yes, Sir, I have." Harry, angry with himself for not having done so, got to his feet.

"You here in connection with the telegraph we got yesterday from western Virginia? Something about shoes?"

"Yes, Sir. And the Pleasants matter."

The smallest boy, whom Harry remembered was called Tad, gave a particularly loud whoop and then charged out of the room, his hollers echoing behind him. The President smiled.

"You've gotten somewhere with it?"

"That's why I'm here, Mr. President."

Lincoln turned to the others in the room, all now standing.

"My apologies, gentlemen. I must see this man first. I'll be with you by and by."

There was grumbling at this. One man, in checked pants, blue coat, and yellow waistcoat, lurched forward as though to reach for Lincoln's arm. He began talking about his brother's need for a postmaster's job in Indiana. Hay, who'd been standing in the doorway, hastily interceded.

More commotion, this time out in the hall. A moment later, Pinkerton and Leahy entered, the former carrying a pair of shoes, the latter hefting Louise Devereux's saddle. It was as Harry had asked.

"Evidence, Mr. Lincoln," said Pinkerton.

Lincoln's grin was slight, but genuine. "I hope you have not also brought the horse that goes with it."

EXCEPT for the additional markers indicating the increased troop strength in the capital, the map sitting on the President's easel looked exactly the same as before. Harry supposed it must depress him.

Lincoln settled into a rocking chair, as might a large, ungainly bird into a small nest. The older of the two boys, Willie, had remained with his father, and now leaned against the arm of the rocker, still saying nothing.

Leahy placed Louise's expensive riding saddle gently on the marble-topped round table in the midst of the group. Stepping back, he reached within his coat and withdrew the revolver they had found in Louise's room, setting it down as carefully and making certain the barrel pointed at no one. Pinkerton set the shoes beside it.

"Glad to see you well, Raines," Leahy said gruffly, taking an awkward seat on a small, upright chair.

Pinkerton remained standing. "I have news," he said. "There may be no need to proceed with this business, Mr. President. Major Pleasants' family has had his body exhumed from the grave. They say it has no face."

All eyes turned to the President, who summoned forth Hay.

"I think it might be a good idea for Willie and Tad to pay a visit to the kitchen and see what the pastry chef is working up today. He'd probably appreciate some help tasting things."

Willie moved obediently off with Hay.

"It's true, Sir," Harry said. "The Confederates out there at Manassas left the Union dead till last, and some pigs got at them. Ate the faces off of several. But the blond hair was still there, and the body was in the major's uniform. It was him, Sir. I haven't the slightest doubt."

"That may be, Raines," Pinkerton said. "But you never showed the widow the remains. Senator Quigley has asked that Pleasants be officially listed on the casualty rolls as missing. I understand Secretary Cameron has agreed to it. With no Major Pleasants, we have no murder of Major Pleasants. No grounds for a legal proceeding. Case closed, probably."

"Then Louise Devereux can go free!" Harry said.

"No," pronounced Pinkerton. "There are other charges pending against that woman."

"All of them spurious," said Harry.

The President coughed, for emphasis. He was staring intently at Louise's saddle. He noticed the scar and bullet hole near the pommel.

"I think we should go ahead," he said, finally. "If only to alleviate some curiosity. Now, I have never been a judge but I have read the law and practiced it for a year or two, as you may know. I've read through the various Army manuals. This is a military matter, in most respects. So, as commander-in-chief, I'll preside over this inquiry. But for now it's an unofficial inquiry, agreed?"

All assented.

"I'll hear from Mr. Raines first," Lincoln said. "And I'd be grateful if it was without interruption."

"Yes, Sir," said Harry. "I'll tell you what I know for fact, as well as what I believe to be true. First, I'd like to show you something that I think will settle the question of whether Louise Devereux is a Southern agent. But, Mr. President, I'd appreciate it if we could treat this with the utmost discretion."

Harry took the carefully folded paper from the pocket of his coat and brought it to Lincoln as though it were some fragile relic. He could sense the stares of the others in the room, but kept his back to them.

"I know what this is," said Lincoln, softly. "I have seen far too many of them. But I fail to ken the bearing."

"That's her mother, Sir. Louise is a Southern lady—New Orleans born. But she could not possibly be a Southern agent, as you can plainly see."

Lincoln returned the paper to him, folding it first. "I will accept that, Mr. Raines. These few printed words are most eloquent on the question."

The door opened without prior announcement and Lincoln's other secretary, John Nicolay, entered, bringing Lincoln a note. The President glanced at it, read it once more, then set it down.

"Mr. Cameron, the secretary of war, has Senator Quigley and his daughter in his office over at the War Department. They've heard of your presence here, Mr. Raines, and have raised a complaint about it. They are sure Major Pleasants is a Confederate prisoner of war and fear you're only going to do his reputation and their happiness more injury."

"That is not my intent, Mr. Lincoln."

"But it could be the result. My respects to the secretary of war, Mr. Nicolay. Tell him we shall all join him directly."

The secretary gave a quick nod of the head, then vanished from the room.

"We go there?" Pinkerton asked.

"I'll not have that poor widow inconvenienced further. Besides, I want to check on the wires from Virginia when this is done. There is a Colonel Beals with them. Who is he?"

"The major's immediate superior, Mr. President," Pinkerton interjected. "Not one of our most competent officers."

"It seems he swears he saw Pleasants carried off by the enemy. Alive."

"Then he swears a lie," Harry said. "It's a different tale from his previous swearings."

"Your confidence is encouraging," said Lincoln. "Let's join the others."

THEY made an odd procession along the path across the grounds of the President's House to the gray brick War Department building at Pennsylvania and 17th Street. Pinkerton led the way, carrying the pair of shoes they'd brought back from Little Orleans. Leahy followed, hefting Louise's saddle on his shoulder. Lincoln was next, tall hat in place, hands together behind his back. Hay and Harry brought up the rear, along with a soldier bearing a loaded musket.

Lafayette Baker and a squad of soldiers were waiting at the street, but Lincoln simply ignored them.

"Mr. Hay says you are under a charge of murder, Raines," said Lincoln, quietly, as they passed into a grove of trees.

"It's that Fetridge business," said Pinkerton. "That sergeant killed down by the canal."

The great gray eyes had some humor in them. "How plead you?"

"Plead? Sir, I've killed no one. Not once in my life. I was nearly killed myself that same night. Possibly by the same person who murdered him."

"I recall now someone saying you'd been injured."

"Your Provost Guard seems to have an inexhaustible supply of charges," Harry said, "which they proffer as they see fit."

The President's eyes fell to the gravel. "I'm reminded of a client I once had. He was brought up on what must have been a dozen charges. Every time the judge asked him how he pleaded, he replied, 'I stands mute.' "

Pinkerton laughed at this. Leahy remained as dour as before.

"He complained to the judge about the prosecutor's competence, and my competence, and the judge's competence," Lincoln continued. "Finally the judge told him that after the trial he could appeal to the Court of Errors. He replied, 'Show me a court that ain't a Court of Errors.'"

The President let fly a loud, startling guffaw, followed by a trail of high-pitched chuckles, though he'd doubtless told this story dozens of times.

"Mr. Raines," the President said. "You may stand mute on this question of murdering a sergeant. I remember now that we received a letter from a Miss Clara Barton—one of the volunteers at the hospital. She asked my intercession in your case, having attended you with the doctor when you were brought into Mr. Baker's little jail. She says you were in no condition to have held a pistol, let alone to have fired one with any hope of hitting a mark. I am told she is an honest and fair-minded woman. There will be no charges brought against you. You have my word on it. As for Sergeant Fetridge, how many of our poor soldiers have been killed in that neighborhood?"

"A dozen at least, Sir," said Pinkerton. "Cutthroats. Brawls. That section resists policing."

"So there you are," said the President. "But on the matter of Major Pleasants, do not stand mute. Have your say. I'll not let them intimidate you."

MRS. Pleasants was seated on a curved-back wooden chair in the anteroom of the War Department. Her eyes were moist and reddened. Harry felt a pang of guilt for having to continue heaping miseries upon her.

She looked with some curiosity at Pinkerton, who was carrying the pair of shoes from Little Orleans, and with outright astonishment at Leahy and the saddle. At the sight of Lincoln, she thrust herself to her feet.

"Mr. President, I . . ."

"Please stay seated, Madam," he said. "There's no ceremony here." He halted and took her hand in both of his. "Your father is inside?"

She nodded, on the verge of tears again.

Lincoln patted her hand. "This will not take long. And then you can rest easier. It will all be laid to rest."

She was about to seat herself once more when her eyes caught Harry's. He bowed.

"Mrs. Pleasants."

"Mr. Raines." The two words came as chips of ice.

CAMERON seemed disturbed to have so large a party in his office, but tried to conceal his displeasure. Not so Colonel Beals. He leapt up as though in a fit of apoplexy.

"Mr. President, that man is a murderer! You must have him arrested!"

"We're not here to arrest anyone," Lincoln said, settling into a large armchair to the side of Cameron's desk. "We're here to hear what Mr. Raines has to say. Then we'll hear whatever anyone else has to say." He paused, nodding at the center of the desk. "Set the saddle and shoes and all down there—where all can see."

Harry went to the saddle, running a finger along the gash in the leather and sticking it into the hole in the pommel. He waited until he had everyone's attention.

"This is Louise Devereux' saddle, gentlemen—what she rode out to Bull Run on. We fetched it back from Martinsburg, where some Rebel cavalry had left it after taking her horse." Harry reached into a side pocket of his coat, pulling forth the two spent, misshapen pistol rounds he'd been carrying. "This hole was made by this bullet. We dug it out from the saddle. It's the mate of the bullet taken from the body of Major Pleasants." He gave them to Lincoln. "They were both fired by this pistol. Small of caliber but long barreled and accurate."

Lincoln took the revolver, again with some delicacy, but then hefted it as might a practiced marksman and aimed it at the window to his right. Harry had heard that the President had taken to test-firing some of the Army's firearms in the woods behind the presidential mansion, but had discounted the talk as tavern rumor. Perhaps there was something to it.

The man had grown up on the frontier, and had been a captain of volunteers in the Blackhawk Indian War.

"How did you come by this pistol?" Lincoln asked.

"The newspapers got one thing right," said Pinkerton. "Leahy and Raines found that weapon in Louise Devereux' room."

"It was in her dressing gown, Mr. President," said Leahy. "In a pocket."

"Where I've no doubt another party put it," said Harry. "Easy to find, but not in a place where a lady would keep it. Not that a lady would want a firearm that big." He let that sink in. "Miss Devereux was aboard that saddle when the bullet struck, Mr. President. She did not shoot herself. She could not have. Doctor Phineas Gregg—he's a colonel in the medical corps and a surgeon at the hospital in Georgetown—he examined Pleasants' remains. The body had two wounds. There was a bullet still in one, but the other round passed clean through. There is this hole in the saddle. When we found the pistol, three rounds had been fired."

"But Major Pleasants is not dead," said Beals. "He was taken prisoner. I saw the Rebels swarm around him. Saw him throw down his sword!"

"The body in the grave had no face," Senator Quigley said, with great solemnity. "It could have been any man."

For the first time, Lincoln showed his irritation.

"I want no one to interrupt Mr. Raines until he has said his piece," said the President. "If you like, Senator, we'll refer to the victim as a major of infantry with blond hair who had Major Pleasants' height and frame and was attempting to rally Major Pleasants' troops when he was shot down near where Major Pleasants was last seen."

"This is very irregular," said Cameron. Harry saw him steal a glance at one of the shoes on his desk.

"It surely is," said the President, "which is why I want to hear the rest of Mr. Raines' remarks. Continue, Sir."

"Thank you," Harry said, trying to imagine how Lincoln the lawyer might have made this presentation. "It's true that Miss Devereux quarreled with the major the night before the battle. In fact, I was witness to part of their disagreement. But it struck me as a lover's quarrel. I mean no disrespect, Senator, but they were lovers. That is a fact. She went to the battlefield that day, not for the fun of watching men kill each other, but to see him at least one last time, if that's what the gods of war decreed. In a dramatic sense, to rewrite the ending of their romance on a less ignoble note. Otherwise, the last chapter of their story would have been a drunken night in a room rented in a bawdy house, punctuated by an unhappy quarrel. No, gentlemen. Miss Devereux is innocent of murder."

Senator Quigley looked a ghost.

"You've persuaded me," said Lincoln. "Press on now, Raines. Right on through the middle to the end."

"Who else at Bull Run might have killed the Major?" Harry continued. "Who had the opportunity and the desire? You'd say several thousand Confederates, to be sure. But when the Rebel counterattack succeeded, and the Union troops were scrambling up the Manassas-Sudley Road in retreat, the Rebels paused and reformed along the Warrenton Pike. It was several minutes—many minutes—before they advanced again. I was there."

"But I tell you . . ." began Beals.

"Were I you, Colonel," said Lincoln, "I would not employ the words 'butt' and 'I' too close together." He smiled, trying to seem amiable in the remark.

Lincoln's broad if telling jest brought silence. Harry recalled that this dignified, kindly, grandfatherly man had for years been a circuit-riding lawyer, making the ribald rounds of country taverns for weeks on end. He probably knew a bawdy backwoods tale or two.

"There were at least three civilian carriages on that slope," Harry continued. "One carried me and a friend—Miss Caitlin Howard, the actress. We certainly bore the major no malice. He had in fact the night before done me a service by writing me a pass so that Miss Howard and I might attend the Bull Run encounter."

Harry turned now to Senator Quigley.

"Your carriage was also there, Sir. You told me you were not on the field of battle and saw none of the fighting. Your daughter had bravely gone to Bull Run to be near him in his hour of crisis, however. She knew his faults, but he had promised her he would redeem himself in her eyes. And he met that promise. He had left her carriage, having seen to her safety, shortly before he fell."

Now Quigley looked to Lincoln. The senator seemed to have regained his customary repose.

"The third carriage was that of Congressman Fowler of Indiana," Harry said. "As the senator's aware, the congressman and the major were not friends. There was the matter of an indiscretion two or three years ago between the major and Congressman Fowler's wife. The congressman had threatened to kill the major afterwards, and might have done so had Senator Quigley not personally intervened."

Quigley nodded, sadly.

"But the congressman had his wife and her sisters with him in that carriage. I doubt he would have chosen that moment to settle an old grudge. And this was not a closed carriage, like Senator Quigley's. He was in an open barouche. He'd have run the risk of many witnesses."

Harry looked to Cameron. "Mr. Secretary, you had a clerk and several other agents out there in Virginia?"

"I did."

"To what purpose?"

"Observers. They had orders to telegraph the outcome of the battle as soon as it could be apprehended."

"So that you could inform the President before anyone else. A couple of those agents are rough men, are they not? Mining company detectives from your home state of Pennsylvania? Men who've killed before?"

"Bull Run made a lot of men killers, Sir. We don't think the less of them."

"Did one of your men kill Major George Pleasants?"

"I'll remind you, Sir, that I am the secretary of war."

"I mean no disrespect to your office, Sir. I am merely setting forth possibilities. You had reason to be displeased with the major—as concerns Army contracts."

Cameron came forward in his chair. "What do you mean by that?"

"In a moment, Sir. Colonel Beals, I do not wish to impugn

your honor, but I was there in time to observe the advance of Colonel Howard's brigade and the unexpected counterattack by the Confederates. It was a stunning blow, Sir, and those raw, green young Union troops may be forgiven for having run before it. But you, Sir, are a ranking officer. And you seemed to be leading the way."

"I was trying to turn them!" Beals sputtered.

"That was precisely what Major Pleasants was trying to do, and managed to do for a time. At one point, you interfered with him. If he had reported you for that cowardice, Colonel, it could have been ruinous. At the least, you'd not have made general. But Pleasants was shot dead—out of range of the enemy—and he's the one held as the poltroon, courtesy of the report you filed. Only now you have changed it—for the second time, I might note—saying he was taken prisoner and not shot."

"There was confusion . . ."

"Of course there was. A more likely suspect was your late friend, Sergeant Fetridge. He was a patron of the gambling halls, like Pleasants—and Pleasants owed him money. In his off hours, Fetridge was employed by the Palace of Fortune as a collector of bad gambling debts. Fetridge had small taste for musketry and cannon fire, as he demonstrated at Bull Run. But he was no stranger to the club and billy, as applied to unfortunate skulls in the dark of alleys."

"The man is dead," said Cameron.

"He survived Bull Run," Harry said. "No great surprise, as I came upon him taking his rest at a ford at least two miles from the fighting. But he must have had keen vision, as from that distant prospect he swore he saw everything Colonel Beals saw. He swore to it when Beals said he saw Pleasants shot down by the Rebels and again when Beals said Louise Devereux did it as part of a cabal of murderous Southern *femmes fatales*. Pity Fetridge didn't live long enough to swear to Colonel Beals' new story, about Pleasants having been taken prisoner."

"As I told you, it was confusion out there," Beals said. "It took time for my memory to sort itself out."

"I hope that task is now complete," Harry said, "because I

think I shall be calling upon that memory in just a moment."
He picked up one of the shoes. "You asked what went on out
in western Virginia, Mr. President. The business of the shoes."

Both Cameron and Beals had shrunk back in their chairs,
as though the footgear Harry held was a loaded weapon that
might go off.

"What happened, Mr. President," Harry continued, "was
that a small Confederate force—a cavalry troop, with wagons—ambushed a military train at a crossing of the Potomac
out in the mountains near a place called Little Orleans. They
knew exactly when that train was due at the crossing, an hour
close on to midnight, and knew exactly what it was carrying.
It was loaded with shoes, which are in short supply in the
Confederacy and which are almost as valuable to an army as
food and ammunition."

Pinkerton leaned forward. "In all my time as a railroad detective, Mr. President, I never saw a neater job of it. This
wasn't a happenstance, a chance raid. It was a delivery of
goods."

"The scheme of scoundrels, Sir," said Harry. "With a wish
to keep their hands clean. Instead of delivering the shoes outright to the enemy, they merely arranged to have the shoes
shipped up the line, then sold the Confederates the information
of how and when the shipment would be made and where it
would be best to strike.."

" 'They' being who?" asked Lincoln.

"A quartermaster, Captain Colton, thought up the scheme
when he found himself with a surplus of shoes. He enlisted
Pleasants in the enterprise knowing how badly the major
needed money to pay off his gambling debts and other unsavory obligations. Pleasants used Miss Devereux, who has a
number of friends and admirers in Richmond from her time
as an actress there, as a go-between."

"You see!" said Beals. "Even Raines admits the woman's a
Southern agent."

"Only in this regard, and most reluctantly—and innocently," Harry said. "In truth, Pleasants gave her no choice.
He knew something about her past that would have proved a
great embarrassment to her and threatened to reveal it if she

didn't help him. I've just shown you what it is, Mr. President."

"That was her reason for killing him!" said Beals. "Shot him down like a dog on a field of honor!"

"Your memory's got itself all unsorted again, Colonel," said Lincoln. "Did this woman actually travel to Richmond to set up this plot?"

"No, Sir. She simply passed on notes from Colton and Pleasants to some actor friend who had contacts in the Rebel capital. His name is of no consequence. I've put it from my mind. Like her, he was only marginally involved."

"Raines tipped us to what was afoot," said Pinkerton. "He telegraphed from Hancock, and we were able to send along another train full of Union troops. Caught them completely unawares, up to their belt buckles in Army shoes. Killed a few of them and took a number of prisoners. If there had been just a few more of those Rebels there, and we didn't have this embarrassing business of Union quartermasters shipping shoes to the enemy, I'd have called in the newspapers and proclaimed a victory."

"Among the dead was Captain Colton," said Harry. "Louise Devereux and her acquaintances aside, all the principals are dead—Pleasants, Colton, and Fetridge."

"The sergeant was part of this, too?" Lincoln asked.

"Fetridge knew about Pleasants' affair with Miss Devereux from his colleagues in the bawdy house business," Harry said. "He was extracting sums of money from the major to keep quiet about it. He found out about the shoe transaction, too. For keeping quiet about that, he was transferred from the infantry to the quartermaster's and cut in on the deal." Harry stepped in front of Beals. "You ordered the transfer, didn't you, Colonel? What prompted such a nice reward for a notorious skulker? How did a man like that keep his sergeant stripes? Or earn them in the first place?"

"The man was excessively fat," Beals said. "Unfit for combat and the march. That's why I had him transferred. That was my sole motivation. I hardly knew him."

"Like you said, Simon," Lincoln said to Cameron, with a wink. "Highly irregular. Just about all of this."

"There's more, Mr. President," said Harry, holding aloft the shoe in his hand. "Major Pleasants was a West Point graduate. He may have been dismissed from the service for drinking out in Oregon and acquired his commission in a Maine regiment only through Senator Quigley's sponsorship and the Union's urgent need for experienced men. But I found nothing in his record with which to fault his bravery or patriotism, nothing to indicate an inclination to treachery—save this matter of the shoes. How then could he participate in such a treacherous scheme?"

Harry held the shoe before Cameron's face.

"There is only one reason. He felt it would be no disservice to his country and its cause for these shoes to be on Confederate feet." He turned to Leahy and handed him the shoe. "Would you demonstrate, Mr. Leahy?"

The Irishman, who'd seemed lost in morbid thought, instantly rallied and took the object. Using just the thumbs and fingers of both hands, he pried the uppers from the soles as he might peel a banana.

"No better than paper," he proclaimed. "Shoddy."

"Mr. Leahy is an unusually strong man," Harry said. "I am not." With that, he took up the other shoe, pulled the flimsy shoe leather of the sole back from the toe, and then tore the flapping piece in two, dropping both shoe and leather piece back onto the table.

"A man might just as well wear leaves on his feet as these," he said. "The Army did have an honest contract for new shoes with a reliable company from Mr. Cameron's own state of Pennsylvania—a factory in Gettysburg. In May, Mr. Cameron cancelled that contract and entered into a new one with a concern that no one had ever heard of before—some upstart company that just opened for business in Carlisle and counts one of Mr. Cameron's political supporters as its biggest stockholders. I know, for I was considering an investment in it myself until I learned that its remarkable profits were due to poor product."

"Pennsylvania makes the best shoes in the Union," said Cameron weakly. "I have heretofore heard no complaint about their quality."

"That's because what few soldiers they've yet been issued

to are still in camp, with no advance in prospect," Harry said, looking to Beals. "Did Major Pleasants learn that more of these worthless brogans were being sold to the Army? Was it more than even his much corrupted soul could stand? Did his sense of honor for once overcome his weakness and desperation? Was he planning to reveal the whole scheme if it wasn't stopped? Had he already informed Colonel Howard, the regimental commander, and so earned two bullets from his fellow conspirators?"

Nicolay entered. "Excuse me, Mr. President. The ambassador from Great Britain is here. Something about the unwarranted search of neutral vessels."

Lincoln consulted his pocket watch. "A bit more celerity, Mr. Raines. But we'll hear you out."

"I am nearing the end, Sir." He looked to Senator Quigley, who looked away.

"No one has been more appalled and saddened by Major Pleasants' sorry saga than the good senator here," Harry went on. "With his wastrel ways, his debts, his philandering, Major Pleasants was a heavy burden to his father-in-law, and a continuing threat to the senator's good family name and political reputation. I am not the first private agent the senator hired in the major's regard. He was kept informed of every transgression—and in many quarters of this city, they were no big secret."

Harry gave his full attention now to the President, who returned it in kind.

"The shoe plot was that last straw—the one applied to the camel's back. The senator maintains otherwise, but he was indeed at that battlefield. He accompanied his daughter there in the closed coach, as one would expect a dutiful father to do. The coachman would tell me no more, but he let slip that Mrs. Pleasants had not gone out there alone. And I have further proof, of a scientific nature."

He produced Gardner's glass plate and offered it to the President's inspection.

"This is a daguerreotype, taken by Mr. Alexander Gardner, Matthew Brady's man. I apologize for the crack across it, Sir. For that I'm obliged to Mr. Baker, but its subjects remain quite discernible. You'll see a grove of trees. That's Sudley Ford, and the rotund soldier there is the unlamented Sergeant Fetridge. You'll recognize the other man as the senator."

Harry hesitated, expecting a torrent of protest behind him, but there was nothing. Cameron, Beals, and Quigley all remained silent—waiting.

"I do not know how the pistol came to be put in Miss Devereux's dressing gown. Major Pleasants had a key to her quarters, which perhaps Senator Quigley obtained. But the pistol was purchased by the senator in this city a year ago. The meticulous gunsmith made a copy of the receipt."

He could not bring himself to look at the senator, so kept his eyes on a fascinated but troubled Lincoln. The cruelty of what he was doing pained him now, but there was no turning back. He reminded himself of how the major had looked without a face.

"There was a witness to the murder," Harry continued. "A young lieutenant who was badly wounded in the battle. Before he died, he told me he saw the major hurrying toward Miss Devereux, that Pleasants died for the sake of love. Congressman Fowler told me he heard two shots, saw the major fall, heard a third shot, and saw Louise Devereux's horse going wild, having thrown her. He looked to where the shots must have come from, and saw a cloud of gunsmoke hanging in the air by the two carriages. It was nearest the closed coach. Your coach, Senator Quigley."

Harry glanced behind him quickly. Cameron looked like a man with his pants full of worms. Beals, struck dumb at last, was staring open-mouthed at the saddle. The senator's head was down.

"Colonel Howard will verify the details of the shoe conspiracy," Harry said. "He had started to look into it before I came along. I think, if pressed, Mrs. Pleasants, might . . ."

"That will not be necessary," said the senator, wearily. He got slowly to his feet. "I am prepared to take full responsibility for George Pleasants' death."

"Murder," said Harry.

"Call it what you will," Quigley said. "I will take the blame."

• • •

A SAD-eyed Lincoln asked for all to leave but his old friend Quigley. As they filed out, a standing Mrs. Pleasants grasped at Harry's sleeve.

"Where is my father?" she said. "What has occurred? What have you done?"

With an effort, Harry spoke gently. "I have done what you paid me for, Madam," he said. "I have named the murderer of your husband and, as concerns his conduct in the battle, restored his good name."

"Named his murderer?"

"Mrs. Pleasants. Your father has confessed."

Her eyes filled with horror, then went suddenly blank. If Harry had not caught her, she would have fainted dead onto the floor.

THEY went to the bar of the National Hotel. Pinkerton drank sparingly, and Leahy not at all. But Harry felt a strong need. His first whiskey had little effect, so he asked for a second.

"I do not think he will hang," Pinkerton said. "It would be bad politics. And besides, there were those extenuating circumstances."

"None of this is official," Leahy said. "Nothing on the public record. Whatever the President decides to do with him, Quigley'll take his punishment in silence. He won't want his family name damaged anymore."

"Lincoln's a fair man," Harry said, astounded at the depth of guilt he himself felt.

"Pardoned two deserters today, I heard," said Leahy. "Some others last week."

Harry drank, morosely, then heard someone call his name.

He turned prepared to deal with Lafayette Baker—decisively, this time—but found instead Matthew Brady hurrying through the barroom crowd toward him, with his man Gardner in tow.

"Raines! Raines! I've been trying to find you."

"Well, Mr. Brady. You have."

"You went to the President's House? You took that plate?"

"Yes. It was very useful." He looked to Gardner, sheepishly. "I am sorry, Mr. Gardner. I only meant to borrow this. I tried to keep it from harm, but I was set upon by Baker's Provost Guards and it was cracked. I'll pay you what it's worth. More."

Gardner took it, eyeing the crack carefully, but with no visible resentment.

"It's worth little, Mr. Raines. It's not a significant picture."

"On the contrary. It's the most significant photograph in Washington today. It has solved a murder—and I fear ended the career of a powerful senator."

"How so?"

"It placed Senator Quigley on that part of the battlefield where Major Pleasants was killed, unraveling quite a tale. The senator's confessed to the crime."

"But that cannot be."

"It is so, Gardner. He confessed it to the President himself."

"But Raines, this is not the battlefield. This is Sudley Ford. It's a good two miles from where he was shot."

"Yes. So?"

"When I made this photograph, it was when the Rebels launched their counterattack. Next thing I knew, our entire Army was running by. Last I saw of Senator Quigley, he was climbing into a coach with some woman after it recrossed the ford and they headed back for Washington with everyone else. Raines, he couldn't possibly have been on the other side of that hill with Pleasants. You've got it wrong."

Chapter 2 9

AGAIN the day began as a gray thing. Forbidding shrouds of mist hung from the old hospital building in Georgetown like macabre bunting put there to welcome Death, who had made so many visits, in so few days.

Harry let the carriage window curtain fall back into place and leaned back to face his solemn fellow passenger. In his mind, he'd ascribed the male gender to Death. Perhaps the feminine one was more in order. Mrs. Pleasants, sitting on the seat opposite in her black dress, the hatred in her eyes showing through her thick veil, certainly looked the part.

Caesar Augustus, serving as coachman this morning, had halted the conveyance immediately after pulling into the hospital yard—as Harry had requested.

"This is our destination," Harry said. They'd not spoken since he'd called for her at her house.

"This is a prison?"

"No, Ma'am. A hospital. The Union Hospital in Georgetown."

"I don't understand. You said I was to serve a sentence— a voluntary sentence."

"This is what the President asks of you in lieu of a prison sentence. Or if you will, what he desires to be your sentence."

"I am to be confined here?"

"Not confined, Mrs. Pleasants. But you must work here,

every day that you are well, until the war ends. That is his wish."

"I suppose it is entirely pointless for me to once again profess my innocence."

"It is to me. Mr. Lincoln decided this."

"You are his messenger?"

"I'm carrying out his wishes. He didn't want soldiers or police or the likes of Lafayette Baker attending to you this morning."

She fidgeted in her seat, then caught herself, regaining her repose but failing to conceal her reluctance to enter the hospital.

"This is monstrously unfair. And unjust. One of the great injustices of this horrible war."

"Mrs. Pleasants, by law, military or civil, you could have been hanged. The President is not only sparing you that, but any official proceeding, any official record, so that no mark will be placed against your name, or your father's. There will be nothing in the newspapers. No disgrace. You have his word, provided you fulfill the terms of his 'sentence.' You will find other women here performing such service voluntarily, and happy to do so."

One of the horses shifted in the traces, jostling the coach. Harry heard Caesar Augustus flick back the reins.

"Was it necessary to send my father into the Army? It could mean his death."

"That's true for any soldier. But he was not *ordered* into uniform. He agreed it would be inappropriate for him to continue in his senate seat in the circumstance. The colonelcy was offered as compensation. It's in one of the new regiments they're raising. Members of Congress are begging for these appointments."

She still would not move. Harry wondered if ultimately they were going to have to forcibly carry her from the coach to the hospital, just so he could acquit himself of his part in this. He'd brought Leahy along, up on the seat beside Caesar Augustus, in anticipation of this possibility, or a repeat of her fainting scene.

"I did not shoot my husband, and neither did my father."

"Do you at least concede that it was your husband there on the Sudley Road who was shot dead?"

She wiped at an eye. "Yes. All that I said about his being missing was only an attempt to end this ordeal."

He decided to indulge her for the moment. She would soon enough find herself up to the elbows in slop buckets.

"It has ended, Madam. Given the circumstance, I'd say it has ended generously for you."

"To what do we owe Mr. Lincoln's 'generosity,' Mr. Raines? Is all this merely to avoid an embarrassment to his administration?"

"Embarrassment to the administration does its cause no good, Mrs. Pleasants. But I'd say you are mostly obliged to Dan Sickles for this leniency."

"You mean Dan Sickles, the New York congressman? He is a scoundrel!"

"Also now a colonel of volunteers. But it was his shooting of Philip Barton Key in Lafayette Park two years ago that gained you your continued freedom now."

"That was a scandal!"

"Yes it was. He shot down that young man in cold blood for having an affair with his wife. And there was some talk the wife deliberately lured the fellow to his fate. But Sickles pleaded temporary insanity—and the unwritten law that countenances murder in revenge for adultery. His defense attorney, that Edwin P. Stanton, is as wily as he is ruthless. So Sickles was acquitted. The President felt you had as much justice on your side as Sickles—probably more—and that you rightly should suffer no worse a fate. That you are a woman should make no difference."

"But it always does. We don't find Mr. Sickles working in a hospital."

"But we may find him in one, depending on the fortunes of war." He took out his watch. "I'm sorry, Mrs. Pleasants. I'm terribly sorry about it all."

"You did your job well."

"I surprised myself."

She lifted her veil. Her eyes looked very clear now—very bright and alert. He wondered if she was frightened.

"It may surprise you to hear me say that it's important to me that you above all others believe me—that I didn't mean for this happen," she said, "that I didn't go out to that battlefield to shoot my husband. That I didn't shoot him. That he himself had taken that pistol from our house. That the first I saw of it again was yesterday in the War Department office."

"Why should my opinion matter so much? You do not like me."

"No, I do not. But you are the most convinced of my guilt."

"I am convinced mostly by the depths of hatred you bear, Mrs. Pleasants. I believe you bore your husband enormous hatred. Miss Devereux, too."

"I told him to leave that woman. I told him if he didn't— if he had any more to do with her—I'd expose her secret. He agreed to break off their affair. He was reluctant, but I had his promise. Yet there she was at Manassas. All but in his arms."

"It was not at his invitation."

"You speak with a certainty I do not share, Mr. Raines."

"Miss Devereux is my friend."

"You know her secret."

"I do."

"It does not bother you?"

"It bothers me what she might endure as a consequence. I should inform you also, Madam, that the President is also aware of her secret, and would view any revelation of it gravely. Were any such revelation to be attributed to you, I think you would find his leniency revoked and yourself in the Old Blue Jug."

She pulled the window curtain aside to look at the hospital.

"He promised me there would be no more of them—no more bawds and slatterns. Then there on a battlefield, with the lives of all at risk, he leaves me to my fate to rush to the side of that slut."

"Mrs. Pleasants . . ."

"A Negress."

Her eyes were on him now. He could see the hardness of her stare.

"She is only partly that."

"She is a Negro. There is no such thing as part."

"You deceive me in your Abolitionism."

"I am an Abolitionist. I'm ardent in that cause. I am as much Abolitionist as I am innocent of this crime. But because I believe they should be free does not mean I believe they should be in my husband's bed."

The horses twitched and shifted. Caesar Augustus must have been listening.

"I fear you are living in the wrong time, Mrs. Pleasants."

"Mr. Raines, we all are."

A silence came between them and remained. Finally, Harry reached and opened the carriage door, stepping out onto the ground.

"It's time, Ma'am. Please."

She extended her arm. He took her hand, holding it firmly as she alighted.

"You'll find a Miss Clara Barton inside. She is very dedicated and a good and fair-minded woman. She'll be of help to you."

"Thank you." Cold words.

Mrs. Pleasants began walking slowly toward the hospital entrance, her dignified bearing that of a moving statue.

"But when in her company, I would strongly advise against such disdainful talk about 'Negroes.' "

CAESAR Augustus, who had the most to lose on this late night voyage, sat lookout in the bow. Leahy, the strongest of them, rowed. Harry sat on the rear seat, holding Louise Devereux close and comforting her in this last travail. The night air, even there upon the wide river, was thick and close about them.

To his surprise, she had smoked a small cheroot as they'd pulled away from the Maryland shore. The aroma clung to their clothes.

He had his arm around her, lest she lose her seating in the swells. She perhaps mistook this as flirtation, as she rested her head on his shoulder.

"We're almost there," he said.

It was a lie. The Potomac was nearly two miles wide at this

point, and the current swift. Leahy was straining some to keep them on course. Harry promised to spell the man on the return trip, when there'd be no Louise aboard.

The downriver breeze blew long strands of her dark hair against his face. He gently brushed them aside, but they returned.

"I am happy and I am sad," she said.

"I am sorry for your exile," he said. "I will miss you at the theater. All of Washington will. This is unjust."

"Then why could I not stay?"

"With all the haroo we've had in the newspapers, the only question was whether to proclaim you escaped or banished. Were you to remain in the North, they'd clamor to have you in a prison. Or on a rope."

"Though I have done nothing."

"Not much justice to be found in war, no matter what they write."

She lifted her head, looking at him. "And which is it to be?"

"I think you are to be banished. I believe the President feels that is the most efficacious and merciful way to relieve you of your predicament. Once you are officially banished, there will be no charges hanging over your head—unless you return before the war is over."

"Hang. Now there's a word." She sat straighter. " 'Hang there like fruit, my soul, Till the tree die.' "

" 'It seems she hangs upon the cheek of night,' " he responded. " 'Like a rich jewel in an Ethiop's ear; Beauty too rich for use, for earth too dear.' "

"So," she said. "You would have me Juliet."

"Only on the stage, Louise, where you die so beautifully. Otherwise, we very much want to keep you alive. That is the why of all of this."

She took his hand and gently kissed it. Louise was one of those women who must always have a man in her life, he supposed, and now he was all she had.

Once in Richmond, that would quickly change. She might even find herself celebrated as a heroine as well as a theatrical beauty. The Northern newspapers she was carrying in her carpetbag had declared her a Southern spy and agent.

"We're going to try to make a landing near a place called Owens," he said. "There's a woman who keeps a tavern and inn there. Show her this, and she will provide for you. She'll find a way to get you to Fredericksburg. There'll be coaches from there to Richmond."

He handed her a folded piece of paper. In the darkness, there was no reading it, but she placed it within the bodice of her dress.

"What is it?" She asked.

"A letter from me. It's addressed to no one in particular, but declares you under the protection of my family."

"And where will that be of any use?"

"Anywhere in Virginia—perhaps not with common soldiery, but with gentlemen, certainly. And with the woman in Owens."

"Will you come and see me in Virginia?"

"If I can."

"Why not come South with me now?"

"There's a reason named Caitlin."

"That's less reason than you think, Harrison Raines. I think you are a foolishly persistent man in that lady's regard."

He let that pass. She hesitated, as though to speak further on the subject, but instead returned her head to his shoulder.

"You should come South, Harry," she said, finally. "You are a Southerner. Just like me."

"Southern, but not a Rebel."

"Marse Harry!"

It was a command—to hush. Caesar Augustus had heard something. Leahy halted his stroke and sat back, listening.

"Gunboat," he said. "I can hear its paddle wheel."

There was a hazy starlight, and a glow upriver that might mean military campfires. Harry looked downriver, and at last saw the thing, a great black moving patch of darkness, but for the sparks dancing in the air around its smokestack.

"Is it Confederate?" Louise asked. He felt her stiffen.

"Their Navy's mostly bottled up in Hampton Roads," Leahy said. "I expect she's Federal."

"That's as bad as the other," Harry said, wishing Louise would sit upright so he could put on his spectacles.

Drawing abreast about a hundred yards to the beam, the gunboat of a sudden idled its paddle wheel, the clank and clatter and millrace splash of water abruptly giving way to an eerie quiet. Looking hard, Harry could see its stack and wheelhouse silhouetted above the trees of the opposite shore.

"If it's Union, what harm could come to us?" Louise asked, in a whisper.

"They'd take us back to Washington, or some other Federal port, and make us explain ourselves. We'd lose this night."

"They may send a piece of solid shot our way just to be on the safe side," said Leahy, watching the larger craft over his shoulder.

"Harry," she said. "Are you going back to Washington?"

There was an unwelcome element of coyness in her voice.

"I will see you safe to Owens."

The gunboat seemed to be turning toward them. Harry could not tell if the shift was owing to the current or the captain's intent. One shot from its two-pounder bow chaser could put them under in an instant.

"Harry . . ."

"Hush, Miss," ordered Caesar Augustus, who was leaning forward over the bow, straining for sounds from the gunboat that Harry, for one, could not begin to hear.

And then came a noise that could be heard all the way back in Washington. With a great chuff and an eruption of black smoke that rose in a curling ball, obscuring the stars, the naval boat got underway once more, her huge paddle wheel recommencing its great gobble of water. Her bow swung away, upriver.

When it was stern to, Leahy resumed rowing.

"I appreciate the respite," he said, "but we'll have to find another landing spot now. We've drifted too far downstream."

"There's a wide-mouthed creek, the Machadoc, downriver a bit," Harry said. "Follow it in, and we should find ourselves a short walk from Owens—a much shorter one than if we had gone straight across the river."

"Shorter except for the rowin'," Leahy said, taking a demonstrably hard pull on the oars.

"I'll spell you," Harry said.

"No need yet."

Louise held Harry's arm tightly against her, so close he could feel her breast. With gentle but unyielding pressure, he pulled his arm away, and then slipped it around her shoulders. He held her close, but as he might a child.

As the rules of chivalry would instruct, Harry carried her ashore, across what proved to be a wide, shallow marsh. It was a long time to hard ground. Once they achieved it, he left her standing there while he returned to the rowing boat.

"If I'm not back by the very first light, go back without me," Harry told Leahy and Caesar Augustus. "Do so hastily, for there'll be Rebel cavalry patrols—all along this shore."

"It's only a short piece up the road to that village," Leahy said. "She can make it."

"I mean to see her safe," Harry said. "Owens may not be safe enough. I'll see."

"So here we are at last, in Dixie," Louise said, when they had left the others and were on firm ground.

"We've a small ways to go up that road. I'll accompany you there." He started to take her bag, which in addition to her clothing and necessities contained a small derringer pistol and one hundred Yankee dollars—half in gold coin, the other half in banknotes.

He halted.

"Before we go on, there's something you should know, Louise. That official paper that Pleasants took from you and gave to his wife . . ."

"Yes?"

"I have it."

"You have it? Damn your soul, Harry, why didn't you tell me?"

He took her by the shoulders. "Why did you carry this thing, Louise? It proclaims to all the world that your mother was an ex-slave. Where did you think you could go that such a thing wouldn't bear harshly on your life?"

"Only if someone found it."

"As someone did. Your major, and then his wife. The risk, Louise. It's enormous."

"You wouldn't understand, Harry. You couldn't."

"I can understand enough."

She put her hand to his arm. "Harry, that paper says forever and ever that, no matter what, my mother is free. And so I am free. It says that I am free. Have you no notion at all what that means to someone like me?"

"But Louise, you were free from birth. No one would question you. And surely no one would think you a Negro to look at you."

"Just give it to me. It's mine."

There was a light visible at the distant tree line, near what Harry judged to be the road to Owens. He guessed it was a house but wondered why there'd be a lantern or lamp burning at so late an hour.

"Louise, let me keep it. I'll keep it safe."

"No. You have no right to it. It's mine."

"I have the right to try to protect you."

"Give it to me!"

She shouted the last, her voice so high pitched it almost sounded like a scream. Dogs began barking in the area near the lamplight.

He handed her the paper. She placed it within the bodice of her dress, alongside the letter he had given her. Then she turned without another word and started across the meadow grass toward the road.

Harry watched her vanish into the darkness. He stood a long moment, listening to the sound her dress made rustling through the grass, till that, too, was gone.

Sighing, he wearily shook his head, then trudged after her.

WHEN they finally parted, two days later in a Richmond hotel room, she kissed him hard and held him close, then said:

" 'I would have thee gone;
And yet no further than a wanton's bird,

Who lets it hop a little from her hand,
Like a poor prisoner in his twisted gyves,
And with a silk thread plucks it back again,
So loving-jealous of his liberty.' "

Harry knocked on Mrs. Fitzgerald's door loudly enough to arouse the entire neighborhood, but only dogs were stirred at first, both inside and outside the boardinghouse.

Finally, there was a rattle of the lock, and the door opened hesitantly, a single, pale gray eye visible beneath a tumbled hank of gray hair and old-fashioned bonnet. Growling could be heard behind her.

"It's only me, Mrs. Fitzgerald."

"Why d'you pound like that? Y'oud think y'were trying to break your way in."

He had in fact thought of that.

"I tried twice before, this hour," he said. "There was no response."

It was after eight in the morning, and there should have been one. Aside from Caitlin, there were only three other boarders in the establishment. From what Harry knew of them, he guessed they were sleeping off their previous night's whiskey and beer. Mrs. Fitzgerald smelled a little of it herself.

He moved forward, anticipating her opening the door, but she didn't budge.

"I must see Miss Howard," he said.

"Well, she ain't here."

He recalled Caitlin's ghostly complexion when last he'd looked upon her.

"Is she all right? Has something happened to her?"

"She's just fine, no thanks to the likes of you. Only she's gone. Where you been?"

"I had business elsewhere. When is she returning?"

Mrs. Fitzgerald backed up an inch or so, but it was only to improve her hold upon the door.

"A few weeks," she said, a little defiantly. "Maybe more. Maybe never."

"What?"

"She went to New York—with a gentleman. She took a part in a play."

Harry pushed upon the door, apologizing for his impertinence, but steadily, carefully, moving the woman back. When there was room enough for him to pass, he bolted inside and up the stairs.

Caitlin's door was unlocked and ajar. Both rooms were deserted and bereft of any sign of her occupation, save a small vase with a now dried rose in it on the bedroom dresser. He stood there, looking about helplessly, then turned to find Mrs. Fitzgerald in the doorway behind him, taking some pleasure in his discomfort but also showing some sympathy.

"She went to New York?"

"She has a part in a play. *The Game of Love.*"

Harry's sorrow was as painful as a grievous wound. He tried to dampen it with words.

"It is by a clever author named James Brougham," he said. "He wrote it six years ago, with another play."

That one was called *Love and Murder.*

"She left you a letter," Mrs. Fitzgerald said.

"Why didn't you tell me?"

"Mr. Raines, you come bustin' into my house before I have much chance to tell you anything."

He bowed, feeling tears in his eyes. "My apologies, Ma'am, for the intrusion."

"I'll fetch it."

The letter was sealed—a single piece of paper. He read it in Mrs. Fitzgerald's front hall, standing by the light of the still open door.

Dearest Harry,

I am so much aggrieved by this horrid war. I regret I ever asked you to take me to it. Now I wish only to fly from it, and so am doing. New York is a tolerable city, and seems far from the fighting. It is an agreeable play, with an amiable cast, and I am fortunate to find such work in this season. I have no address of my own as yet. I will write when I do, though I know not when that will be.

*I do thank you for all you have done for me. If I have
no happiness otherwise, I can rejoice in my friends.*
                          With much fondness,
                          Caitlin

Her hand, usually precise, had been unsteady, and a drop of
moisture had blurred a cluster of words.

Fondness. No address of her own.

"You said 'with a gentleman'?"

"Oh, yes," said Mrs. Fitzgerald. "Mr. John Wilkes Booth."

Chapter 30

Harry stood watching as the gravedigger finished his task. When the casket was finally lowered, with some clumsiness, into the hole, the man looked to him, wiping the sweat from his brow with a red kerchief. Harry nodded solemnly in reply and stepped forward with a Bible he had brought with him. He wasn't certain the ritual was necessary, this being a second burial, but decided it couldn't hurt, given the excessive amount of sin that had to be expatiated.

He'd chosen the passage at random, thinking most anything would do, but the words seemed appropriate:

> *Now therefore keep thy sorrow to thyself, and bear with a good courage that which hath befallen thee. . . . The souls of the righteous are in the hand of God, and there shall no torment touch them. In the sight of the unwise they seemed to die: and their departure is taken for misery, and their going from us to be utter destruction: but they are in peace. For though they be punished in the sight of men, yet is their hope full of immortality. And having been a little chastised, they shall be greatly rewarded: for God proved them, and found them worthy for himself.*

Harry took a handful of dirt and tossed it onto the pine box below, trying to think of the major in some favorable way.

What came to mind first was that last night in Naylor's Livery, when Pleasants had somehow pulled himself together from his debauch and ridden off into Virginia and the great fight. Somehow there seemed more courage in that than in his mad cavort with sword in hand at Manassas, trying to stem the rout. There is more bravery to be found in the considered act, it seemed to Harry, than in anything undertaken in the high pitch of excitement.

Another image came forth, though not from memory: the major rushing to Louise Devereux' side, only to fall to two bullets.

From that came another vision, the sheer, smouldering loveliness of Louise's face in the heat of passion. He tried to drive that from his mind, for this was a sacred occasion, but could not.

"Where's the stone?" the gravedigger asked, resting between shovelings.

He'd already half refilled the grave with dirt. Harry nodded to the wagon over by the road, where Caesar Augustus stood waiting.

"You want it put in now?"

"As soon as you're ready. I won't leave until it's done."

"All right. Have your Negro bring it over."

Harry took a step closer to the man, his voice turning gruff.

"Caesar Augustus and I will *help* you bring the stone to its place. I'm paying you, Sir. Earn your money, please."

When the time came, the three of them managed the remarkably heavy headstone, but not without some struggle. Harry had spent a substantial part of the winnings held for him at the Palace of Fortune on this burial and arrangement, and the stone was considerable. When the slab was finally standing erect, the three of them stood quietly before it, as though it were some extraordinary work of art.

On the front was carved: *"Here lies a brave soldier of the war."* Nothing more.

"There's no name," said the gravedigger.

"When the war's over, perhaps," Harry said. "For now, this will have to do."

"Never heard of such a thing."

"I fear you will—many times again."

LEAHY found Harry late in the afternoon in the round bar of the Willard Hotel. The Irishman seemed disapproving, as though he could immediately tell Harry had been there the better part of the day.

"Mr. Pinkerton wants to see you," Leahy said.

"He seems to want that every other day."

"This is of some importance. Especially to you."

Harry took a heavy swallow of whiskey. The writer Nathaniel Hawthorne was standing on the opposite side of the round bar. He nodded to Harry, with a smile of appreciation, for Harry had just bought him a drink.

"Raines, it will do you small good to trifle with this man."

Leahy accepted a lemonade from the bartender, draining the glass in a rapid succession of swallows.

"I'm sensible to that," Harry said.

"It wouldn't seem so."

"How's that?"

"You tarried pretty long in Richmond, Sir."

"Some personal business."

"Mr. Lafayette Baker has had a report you paid a visit to Jeff Davis."

"Mr. Baker has excellent intelligence. I did. Davis is a friend of my father's. I took advantage of that."

Leahy chewed over this response for a long moment. "Do you want to explain yourself?"

"I wanted to secure his assistance in providing protection for Miss Devereux. And get some measure of those people in the process."

"Did you succeed?"

"I think so."

"What was it like?"

"My conversation with Davis? It was like a bucket of very cold water in the face."

"I would expect as much. What did you learn?"

"That this war, Mr. Leahy, is going to be a very long and

very nasty piece of work. Very long, very nasty."

They stood drinking a moment in silence, which was interrupted by some shouts and cheers over by the door. There'd been some sort of skirmish out in the mountains of western Virginia, which reports had exaggerated into a significant engagement. Every fresh word of it was being hurrahed.

"The President'll be making more changes," Leahy said, finally. "I don't think Secretary Cameron is going to be tolerated much longer."

"The shoes."

"More than shoes."

The bartender, unasked, gave Leahy another lemonade and waved off payment.

"You have moved here to the Willard from the National," Leahy said.

"I have. A better class of residents."

"This is a Union hotel. The National's full of Southerners. Is Wilkes Booth still there?"

"I am informed he is in New York." Harry set down his empty whiskey glass loudly on the wood. "If you'll excuse me, Leahy. I am going to have a bath."

"Pinkerton wants to see you right away. You know why."

"I suppose I do."

"You'll have to make a choice, Raines. It's what he asks, or moving back to Virginia. Sharing the fate of that poor Devereux woman. Or worse."

"All right, Mr. Leahy. I've faced up to everything else. I might as well face up to this. Where's Pinkerton?"

"At the War Department."

"But afterwards, I'm having a bath. Tonight I must call upon a lady."

"Miss Howard?"

"She has gone to New York, alas."

"With Booth?"

"Indeed she has, Sir. So I must pass this evening in the company of another."

"Not your cousin, Belle Boyd?"

"Oh no. A lady in a whorehouse."

•   •   •

HARRY went upstairs with the first girl in the establishment to approach him, not caring who she was or what she looked like. She proved to be young, and a little pretty, though much overfed and somewhat cross-eyed.

Once in the bedroom, she introduced herself as Melanie, and seated herself on the bed. Harry took a chair, the only one in the tiny room.

"Let's talk for a while," Harry said.

"Talk?"

Harry leaned back, crossing one leg over the other. The boots he'd put on were highly polished.

"How do you like it in this house? Is Miss Turner good to you?"

"Miss Mollie's just fine."

"What about the sister? The younger, prettier one?"

"Miss Ella? We don't see her much. She sleeps all day and spends most of her time in her rooms."

"Where are they?"

"End of the hall. Why you askin' about her? You can't get no poke offa her, Mister. She's not in the business. She just lives here."

Harry got back to his feet, feigning a weariness that, as he thought upon it, was real. Melanie started pulling off her shift.

"No, Miss, that won't be necessary. I fear I am too tired for amour this night. I've been on a long journey, and I've had too much to drink. I'm sorry."

"Why'd you come up here, then?"

"I mean no disadvantage to you, Miss. The spirit is willing, but the proverbial flesh . . ." He shrugged. She finally comprehended.

He put money on the small table by the bed—twice the amount she had quoted him. "Thank you, Miss. Perhaps another night."

Harry took a few noisy steps toward the main stairs, then halted. He could hear voices and sounds of social congress all about him, but the hall itself was deserted. With soft footfalls, he made his way back to the other end of the corridor and a solitary closed door.

Harry rapped on it gently.

"Is that you, Mae?" The voice was very womanly, for someone so young.

He said nothing. From a bedroom down the other way came a loud squawk of laughter. There was banjo music downstairs.

"Don't stand there, girl!" said the voice behind the door. "Come in! I am impatient for my supper!"

Harry glanced behind him again, then put his hand in his coat pocket, around the derringer he carried there, setting a thumb carefully upon the hammer. With his left hand, he turned the knob and pushed open the door.

She did not reach for a weapon, and he was grateful, for that eventuality was what he feared most in this encounter.

"Mr. Harrison Raines—I do declare." Still womanly, her speech was now Southern, theatrically so. She was mocking him.

Ella Turner reclined on a chaise longue by the curtained window, wearing an emerald-green dressing gown and matching slippers. Her legs were bare and much exposed. She pulled the skirt of her robe over them.

She had turned off the gaslight and illuminated the room with candles. The effect was most becoming to her, but she had no need of such enhancement. The lady was a beauty and in the very perfection of her youth. Her fair hair seemed aglow in the golden candlelight.

"I was expecting to hear from you," she said. "I did not expect it would be as an intruder breaking into my room."

"I knocked, Ma'am."

"So you did."

"I needed to see you—discreetly."

"My housemaid Mae will be here directly. Then nothing about your presence here will be discreet."

He closed the door behind him and turned to secure the latch. When he looked back, it was to see the barrel of a small revolver aimed at him.

"That's not necessary," he said.

"I hope not," she replied, pulling back the hammer of the piece. "But I fear you mean me harm."

"No, I only want to relieve my curiosity. I won't stay long, I promise. May I sit down?"

There was a lone armchair, set beneath the gas lamp. He wondered if Booth had sat there, when not otherwise occupied. She nodded her assent, and he moved toward it. Deciding the derringer was pointless at this juncture, Harry removed his hand from his pocket, and sat down, crossing his legs.

Ella kept the pistol on him.

"You keep your boots as well polished as Mr. Booth's."

"No, just tonight. As I was calling on a singularly handsome woman, I wished to look my best."

The pistol lowered to her lap. She smiled sweetly. More mockery. This girl was not much older than Belle Boyd, but seemed a woman to hold her own with kings and presidents.

"I do enjoy the company of gentleman callers, Sir, but you are not the one I would have tonight." Another smile, not sweet.

"I'll be brief. I need to know the answer to a question that plagues me still."

"At what consequence to me, Sir?"

"None, Ma'am."

"Are you certain? The answer may displease you."

"I'll make it my promise. As a gentleman. A Virginia gentleman."

"*D'accord.* Now what do you want?"

"Who killed that sergeant they found me with? You were there. You surely must know."

Now she set the pistol on the table beside her, and sat straight up. The movement exposed her leg again, but she did nothing about it.

"If that is all you wish to know, Mr. Raines, then you need not tarry here long." She eyed him as might a cat. "I killed him. Shot him dead through the back as he raised his club to strike a blow."

"You did it? Not Booth?"

"My darling Wilkes, Sir, could not harm a flea. Surely you know him that well, like him or not. No, Sir. I am your villain, though you might count me your heroine. Because when my bullet ended that lout's life, he was fast at work trying to end yours."

"Then I am grateful to you, Miss Turner. And obligated. Forever obligated."

A very mocking smile now.

"Don't be," she said, "for I almost let it happen. But I dared not. Once he'd finished with you, I feared he might then turn on Wilkes. I could not bear to have a single bruise on that noble face, Mr. Raines. Do you understand that?"

He did, though he didn't like it. "My thanks just the same."

"Some day I'll ask a favor of you."

"I've already given it. I didn't tell anyone I thought it was you, and I was asked—repeatedly."

"Then my thanks. I guess we're quits now."

He rose. "One thing more," he said. "When is Booth coming back?"

"Ah, the spurned Lochinvar. Your lady is with him in New York, isn't she? In that play. You fear she will not return until he does. That she will follow him wherever he wanders. That she may never come back." She rose and went to a sideboard, pouring herself a glass of wine from a decanter. "Sherry?"

"No thank you."

"You needn't fear, Sir." She turned to face him, taking a sip, her eyes staring at him over the rim of the glass. "He will tire of her again as he has in the past. He must have two dozen women in that city, and they will come calling on him, rest assured. If he invited Caitlin Howard there, it was to spite you; not for love. In the end, he always returns to the same woman."

"You."

She bowed to him slightly, careful not to spill her glass.

"But you must promise me, Mr. Raines, and I do indeed want your word as a Southern gentleman on this. No harm must come to Wilkes from your quarter. We're even now. I will keep your secrets safe, but I will have your word on Mr. Booth's safety."

"What secrets have I for you to keep safe?"

"One is that this afternoon you took an oath to loyalty to

the Union and became a member of the U.S. Secret Service, rank of captain."

He was stunned.

"What on earth makes you say that?"

"Something on earth called Lafayette Baker. He is one of my sister's best customers, you know—if I may use that term about someone who does not pay for anything. But he let slip this news this very evening. He wasn't made very happy by it."

"I'll see that he's made even less happy—if he doesn't start guarding his mouth. What other secret of mine are you safe-keeping?"

"That you have made such a botch of your mission."

"What do you mean?"

"You have let the murderer of Major Pleasants go free."

"Mrs. Pleasants? You should know that I delivered her this morning to the Union Hospital in Georgetown, where as penance she will work among sawn limbs and spilled guts the rest of this war."

"As well she should. But I am not speaking of that poor woman. I mean Louise Devereux, whom you have just delivered safe to Richmond City."

"What are you saying? Louise is innocent. She resides now in Richmond at some peril."

Ella laughed, a pretty sound. "As a Southerner, have you heard the tale of Brother Rabbit?"

"Bre'r Rabbit? Yes. That's an old Negro story."

"He begs not to be thrown into the briar patch? He begs any fate but that. So that's where they throw him. But that is where he most longs to be! That is where he's safest!" She paused for another sip of sherry, then raised her glass. "My compliments, Sir. You have tossed that lady rabbit right into her briar patch."

"That's nonsense, Ma'am."

"She's a Confederate spy, Sir. *Agent provocateuse.* She recruited my poor Wilkes into this murky business. And her hapless lover, Major Pleasants. Wilkes' Southern sympathies you know. But Pleasants sickened of what they were doing. He was going to betray her to Federal authorities. Threatened to do that right in this very place, the night before he died. She tried to kill him, but that tiny pistol of hers missed by a mile. So she took a gun of his that he kept here and went off the next day to do the job on the battlefield if the Confederates didn't. Are you sure you will not join me in a sherry, Mr. Raines? You seem distraught."

"Louise could not possibly be a Southern agent. As your Mr. Booth must have told you, she is an Octoroon. Her mother was a slave. Louise had her mother's freedom papers! Pleasants took them. And then his wife found them."

"Just as Miss Devereux intended. That woman has nothing darker than Spanish in her, Raines. She is as white as you or I. Do you think for a moment that a woman in her position, were she actually Negro, would carry a piece of paper around proclaiming her so? Do you think any Southern woman, white or taken for white, would travel through the South from New Orleans to Richmond with such a thing? That paper had only one purpose, Harry Raines, and that was to fool the likes of you."

"But she could not have shot the major. The bullets from that revolver—one of them struck her own saddle."

"I'm sure one did. What you must ask yourself, Sir, is *when* it was fired. And by whom."

Harry stared at the floor, his thoughts in a rush.

She came up to him, looking into his face. "Poor man, I see you are doing that now."

"Louise Devereux is merely an actress."

She opened the door, preparing politely to turn him out into the night. "And an extremely good one, wouldn't you say?"

He flushed, hoping she'd not notice, but she did.

"I don't think you're a fool, Harry Raines," she said. "Not at all. You're a roomantic. It's different, but just as dangerous in this kind of game."

She put her hand on his arm, in Southern fashion.

"Don't despair," she said. "You haven't failed. You've wreaked a lot of havoc among some evil men. Righteousness has prevailed, with dead bodies to show for it. If the fair sex has fared better at your hands than the men have, why, that's what Southern chivalry is all about, isn't it?"

To his surprise, she stood on tiptoes and kissed his cheek. "Let us be friends, *Captain* Raines. In your new capacity, I'm sure you and I will have ample occasion to be of use to one another again. It's going to be a very long war."